Lila's Journey

By

Jane Coletti Perry

Overland Park, KS

Lila's Journey

ISBN 13: 978-1-961907-67-6

Published by:
Mustard Seed Press
Overland Park, KS

Copyright © 2024 by Jane Coletti Perry. All rights reserved.

This book, or parts thereof, may not be reproduced, stored in a retrieval system, or transmitted in any form or by any means, electronic, mechanical, photocopying, recording, or otherwise, without the written permission of the publisher.

This story is a work of fiction. Any resemblances to actual people, places, or events are purely coincidental.

Front cover design by Mustard Seed Press

Printed and bound in the United States of America

Praise for *Lila's Journey*

Award-winning author Jane Coletti Perry deftly weaves the story of a young, determined Lila Bonner and her quest for survival in all that life hands her. Having already lived a life filled with heartache well beyond her years, Lila meets a young man who aids her journey traveling the Santa Fe Trail in 1866 while capturing her heart. Ms. Perry skillfully paints a picture for the reader's eye that describes the unexpected twists and turns, making this story a must-read for any age.

--Deborah Swenson, Award-Winning Author of *Till My Last Breath and Till My Last Day.*

Dedication

To my mother
who taught in a one-room school.

Acknowledgments

I have loved discovering Council Grove, Kansas. I could not have found a more historically rich or welcoming community for the setting of *Lila's Journey*. It will forever hold a special place in my heart.

I have many people to thank. I am indebted to Kelley Judd, Morris County Historical Society Treasurer who has graciously given me more than one tour of historic Council Grove (along with wife Jill), answered my many questions, taken pictures, and been supportive in every possible way during my research; Ken and Shirley McClintock shared stories and history of Council Grove at their charming restaurant, Trail Days Café and Museum; the Council Oak Chapter of Daughters of the American Revolution welcomed me and other Olathe DAR members to share local history and answer questions, all of it helpful in my research.

To my beta readers, thank you. Women Writing the West member/author Deborah Swenson and author Janie Paul read the entire manuscript for content, clarity, accuracy, and the thousands of writing details that need attention. I am grateful beyond words for your support and contribution to this book.

Thank you to Nancy Moser and Mustard Seed Press for designing the cover and formatting the manuscript into softcover and eBook editions. Your talents continue to amaze me and are appreciated.

I'm grateful to Krista Soukup and Janell Madison at Blue Cottage Agency for your expertise, support, and friendship. Your marketing talents are the wind beneath any project I undertake.

Thank you, Jan Kirk, WWW member, for gifting me *The Santa Fe Trail: Its History, Legends, and Lore* by David Dary from your husband's library. Scholarly and thorough, I relied on this wonderful resource more than any other during my research. I would recommend it to any serious reader of Santa Fe Trail history.

To my dear husband, Dick, I give my biggest thanks for supporting my writing endeavors no matter how long they take. After I have spent the day at the computer and we sit down to a meal you have prepared, I am grateful and count my blessings. You are the best.

Santa Fe Trail Map by Doug Holdread

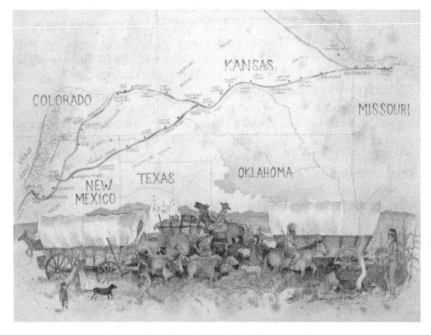

Permission from Santa Fe Trail Association

I Hear America Singing

I hear America singing, the varied carols I hear,
Those of mechanics,
each one singing his as it should be blithe and strong,
The carpenter singing his as he measures his plank or beam,
The mason singing his as he makes ready for work, or leaves off work,
The boatman singing what belongs to him in his boat,
the deckhand singing on the steamboat deck,
The shoemaker singing as he sits on his bench,
the hatter singing as he stands,
The wood-cutter's song, the ploughboy's on his way in the morning,
or at noon intermission or at sundown,
The delicious singing of the mother, or of the young wife at work,
or of the girl sewing or washing,
Each singing what belongs to him or her and to none else,
The day what belongs to the day —
at night the party of young fellows, robust, friendly,
Singing with open mouths their strong melodious songs.

WALT WHITMAN

Chapter One

March 1866

The minute her pa stumbled through the doorway, drunk again, Lila Bonner felt the air in the already cold room change. Now it was frigid. Pa cursed the dilapidated shack and its meager furnishings in the room—the rough table and chairs, the cot where Lila slept, the rusty stove—before his eyes focused on her. She hated it when he looked at her like this, his bloodshot eyes full of anger, his mouth a grim line.

"What you lookin' at, girl?" he slurred as he grabbed the table to steady himself.

"Nothing, Pa," She tried to sound pleasant. "Set yourself down," she encouraged, pulling out a chair for him.

"Think I'm helpless, do ya?" he yelled as his hand struck her across the face. Lila fell backward to the floor holding her cheek. "Don't need no help. 'Specially from the likes of you," he bellowed.

Dazed by the blow, Lila didn't move for a moment before rising to her feet. Tears stung her eyes. "Pa, please." She made her appeal softly.

"Please what?" he growled and lowered himself into the chair. "I walked into town for some poker and lost every hand." He laughed harshly before turning his gaze to Lila, and his crooked smile disappeared. "You look just like her, ya know? And now she's dead."

Lila held her breath, waiting for his next outburst. It didn't come.

He stood and lurched toward the door. "Can't stand lookin' at you. Can't stand bein' in here. I'm sleepin' in the barn," and he disappeared into the cold night.

Lila's heart thudded in her chest. This is how it had been since Mama died three months ago just before Christmas— outbursts of rage followed by deep despair. At first Lila had blamed his behavior on grief. Mama was the heart and soul of their family, and they were both lost without her. Then Lila blamed the whiskey when Pa took to drinking.

Now she didn't know what to blame, but his outbursts were becoming more frequent and more violent. She didn't know how much more she could take. She dragged their old trunk from the back bedroom and shoved it against the front door. Maybe this would keep Pa out if he came back later. Maybe she could sleep through the night.

Maybe.

**

The sky dappled pink in the first light of morning. Lila yanked the shack's door shut behind her and took a deep breath, filling her lungs with damp spring air. She touched her cheek, hoping the swelling had gone down enough to go unnoticed. There wasn't time to sort this out now, and Lila willed the worry to leave her mind.

She hugged her homespun wool cloak tight and ran across the yard, her chestnut brown curls tangling in the wind, the muddy earth soft under her boots. She opened the back door to the Beatty's house and hurried down the stairs into the basement kitchen. They would be overwhelmed with hungry travelers soon enough.

"Mornin', Mrs. Beatty," Lila managed a smile and hung her cloak on a peg. "I'll start the johnny cakes."

"Good morning, Lila." Mrs. Beatty glanced up as she mixed biscuits, then stopped and frowned. "Lila, what happened?"

"What happened?" Lila repeated the question in an offhanded manner.

"To your cheek. It's bruised."

"Oh, that. It's nothing. The door sticks, and it whacked me in the face."

Mrs. Beatty said nothing, and Lila knew her excuse had fallen short. Mrs. Beatty studied Lila for a moment longer before turning her attention to the five Beatty children cleaning the soot off the chimney lamps. "Mind that chimney, Benjamin," she warned the youngest child. "They are expensive and hard to come by, young man."

"Yes, Mama," he nodded.

The Beatty family owned the two-story limestone home set on acres of rich Kansas farmland which served as a stagecoach stop thirty-five miles west of Independence. The Santa Fe Trail covered 770 miles from Independence, Missouri to Santa Fe, New Mexico, and ran along their property line, affording commerce with traders, trappers, homesteaders, and adventurers heading west. While a fresh team was hitched up to the coaches, the Beattys provided the passengers with johnny cakes for breakfast and suppers of stew and hash.

Lila welcomed her work in the kitchen, anything to get her mind off Pa. The johnny cakes sizzled on the hot griddle and she transferred them to a pan on the stove's warming shelf. Balancing a tray of tin plates and cups, she set the trestle table which stretched the length of the basement room. The walls were the same white limestone as the house and caught the warm reflection of the kerosene lamps hanging from overhead beams.

Mrs. Beatty shooed the children into action once they'd finished the lamps. "Time you brought in the eggs. No dillydallying!" She brushed aside a wisp of graying hair and turned to Lila. "Not too soon to start the bacon."

Lila heard horses thunder into the stable yard, the reinsman barking commands to the blowing, whinnying team as the coach came to a stop.

"They're here already," Mrs. Beatty heaved a sigh and wiped her brow before setting out a pan of hot biscuits.

"Expecting a big rush this week?" Lila asked.

"Lord, I hope not. Last Thursday we served seventy-five. Can you believe that? Seventy-five!"

Through the window Lila glimpsed the passengers climb out of the coach and stretch, some heading to the privy out back and others washing up at the pump outside the door.

Mrs. Beatty greeted the arrivals as they found chairs at the table. "Breakfast is coming right up." Lila tended thick slices of bacon sputtering in the skillet that gave off a smokey aroma from the stove, then piled them onto a platter and brought them to the table.

"Smells good enough to eat."

Lila turned to the young man seated at her elbow as he rubbed his hands together in anticipation. "Yes, sir," she nodded.

With a few discreet glances, Lila sized up the travelers. She was certain the three men with greasy beards wearing slouch hats and canvas pants stuffed into tall boots were trappers. One had let loose a stream of tobacco juice before coming inside. At least he had the decency to spit outside, Lila thought. The young man who had spoken to her was more puzzling. He wore working man's clothes, but his dark brown hair and beard were clean and neatly trimmed, nor were his hands calloused like a laborer's. Unusual for a westward bound man.

The travelers devoured the biscuits and gravy, johnny cakes, and bacon without uttering so much as a word. Lila and Mrs. Beatty shared a quick smile of satisfaction while keeping the table well supplied.

"You serve right tasty food, Ma'am," one of the trappers said, sopping up the last of his gravy with his third biscuit.

"If you pass through here in summer, you'll have the best berry cobbler anywhere," Mrs. Beatty said with pride.

Breakfast concluded in twenty minutes while the team was changed out, and the passengers gathered their belongings for the next leg of the journey. Lila watched them board the stage through the open door and felt the spring air gust cold with a shiver.

Smokey, the reinsman, walked around the team to double check the harness. Although he trusted Mr. Beatty's handlers, it was his responsibility to keep his passengers safe. Coming front to his lead horse, Smokey gave the soft muzzle a pat. He climbed into the box and eyed the clouds in the west. One of the best drivers on the trail and a veteran of the Civil War, Smokey always kept a sharp eye on his surroundings. "Weathers comin'. Best be on our way."

Lila saw Pa holding the harness of the lead horse until the coach was loaded. No one could have guessed how drunk he'd been only hours earlier. No one knew how skillfully he hid his drinking. To the casual observer, nothing appeared out of the ordinary. Only Pa and Lila knew the truth.

And the truth broke Lila's heart.

The Beattys had been good to Lila's family. She had moved with Pa and Mama from Indiana two years ago after the crops failed. Her older brothers stayed behind, determined to make a go of it, but Pa was sure his dream was out West. He was good with animals, and the Beattys hired him as a stableman to care for the teams of horses and mules so vital to running the station. The Beattys had a crumbling cabin on their property Pa said he would fix up while he "got back on his feet," and then they would find a place of their own.

But he never got around to fixing it up, and last winter when the cold and snow came in through the slats, Mama came down with a cough that wracked her body. Then came the fever, and two weeks before Christmas Mama died. It was a staggering loss for Lila.

The tin canister on the shelf in their make-shift kitchen had a thin roll of bills in it. One night after Pa had been to town, Lila noticed the next morning the roll of bills was thicker. That was a month ago, but lately the roll of bills was thin again, and Pa still hadn't gotten back on his feet.

Lila watched Pa step away from the lead horse, and with a crack of the whip the stage rattled out of the yard onto the highway, leaving a heavy silence in its wake.

Chapter Two

Lila latched the Beatty's dining room door against the chill, but her thoughts continued down the road with the stagecoach. "Ever wonder about folks like them?"

"What do you mean?" Mrs. Beatty asked, pouring water from a bucket into a dishpan.

"Where they're headed . . . what they're looking for." Lila brought a tray of dishes to the kitchen counter and rolled up her sleeves. "I usually don't pay any mind, but don't you sometimes wonder how it turns out for them . . . searching for their dreams." She sighed, "I think everyone should have a chance for that."

"I've no time searching for anything, Lila. Busy enough with work right under my nose."

Lila jumped as a crack of thunder split the peaceful morning. "Gracious! Where'd that come from?" Rain suddenly pelted the house.

Mrs. Beatty glanced out the window. "Those folks are heading right into that weather. Don't envy 'em that."

They scrubbed down the table and stacked the tin ware into the cupboard while the wind whipped rain across the yard. The oldest Beatty children swept the floor until a rattling sound drew them to the window.

"Look, Mama," Jerimiah said. "Corn snow."

Mrs. Beatty peered over his head at ice pellets hitting the window. "Oh, Lordy. Thought we were done with winter."

An hour later they heard a coach pull into the yard now covered with sleet, the booming voice of Smokey halting his team. Moments later the door burst open, and passengers surged into the dining room, the same passengers who had just left. The men were drenched, their clothes splattered with mud.

"Sakes alive you're soaked!" Mrs. Beatty exclaimed. "Take your coats off." She pulled chairs close to the cookstove where they draped their soggy garments. "Lila, get the coffee going. "Jerimiah, Samantha," she called up the stairway. "Fetch towels." The onslaught of muddy passengers and drenched clothes upended the room. It looked and smelled more barn than dining room.

Smokey joined them after taking the team to the barn and peeled off his rain-soaked coat and hat, ice crystals dripping from his thick beard. "We rode smack dab into it," he declared.

"Never seen such a gully washer," one of the trappers said.

Smokey continued. "Before I knowed it, the left front wheel was sunk in the mud."

"Took a mighty lot of pushing to get it free," said the young man as he wiped his head with a towel.

"Gonna put us behind schedule," Smokey said, "but it made no sense to go on—the road's like muck."

When the coffee had boiled, Lila brought steaming cups to the table where the passengers dried off with rags and towels, unsure how long they'd be waiting on the weather.

Lila handed the young man a cup. "Best get warmed up before you catch your death."

The young man nodded. "Much obliged."

**

By afternoon a blizzard had taken hold. Mr. Beatty and Pa came in from the barn, red-faced and covered in snow.

"Don't think you'll be going anywhere today, Smokey," Mr. Beatty said, stomping his boots.

"Sure 'nuff a bad one," Pa added, brushing snow from his coat. "Your team is watered and fed. No need to worry 'bout them."

When it was obvious the travelers would be staying the night, Mrs. Beatty gathered blankets from upstairs. It was a crowded table as the entire Beatty family and Pa took supper with the travelers. Lila and Mrs. Beatty baked a double batch of cornbread, added extra carrots and potatoes from the root cellar to the pot of stew, and sliced a platter of ham.

After supper the men brought in armloads of wood covered in snow that dripped onto the floor and steamed when fed to the stove. The trappers lit their pipes, and smoke hovered over the trio while they played poker from a deck of dog-eared cards. The young man turned up the wick on a kerosene lamp and opened a book from his satchel. Curious, Lila paused beside him while offering coffee refills as she made her way around the table.

"More coffee?"

"What?" He looked up. "Oh, yes, thank you."

She filled his cup and glanced over his shoulder at his book. "You're reading Whitman's verses."

He couldn't hide his surprise. "You know Walt Whitman?"

Lila felt the color rise in her cheeks. "Why, yes. I—we studied him in school—back in Indiana." She cleared her throat. "You seem to know him, too."

The young man replied, "I suppose I do." Lila found his steady gaze unsettling. "Did you enjoy his poems?" he asked.

"Very much. I remember one especially—about America singing. It's my favorite." Lila still thought of herself as "the girl sewing or washing" in the poem. Those words had leaped from the pages into her heart, making her feel part of something important, something greater than herself. She suddenly caught herself staring into the young man's brown eyes and quickly looked down at the coffee pot. "Didn't mean to bother you."

"Not at all, Miss—" he raised his eyebrows.

"Bonner."

"Miss Bonner, I'm Mr. Reynolds. You obviously enjoy reading, and I find that commendable. Certainly not a bother." His mouth turned up in the slightest smile.

Lila felt the color in her cheeks deepen. Not only was his appearance different, so were his manners.

The wind rose in a fierce howl, rattling a loose shutter, and Mrs. Beatty stuffed rags under the door and across the windowsill to keep snow from blowing in. The travelers gravitated toward the stove in the kitchen end of the dining room as it struggled to keep the room warm. The trappers eventually folded their cards, wrapped themselves in blankets, and found places to sleep on the floor. Before Lila and Mrs. Beatty left the kitchen, Mr. Reynolds approached Lila.

"Miss Bonner, I know there's not much left of the evening, but since we're going to be here for the night, perhaps you'd like to borrow my book."

"I couldn't . . . I . . ."

"Please, I insist. I have other books with me."
"You don't mind?"
"Here." He handed her the slender volume.
"I'll be very careful with it and return it first thing in the morning. Thank you, Mr. Reynolds." Lila hesitated. "If you don't mind me asking, where are you traveling to?"
"Council Grove, Kansas. About a hundred miles from here."
"What will you do there?"
"I'm taking the position of schoolteacher. They've just opened a new school."
Lila ran her hand across the book cover. "That explains this," she said wistfully.
"Now that I answered your question, perhaps you'd answer mine." Mr. Reynold gave Lila a perceptive look. "You were obviously a good student. Any opportunity for you to continue your education?"
Lila gave a harsh laugh. "Too many demands to keep body and soul together, sir." She tucked a stray curl behind her ear and in a gentler tone added, "But I thank you kindly for lending me your book. I look forward to reading it."
"You're welcome. Good night, Miss Bonner."
"Good night, Mr. Reynolds."
A small room off the kitchen stored sacks of flour and corn meal, a box of old clothes, and a cot used in emergencies for sick travelers. When the weather was especially bad during the winter Lila often slept there. Wrapped in the warmth of her cloak she carried a lamp into the storeroom with the book of verses. The room was freezing. Lila propped open the door for heat from the kitchen and settled onto the cot under a quilt.
If cooking was a respite from her daily worries, reading was the opening to another world altogether, a world of wonder and delight she had only caught a glimmer of through the borrowed books of her former teacher. Now she held one of those treasured books she could read until tomorrow. Between blowing on her hands and rubbing her ice-cold nose she read page after page until the words swam before her tired eyes and she nodded off to sleep.

Chapter Three

"Lila!" A rough hand shook her hard.

Lila opened her eyes. A dark figure loomed over her. "Pa? Is that you?" She pulled up on her elbow. "What's wrong?"

"I been lookin' for you." He leaned into her face, stinging her eyes with the stench of whiskey.

Lila recoiled. Drinking two nights in a row was unheard of, even for Pa.

"Why didn't you come to the house?"

"Weather's so bad . . . it was late . . ." She pulled the quilt closer, and the book fell to the floor.

"What's this?" Pa swayed as he bent over and picked it up. "Where'd you get this?"

"Pa, lower your voice. You'll wake the guests."

"Don't be tellin' me what to do, missy." He looked at the book with disgust. "Stupid girl." His lips curled in a sneer. "How many times I told you don't waste time on books?" He waved it in the air. "Nonsense is what this is. I need you workin', not readin'."

"Alright, Pa, I will. But, please, give me the book." Lila reached for it, and he clamped down fiercely on her wrist, wrenching her hand backward, ripping one of the pages.

"Pa!" Lila cried out in pain.

"Now look what you done!" Pa slammed the book to the floor.

Lila stared in horror at the book, her wrist throbbing and burst into tears.

Pa stood silently over Lila, watching her sob. Suddenly he was on his knees begging forgiveness, his own tears flowing. "Lila, honey, I'm sorry. I didn't mean nothin'. Please don't cry. I need my sweet Lila. I need you darlin." He buried his face in her lap and wept, pulling her close.

Lila suppressed a gag against the smell of whiskey and the revulsion of his head pressing against her chest. "Pa, stop it." She choked back a sob. His arm reached to stroke her hair, and she pushed it away. "Pa, stop." She forced herself to sound firm. "You must be really tired, Pa. You should rest a spell before breakfast." He didn't argue, and she angled his sagging body onto the cot. He fell to snoring as Lila retrieved the book and fled to the kitchen.

Pa's striking her was bad enough, but his depraved longings were a terror all their own. One minute he hated the sight of her, the next minute he was stroking her hair, forcing himself on her. Maybe it was her chestnut hair and expressive hazel eyes that reminded him of Mama. Lila favored the mother she adored more and more with each passing year. One thing had become very clear to Lila—the reasons no longer mattered. She was done living in that shack with Pa. If she wanted to survive, she had to leave.

She wiped her cheeks and hung her cloak. Her hands shook as she lit a kerosene lamp and added kindling to the embers in the cookstove while Pa's drunken rant lingered to taunt her. *Stupid girl. Stupid girl.*

"You're up early."

Lila whirled around. "Mr. Reynolds, I didn't know anyone was awake."

He smothered a yawn. "Truth be told, I'm not sure I ever went to sleep. Wind howled most of the night."

Lila avoided his gaze and looked down at her fidgeting hands. "Mr. Reynolds, I have unfortunate news."

"Oh?"

"I'm afraid . . ." Lila raised her chin. "I've spoiled your book. I'm deeply sorry, and I will pay you for the damage." She fought back tears.

A frown creased Mr. Reynold's forehead. "Surely, it's not as bad as that, Miss Bonner, to cause you such worry. Perhaps it can be mended. It wouldn't be the first time one of my books has needed repair." He followed her gaze to her hands clasped in front of her and inhaled sharply. "Your wrist. Miss Bonner, what happened?"

Even in the dim light, Lila couldn't hide the red mark Pa had left, and she fumbled to cover it with her hand. "Not sure how it got there—you know how it is—always something happening in the kitchen." She feigned a smile and handed him the book. "If you could let me know what I owe you for the repair."

After breakfast Mr. Beatty and Pa cleared a path from the main door to the privy. Through the frosty window Lila watched Pa gather an armload of firewood, seemingly unaffected by last night's dinking. By mid-morning the snow had stopped, and although it wasn't deep, the relentless wind kept the travelers bound inside.

"Miss Bonner, might I have a word?" Mr. Reynolds rose from the table while Lila cleared the last of the noon time dishes.

"Of course."

"You owe me nothing to repair the book. I've mended much worse. You should see some of my classroom books at the end of the term."

"But Mr. Reynolds—"

"Please." He held up both hands. "The matter is closed."

Lila paused. "Thank you. I appreciate your generosity." She started to leave. "Do you mind, Mr. Reynolds, could you tell me about Council Grove?"

"What about it?"

"Is it the kind of place where someone like me could find work? Folks on the trail been talking about the Hays House Restaurant there the past few years. It's getting quite the reputation. Sounds like a place I could get a job."

"Is your family thinking of moving there?"

Lila's head dropped. "It's only me and Pa now, but," she whispered, "he's not my real Pa."

"I see." Mr. Reynolds glanced at her wrist, then looked at her with concern. "Surely, you're not thinking of going there on your own?"

"No, of course not. But if I did go, what would my prospects be, do you think?"

"The town is growing fast. You might find employment, but I wouldn't recommend you go by yourself. The West isn't a place for a young woman on her own."

"I've worked for Mrs. Beatty near two years in the kitchen. She's taught me ever so much about cooking and shared her family recipes."

Mr. Reynolds smiled agreeably, but Lila could tell his opinion hadn't changed.

Lila leaned forward, making her case. "I can do more than cook. I can read. I could help teach in a school like I did back in Indiana." Her voice rose with conviction. "I know there's a school because that's where you're going." Distracted from their game by the rising voices, the trappers stopped play and looked up. Suddenly self-conscious, Lila lowered her voice. "What about fare for the stage? We've been saving up, but I don't know if we have enough."

The rest of the afternoon Lila's mind whirled while she thought about the meager roll of bills in the kitchen canister. Wrapping herself in cloak and hat, she stepped outside and found the wind's fury had receded, its biting teeth reduced to an occasional gust. A feeble sun hung behind the clouds as she trudged across the frozen yard to the little shack.

The stove was cold, and dirty dishes littered the table. She went to the bedroom and pulled out Mama's carpet bag from under the bed. It didn't take long to gather her things—a night gown, an extra change of clothes, her only good dress, and her most precious possession, a daguerreotype of Mama. She removed money from the bottom of the carpet bag where Mama had secretly stashed what little she could over the years. There wasn't enough for the fare to Council Grove, but she could buy a ticket as far as Overton and take her chances there. She slid the bills into her skirt pocket and left the shack without touching the money in the canister.

She would have to board the stage without Pa knowing—he'd never consent to let her go. But how would she accomplish that? Sometimes he stood with the team until all the passengers boarded. Could she board at the last minute and hope Smokey would drive away against Pa's protests? Every nerve in her body was frayed when she entered the kitchen. Lila stuffed her carpet bag under the cot in the storeroom and turned her attention to supper.

By late afternoon a lone rider arrived from the west. When he took supper in the dining room, the stranded travelers gathered round eager to hear his report on the travel conditions.

The wind had blown the road clear, he said, and he figured they could travel west just fine. "Signs of moonlight, too," he added.

"I like the sound of that," said Smokey. "Once we have our supper, I say we harness up the team and head out." The travelers heartily agreed, and their excitement grew at the prospect of resuming their journey.

Chapter Four

This evening? A wave of panic swept over Lila. The stage was leaving in only a few hours! Her heart hammered in her chest. *I can't go,* she thought. *I'm not ready — I don't have a ticket — I can't leave Mrs. Beatty without help — I can't do it!* Then she looked down at her hands working the dough and saw them trembling. The red mark on her wrist had faded, but there would be other marks, other humiliations, she was sure of it.

Supper was finished. Lila had forced down only a few bites of biscuit, partly from lack of time but mostly because her stomach was in knots. She pulled Mrs. Beatty aside.

"You've been good to my family. I want you to know how much I appreciate your kindness."

"Why, of course, dear. But why are you telling me this now?" Mrs. Beatty frowned, confused.

"Because I need you to do something for me."

"What is it?"

Lila handed her the bills from her pocket. "This is for my ticket to Overton. If you'd give it to Mr. Beatty, I'd be grateful."

"You want a ticket to Overton? Whatever for?"

"Just give it to him. I have to leave tonight, on the stage. Before Pa knows."

"What's happened, Lila?"

"Since Mama died, he's taken to the bottle. He's drinking too much. Getting too familiar."

Mrs. Beatty gasped. "Oh, child, why didn't you tell me?" She grasped Lila's hand.

"I can't stay with him anymore." Lila slowly withdrew her hand. She backed away from Mrs. Beatty to the storeroom and returned wearing a man's coat, her skirt stuffed into britches, her curls tucked in her woolen hat, carrying the carpet bag.

The passengers were filing out the door to the stagecoach. Lila could see Pa standing beside the team of horses, and she hurried into line behind the last passenger, Mr. Reynolds. He turned and his eyes widened.

"Miss Bonner?"

Lila put her finger to her lips, pleading with her eyes. She leaned in with the other passengers and inched toward the stagecoach.

Mr. Reynolds frowned in disapproval. "Miss Bonner—"

"Please. Don't say my name," she implored in a whisper.

"But surely, you can't—"

Lila grabbed his forearm. "I have to," she begged under her breath.

Mr. Reynolds held her pleading gaze for agonizing minutes before he patted her hand and left the line to walk over to Pa. *Please don't tell him. Please don't tell him.* Afraid of being found out, she lowered her eyes to the ground and took another step toward the coach.

"Mr. Bonner, good evening to you." Mr. Reynolds positioned himself in Pa's line of sight. "I wanted to thank you for everything you and the others have done for us while we've been stranded. Much obliged."

Lila felt a hand on her arm and turned. Silently Mrs. Beatty pressed coins into Lila's hand, regarding her with eyes brimmed in tears. Lila squeezed her hand, blinking back tears of her own.

Only one passenger stood between Lila and the coach door. *Hurry. Please hurry.* Mr. Reynolds continued to talk, and Pa remained beside the team of horses. Lila reached the door, hoisted herself up into the carriage and sat, her heart thudding so she was certain everyone could hear it. Moments later Mr. Reynolds climbed aboard, squeezed in next to her, and closed the door.

Smokey hollered at the team and snapped the whip, jerking the coach into motion. Lila leaned toward the window and could make out Pa in the twilight as he walked toward the barn. If her brothers could see him now, they wouldn't recognize what he'd become, how far he'd fallen. Her heart ached at the loss of her family, of her brothers back in Indiana, but especially of Mama and Pa when their family had been whole and happy before it was diminished. She turned to Mr. Reynolds and whispered in a barely audible voice, "Thank you kindly."

"Where are you traveling?" he asked casually.

Lila took a deep breath to calm herself and felt the tension ease from her shoulders. "Overton. I hope to find work there as a cook."

"Overton? There's nothin' in Overton but a couple a homesteads and a stable for changin' teams," said one of the trappers. "Ain't nobody hirin' a cook there."

Lila frowned. "But I thought . . ." Her heart fell to her stomach at the realization of her plight as the Beatty's grand limestone house with green shutters—that blooming flower on the Kansas prairie—disappeared behind a rolling hill.

"I've heard Council Grove is a satisfactory destination," Mr. Reynolds offered. "If you need an extension on your ticket, perhaps someone onboard could assist you."

Lila heard the empathy in his voice. She spoke earnestly as she searched his face. "Mr. Reynolds, that would be the kindest thing anyone's ever done for me. I would repay this person in full as soon as I'm able."

"I'd expect nothing less." He smiled, his eyes full of encouragement.

The coach swayed as it picked up speed traveling into the moonlit night. Lila wasn't bothered by the discomfort of the hard coach seats and biting cold; her worry came from Pa discovering her escape. In the first hours, Lila feared he would catch up to the stage and force her back home with him. But with each mile down the road, she was more certain she had left Pa behind for good. Lila sank into her oversized coat and britches and closed her eyes, allowing herself to feel safe as the miles lengthened behind her and a future stretched ahead.

Something stirred deep inside her, something buried but not forgotten from a poem memorized years before: "*I hear America singing, the varied carols I hear . . . Each singing what belongs to him or her and to none else . . . their strong melodious songs.*"

It lifted and circled and hummed until it sang full-throated with the turn of the wheels, daring her to be hopeful as the coach rocked its way west.

Chapter Five

They arrived in Overton in the early morning hours, and Lila discovered the trapper had been right in his assessment of the town. It consisted of a changing station which was a squat, rundown barn and an operator who lived in a dugout beside it. Her insides quivered at the thought of being dumped here with nowhere to go, and she breathed a silent thank you to Mr. Reynolds for his generosity.

The passengers got out, and the men walked away from the station to relieve themselves. There was enough moonlight for Lila to find her way through the tall grass to an outhouse beside the barn. Her boot caught on a twisted vine, and she fell into a thorn bush. *I should have squatted beside the road,* she thought grimly, while pulling a sticker from her palm as she sat in the outhouse.

When the team of horses was changed out, they continued down the highway. "Mr. Reynolds, do you know what time we get to Council Grove?" Lila arched her back to stretch her cramped muscles.

"The driver said it will be after dark tonight."

"Knew we should've taken mules," said one of the trappers to his friend. "Ain't used to ridin' coaches," he explained to Lila. "Ridin mules is better. Got more say in how the travelin' goes."

The fickle March weather was fair by midday, and the canvass curtains were raised, allowing a view of the countryside. High rolling prairie was dotted with stands of trees and endless contours of thick grass the color of hay. Lila was sure the blue and white dome of sky was within her reach, should she choose to touch it. The passengers dozed or were lost in their own thoughts as they rocked side to side. Mr. Reynolds returned to reading one of his books, which gave Lila a chance to glimpse him unnoticed.

Mr. Reynolds was nice looking, no denying that. Penetrating brown eyes, strong chin, broad shoulders. But what was Lila to make of him? He seemed very kind, but what did she really know about him? She didn't want to admit it, but she was indebted to him. There was no way she could make it to Council Grove without his help. She fingered the coins Mrs. Beatty had given her safely tucked in a coin purse in her pocket. Those coins plus the dollar bill she set aside from her ticket money would have to be rationed out over the coming days until she found a job. In the meantime, she hoped Mr. Reynolds was as nice as he seemed and not a masquerading rogue, pretending to be something he wasn't.

"Can I trust him?"

"Sorry, did you say something?" Mr. Reynolds had put down his book and was looking at her.

Lila took a sharp intake of breath. "Oh, no." She gave a shy smile and recovered her error with, "I must have been mumbling in my sleep." Mr. Reynolds resumed reading, and Lila's gaze returned to the landscape. *Mr. Reynolds has given me no reason to think poorly of him and every reason to think highly of him. Mama always said, "Your heart knows the truth," and my heart says he's trustworthy. Still, I have to be wary.*

**

Lila stood in front of the mirror above the chest of drawers in the boarding house bedroom and smoothed the wrinkles out of her dress the best she could. Her stomach growled as she ran a hairbrush through her tangled hair with little success. "What a mess." She leaned into the cloudy mirror, searching for her image, and pinched color into her cheeks while trying not to worry about her desperate situation. She'd gotten away from Pa but had no means of taking care of herself. Had she exchanged one dire situation for another?

There was a light tap on her door. "Miss Bonner?"

"Yes." She tossed the brush onto the dresser and opened the door. "Good morning, Mr. Reynolds."

"Good morning, Miss Bonner. I trust you slept well?"

"After being thrown around in the coach for the past day and night, that bed felt mighty good, thank you. And you?"

"Slept like a log. Can I interest you in breakfast, perhaps at the restaurant across the street?"

"Mr. Reynolds, I appreciate the offer, but I don't want to put you out. There's really no need."

"I beg to differ, Miss Bonner. We're both new in town, and you're here on your own. We can make new acquittances together."

Once again, Lila was caught up in the man's kindness. "Thank you, sir. I'd welcome the company."

The sun peaked through hazy clouds as they left the boarding house affording them their first daylight view of Council Grove. The surrounding tallgrass prairie, a vigorous forest at the edge of town, and water from the Neosho River that meandered through town made it an appealing place for a settlement, or so Lila had been told by the other travelers. The broad main street was dotted with wooden buildings on both sides: two inns and the boarding house, a limestone mercantile, a handsome brick bank, one hotel, two restaurants, a livery and blacksmith, and houses, both log and wooden, set off from the main street.

Lila noted the early morning shoppers and traders of Council Grove, townsfolk mixed in with rough looking drovers and teamsters, then gave her full attention to the one-story clapboard building across the street with a set of double doors and an overhead sign with huge letters identifying Hays House Restaurant.

There was more riding on this meal than filling her stomach. She meant to find work here—any kind of work—at this well-known eating establishment. Working at Hays House was the quickest way to pay off her debt to Mr. Reynolds and get herself established in Council Grove. She had no back-up plan and desperately hoped they would hire her.

The aroma of bacon and coffee met them at the front door. "Sit yourselves anywheres," a plump women called from the kitchen at the end of the large dining room. She and Mr. Reynolds found a small table beside a stone fireplace at the opposite end of the room. Logs crackled and sent sparks up the chimney. The floor was rough wood planking surrounded by whitewashed walls, the ceiling supported by sturdy wooden posts. Sunshine spilled into the room from windows that looked out onto Main Street.

"Seems like a nice place," Lila whispered noticing customers at nearly every table.

A young lady slightly older than Lila brought their order of fried eggs, potatoes, and bacon to their table. Lila hadn't eaten a full meal for over two days and dove into her food without another word. Brushing the last crumbs of biscuit from her mouth Lila wondered aloud, "Do you think a family runs this place?" she scrutinized the employees. "I see a woman doing the cooking, I think I see a man through the swinging door behind the kitchen, and the waitress might be their daughter."

"Only one way to find out." Mr. Reynolds nodded in the direction of the kitchen.

"Introduce myself and ask if they are hiring." Lila stood and made her way toward the woman frying breakfast at the cookstove. "Excuse me." The woman took no notice and slid eggs onto a plate. "Sorry to bother you—"

"Can I help you?" It was the young lady who served the dining room.

Lila turned. "Oh, yes. I was hoping—that is—my name is Lila Bonner, and I'm new in town." She thrust out her hand.

The blond-haired young lady had an abundance of freckles on her upturned nose and the appearance of dimples when she spoke. She looked at Lila's hand and offered hers with a questioning look on her face.

"I'm looking for a job. I'm a cook with two years' experience at the Beatty Stagecoach Stop west of Independence. I was hoping you might be hiring. I'd be willing to do anything—cook, serve dining room, stock supplies, cleanup—anything."

"How do I know you can cook?" The round-faced woman from the cookstove was at her elbow, eyeing her. She came up to Lila's chin, her white hair pulled back in a bun; a feed sack apron strained across her ample figure.

"Well, ma'am," said Lila, "my friend, the new schoolteacher for Council Grove, just came from the Beatty's. He can vouch for me. Or I guess I could show you." Lila lifted her eyebrows ever so slightly.

"We don't get newcomers lookin' to be cooks here. We run a family business—me, my husband and daughter. Been open ten years. Sorry Miss—"

"Bonner."

"Miss Bonner. Don't need any help. Now if somethin' happens, you know, out of the blue, maybe then."

Lila put on a brave face as her heart sank. "If you're shorthanded even for a day, I'd be willing to help out. I'm staying at the boarding house. Thank you kindly, Mrs. —"

"Hays. Everybody calls me Edna." She nodded toward the waitress. "This here's my daughter, Stacy."

"I'll be in again. Breakfast was very good — especially the biscuits and sweet cream butter."

When Lila returned to their table, Mr. Reynolds didn't need an explanation. "Judging from your expression, they're not hiring."

Lila slumped into her chair. "Only if they come up shorthanded. That leaves me hoping they have some kind of difficulty. Not very charitable of me."

"The day has just begun. Come on, I have errands to do."

Down the street was The Last Chance Store with a large hand painted sign in front: Beans Bacon and Whiskey. Modest in size, the mercantile was built from local white limestone, and the wagons and horses tied up in front indicated there was a brisk trade taking place inside.

"Last Chance," mused Lila as they entered. "Interesting name."

"It's over 600 miles from here to Santa Fe if you take the Cimarron cut off — further if you take the mountain route. No other place to trade once you leave Council Grove. You'd best be prepared before you head out," Mr. Reynolds said.

"Where'd you learn all that?" Lila asked.

"Been reading up on Council Grove since I knew I'd be moving here."

Lila took new interest in the store that held such importance for anyone embarking on the Santa Fe Trail. She wandered the aisles stacked with hand tools, breaking plows, tents, dry goods, candles, and whiskey kegs. As she passed the coffee beans, rice, flour, corn meal, and bacon, she felt her coin purse and stopped. To save money it made sense to buy a few items for supper and avoid paying for board at the boarding house. She picked up a box of crackers, a wheel of cheese, two apples, and met Mr. Reynolds at the counter to pay.

After he paid for his purchases, Mr. Reynolds reached in his jacket pocket. "Oh, I nearly forgot. Can I post a letter here?"

"Sure thing," the man behind the counter replied. "It'll go out tomorrow. We have a postmaster who picks up and delivers." He nodded to a pile of letters on the floor next to the counter. "That's the delivery right there." He gave a gap-toothed smile. "We don't have mailboxes. But I take care of the letters—nothing gets lost on my watch."

Lila and Mr. Reynolds shared a skeptical look before she asked him, "Do you have family back home?"

"Something like that," Mr. Reynolds replied.

"Reminds me," Lila said, "I should write my brothers, let them know where I am."

In the afternoon Mr. Reynolds had an appointment with the school superintendent, and Lila sought out the lady who ran the boarding house, a widow named Mrs. Bauer. She found her in the small kitchen off the dining room peeling potatoes.

"Mrs. Bauer?" Lila knocked tentatively on the doorframe.

A rather stern looking, middle-aged woman with dark hair raised her head. "Yes? Are you in need of something?" A frown creased her forehead.

Lila cleared her throat. "I don't mean to interrupt."

"Miss Bonner, isn't it?" Mrs. Bauer resumed peeling potatoes. "What can I do for you?" Her question sounded more like a command.

Lila's words tumbled out. "Mrs. Bauer, I'm in need of a position to support myself. I'm new in town, on my own, and can do most anything—clean, cook, do laundry. Mr. Reynolds, the new schoolteacher, can vouch for me. I'd be willing to help out anyway I can. I'd be most obliged if you'd consider me."

Mrs. Bauer stopped work for a second time and gave Lila a penetrating look with steel blue eyes. "You're pretty young to be out on your own. You're not a run-away, are you?"

"Oh, no, ma'am. That is, there was only me and my pa and things weren't going well and so I . . ." her words hung in the air, heavy with innuendo.

"I don't run a charity, Miss Bonner. Can't afford to. This place is all I have to stay alive."

"I don't expect charity, Mrs. Bauer. I'm a hard worker, grew up on a farm. I can do chores—chop wood for kindling and such. If you can't hire me, maybe I could work for my room and board, or whatever you think is fair." Lila returned her steady gaze and could tell Mrs. Bauer was giving her words consideration.

"Grew up on a farm, you say?"

"Yes, ma'am. Helped with spring planting and putting food by after the harvest."

The room grew silent but for the sound of the knife slicing through potato skins. Lila waited.

"There's days I could use an extra pair of hands, Lord knows." Mrs. Bauer straightened. "How about this. I try you out for a week or two doing odd jobs and see how you do. If your work is satisfactory, you get room and board. If you fall short, the agreement is off. Do we have a deal?"

"Oh, yes, Mrs. Bauer. Thank you." Lila extended her hand, then hugged the surprised woman. "I won't disappoint you, I promise. When do I start?"

"Table needs setting for dinner, you can start there. Tinware's in the cupboard in the dining room."

A long trestle table, much like the Beatty's, with mismatched chairs took up most of the dining room. Adjacent to it was a parlor with a pot belly stove flanked by well-worn stuffed chairs, foot stools, and two rockers with a brightly colored, braided rug on the floor. But the star of the room was a walnut mantel clock with a gold face, sitting on a side table. Lila thought it must be a family heirloom brought here from far away. It graced the simply furnished parlor with elegance.

Lila made short work of the table setting and stood back, hands on her hips with a pleased nod. Activity out on Main Street drew her attention to the front window. She glanced up and a cry escaped her lips. Disappearing into The Last Chance Store she caught sight of a familiar figure. It was a quick look but enough to send a shock through her system.

It was Pa.

Chapter Six

Lila stood frozen, her hands to her mouth.

Mrs. Bauer burst through the swinging door from the kitchen. "Whatever is the matter, Miss Bonner?"

Lila's voice choked with fear. "Mrs. Bauer, you can't tell him I'm here. Please. He can't know I'm here."

"What on earth are you talking about? What's happened?"

"It's my pa. He's come looking for me, and I can't go back with him. I can't!" Tears welled in her eyes.

At that moment, Mr. Reynolds arrived back at the boarding house. "Good afternoon, ladies. How —" He stopped abruptly. "Good heavens. What's happened? Miss Bonner, you're white as a sheet." He reached for her elbow to steady her.

"That's what I'd like to know," Mrs. Bauer said. "I heard a shriek, came running out here and she's making no sense. Going on about her pa and I don't know what all."

"He's here." Lila's voice was small. "He's looking for me."

"You saw him?"

"Yes, going into the Last Chance Store."

"Would someone tell me what's going on?" Mrs. Bauer's voice rose.

Mr. Reynolds turned to her. "Mrs. Bauer, there's been a misunderstanding. Miss Bonner has had a fright which I will straighten out. If you would be so kind as to fix her a cup of coffee or tea, I am stepping out for a moment but will explain the situation when I return." He led Lila to a rocking chair, nodded to the landlady and left.

"Where are you going?" Lila called after him.

"Last Chance," he called over his shoulder.

**

The coffee Mrs. Bauer gave Lila was strong and bitter, left over from the morning pot. Lila didn't mind. It was hot and comforting as it slid down her throat while she waited for her nerves to settle and Mr. Reynolds to return. While the minutes ticked away on the mantel clock in the parlor, Lila's fear was compounded by her embarrassment over the fuss she had caused at seeing Pa. It wasn't like her to fall apart so completely, but then, she'd never run away before either.

The minute Mr. Reynolds returned, her heart pounded anew.

Lila shot from her chair. "Well?"

"He wasn't there."

"But I saw him go in."

"I went through the store, front to back. Even talked to the owner. Your pa's not there."

Lila sank to the chair. "I know it was Pa. He must have slipped out somehow."

"Perhaps you were mistaken. You thought you saw your pa, but it was someone else." Mr. Reynolds lowered into a nearby chair. "There's only one way for customers to leave the store and that's by the front door." He leaned forward and waited until she looked up at him. "I think it's more likely you saw someone who looked like your pa, and that was very frightening for you."

"I want to believe you. But—"

"Excuse me." Mrs. Bauer appeared from the kitchen, a dish towel in her hands. "Could I have a word, Mr. Reynolds?"

"Of course." He rose and followed Mrs. Bauer from the room, leaving Lila alone to sort through what she was sure she had just seen—Pa in the flesh, here in Council Grove.

When Mr. Reynolds returned Lila could sense something was wrong. "Mrs. Bauer is very sorry for your troubles, but—" He looked away momentarily.

"But what?"

"She's backing out of the agreement she had with you. Says she can't afford any trouble here at the boarding house. She's sorry. So am I."

The room was silent again but for the mantel clock and the occasional whinnying of a horse on Main Street. "I see." Lila rose. "If you'll excuse me, Mr. Reynolds, I'm going to my room for a spell. Thank you kindly for looking for Pa. I'm most grateful." She quickened her steps to her room and shut the door before tears spilled down her cheeks.

Lila sat on the edge of the bed. The fright at seeing Pa, then doubting the truth of it, and now losing compensation for work, however meager, was too much. Even though she had escaped his grip, Pa still had a hold on her, that much was clear. Unless she wanted to live her life looking over her shoulder, Lila knew she had to rid Pa from the emotional claim he held over her.

Lila took her time. She released a deep breath and poured water into the wash basin. Her hands trembled as she splashed cold water on her face and dabbed herself dry. *I thought leaving Pa behind would mean a new start. Turns out leaving him behind won't be that easy.*

There was a light tap on the door. "Miss Bonner?"

"Yes."

"It's Mr. Reynolds."

"A moment, please." Lila smoothed a stray curl, knowing it would do nothing to hide her puffy cheeks and went to the door.

"I thought, perhaps, you might like to see the new school. I have to finish unpacking books, if you'd care to accompany me?"

"I'm not sure I'd be very good company, Mr. Reynolds."

"It would make short work of the unpacking." He raised an eyebrow.

Lila felt a small surge of something. Normalcy. Hope. "I think, Mr. Reynolds, I like your suggestion. Let me get my cloak."

**

The new clapboard school perched at the top of a hill overlooking the town's cluster of buildings like a matronly schoolmarm eyeing students in her charge. There hadn't been enough money to install a proper belfry, but the townspeople had promised it for the future. The classroom smelled of new lumber and fresh paint.

"Oh, what a lovely school, Mr. Reynolds," Lila declared once inside. She turned in a slow circle, eyes wide, taking in the new bookcases, the freshly polished desks in perfect rows that faced the front of the classroom and the teacher's desk and nearby pot belly stove. Three windows on each side of the room allowed a view of the prairie grass waving in the March wind. "We started out with a one-room dirt floor back in Indiana."

"Folks here are mighty proud of it—as they should be. I'm lucky to have secured the job here." He turned to one of the crates that lined the walls and rolled up his sleeves. "Now to work. Most of these crates have textbooks. They go on the shelf under the windows." Lila nodded and the two began emptying the books into neat rows on the shelves.

"Look what I found." Lila held up a slim book, her face wreathed in a smile. "My first reader." She leafed through the pages and grinned. "I loved the stories my teacher read from these. Do you have all the McGuffey's?"

"The first three sets."

Reluctantly she closed the book and carried an armload to the bookshelf. "What about these?" Lila pointed to rolled-up maps lying on the floor.

"I'll need a toolbox to get those up. That's for another day."

"And these boxes?"

"Slates and chalk."

They were unpacking the last of the ink pots and pens when Mr. Reynolds spoke. "Miss Bonner, about what happened earlier." He turned to Lila. "I hope I'm not overstepping, but I think your worry about your pa got the better of you."

"Oh?"

"Do you really think he has the capability to come after you? To take you back with him to the Beattys?"

Lila stopped working and turned the idea over in her mind before answering. "When you put it like that, I'm not sure he *is* able to come after me. He doesn't own a horse. He'd need to borrow one."

"That's what I've been thinking," Mr. Reynolds answered.

Lila continued. "He'd have to up and leave the Beattys, which he can't afford to do. He needs that job."

"I was hoping you could see that, too. I think your worry is making you fearful in a way that clouds your judgement."

"That's possible," Lila conceded. "You are right, I was very frightened when I saw, when I *thought* I saw Pa. Then I was embarrassed I made such a fuss. Then I was upset Mrs. Bauer didn't want me to stay on as a helper." She drew an exasperated breath. "Then I was furious that Pa—even though he wasn't here—could cause me such trouble. I'm still mad. I've got to find me a job before I starve."

"No talk of starving, Miss Bonner. You are far too clever for that." Mr. Reynolds brushed his hands together in a finishing manner. "Let's call it a day and head back to the boarding house."

The March wind whipped Lila's cloak as the pair walked down the hill to Main Street. Knowing a supper of cheese and crackers waited in her room, Lila considered Mr. Reynolds' lighthearted dismissal of starving. She'd at least have *something* to eat, by golly. But thoughts of starving disappeared into the blustery air, replaced by the excitement of being in the Council Grove brand-new schoolhouse. To be in a classroom again, looking through her very first McGuffey Reader brought back a flood of forgotten memories. She hadn't wanted the afternoon to end, so enjoyable was the task.

"Mr. Reynolds, I was glad to help with the unpacking and getting things ready for school. If you need more help with anything—the books or supplies or even helping the students settle in, please let me know. I'd be glad to lend a hand."

"Glad to hear that, Miss Bonner. Glad to hear that."

Chapter Seven

Lila was up before the sun. There were two places left to inquire about employment that she knew of—Last Chance and the livery. She knew the livery would be open early and decided to go there first. She bit into her last apple while she decided to wear her everyday dress instead of the pants and shirt she had worn when she fled from Pa. She would wear those old work clothes if she got the job but could at least appear as the girl she was when making her first appearance.

"You serious about mucking out stalls?" The dark complected man was built bull strong with a square jaw. He gave a derisive laugh. "What would I want with a scrawny thing like you?"

Lila drew herself up. "Sir, I've mucked out many a stall growing up on our farm."

"Horses?"

"One or two."

"Know how to handle 'em, do 'ya?"

"Well enough."

"Hmm." He let loose a stream of tobacco that landed in front of her boots. "Never hired a girl before. That lazy Farnum boy only shows up when it suits him, hafta say."

"I'll show up whenever you say so."

The man eyed her closely. "Hmm." He spat again and shoved his hands in his pockets. "Like I said, ain't done this before. So, ya think you can pull your weight?"

"Learned from the best—four older brothers. And my pa, of course."

"Well, then, let's see what ya got. I don't 'spect no half measure of work."

"No sir, Mr. Jensen. Full-out hard work." Lila extended her hand. "Thank you very much. When can I start?"

"See that pitchfork over there?"

**

She hadn't dreamed she'd be hired on the spot, otherwise she'd have worn the undesirable but much preferable work clothes. By midafternoon Mr. Jensen had run out of chores. Lila raked her boots against the foot scraper beside the livery door and headed back to the boarding house. Filthy and hungry she went out back to the pump behind the kitchen to clean up.

"Sakes alive," she muttered, inspecting the hem of her dress covered in mud and muck. She held it under the pump, gave the handle a few jerks and rubbed the soiled places as best she could. Grabbing a rag drying on a nearby bush, she swiped the remnants of mud and manure off her boots, aware that although they looked clean, they might smell otherwise. She finished washing up with cold water, wishing for the bar of lye soap on the washstand in her room.

By suppertime Lila was famished. *No cheese and crackers tonight.* She draped her damp dress over the footboard to dry, changed into clean clothes, and pulled her hair back into a soft coil. The aroma of fried potatoes and onions made her mouth water as she stepped into the dining room. Mrs. Bauer was setting out platters of hash topped with fried egg next to baskets of biscuits.

"Good evening," Lila flashed a small smile to Mrs. Bauer who had been cordial but cool to her ever since the incident about Pa.

"Miss Bonner," she nodded and returned to the kitchen.

The table was full of men, seven in all, a cowboy in boots and spurs with hair to his shoulders, some in workmen's clothes, others who looked like travelers on the trail, all generally clean but for one man in grubby hunting clothes. They took turns giving Lila side-ways looks. One man not hiding his curiosity gave her a long hard stare. Averting her eyes, Lila pulled up the nearest chair and sat.

"Miss Bonner, nice to see you." Mr. Reynolds slid into the chair next to her.

Relief flooded her. "Good evening, Mr. Reynolds." Lila took a biscuit and passed him the basket. "How was your day?"

"Almost ready for school to open." He scooped a helping of hash onto his plate. "And how was yours?"

Trying to balance her ravishing hunger and polite conversation, Lila told him between mouthfuls about her unexpected employment at Mr. Jensen's livery. "Before I knew it, I was mucking out the stalls." She paused to wipe her mouth and, in the silence, realized all heads at the table were turned in her direction.

Lila felt her cheeks flush.

"Young lady like yourself, workin' at the livery?" One of the men shook his head.

"Nothin' wrong with that," said the unkempt hunter.

Another man gave Lila a leering smirk that slithered down her spine. "Perhaps the lady would like some company later this evening?"

"Excuse me." Mrs. Bauer stood at the kitchen door, arms folded rigidly across her chest. "What folks do on their own is no concern of mine. But while you're a guest at the boarding house—and you are my guests—everybody treats each other right."

She retreated through the swinging door, leaving an awkward silence in the room. After an interval, one of the men cleared his throat and the meal resumed. Lila finished eating and carried her plate to the kitchen. "No call for boarders to clear their plates." Mrs. Bauer's tone was brusque.

"I know," said Lila. "Only want to make myself useful. Besides, it gives me a reason to leave the table."

"Hafta watch out for some of the men in a town like ours," Mrs. Bauer continued. "I have rules in my boarding house, and I hold folks to 'em. We have a decent town and most folks passing through are decent, too. Then there are others . . . well, you can't be too careful, being a young girl like yourself."

Lila set her plate on the counter. "What do you mean?"

"I mean, Miss Bonner—"

"Please, call me Lila."

"Lila, there are some men who take advantage of women no matter their age. There are horse thieves, stagecoach robbers, cattle rustlers—real scalawags you need to watch out for. You are an attractive young lady, if you hadn't noticed, which makes you a target of unwanted advances. So, I'm saying be on your guard."

Lile opened her mouth, then closed it, struck by Mrs. Bauer's blunt warning. "Thank you for saying what you did in the dining room . . . and for saying what you did just now. I'll be careful, Mrs. Bauer."

**

Lila sat on her bed gazing out the window that overlooked Main Street, her stomach full, her body tired but her mind at rest. She had a job. Even though it was exhausting and smelly, working at the livery was a life saver until something better came along. Streaks of daylight remained in the darkening sky, allowing her to watch the town put itself to bed. The only disturbance was from the saloon two doors down which was lit up with raucous laughter and tinny piano music that floated in her window.

A wagon loaded with supplies left town and rumbled past five figures on horseback at the end of Main Street. Lila stared at the silhouettes, tall in their saddles, bare-headed and knew from their bearing they were Indians. Her chest tightened ever so slightly. Lila's experience interacting with Indians was limited. The town of Olathe near the Beatty's stagecoach stop was a melting pot of sorts, and the few times Lila had ventured there she had encountered a mix of people: fur traders with French names, slave owners and abolitionists, immigrants from Germany, Jewish businessmen heading to Santa Fe, and freed slaves. American Indians were part of this mix, but she'd only seen them from afar.

The five riders held their mounts, watching Council Groves, but for what purpose? Lila kept them in her gaze until they turned their horses and with a single whoop, sped off into the night. She shuddered involuntarily. Suddenly chilled, she turned back the quilt on her bed and crawled under it.

She was certain she'd fall asleep instantly, but when she closed her eyes a bizarre parade of images assaulted her: the men from the boarding house making lurid banter at her expense, a full-fledged war party of Indians bearing down on Council Grove, the specter of Pa lurking outside her window. Her eyes popped open. She lay still, straining for the faintest sound of danger but heard only the raspy snoring from the boarder in the room next to hers.

Chapter Eight

Mr. Reynolds swung the ax high and split the log clean in two. He repositioned the half, swung again, and the two splits toppled over. The sun was hot for April, and he wiped his brow with his forearm before continuing. Lila gathered an armful, disappeared into the schoolhouse, and returned for another load. "The wood box is nearly full."

"This will be the last of it then." He heaved a breath and sat on a stump beside the uncut logs. Lila sat on the ground beside him.

In the three weeks since arriving in Council Grove, Lila's life had settled into something of a routine. Mr. Jensen was a gruff but fair employer. Mucking out the stalls, filling water tanks, and feeding horses made for cracked blisters on her hands. The first coins she earned would not go to paying off her debt to Mr. Reynolds but toward a pair of work gloves at Last Chance. Her next earnings would buy work boots so she wouldn't have to scrub hers every night before supper. Lila regularly stopped by the Hays House to ask if they needed help in the kitchen or to run the odd errand. In spite of being turned down, Lila persisted in a pleasant way, even buying an occasional cup of coffee, which she couldn't afford. Edna Hays made note of that and discreetly refused Lila's coins at the register. Her generosity caught Lila off guard, and she gave her unspoken thanks with a grateful smile.

Although helping at school brought no prospect of income, Lila made time in her day whenever possible to stop by the school. Whether she listened while a student read to her during class or helped tidy the classroom at the end of the day, she couldn't ignore the draw she felt to the school.

Sitting in the warm sun, Lila scanned the schoolyard and beyond. The landscape possessed a vibrant beauty—yellow and red blooming wildflowers in grassy fields, a beautiful grove of fine timber at the end of Main Street, gentle hills in the distance, and powerful clouds racing the azure sky. Movement in the corner of her eye drew her attention to a young boy before he disappeared around the corner of the schoolhouse.

"Mr. Reynolds, I do believe one of your students has been spying on us." The corners of her mouth turned up. "Or maybe he doesn't want to go home quite yet."

"Ah, I think I know who that might be. Mr. Charles Bellmard—Charley. He's a good youngster, smart. He hangs around the schoolyard sometimes. Always by himself."

Lila was facing the corner of the schoolhouse where Charley had disappeared and saw his dark curly head peek from his hiding place again. "He's a good student then?"

"A very good reader."

"What about friends?"

"From what I can tell, he's somewhat of an outsider. Mr. Piper told me his dad comes from a family of French fur traders. He married a Kaw Indian who died when Charley was a baby, so the father raised him. They live in the woods north of Council Grove. His father has taught him how to trap and takes him out of school for weeks at a time when they go hunting."

"Have you met his father?"

"Oh yes." Mr. Reynolds chuckled. "Soon after I got here, I found where they live—a primitive cabin—and was met with a shotgun blast as I approached. I had wanted to tell Mr. Bellmard what a good student Charley is and the importance of school attendance. As you can imagine, I changed my mind. We hollered a few exchanges. I invited him to stop by the school. So far nothing. But I'm not giving up. Charley is smart and someone needs to stand up for him."

"You're just the person to do that, Mr. Reynolds. If anyone can get Mr. Bellmard to listen, it'll be you."

The surprising authority in Lila's voice caused Mr. Reynolds to stop. He stared at Lila a moment before he pulled his handkerchief from his pocket and mopped his brow. "Miss Bonner, we've known each other for a while now, having met under rather dire circumstances. Would it be inappropriate to call each other by our Christian names?"

Lila stood. "I think of you as a friend, a very kind friend indeed." She hesitated a moment. "It would please me to use our Christian names, Mr. Reynolds."

"Call me John." He gave a half grin.

"You may call me—"

"Lila. I remember from before." He extended his hand, and they shook as in a friendly first introduction. Lila returned the smile, her cheeks warming.

**

Lila scraped manure off her boots while Mrs. Bauer worked the pump to fill the kitchen buckets. The livery had been busy well past supper with a heavy volume of travelers passing through town. Lila hoped there might be a plate of food left in the kitchen. She was famished.

"Do you mind if I ask you something?" Lila asked.

"What's that?"

"Are there Indians around here? I mean, I've seen one or two at Last Chance, but that's all."

Mrs. Bauer wrinkled her brow. "What brought this on?"

"The other night I was looking out my window. I saw riders at the end of Main Street. They were sitting on their horses watching the town for what seemed like ages. Just watching. They were Indians, Mrs. Bauer. Gave me the willies. Now why would they be doing that?"

"You're asking the wrong person. I don't pretend to understand Indians and their ways." Mrs. Bauer placed a second bucket under the spigot and pumped. "The Kaw tribe has been here a long while, since before we arrived. They live on the reservation a few miles south. They hunt and keep to themselves for the most part, trade in town at times."

Lila laced up her cleaned boots and wiped her hands on her pants. "Do you ever have any troubles?"

"Some settlers up north of here was raided a few years ago. Whole family killed by a few renegade Cheyenne. Terrible business. Sometimes the tribes go at each other, too. But it's been quiet for the most part, thank the Lord."

A whole family murdered. Lila had only heard rumors of such atrocities, but never from those who lived close by. She searched the horizon behind the boarding house for what she didn't know and shrugged off a shudder. "Guess it's different from what I'm used to."

"Nothing you can do about it but mind your own business. And be on the lookout." Mrs. Bauer picked up the buckets.

"Let me take one of those," Lila offered.

"Don't think I don't know what you're trying to do, Lila. You're still a paying guest and I'll not be needing your help."

"I'm not trying to get a job, Mrs. Bauer. Just offering to help—like any decent able-bodied person would."

Mrs. Bauer sniffed. "By the by, if you can't get those boots any cleaner, you'll drive my last paying boarder out of the dining room." She turned on her heel, wedged the door open with her toe, and let the door slam behind her.

Lila stood staring, her appetite and thoughts of food gone.

**

The school children had scattered for home long ago. Only Lila remained on the schoolhouse steps, Charley beside her, reading aloud from the McGuffey Reader. Reaching this level of trust with Charley had unfolded in stages. On the odd day when Lila finished early at the livery, she'd hurry back to the boarding house, change into clean clothes, and come by the school, often to find Charley hanging around the schoolyard by himself. Sometimes Mr. Reynolds gave him jobs. Lila tried to engage him in conversation to no avail. Lila understood the loneliness of an independent child and despite their difference in age, imagined what it must be like for him. It wasn't until Lila pulled one of the readers from the shelf and asked him to read to her one afternoon that Charley opened up.

He hunched over the book and traced the words with his finger.

"The . . . frog can see the dog. See the frog on a . . . log." Charley turned to Lila with a look that sought approval, his coal black eyes shining.

"Very good. Go on."

He nodded, pleased. "This is a fat hen. The hen has a nest in the box."

A shadow fell over the page. They looked up into the face of Louis Bellmard, Charley's father, peering down at them. His skin was weathered in a deep tan, his dark hair pulled back in a braid and dark eyes that glinted black as night like Charley's. "The boy should be home now. School's over." It wasn't a threat, but rather a statement that would take no counter.

Lila stood abruptly. "Mr. Bellmard. How do you do?" She extended her hand. "I'm Miss Bonner. I help out here at school. I—"

"You're not the teacher. He came by once."

"That I did, Mr. Bellmard. It's good to see you." Mr. Reynolds appeared at the school door.

"Came to collect my boy." He turned to Charley. "Chores waiting for you."

"Of course. We won't keep him from his chores, right Charley?" Mr. Reynolds gave Charley a smile. "Mr. Bellmard, if it's all right with you, I'd like to send a book home with your son."

Charley's mouth fell open, and he turned to his father.

"What book would that be?"

"A reading book. We have an extra set of older books. Charley has been doing so well—I'd like to see that continue."

Mr. Bellmard frowned. "Never given such a thing any thought." Charley grabbed his dad's hand but kept his eyes to the ground.

"What could it hurt?" Mr. Reynolds's voice was encouraging.

"Hmm. Probably nothing." He looked down at his son. "So long as chores come first."

Charley nodded vigorously. "Yes, Pa."

They watched Charley and Mr. Bellmard walk away, Charley clutching the primer close to his chest. He looked back once, then turned, and hurried to keep step with his pa.

"You may have won a small victory, Mr. Reynolds—John," Lila corrected herself as they watched the pair leave the school yard.

"Maybe," he agreed. "We'll know for sure when it's hunting season. Old habits are hard to break. Speaking of that, I found something you might be interested in."

Once inside he led her to the bookshelf. "I finished sorting a small crate of books Mr. Piper found. They're odds and ends, some are retired readers, others are single volumes. Help yourself. Borrow whatever you want."

"Oh, Mr. Reynolds—John—that would be lovely." Lila fell to her knees and scrutinized the spines of each book, setting aside a few as she went. In no time she had a stack of five, then put three back not wanting to appear greedy and knowing her exhaustion at the end of each day would limit her reading time.

They walked down the school hill together, Lila's new books clutched to her chest with the same pride as Charley had with his own reader. When they reached Main Street Mr. Reynolds paused. "I have errands at Last Chance. I'll see you later at supper."

"Posting more letters home?" Lila teased lightly.

"Something like that," he replied with a smile Lila had grown accustomed to. The breeze blew his dark hair over his forehead which he brushed aside and strode toward Last Chance.

As he walked away, Lila wondered and not for the first time about John's family. He was very faithful in writing them, yet he never spoke of his family, which she found curious. Someday maybe the opportunity would arise when she would ask him about that.

Chapter Nine

"Lila, could I speak with you?" Stacy Hays stood in the doorway of the boarding house dining room, shifting from one foot to the other, her brows knitted in a frown.

"Of course." Lila excused herself from the table.

"It's Ma," Stacy whispered. "Her foot is hurt bad—dropped a jug on it—and doc told her to stay off it a few days, and she won't listen and it's gettin' worse."

They moved out of earshot into the parlor. "What can I do?"

"Can you help out? Maybe then Pa and I can make her sit so the swelling will go down because it if gets any bigger I don't know what—" She broke off and tears filled her eyes.

"She's in a bad way?"

Stacy nodded.

"I'd be glad to help, only—"

"What?"

"I have to keep hours at the livery. I can come by when I'm finished and stay as long as you need me."

"We'd be grateful for that. Thank you."

**

By the time Lila changed and rushed to Hays House the supper crowd had thinned out. She hadn't even stopped to eat, hoping once again for leftovers. If she lost any more weight, she'd need suspenders to hold up her work pants. Mrs. Hays sat in a corner of the kitchen area, her left leg propped up on a footstool, barking orders to Stacy and her father who were flying between the cook stove and customers in the dining room.

"Am I glad to see you." Stacy brushed past Lila balancing a tray with bowls of chili.

"There's an apron in the back," said Mrs. Hays and gave a weary smile. "Glad you could come."

"I asked for work more times than I can remember," said Lila. "I should thank you."

In the two remaining hours before closing, they kept ahead of a small but steady stream of customers until nine o'clock when Stacy locked the doors and pulled the shade. Lila, Stacy, and Mr. Hays washed the dishes, swept the dining room, cleaned the cook stove, and closed out the till. When Mrs. Hays mentioned baking a cobbler for tomorrow's customers, Lila felt the last of her energy seep away. Steadying herself at the kitchen counter, she asked, "Mrs. Hays, would you mind very much, I haven't eaten since breakfast and—"

"Oh, child, shame on us. We had no idea." She tried to stand, winced, and fell back into her chair.

"Edna, you stay put," Mr. Hays said. "We'll see to Lila."

"Herbert," she replied, "there's cheese in the back. Stacy, isn't there some leftover apple dumpling?" She turned to Lila. "I'm so sorry. Get yourself a cup of water and sit a spell. We'll fix you right up."

For the next week Lila worked from sunup to sundown at the livery and the Hays House. She fell into bed exhausted when she returned to the boarding house after dark, nevertheless counting her blessings to have two jobs, even if one was temporary. Returning to the kitchen brought sunshine back into her life. The aroma of coffee and fresh baked biscuits, the bustle of activity in the restaurant were comforting reminders of the Beatty's stagecoach stop. Seeing the parade of adventurers pursuing their dreams on the Santa Fe Trail served as a distraction from her daily battle to survive. The Hays family had an easy familiarity about them, and a plate of warm food that came with the job was worth a salary all its own.

**

"M-m-m, this is mighty good."

"Would you like another helping?" Lila smiled, barely looking at the man while she carried dishes from another table.

"I would indeed. Thank you."

Lila halted and turned. She stared at the man with a thick dark beard and bushy eyebrows, finishing his bowl of rice pudding. "Smokey, is that you?"

The man returned her stare. "Smokey it is. Who be you?"

"Lila, Lila Bonner from the Beatty's place. I worked in the kitchen."

He frowned and then a look of recognition spread across his face. "The young 'un who worked with the missus in the dining room. I remember you."

"I can't believe seeing you again. You driving a stage?"

"Yup. Headin' to Santa Fe again. Got a full load."

"You must be mighty busy."

That was all Smokey needed to launch into a story about his last drive where he avoided catastrophe with a twister in western Kansas. When his narrative was over, he gave Lila the once over. "You workin' here now? On your own?"

"Yes . . ." Lila set her tray on the counter and sat in a nearby chair. "How are the Beattys? How's Pa? He doin' all right?"

"Beattys are fine. Your pa is same as ever, from what I can tell."

"That's good to hear." She paused to consider how to proceed. "I have a favor to ask. This may seem strange, but Pa can't know I'm here. It's better if we don't cross paths."

"What goes on 'tween family folk ain't none of my business."

Lila expelled a breath. "I'd be much obliged, Smokey." He nodded but his eyes lingered as though he was looking for unspoken answers in Lila's face. She prayed he was trustworthy and wouldn't divulge her whereabouts to Pa. "It's good to see a familiar face again. Now, how about another serving of rice pudding? It's Mrs. Beatty's recipe."

The rest of the evening while Lila served customers her thoughts turned to the day three months ago last March when she had watched a coach load of travelers leaving Beattys "searching for their dreams." Wasn't that how she put it to Mrs. Beatty? Which begged the question now, what was she searching for? What was her dream?

There had to be more to her dream than getting away from Pa. There had to be something to go *to*. Like Whitman's poetry she believed everyone has their place, their song to sing. Why was finding her place, her dream, so difficult? Lila set a tray of dishes at the sink and looked at her chapped hands and her falling-apart boots. "Some dream. More like a nightmare."

She helped close the restaurant and crossed the empty street to the boarding house. Had she made a mistake in striking up a conversation with Smokey? He could reveal her whereabouts to Pa. She wondered what the odds were Smokey would keep his word, when a tall figure stumbled into her path and fell against her.

"Watch where you're going," Lila admonished. As she brushed past him, the man reached out and grabbed her arm.

A deep voice slurred, "Wha's your hurry?"

"Let go of me." Lila pulled against his grip, but he held fast.

"Where you goin' tha's so important?" He blocked her way and grabbed her other arm.

"I said let go of me!" Lila shouted and struggled against his tightening clutch.

"Yer goin' nowhere." He pulled her from the street and shoved her against a hitching post. "Not till I git my good night." His foul breath swamped her, and he covered her mouth with his.

From some primal place came a response that Lila knew was her only chance. In one swift motion, she raised her knee and with all the force she could muster planted it into his groin. His holler raised the alarm that her own call for help hadn't. Lila suddenly found herself surrounded by Mr. Hays, Stacy, John, and Mrs. Bauer. Rowdies from the boarding house poured into the street and raised fists on the offender. They beat him until Mr. Hays shoved his way to the crumpled man and sat on him, sending John and another to fetch the sheriff.

"Good heavens, Lila, do you go lookin' for trouble or does it find you on its own?" Mrs. Bauer put her arm around Lila and with Stacy's help led her inside the boarding house to the parlor. "I'm brewing you a strong tea with spirits in it, and I won't take no for an answer."

Stacy and Lila sat on the davenport. "Are you all right?" Stacy looked as terrified as Lila felt.

"I think so," but Lila's trembling hands belied her words, and Stacy reached out and pressed them between her own.

"Wish we had gotten there sooner. By the time we got the door unlocked—oh, Lila I hope he didn't hurt you."

Lila forced a steady voice. "He came out of nowhere. Just grabbed me." Terrible thoughts took hold while she sat there. What if running away was worse than staying put with Pa? What if worrying about Pa tracking her down wasn't as real as the bad sorts in her midst who were ready to do her harm this very minute? This place could eat her alive if she weren't careful.

By the time Mrs. Bauer brought the tea, the noise from the street had quieted. The liquid was hot and potent. "Drink all of it—you need it," she ordered Lila. Lila took another biting swallow and looked up as John came through the door.

"Are you all right?" He sat opposite her, worry written on his face.

"I am, thank you. I should have been paying attention."

"This is not about you, it's about the man who attacked you."

"Where is he?"

"Don't worry about him. Sheriff's got him."

"I'll see she gets to bed," said Stacy. She helped Lila to her feet, and they left Mr. Reynolds who watched them until they reached the safety of Lila's room and closed the door.

Chapter Ten

The sun streaming through the window signaled she had overslept. Lila rolled over and winced. Why would her back hurt?

Then reality penetrated her morning daze, and she remembered last night—the shove against the wooden post, whiskers raking her face, the hands groping her body. She sat up in bed and pulled the covers to her chin. Of all the things that happened last night, it was his whiskey smell that sent a shudder through her this morning. That was the smell of Pa, and it brought a chill no pile of quilts could set right.

She huddled deeper into the covers and leaned her head against the iron headboard. What day was it, Tuesday? Wednesday? Why couldn't she focus on something so simple? The last thing she remembered was drinking Mrs. Bauer's tea to calm her nerves. She had slept soundly for which she was grateful, except now she felt unable to think clearly. She swung her legs over the side of the bed. Her livery pants and shirts lay in a nearby heap, soiled with dirt and dung. Her stomach recoiled and she reached under the bed for the pisspot. Not a good start to the day.

Lila shook off her dirty clothes outside the back door and took deep breaths of fresh June air to help clear her head and settle her stomach. By the time breakfast was prepared she felt well enough for fresh biscuits and coffee. Out of habit she carried her dishes to the kitchen where Mrs. Bauer stopped her.

"Lila, what in the world were you doing out so late? And not for the first time I might add." Mrs. Bauer stacked dirty dishes at the counter. "There's bound to be trouble that time of night." She faced her, waiting for an answer.

Lila felt cast as the disobedient child in need of reprimand. "I need the money, plain and simple."

"You're working? Doin' what?" Mrs. Bauer waited, eyebrows arched.

"What do you think I'm doin'?"

"You're not working at the Red Horse, are you? Cause if you are—"

"Mother Mary, of course not!" Lila put both hands on her hips and stared down Mrs. Bauer. "How could you think that?"

"Well, I—"

"I'm working at the Hays House. Have been for two weeks till Mrs. Hays gets back on her feet."

"I didn't know they hired—"

"Well, they do hire. And they're mighty nice folks, too. Now if you don't mind, I'm late to the livery." She turned on her heel and left the kitchen.

**

Jenson Livery was painted above the hayloft doors on the front in bright red paint. The livery was much larger than their barn back in Indiana, built of rough timber with a wide front door that slid open on a rail, stalls along both walls that ran front to back, and a hayloft above. Mr. Jenson confined his office business to a battered wooden table and chair near the door where he exchanged money with customers. He could accommodate a few wagons out back but most clientele were cowboys and travelers seeking a place for their horses for a night or two.

"Bout time you got here. Yer not gettin' lazy on me, are ya?" Mr. Jenson asked, not really caring for an answer and returned to his work.

Lila assured him she was not getting lazy and grabbed a pail and shovel. To her relief there were only five stalls that needed cleaning. She mucked out each stall, forked over fresh straw and filled the water tanks, the twinge in her back barely noticeable. It was important to be thorough. Lila knew the first able-bodied man or boy who showed up looking for work would be hired on the spot, and she'd be out of a job. At the very least she didn't want to give Mr. Jenson a reason to terminate her, other than the obvious. She was a girl.

By mid-afternoon with chores done, Lila cleaned her shovel and boots. Being so accustomed to the barn smell, she hardly noticed whether her boots were clean anymore. It was the straw under her shirt chaffing her skin that drove her home to change as fast as possible. A calendar hung on the wall beside the sliding door with an advertisement for a hardware store in Denver. The date she couldn't recall earlier in the morning leaped from the calendar. Today was Tuesday, June 15. Her seventeenth birthday.

She walked back to the boarding house, the sun riding high over Council Grove, its townspeople animated with purpose and place. A mother trailed by four children going into Last Chance to shop, families loading wagons with goods heading out of town, a stagecoach discharging passengers at Hays House, a group of men in conversation in front of the bank. After three months of tedious work, this was still not her place, nor had she found her purpose.

The importance of this special day brought an ache to her heart. She remembered birthdays past when Mama saved enough sugar and flour for a vanilla cake with icing always decorated with a single wild rose plucked from a bush in the yard. "My little wild rose" is what Mama had called her, their only daughter with four older brothers. The memory brought a lump to her throat.

"Miss Bonner—Lila." Mr. Reynolds waved as they approached the boarding house from opposite directions. She pushed back the tears and brightened when he caught up with her inside. "I'm so glad to see you. I've been worried. How are you?"

There was that look he gave—so sincere and genuine—that always undid Lila. It was like he could read her thoughts. "I'm all right, thank you. Mrs. Bauer's tea, whatever was in it, I slept like a log." She managed to smile.

"I'm glad to hear that." He returned her smile. "Say, I have some news, an invitation really."

"Oh?"

"Next Sunday is the annual school picnic. From what I hear it's quite an event." He went on to explain that after church the whole town gathered at the school grounds to celebrate the end of the school year. "You must come. You haven't been able to help at school for weeks, and the children have been asking about you."

A social event with townspeople and food and games and... "I'd love to come if I don't have to work."

"Mr. Piper said businesses close down for a couple of hours—the livery, the mercantile included. I'm sure the Hays family will be there, too. I don't think you have to worry about work."

Thoughts of the picnic carried Lila all the way to her room, and she nearly tripped at her door. On the floor was a pair of boots, second hand, but still useful and recently polished. She picked them up. "Where in the world?" She looked up and down the empty hall, pondering her benefactor. Mr. Reynolds? The Hays family? It didn't really matter who the kind-hearted person was. Now she owned two pairs of boots and could relegate one for barn work and one for everyday wear. Such luxury.

She quickly changed into a skirt and blouse and her new boots; they were a bit large but if she laced them tightly, they would do fine. Before leaving for the Hays House, she ran into Mrs. Bauer setting up the dining room for supper.

"Mrs. Bauer, did you see anyone leave a pair of boots outside my door? Perhaps Mr. Reynolds, or Stacy?"

Mrs. Bauer ran her hands over her apron. "I had an extra pair, hardly ever wear them."

Lila stood speechless. "You?"

"Do they fit?"

"I . . . how can I ever thank you? I—"

"Now don't go on and on. You have a job waiting. Better get goin'."

Lila backed out the door, expressing her gratitude while dumbfounded by Mrs. Bauer's generosity. The woman was hardly civil to her, never mind kind. Where had this come from?

Chapter Eleven

Lila nestled two cherry pies into a basket and covered it with a gingham cloth before returning to the stove. She had been at Hays House since early morning frying batches of chicken for the picnic with Stacy and Mrs. Hays, whose kitchen was fully engaged now that her foot was completely healed. Edna hovered over the sputtering fry pan and turned the chicken one last time. "Get these into the basket, and we should be on our way, Stacy."

Saturday evening Lila reserved the tub at the boarding house and indulged in a hot soaking bath in her room. She couldn't remember the last time she'd had a tub bath. She slid down until the hot water was up to her neck, smelling the sweetness of lavender soap that she'd splurged on at Last Chance.

She closed her eyes and let the steam rise until her cheeks tingled. This was heaven. She swore she could feel the layers of dirt lift from her body. She ducked her head under until thoroughly soaked, then lathered her hair and scrubbed with vigor. It would take considerable brushing to untangle it, but it was worth every stroke to feel so deliciously clean. She owned only one other dress—the green one that still looked smart and complimented her coloring. She'd wear it with a matching ribbon to tie back her hair.

Skies had threatened showers in the early morning, but the sun cast rays through the clouds as the procession of buggies and wagons made their way to the school yard. Lila and Stacy hopped down from the wagon and helped unload the food baskets and jugs of water. They found a place to spread blankets under the stand of trees where Mr. Reynolds and parents were setting up a table for food.

"Ah ha, Mr. Reynolds, looks like a nice crowd for the picnic." Mr. Hays thrust his hand forward in greeting.

"Indeed, it does. So good to see the Hays family." He turned. "And Lila—" He stopped mid-sentence, his eyes wide.

"Good morning," Lila smiled. "Lovely day for a picnic."

Mr. Reynolds stood mute, staring at Lila, the wind ruffling strands of her hair, gently billowing her dress. "I . . . that is, you look . . . "

"Cat seems to have your tongue, young man," Mr. Hays teased.

Mr. Reynolds' tanned face turned red. "I mean, yes, it is a lovely day for a picnic. So glad you came." His eyes never left Lila.

Activity swirled around them, women setting out food on the table, men starting up a game of horseshoes, children playing tag, but for that moment Lila was captured in his gaze, unaware of everything else.

"Your pies, Lila."

The words barely registered. "What?" Lila didn't know who had spoken.

"I said, you should set out your pies." Mrs. Hays had a bemused look on her face.

"Oh, my pies. Yes, of course." Lila tried to hide her blush with the busyness of unloading the food baskets.

Stacy gave her a playful nudge and whispered, "As I live and breathe, if I don't see two people smitten." She giggled. "Why didn't you tell me?"

"Mr. Reynolds smitten? What a silly notion, Stacy." Lila reached for a knife and cut slices of pie, ignoring Stacy's know-it-all grin.

"Well, I notice you're not denying that *you're* smitten."

That's when a realization hit Lila like a thunderbolt. She couldn't deny the charge because it was true. As careful and cautious as she was in matters of trust, she *was* smitten.

**

Lila circulated among the families while looking for one particular student. When she didn't find him, she made her way to John who was visiting with Mr. and Mrs. Piper. After an introduction and short conversation, Lila pulled him aside. "John, where's Charley?"

"Looks like he's not coming. I was hoping Mr. Bellmard would come for Charley's sake."

"Isn't there something we can do?"

"Short of going to their cabin and bringing Charley here, no there isn't."

Lila brightened. "That's it. We could go to their house and ask Mr. Bellmard if we could bring Charley to the picnic."

"You mean, now? But the picnic has already started."

Lila would not be deterred. The Bellmard cabin was a fifteen-minute walk from school. John would not hear of Lila going alone so she convinced him that the picnic would continue during his short absence, and they would search for Charley together.

A canopy of trees arched overhead as they walked the sun dappled path through the woods. The musty smell of earth and leaves stirred underfoot. They reached a clearing where the Bellmard cabin stood with a lean-to that housed a horse and a chicken coop full of squawking poultry. John approached the cabin door with apprehension, remembering Mr. Bellmard's previous shotgun welcome.

"Let's hope this goes better than last time." He knocked.

Presently the door opened a crack exposing one of Charley's coal black eyes. "Mr. Reynolds. Miss Bonner." He threw the door open and grinned.

"Who is it?" Behind Charley loomed the tall figure of Mr. Bellmard. "Oh, it's you." He seemed taken aback. "What do you want?"

"Good morning, Mr. Bellmard. We don't mean to intrude, but we have a favor to ask that concerns Charley."

Mr. Reynolds invited them to the school picnic, but made clear if Mr. Bellmard was busy, they would be happy to take Charley back with them. While they discussed the picnic, Charley pulled on his dad's arm and whispered in his ear.

"Charley says he can't go cuz he don't have any food to bring," said Mr. Bellmard.

"Oh, Charley." Lila knelt beside him. "I made two cherry pies—one from me and one from you. How about that?"

Charley looked sullen. "Not the same. I should bring something of my own."

"It's not necessary," Mr. Reynolds began.

"Wait. I know." Charley burst out the door and ran to the chicken coop. "I can bring eggs," he called over his shoulder.

**

They arrived back at the picnic as Mr. Piper was finishing his remarks to the crowd about the successful school year. "The first term in our long-awaited new schoolhouse has concluded, and we couldn't be prouder of the students, our new teacher, Mr. Reynolds and the townspeople of Council Groves for this splendid new school." The crowd clapped with enthusiasm, and there were more than a few whistles of approval.

While the superintendent finished his speech Lila and Charley ducked into the school to make a label for Charley's eggs. Lila pointed out it wouldn't do for picnickers to think these were hard boiled, and Charlie giggled at the prospect of such a messy misunderstanding. Lila watched him set his box of eggs labeled "Bellmard's fresh eggs" on the food table with such pride her eyes misted over.

The feasting began and lasted into the early afternoon—fried chicken and hams, green beans and scalloped corn, rolls and bread with apple butter, fruit pies and frosted cakes, ice water and lemonade—the parade of food was impressive.

Mr. Reynolds organized the children into teams for a gunny sack race and a relay of pass the baton, but the favorite was the three-legged race. After the first race, the older boys and girls wanted stiffer competition from the crowd, and began chanting "Teacher, teacher" as they pressed around Mr. Reynolds.

"Who would I partner with?" Mr. Reynolds held up his hands in a quandary.

"Miss Bonner, of course," shouted Billy Riley, "our other teacher."

"Oh, I don't think Miss Bonner—" began Mr. Reynolds

"You think wrong, Mr. Reynolds," Lila announced as she made her way through the circle of students. "I'm game if you are." She gave Mr. Reynolds a challenging grin.

"Well, if our teachers are game, then the school board should be, too," said Mr. Piper. "Come on, Harriet." Not to be outdone, John Higgins, Pastor of the Presbyterian Church, and his wife joined them along with Mr. Osgood from the bank and his wife.

Mr. Reynolds took off his jacket and rolled up his sleeves. "Get ready, Riley brothers." Lila took her cue and rolled up the cuffs of her shirtwaist. The couples lined up with the children at the starting mark. Lila looked down at her left boot securely tied to Mr. Reynolds' right boot with a bandana. "Are you any good at this?" she whispered.

"You'll see." Before she could think twice, he grabbed her hand tightly, someone hollered, "Go," and they were off. He urged her forward, and she matched his stride, grateful her long legs allowed them to find a steady rhythm. She heard the noise from the crowd but was more keenly aware of John's hand clutching hers, their bodies surging forward in unison.

The field of competitors fell behind except for the Riley brothers who stayed even with Lila and John while at the same time interfering with their progress by drifting in their pathway. To her amusement Lila discovered John very competitive and not above using a sharp elbow when the Rileys bumped into them. The lead changed back and forth, but in the end, it was Lila and John who leaned forward across the finish line first, nosing out the brothers. The crowd cheered wildly.

Breathless, Lila raised her arms in triumph and saw Mr. Reynolds' admiring smile. "Well done, Miss Bonner." He grabbed one of her hands, and together they took an exaggerated bow to the crowd.

Charley ran to the finish line and circled them chanting, "Teachers won, teachers won."

**

The sun settled, and one by one constellations glimmered in the early evening sky as Lila and John sat on the steps of the boarding house recounting the day's events. Lila's insistence on bringing Charley to the picnic was affirmed at every turn. He was an asset as a team member, and the children engaged with him in ways they hadn't before. A few of the older boys who had whispered "half breed" under their breath since the term began were now grudgingly accepting him. Since he didn't have a family to eat with, Lila and John made sure he shared their picnic blanket. He ate voraciously.

"I'm glad we fetched him," John said. "It was the right thing to do." He leaned back and scanned the darkening sky. "Look, Lila. The Great Bear." He pointed heavenward. "See the outline?"

"Great Bear? I don't see one. But the Big Dipper—I see that."

"They're the same thing but with different names. Also called Ursa Major."

Lila looked at him quizzically. "You know a lot about the stars."

"I find them interesting, a good addition to a science lesson. Like Orion, the Hunter. He shows up in the winter sky, with his bow and arrow."

"A bow and arrow? Really?" Lila marveled at this new information and at John who continued to amaze her with his wealth of knowledge. She took a deep breath and savored the day, the new friends she had made, the food and laughter they had shared. The worries that weighed on her for longer than she could remember were put aside for one glorious, happy day. She studied John's profile. "Thank you," she said simply.

He turned with a confused look. "For what?"

"For today. For inviting me to the picnic."

He smiled, the way that made her breath catch. "I'm glad you came. It was a special day."

Her thoughts spilled out. "This was the best day I've had since I came to Council Grove. No, since before that." She fell silent and gazed at her lap. "Since Mama died." She raised her head. "I have you to thank for that."

"I'm happy for you, Lila." A man in the street passed them and nodded a greeting. "You know, this town is growing on me," he continued as he watched the man walk down the street. "There's fine folks here, I have a good job. I could see myself settling here."

"You could?" Lila swallowed her surprise. John was sitting here, sharing for the first time his thoughts about the future. She knew she had no claim on him. Still, she dared to wonder who he'd want to settle down with.

"I'd like to have a small piece of land here in town. Or nearby. Build my own place." He gazed at her again, then something fluttered across his expression that pulled him away.

Lila could see it. "Is something wrong?"

It was gone in an instant. "No. Everything is fine."

One moment their minds seemed to think as one. The next moment...

What is it, John? What are you keeping to yourself?

Chapter Twelve

"Is this something to be worried about?" Lila held a scoop of boiled potatoes midair waiting for John's reply as the boarders passed the supper of stew meat, potatoes, and corn bread around the table. Two weeks had passed since the picnic, and John had found work for the summer at Last Chance when travel on the trail was especially busy. He quickly discovered the mercantile was the social center of the town and the hub of its information, reliable or otherwise, and brought news to the boarding house every evening.

"The man I overheard was a scout for the wagon train at the campgrounds. He said there's a dispute between the Cheyenne and the Kaw." Other boarders dropped their conversations and listened in.

Lila was familiar with the campground outside of town called the Council Grove rendezvous where wagon trains formed up before leaving for Santa Fe. The beautiful grove of elm, oak, cottonwood, walnut, and sycamore was attractive for settlers and useful for travelers heading west. Water from the nearby Neosho River was an added bonus, and the bed of gravel rock afforded freighters and wagons easy crossing from the campgrounds into Council Grove and points west.

She had stood at the end of Main Street watching from a distance as the wagons gathered individually and in groups into one large train before moving out. The sheer number of people and wagons made it a breathtaking sight. Now there was news of danger to not only the wagon trains but to Council Grove. "Will there be trouble for the wagon trains?"

"It doesn't look that way. This feud seems to be between the tribes." John's expression was one of reassurance.

Lila ignored the shiver of fear that ran down her spine. "What about us? Are we in danger?"

"The Indians don't have a dispute with folks in Council Grove." He seemed quite certain in his answer. "Be that as it may," he continued, "it's probably best that you don't make visits to Charley's by yourself. Until we hear things have settled down." Lila had visited the Bellmard cabin the previous Sunday to take Charley another reader along with two freshly baked biscuits from Hays House. Charley's bright-eyed smile greeted her as always, and Mr. Bellmard, a forbidding presence, had at least nodded a thank you for the biscuits. "We'll both go to visit Charley next time," John added.

Lila hoped he was right in his assessment of the Indians but couldn't suppress her anxiety for the families in the wagon train poised to leave on their cross-country journey or for the good folks in Council Grove striving to secure their growing town.

**

Mrs. Bauer told Lila she'd like to speak with her after supper and to please meet her on the front porch. The porch was really a wooden stoop that was part of the walkway in front of the boarding house where Mrs. Bauer had set out two old rockers which the boarders enjoyed in the evenings. Lila immediately began a mental inventory of offenses she may have committed to get ahead of the charges and found herself in a state of nerves by the time she and Mrs. Bauer sat down.

"Lila, I've been watching you for some time now," she began.

Lila moaned inwardly thinking this was worse than she had thought. Even the memory of the one kindness Mrs. Bauer had shown by giving her boots didn't offer hope now for a good outcome.

"You never missed a day at the livery, and you took on a second job when Edna hurt her foot. You're reliable."

Lila nodded, amazed, and held her breath lest it interrupt the flow of the conversation.

"Business has been good. Truth is I could still use some help. I don't mean to complain, but my rheumatism acts up now and again." She shifted in her chair and gave Lila a reproachful look. "Besides, it seems to me it's time for you to quit associating with those ne'er-do-wells at the livery."

Lila chose her words carefully. "If I quit the livery, I would need a job."

"That's what I'm offering. Free room and board with a small—and I mean small—salary."

Lila could barely contain herself. "Mrs. Bauer, I would be most grateful to work for you. That is a very generous offer, and I thank you kindly." She wanted to fling her arms around this aloof and brittle old lady but held herself in check.

This could change everything. If room and board were free, the stipend, however small, could be saved and she knew exactly the place to keep it safe: in the bottom of mama's satchel under her bed. She would keep busy with chores at the boarding house no doubt, but not as exhausted as she'd been the past months. Why, she might even have time after supper to read from the books John had loaned her. That thought was one of pure bliss.

"And besides . . ." Lila's ears perked up as Mrs. Bauer continued, "maybe we could put some meat back on those bones, Lila. You're no bigger than a corn nubbin."

Lila could hold back no longer. She leaped from the rocker and hugged Mrs. Bauer around the neck.

**

Only one more day and Lila would be done working for Clive Johnson and the other "ne'er-do-wells" at the livery. Mucking out the horse stalls in the surprising June heat was insufferable. The ungodly stench, the sweat, the hay sticking to every part of her body made leaving the job that much sweeter for Lila. Still, it had provided for her when nothing else had presented itself, and for that she was grateful. Manure and all.

It made Lila's head spin, in a good way, to go from a livery worker to a domestic. Mrs. Bauer ran a high-quality boarding house and declared with regularity, "No bedbugs here. No dark, musty rooms either. I run a clean, sanitary establishment." On Lila's first day of work at the boarding house they carried the rugs from the parlor and Mrs. Bauer's room to the clothesline out back for an overdue cleaning. They whacked them unmercifully with carpet beaters until clouds of dust rose and sneezing ensued. Still, it was preferable to anything required at the livery. They returned the rugs to the rooms after airing all day, which gave Lila a chance to see Mrs. Bauer's living quarters.

Her room was comfortably large and furnished with a tall wardrobe made with beautiful wood inlay, a table and chair, and a trunk bound with leather straps. A perfectly stitched quilt in the popular wild goose pattern covered the bed, and above the iron headboard hung a sepia family portrait in an oval frame. Lila stepped close and studied the portrait of a young woman holding a toddler on her lap and a broad-shouldered man standing behind her with a young boy at his side.

"A lovely picture. Your family?"

When there was no reply, Lila turned to Mrs. Bauer. She was staring into the distance, a stricken look on her face. "It is my family, it *was* my family."

Lila immediately regretted her intrusion. Mrs. Bauer's expression told her she had unwittingly stumbled onto a tragedy related to the family in the photograph. She didn't know how to proceed. "Mrs. Bauer, I didn't mean to pry."

Mrs. Bauer lowered herself into the chair and kept her gaze out the window. "Little Gretchen had always been sickly, but we never dreamed she wouldn't survive the crossing." Her voice was a whisper.

"Oh, Mrs. Bauer." Lila went to her side and knelt by the chair.

"Once we got to Kansas things were better. My Hans was a hard worker, and we worked a small farm not far from here. Did all right for a while. And Karl was growing into a fine young man. So strong." Her face glowed at this memory, but her features quickly darkened. "Our happiness wasn't meant to be."

Lila's heart quickened while Mrs. Bauer continued.

"It was a terrible accident. Hans was plowing behind our horse, holding the lines, and it bolted and dragged him. Karl was putting seed in the furrow, and the horse ran him down and . . ." She couldn't finish. "Hans was never the same afterward. He adored that boy, blamed himself." Tears streamed down her face. "He just gave up, that's all. Just gave up after we lost Karl."

Lila clutched Mrs. Bauer's gnarled fingers and blinked away her own tears. Many a day Lila had felt like an orphan since running away from Pa. She knew what it was like to be without family, but not like this, not through the kind of loss that ravages the heart so completely. Mrs. Bauer had come to America hoping for a better life, and in doing so, everyone she loved had been taken from her. As painful as the loss of Mama was for Lila, she knew Mrs. Bauer had suffered three-fold.

They sat in silence for a long time, their hands clasped together.

Chapter Thirteen

Lila slid the chalk and slate into her satchel along with jerky and slung a canteen over her shoulder. She knew John would not approve of her visiting Charley by herself, but her work was done until suppertime and the beautiful Sunday afternoon beckoned. The rumors of Indian troubles had died down, and the Bellmard cabin was a short walk from town. She was certain it didn't pose any risk.

Lila relished the quiet walk through the woods. The longer she lived in Council Grove the more she appreciated its unique grove of trees situated on the prairie. The sycamore with their shaggy white bark that hugged the Neosho were the tallest but the cottonwood were her favorite, their leaves fluttering in the gentlest breezes. She cast her eyes skyward through the shimmering green canopy and inhaled the sweetness of summer.

Lila never knew what to expect at the Bellmard cabin — sometimes Charley greeted her with his shy smile, sometimes the place was deserted. The smell of wood smoke reached her before she arrived in the clearing where she saw Charley's father splitting wood and Charley stacking it beside the cabin.

Lila waved. "Good afternoon."

Charley stopped his work and grinned. "Miss Teacher's here."

"I can see that," Mr. Bellmard replied in a gruff tone. He continued swinging his ax. "I suppose you'll be wantin' him to stop workin'."

"Only when chores are done, Mr. Bellmard. I'm happy to lend a hand with the stacking," she offered.

"Won't be necessary. Charley can do it."

Lila was used to Mr. Bellmard's abrupt manner, so she positioned herself on the wooden step of the cabin and watched for the next half hour while father and son worked their way through the wood pile until it was chopped and stacked.

When finished, Charley plopped down beside Lila. She pulled out the slate and handed him the chalk. "I thought we'd do sums and subtractions today."

Charley made a face. "Don't like those much. Specially the take-aways."

"But if you practice them, you'll get better and soon they'll be easy."

Charley rolled his eyes.

"I promise, one day these will be as easy as falling off a log." Lila wrote two problems on the slate for him to solve. She dug in her satchel and pulled out a piece of jerky. "This is for energy. You deserve it after your hard work."

Charley grabbed the jerky and bent over the slate, counting out the answers on his fingers. When he tired of the math problems and Lila could no longer coax him with jerky, he ran inside for his McGuffey reader and read to Lila for another half hour. She was heartened to see his enthusiasm for reading hadn't diminished although his skills had fallen some from lack of regular lessons.

The afternoon had slipped away, and Lila returned the materials to her satchel. "Time for me to go, Charley. You've done very well." She rose and tousled his head. "I'm proud of you."

"Want to show you something." He grabbed her hand and took her behind the cabin, proudly showing her a goat munching grass. "Just got her. Now we git milk."

"Well, isn't that something."

"Pa and me gots to build a pen for her."

"Yes, I see that. Do you take care of her?"

"Yup. She's got a name."

"Which is?"

"Jolie. Pa says it means pretty in French."

"I think Jolie is lovely."

Charley waved at Lila until she was at the edge of the clearing and turned into the woods toward town. It was none of her business, but Lila was concerned with this new addition to the livestock at Bellmards. When Mr. Bellmard took off to set his traps and left his son alone, Charley was responsible for the chickens and now the goat. No small task for a boy not yet eight years old, never mind the possible dangers from Indians and animal predators. Of course, the other choice was to take Charley with him and leave the animals on their own. Neither option was suitable.

Lila was deep in thought when she first heard faint rustling behind her. She turned, expecting to see squirrels chasing through the brush but saw nothing. All was quiet while she stood still, so she continued her walk down the path that wound through the trees. She passed a cluster of elms and heard a soft crunch some distance behind her, this time sending off an alarm inside her head. Was someone following her? Her pulse quickened and she lengthened her stride.

Lila was still a long way from town. Too late she regretted ignoring John's advice about walking here alone. Up ahead the trees were dense, and she decided to take cover behind a large sycamore. She couldn't be sure if the sounds continued, so loud was the pounding of her heart. Lila knelt behind the tree, making herself as small as possible, holding her breath.

She waited. Nothing happened. Just when she decided it was safe to move from cover, two young braves in buckskin appeared on the path, footfalls as silent as falling leaves. Lila pressed into the tree. They walked past her, then cut off from the path and headed north through the dense wood. For what purpose they were walking in this part of the woods, Lila couldn't guess. They wore sheathed knives at their waists yet didn't appear threatening, but she was shaken to her core and couldn't move her legs fast enough to run the rest of the way to town.

**

Lila knew better than tell John about the Indians in the woods. She could almost hear his reprimand: "What were you thinking? Didn't I say it was unsafe to go alone?" And he was right. She had no idea whether the young braves had ill intent or cared not at all that she passed through the woods. She had been lucky nothing happened. She wouldn't be so foolish again.

When she next saw John, she took great care to avoid mention of Charlie and tutoring or anything to do with school.

John, however, brought it up himself. He strode into the boarding house after Lila finished the noon meal cleanup, his face flushed with excitement.

"Mr. Piper has allowed there's enough in the budget to purchase a few extra books next term. I'm going to start a school library." He beamed.

"That's great news." It was a big concession considering the school budget had been spent on the new schoolhouse. "I've got time before the boarder upstairs checks out. Tell me about it."

They sat in the rockers on the boardwalk in front of the boarding house. "We can't afford many, but one for each age group would be a good start." John got up and began pacing as he talked. "We'll have to get a list together, which will be hard — there are too many great books to choose from."

Lila watched him pace, amused.

John paused and asked, "Would you like to help make a list?"

Lila sat up. "Me? Really?"

"Any suggestions at all. I have some ideas, but I'd like to hear yours as well."

"I remember my teacher read *Treasure Island* to our class — it was wonderful."

When they finished making a list of titles, Lila said, "I have another idea for the library."

"Go on," John said, his interest piqued.

"Emma Simpson brought a copy of *Youth's Companion* to school a while back. It's full of stories and puzzles. Maybe I could ask her parents if they'd be willing to donate old copies to the school, to our new library."

"I think that's brilliant, Lila." John contemplated for a moment. "Lila, how many years of school did you finish?'

"Four."

"This gives me another idea — about you."

She tilted her head. "Like what?"

"You should finish school and get a diploma. Your reading is far beyond the years you spent in school, and you catch on to new concepts quickly."

"I don't have time to study."

"I think you do. When you're at school helping, you can sit in with the older students for reading and math. You could work at your own speed as you have time." John leaned forward with enthusiasm. "Lila, I don't think it would take long for you to fulfill the requirements for a high school diploma."

A diploma. Lila was amazed at the idea. "I never gave this any thought. Ever since I quit school, I've had to work, either on the farm or for income."

"I'll find extra math and reading books for you. Keep them here at the boarding house."

Lila began to grasp his excitement. If she had her own textbooks she could study whenever she had free time, especially in the evenings. "You don't mind if I spend part of my time at school learning for myself when I'm there to help the children?"

"Not at all. It's a good thing all around." John smiled, triumphant at the proposal.

"That's so generous of you . . . I don't know how to thank you."

"Seeing you receive a diploma would be thanks enough, Miss Bonner." He grinned again.

Lila liked the sound of that. Very much.

**

The summer months were favorable for wagon trains heading to Santa Fe, and the remaining two weeks in June were busy in Council Grove. No sooner would boarders check out than newcomers would arrive. Lila kept busy in the yard, laboring over a boiling pot, laundering sheets and drying them on the clothesline. She and Mrs. Bauer had a full dining room for most meals and kept the stove hot from early morning till evening.

Lila had no time to visit Stacy, but Hays House was swamped with the tide of travelers as well. Most of John's work involved unloading the arrival of supplies—sacks of coffee and cornmeal, barrels of flower, cones of sugar, apples from Missouri during season, as well as lantern oil, matches, ax heads, rope, saddles, scythes. The aisles of Last Chance were stacked high.

In the midst of work no matter how busy she was, Lila always stopped to watch whenever a wagon train drove down Main Street as it began its journey on the Santa Fe Trail. Lila stood beside Mr. Hays in front of the restaurant watching the wagons leave town one June morning and noticed something for the first time. "Are those tree limbs stowed under their wagons? Seems to me that would make their load heavier."

"Heavier, maybe, but very important. It'll be the last lumber they can get on the trail. If they get a broken axel between here and Santa Fe, they'll be mighty glad for those sturdy limbs to repair it. Could be lifesaving."

Lila tried to imagine traveling hundreds of miles without encountering trees like those so plentiful in Council Grove. She couldn't.

Lila didn't mind the hard work at the boarding house, but there was something else she *did* mind. The school picnic had been an unforgettable event for her. Vivid images of John came to mind when she recalled that day—the way he spoke to the crowd with ease and confidence, the way he grinned before asking for second helpings of fried chicken, the way he grasped her hand in their victory bow that had caught her breath.

But in the following weeks, Lila felt John growing more distant, as though something had come between them. They would be having a great conversation about nothing in particular and then his demeanor would change, as if he suddenly remembered something important, and he would retreat. She didn't understand. She felt their friendship was truer and deeper than it had ever been, and his pulling away made no sense.

**

"Thanks, John. You really don't need to do this."

"'Many hands make light work.' My mother always said that." Every window of the boarding house stood open begging for a breeze from the motionless evening air while John helped Lila fill water buckets at the pump. "Molasses came in today. First time in ages."

"I'll tell Mrs. Bauer. She'll be pleased." Lila set another empty pail under the spigot and John worked the handle, every downward thrust a defiant screech.

When the buckets were full, they headed for the door. "Oh, by the way, I have some news. I have company coming in a few days."

"Really, John? That's exciting. Who is it?"

"Family. From St. Louis. I'd like you to meet them."

"Of course. I look forward to it," Lila smiled and wondered if now she would at long last get some answers about the mysterious Reynolds family.

Three days later was the first day of July, sunny and sultry. Lila's work dress was damp at her neck and a trickle of sweat ran down her temple. She finished the breakfast clean up and sat for a moment in the parlor to fan herself before sweeping the bedrooms. A stagecoach clattered to a stop across the street at Hays House stirring up dust and causing curious onlookers to halt their business. She watched John emerge from Last Chance and stride over to meet the coach as passengers disembarked. He took the arm of a young lady about her age and led her toward the boarding house.

Lila stood. *John has a sister.*

They came into the parlor. "Oh, I'm glad you're here, Lila," John said. "There's someone I want you to meet." He turned to the young lady. "Lila, I'd like you to meet Fanny Elwood, my fiancé."

Chapter Fourteen

Lila stood motionless. Surely, she heard wrong.
"How do you do?" Miss Elwood extended her hand with a smile.
His fiancé? Lila couldn't get her breath. She searched for air to fill her lungs, her arms dangling at her sides. "Miss..."
"Elwood," the young lady finished for Lila.
"... Elwood. How nice..." Lila reached for the young woman's hand more to steady herself than in a greeting. She had clear blue eyes and wavy brown hair neatly combed into a stylish chignon. She looked fresh and composed in her traveling costume of navy skirt and matching jacket, unlike the other travelers who were dirty and disheveled from their journey. Of course, John would fall for a woman who looked exactly like this, so attractive and worldly.
Lila found her voice. "Welcome to Council Grove." She turned to John, imploring him to say something, but his eyes never met hers.
"Is Mrs. Bauer here?" he asked. "I should get Fanny settled in a room."
"She's in the kitchen." Lila was desperate for air. She smiled weakly and backed away. "If you'll excuse me, I have things to do."
Lila blindly made her way down the hall to her room and closed the door. Engaged? It can't be true. She lowered herself onto the bed and drew in air. When did this happen? Had John been engaged the entire time she'd known him? Her mind raced searching for answers and remembered the letters he wrote home and mailed at Last Chance. "For your family?" she had asked. "Something like that," he'd replied. Lila felt sick. How could she have been so naïve? She had created a relationship between herself and John out of whole cloth.
Her eyes brimmed with tears. Every kindness he'd shown was charitable and nothing more. There was no romance blossoming between them. The coach ticket he'd bought for her

escape from Pa, the books he'd loaned her, the hours they'd spent together at the school, the confidences they'd shared — all of it meant nothing to John Reynolds. He was marrying someone else. The pain she tried to smother erupted; she leaned over and sobbed into her hands.

A man like John who understood hard work yet appreciated book learning was one in a million, and she knew it. She would be happy with either quality in a man, but he possessed both. She had dared to hope she shared a future with John. He had thoroughly captured her heart, and now he was gone like mist in the morning.

She cried until she could cry no more, lost in her tears, lost in her hopes, lost in every way she could imagine. Completely spent and empty, Lila stood and went to the dresser for a clean handkerchief tucked in the top drawer. She caught her tear-stained reflection in the mirror and stopped to wipe her cheeks. How pathetic she looked. She didn't want to see anyone, didn't want to talk to anyone but knew Mrs. Bauer would soon need her help with morning chores. Tucking a strand of hair behind her ear, she smoothed her dress in an attempt to gather her wits. It didn't help.

"Lila, where are you?" Mrs. Bauer called from a distance.

"Coming," Lila replied, and stepped into the hallway.

"There you are. Could you make up a bed for our new lodger, Miss Elwood, in Room Three? She'll be here indefinitely."

The request bit like a knife in her flesh. *I have to make up her bed?*

**

Lila stumbled through the day, washing dishes, peeling vegetables, oblivious to details, weighed down by this new reality. She chastised herself for not seeing the truth of her relationship with John. He was the most decent man she'd even known — not a deceitful bone in his body. Or so she thought. Was it possible he hadn't been as honest with her as she believed? She relived their time together in Council Grove, recalled conversations and searched her memory for any indication John was engaged.

Try as she might, her thoughts always circled back to the glorious day of the picnic. She remembered vividly John's expression when he first saw her arrive, how he stared at her, unable to speak. It was etched in her brain. She knew John was seeing her as though for the first time, no longer as a friend but as a lovely young woman. She knew it as surely as her name was Lila Bonner. So how could that square with the stunning revelation that Fanny Elwood was his fiancé? As the hours ground away, her pain shifted. By suppertime tiny embers of what she could only conclude was John's dishonesty flickered then sparked into simmering coals of anger.

"He led me on, that's what he did," she thought to herself, then replayed the idea until she was muttering under her breath as she dished up the corned beef. "He led me on. How could he do that?" She marched the platter of meat to the dining table and delivered it with a thud. The boarders turned in surprise, John most of all.

He sat beside Fanny and looked up startled. "Good evening, Lila."

"Mr. Reynolds," Lila nodded curtly. She caught a glimpse of his frown as she left the room.

In the kitchen Mrs. Bauer took a pan of biscuits from the oven and slid them into a basket. "Don't go thumping these onto the table, young lady. You've been in a mood all day—what's gotten into you?"

"Don't know what you mean." Lila grabbed the basket, and Mrs. Bauer took hold of her arm.

"Yes, you do. It's written all over your face."

Lila felt crimson creep up her neck and blinked back threatening tears. "I'm fine." She deposited the biscuits and made an excuse to Mrs. Bauer to use the outhouse, seeking privacy in a sour, dark place which fit her mood perfectly.

She had a big problem. John was engaged and his fiancé was here permanently. In addition to having her dreams crushed, she was living under the same roof with them in the boarding house and would be serving them meals at least twice a day. She couldn't escape to the outhouse during every meal or dodge them whenever they walked into the parlor.

"I'm going to be bumping into them all the time," she moaned in the stink of the privy. "Them and their happily-ever-after."

She didn't think she could bear it.

She left the outhouse deep in thought. Too late she heard the squeaking pump handle and stumbled into John filling a bucket. She froze.

John looked up. "Lila."

"Sorry. I didn't see you."

John straightened and gave her a look. "Is everything all right?"

It seemed an eternity before she could speak. "Yes."

He gave her a steady gaze, the one she had come to know all too well, the one that read her thoughts, that now told her he didn't believe her. "You're upset about something. What?"

She tipped her head back, looking at the sky in exasperation and calmed herself before returning his gaze. "I was very surprised today to meet Miss Elwood. You never spoke of her."

It was his turn to look away. "I see." He ran his fingers through his hair.

She waited. The boiling rage she tried to tamp down churned inside. "You don't have to explain yourself to me, John Reynolds." She picked up her skirt and climbed the back steps.

"Wait, Lila—"

The door banged shut.

**

The next weeks were a blur of chores, suppressed heartache, and more chores for Lila. She did her best to put on a brave face each morning as she served breakfast to the hungry boarders while avoiding any glances at John and Fanny. If she saw John coming from a distance, she did an about face to avoid an encounter. If she found herself unable to escape his presence, she made up a reason to excuse herself. It was exhausting. She watched with sadness as John and Fanny visited the schoolhouse where she had spent so many happy hours and wondered if this, too, would be lost to her once school resumed in the fall. Worst of all, John seemed oblivious to the pain he had caused her.

One morning when John cornered Lila in the kitchen, he began chatting as though nothing had changed between them. "Lila, we haven't had a moment's time to visit. You've been so busy lately."

"More to the point, you've been very busy since Miss Elwood arrived." Lila's voice was stiff.

"Well, that's true, but I have the distinct feeling you've been avoiding me."

His frankness caught Lila by surprise, but she did not respond with equal candor. "Not at all. As you said, I've been busy."

"I wonder if you're too busy to do a favor for me?"

Lila scraped potato peelings into the slop bucket. "That depends. What's the request?"

John relayed that in the weeks since Fanny had arrived in Council Grove, she had felt isolated. He wondered if Lila could arrange an outing, perhaps a picnic, with Stacy and other young ladies. Extend the hand of friendship and make her feel welcome.

Lila nearly sent the bucket across the floor. *Become friends with John's fiancé? Not bloody likely!* She wanted to scream at him and his thick head. Did he not know he had broken her heart into a million pieces? Was he that dense?

She finished scraping the peelings until every last bit was in the slop bucket. Controlling her seething anger she replied through clenched teeth, "I'll give it some thought, but I really don't think I'll have time."

Chapter Fifteen

Mrs. Bauer had summoned her.

Lila thought their arrangement was working out well and hoped Mrs. Bauer was pleased with her work. In the days following Mrs. Bauer's heartbreaking revelation of the loss of her family, Lila could think of little else. She had come closer to understanding this very private woman who worked hard but shut herself off from the world. Lila remembered asking her to come to the school picnic to which she had said, "Don't have time for such nonsense. Have a business to run." Lila had been taken aback by anyone would think a picnic was nonsense, except perhaps someone so wounded by life she kept everyone and everything at arm's length. Since that day, Lila had come to see Mrs. Bauer differently.

"Have a seat, Lila." Mrs. Bauer sat in the rocker by the window. The only remaining place to sit was on the bed where Lila lowered herself. Mrs. Bauer looked her straight in the eye. "What's eatin' you, Lila?"

Lila's eyes popped wide. "Excuse me?"

"Somethin's botherin' you, has been ever since Miss Elwood arrived. The air in the house is off kilter. You're so upset, you can't give Mr. Reynolds two civil words, backing out of the room whenever he walks in—what's goin' on?"

Lila twisted the handkerchief in her hands and stared at her lap.

"Silence is not an answer," Mrs. Bauer persisted.

"I know."

"Are you sweet on Mr. Reynolds?"

Lila's head jerked up. "No, of course not... that is... I—"

"Lila, I wasn't born yesterday. I see the way you look at him. He's a fine young man with good prospects. Now all of a sudden, this Miss Elwood shows up and everything's changed. Mr. Reynolds is no longer available. He's engaged." Her expression was one of sympathy and her voice softened. "I think I understand."

Lila couldn't believe her embarrassment was playing out in front of her employer. "I never meant—" She stopped before her voice broke.

"There's no shame in caring for someone."

Lila raised her head. She knew the sound of that voice, those tender words—it was a mother consoling a child. The ache in Lila's throat nearly strangled her. "Thank you," she whispered.

Mrs. Bauer let the moment between them take hold. "Why are you here in Council Grove?" she asked quietly.

Lila took a shaky breath. "To get away from my pa."

"To be safe?"

"Yes."

"And are you safe?"

"I think so."

"Good. Does Mr. Reynolds know how you feel about him?'

"No."

"You didn't tell him?"

"Of course not." Lila was indignant.

"So, he has no idea he broke your heart."

Lila dropped her head in silence.

"That's what I thought. Now, did you come here to find a husband?"

"No, ma'am. I came to find my own way."

"All right then. Seems to me things are working out just fine for you. You're here, you're safe, and you've got your whole life waitin' to be lived. No need to be sad or frettin'."

Lila nodded and dabbed her handkerchief to her eyes, attempting to smile.

Mrs. Bauer rose and returned Lila's smile. "There's some strudel left in the pantry. I say it's time to finish it off."

**

The July heat had settled over the parched town, making everyone irritable. Days stretched into weeks without rain, and it became practice for every man, women, and child to search the heavens for rainclouds that never materialized. The Neosho shriveled, the well water fell off, farmers prayed for rain, and the sun beat down mercilessly.

It was almost closing, and Hays House was empty but for a handful of customers. Travel on the trail was at its peak for the year, and those heading west were almost always bedded down early at the campgrounds. Two men dressed in buckskin seemed reluctant to leave, loitering over coffee until Stacy hovered beside their table with a perturbed look on her face.

"What's yer hurry, sweetheart?" one of the men said.

The gold standard for Hays House was "the customer is always right." Even so, Stacy rolled her eyes at the sweetheart reference. "We're closing in a few minutes, sir."

The other man finished his coffee. "Let's head over to the Red Horse. More time to drink over there."

His friend guffawed. "Good idea, Skaggs."

Lila wiped down a table nearby and noticed how one of the two men shifted his eyes away whenever she looked in his direction. She overheard his name was Bill and thought there was something familiar about him but didn't know what. It was likely he reminded her of the tens of dozens of adventurers wearing buckskin heading west.

When the men finally departed, Stacy balanced a tray of dirty dishes into the kitchen where they began washing up. That's when Lila told Stacy about John's request that she plan an outing for Fanny.

"How John had the gall to ask me that, I'll never know."

"You're not responsible for entertaining his Miss Fanny." Stacy plunged her hands into the wash tub and began scrubbing plates.

"It would take a miracle for me to be friends with Fanny Elwood." Lila gave Stacy a sideways look while she dried the plates. "You don't suppose—"

Stacy cut her off. "If you're asking me to plan something for you, the answer is no. I've got enough to do."

"But Stacy—"

A commotion drew their attention to the dining room, and John suddenly appeared at the kitchen door.

"John, what are you doing here?" Lila paused her work in surprise.

"Sorry to barge in," he began," but there seems to be trouble brewing at the Kaw reservation. We just received word from the sheriff that folks should be inside their homes and stay put till whatever this is blows over."

Stacy and Lila looked at each other in disbelief. In truth Lila had grown used to seeing Indians in town on occasion, sometimes trading beads and pelts outside Last Chance. She deemed them harmless and, in some cases, sad as the tribe lost increasing amounts of land and withdrew to the south. There had been no indication that trouble was expected from the Kaw.

Herbert Hays appeared at the kitchen door. "You best get along home, Lila. Go with John, and we'll finish up here."

"What could be happening at the reservation?" Lila asked.

"Never you mind." Edna Hays stepped into the kitchen. "You heard John. Now, off with both of you."

Lila rolled her blouse sleeves down as they made their way to the door. "What brought you out looking for me?" Lila arched her eyebrow.

"Mrs. Bauer wanted me to fetch you. Thought this is where you'd be."

And not your concern for my safety. The thought sat bitterly in Lila's heart.

John opened the door and guided Lila out, his hand under her elbow. She flinched and pulled away. She did not need or want any assistance from him.

Chapter Sixteen

A blood curdling scream jolted Lila awake. She sat up, heart pounding, and grabbed her shawl in the dim light before a second whoop came from down the street. By the time she reached the hallway boarders were spilling from their rooms, confused and alarmed.

"Sounded like Injuns," an elderly preacher traveling to western Kansas with his wife spoke first. He wrapped a protective arm around her as she leaned into him, clutching her robe.

"Indians!" The expletive came from Fanny standing beside John at the end of the hall. In the early morning light, her disheveled hair and terrified expression revealed a Fanny that Lila had never seen before. The sheen was gone, the perfect veneer cracked and distorted revealing a vulnerable person no different than anyone else standing in the hallway. John put a reassuring arm around her.

Two men from the rooms upstairs arrived at the hallway the same time as Mrs. Bauer. "What the hell is goin' on?" one of them asked.

"I don't know." Mrs. Bauer's face was drawn with fear.

Thunderous pounding rattled the front door. "Help! Let us in!" John was at the door immediately and ushered in a young man and his family, then secured the door behind them.

"Mr. Shaw? Mrs. Shaw?" John recognized the family that farmed a few miles outside of town. "Are you all right?" Mrs. Shaw held an infant and four other children clustered around the parents. Lila now recognized the children from her time helping at school.

Mr. Shaw gathered his breath. "We're all right. We didn't hear about the troubles till early this morning and made a run for it. Safer in town than on the farm. There must be a hundred Indians out there, and we don't even know why."

"A hundred—" Fanny put her hand to her mouth as though trying to stop the words from escaping.

By now everyone in the boarding house had gathered in the parlor. Frightened as she was, Lila wanted to see what she could from the windows that faced Main Street. She edged close and peered out. The rising sun revealed two groups of Indians mounted on horseback, one on each end of Main Street. They sat tall, bare chested and feathered on their mounts and even her inexperienced eye could tell these were enemies facing off to do only God-knew-what in the middle of their little town. She looked again and her stomach clenched. Their bronze faces bore the bright colors of what she could only assume was war paint.

Her breath left her. She backed away from the window and turned to the one person she had grown to rely on. "John, what does this mean? What's happening?"

John had been looking out the other parlor window. "I don't know." Although his voice was calm, he couldn't mask the worry on his face.

"What should we do?" asked the preacher.

It quickly became clear there was nothing they could do to change the situation. They would have to wait and see what the Indians did. There were four windows facing Main Street, two in the parlor and two in the dining room. Except for Mrs. Shaw and the children, everyone went to the windows for a look, and over the next half hour, they pieced together a theory. The Kaw Indians were on the west end of Main Street, and their longtime enemies, the Cheyenne were on the east end. For reasons unknown to them, the two tribes were preparing to do battle with each other.

"Probably has somethin' to do with horses," remarked one of the men who boarded upstairs.

"Horses? Why do you say that?" asked the preacher.

"I lived west of here the past three years, trying to make a go of it." He continued. "The Cheyenne and Kaw are always at each other. Now that the Kaw are being moved off to Oklahoma, they've got hardly nothin' left. Wouldn't be the first time they stole Cheyenne horses."

"Or maybe the Cheyenne stole Kaw horses," said Mr. Shaw. "Then again, maybe has nothin' to do with horses. We don't know the half of what goes on between tribes."

The whoop and cry of Indians rang through the air. Hooves pounded the street, and the boarders strained at the windows to see five braves from the Kaw tribe pull their mounts to a halt directly in front of the boarding house. Facing the Cheyenne enemy, their horses reared back on hind legs and the braves fired their shotguns into the air with more blood curdling screams. One of the warriors with a heavily painted face expanded his bare chest and struck it with his palm, then led the other four back to rejoin the rest of the Kaw warriors.

"Everyone, away from the windows," John shouted. "Into the kitchen. Now!"

Wide-eyed with fear, the group gathered in the kitchen on the back side of the house. With only one window facing the open prairie to the south and a back door that led outside to the pump and outhouse, Lila understood why John thought this the safest place from stray bullets. The commotion had startled the infant who began wailing, and Mrs. Shaw bounced and shushed the baby who cried harder. The crying unleashed the pent-up fear of the youngest child, a toddler who began sobbing and clutching her mother's skirts and soon the five-year-old joined in the wailing.

"Oh, dear," Mrs. Bauer muttered. "Can't have this." She turned to John. "Think it's all right for me to fix the young'uns some vittles?" John nodded. "All right then. Lila, let's get to it. You can help too, Miss Elwood," and with that Mrs. Bauer started a fire in the stove and gave directions for making coffee and oatmeal. They pulled in extra chairs and lit the lamps.

"Have you ever seen anything like that?" It was the younger of the two men who had told them his name was Sam. "It was like they were showing off to the other tribe. Or giving a warning."

"Bloody savages. The only good Indian is a—"

"Excuse me," the preacher interrupted, "but may I remind you we have ladies present. This is a fearful time. Let's not make it worse with that kind of talk."

"And what kind of talk is that, old man?" He drew himself up before leaning into the preacher's face. "Ain't nobody in charge of me around here." He turned to John. "And that includes you."

The children immediately sensed the tension, their whimpering subsided, and the room grew silent. "Look, Ben—that is your name, isn't it?" John began. "We've got a serious situation on our hands. We want to keep everyone safe. That's all *I'm* trying to do."

Ben gave him a hateful stare but kept his peace.

Indian whoops suddenly exploded from the street. Fanny clapped her hands over her ears and her frying pan clattered to the floor. The startled infant began crying again.

John looked desperately at Fanny then his gaze swept over the faces in the room. "I'm going to have a look out front."

"Me, too," said Mr. Shaw and with the other men following, they left the kitchen.

Lila went to Fanny's side and picked up the pan from the floor. Fanny's hands shook as she sliced the bacon. All color had drained from her face. "I can help if you'd like?" Lila offered.

Tears sprang to her eyes. "I can't do this." Fanny bolted from the kitchen and fled down the hall to her room.

Mrs. Bauer watched her departing figure. "Must be frightened to death," she said to no one in particular, "but then, aren't we all?" She turned to the pot of oatmeal and gave it a few swirls with her wooden spoon. "Now who's ready for breakfast?" She gave the children a smile, and in that moment when fear was snarling at the door, Lila's heart was filled with gratitude for Mrs. Bauer's strength and kindness.

When the men returned to the kitchen, Lila had finished frying the bacon and the coffee had boiled. A tense calm hung over the room. Mrs. Shaw was settled in a chair near the window nursing the infant, and the children sat on the floor nearby scooping oatmeal from their bowls.

Lila tried to read John's expression. "What's happening?"

"Same thing that happened before, only this time it was the Cheyenne taunting the Kaws, riding to the end of the street, whooping and shooting. Then one of them threw a spear in the dirt in front of the Kaws before racing back. I don't know if this is some kind of ritual before they come to blows or what."

"This could go on for hours," Sam added.

Ben spoke up. "It better not. I ain't waitin' around all day for these redskins to do whatever it is they're gonna do."

Mrs. Bauer shot John a nervous look before turning to Ben. "Now before you get in an all-fired hurry, we got bacon cooked up." She pulled cups and plates from the cupboard. "Set a minute and have some coffee."

John reached for a cup, then glanced at the kitchen with a frown. "Where's Fanny?"

Lila pulled him aside. "She's very upset. Went to her room."

"I should go—" Then he paused. "That is, someone should check on her. Maybe it's not proper if I go to her room. Lila, would you, could you please make sure she's all right? I'd be ever so grateful."

**

Lila stood outside Fanny's door and heaved a sigh.

How did she get herself into these situations? Here they were facing what could be an imminent Indian attack, and she was on a mission for John to check on the welfare of his precious Fanny whom she didn't care for one whit.

Fanny has no backbone Lila thought with resentment. Like Mrs. Bauer said, they were all scared. Why should Fanny be excused to run and hide at a time like this? If she were being totally honest with herself, Lila would have to admit every Indian war whoop she heard shook her to the core. She was just as fearful as Fanny.

Lila tapped on Fanny's door. "Fanny, it's Lila." She waited. "Are you all right?" She heard coughing and gently pushed open the door. "John wanted me—" Fanny was sitting on the bed, vomiting into the chamber pot cradled in her arms. "Oh, my goodness." Lila hurried to her side and held the pot until Fanny's retching subsided. There was an awkward silence as Lila poured Fanny a glass of water and waited for her to regain her composure.

Lila searched for words. "I didn't realize you were ill."

Fanny hung her head. "I'm not ill . . .unless being scared to death is an illness."

"Being scared is nothing to be ashamed of. We're all scared."

"But you all carry on in spite of it. I simply . . . fall apart." She sipped the water and turned to Lila. "How do you do it?" She dabbed her face with a handkerchief.

"I don't rightly know. It helps to focus on the others, though. Like the children. Helping them to be calm and feel safe." She paused. "I was going to my room for some old primers just now. Thought I might read to them to take their mind off what's going on outside." She stood. "Why don't you join us—as soon as you feel steady. You could read to the children, too."

Fanny nodded silently, and as Lila moved toward the door, Fanny grabbed her hand. "Please, don't tell John how poorly I've behaved. Please?"

"Of course not, Fanny." The pleading look in her eyes was enough to make Lilia feel sorry for her. Almost.

Lila made her way down the hall to her room with a sense of frustration. She gathered books from under her bed, muttering to herself. "Drat it all! Now I'm in the middle of it. I don't want to know any secrets those two are keeping from each other, yet here I am." She found the old primers John had given her when she heard shouting from the other end of the house. She grabbed the books and ran.

Chapter Seventeen

"Dear God, what happened?" The words flew from Lila's mouth when she reached the dining room. Shards of broken glass littered the floor beneath a shattered window.

Ben Thornton was propped up against the interior wall of the room, bleeding from his side. "Goddamn Indians," he cursed through clenched teeth.

"Watch your mouth," Sam warned, standing over him. "You got no one to blame but yourself. Going out there was a stupid thing to do."

Mrs. Bauer hurried into the room clutching dish towels. "Lila, fetch some water."

"Don't go outside—it's too dangerous," John cautioned. "I'll go," and he disappeared out the kitchen door.

Even before Lila knelt beside Ben, the coppery smell of blood overwhelmed her. She and Mrs. Bauer applied pressure to the wound. Ben struggled to muffle a cry as they pressed down to staunch the bleeding.

"You know we got to stop the flow of blood, Mr. Thornton." Mrs. Bauer's tone was matter of fact. They held the cloths firmly in place until John returned with a basin of water. Mrs. Bauer wiped down the wound, and with Lila's help they wrapped the towels around his midsection as tightly as they could. Lila ripped strips from one of the towels to hold the make-shift bandage in place. "That should hold you for now, Mr. Thornton." Her voice was reassuring but the look she gave Lila said otherwise.

Ben tilted his head back against the wall and took a jagged breath. "I just want to leave this God-forsaken place."

"Your chances of leaving this God-forsaken place have gone down considerably." John leaned over Ben. "And now you've put the rest of us in a more dangerous position."

Beads of sweat appeared on Ben's forehead. "I'm sick of you ordering me around," he sneered through his pain. "You don't know nothin' more than anyone else."

"I don't pretend to," John came back. "But I do know it wasn't safe to go out into the street."

John turned on his heel, broken glass crunching under his boots, and Lila followed him into the kitchen. "Whatever happened, John?"

He took an exasperated breath. "Thornton decided he wasn't going to wait any longer and took off for the livery to get his horse. Next thing we knew there were gunshots, and he went down in the street."

"Dear God! How did he get back inside?"

"Sam and Mr. Shaw helped me bring him back inside."

"You went out to get him? John, it's too dangerous. You said so yourself."

"I know. But we couldn't just leave him out there."

"Maybe you should have. He's an ornery cuss."

The corners of John's mouth turned up. "'He's an ornery cuss?' Where'd that come from, Miss Bonner?" He couldn't hide his amusement, even in the midst of their terrible situation.

Lila felt her face redden. "Well, he is. Mrs. Bauer just dressed his wound, and does he thank her? No indeed. He goes on being ungrateful and selfish. I can't abide him."

"His selfishness has caused us new problems, that's for sure."

"Like that bullet that's still inside him?"

John nodded. "Sooner or later, it's going to fester."

**

Lila sat on the kitchen floor after finishing a story for the children who sat circled around her. She closed the primer and turned her attention to Mrs. Bauer. "How long's it been?"

Mrs. Bauer opened the pocket watch pinned to her blouse. "About four hours, give or take." She snapped it shut and finished cleaning up the breakfast dishes with Fanny's help. Lila noted Fanny was at least lending a hand and appeared to be over her fit of nerves.

"Only four hours? Seems like an eternity," Lila muttered under her breath.

The morning had been torturously slow. Moments of calm were interrupted by sporadic shooting and war whoops from the street followed by an eerie and unsettling silence. The men kept watch from the front windows while the women kept the children entertained in the kitchen. The chamber pots were full, the stink permeating the rooms. John thought it safe enough for Pastor Johnson to empty them in the outhouse so long as he carried a rifle.

As the hours ticked by, the captives in the boarding house grew restless, feeling powerless to change the stalemate in the street. When the sun had climbed directly overhead, Mrs. Bauer enlisted Fanny's help in making corn bread. "Better to get ahead of hungry folks in a situation like this," she told Fanny. Mrs. Johnson took over caring for the Shaw's infant while Mr. Shaw watched his family safely to the outhouse and back, and Lila took it upon herself to check on Ben's bandages. Although she had little experience nursing gunshot wounds, Lila felt confident from watching Mrs. Bauer that she was up to the task.

As she approached the parlor, she overheard the men talking in the dining room and paused outside the door. They spoke in near whispers. She strained to catch their words and leaned close to the door. After several minutes one thing became clear to her: the men considered their situation dire. They worried the confrontation between the tribes that had been contained up to this point might at any moment erupt. Until now it had been a prideful show of prowess between tribes. If the wrong Indian got wounded or killed, it could lead to an all-out war in the street and spill over to the townspeople. It could turn into a blood bath.

Lila's mind raced. A blood bath? One of the men had uttered those very words—maybe Mr. Shaw, maybe Sam Curtis—but there it was. The men were protecting the women from both physical harm and the knowledge of their vulnerable situation. This new information left Lila thunderstruck. She stood by the door unable to remember why she was there in the first place.

A blood bath.

Then she remembered Ben's bloody bandage and pushed through the door. "Thought I'd check on Mr. Thornton," she spoke with forced cheer to the men in the room and moved to the parlor. Ben lay on the floor covered with a blanket, his head on a pillow. When Lila unwrapped the bandages, her stomach lurched. The wound oozed and was warm to the touch. It didn't smell putrid, but she guessed it was only a matter of time. "I'm changing your dressing, Mr. Thornton," she whispered. He didn't seem to know she was there.

"That doesn't look good." Pastor Johnson was bent over her shoulder, eyeing the wound.

"No, it doesn't," Lila agreed. "We should think about moving him to a bed."

After a meal of hot corn bread and bacon sandwiches, everyone remained in the kitchen. John cleared his throat. "I suspect many of you have been thinking the same thing I have — that Mr. Thornton needs a doctor."

Pastor Johnson agreed. "He's in a bad way. Infection is settin' in."

"But how are we going to get a doctor here?" Sam asked. "You do have a doctor in town?"

"Doc Watson. Has a practice a block off Main Street," John said. "I know he'd come if we could send word."

"I don't see how we're gonna do that." Mrs. Bauer's face creased with worry.

"Unless one of us wants to venture out when things are quiet out there," John offered.

Lila spoke up. "Who would volunteer to do such a dangerous thing?" She trained her eyes on John.

No one spoke. Some avoided eye contact, others turned toward John waiting for an answer.

"I know the Doc. He's delivered our last two young'uns." It was Mr. Shaw. "I'd be willing—"

"Jonah, no." Mrs. Shaw rose from the rocker, their baby snuggled peacefully in her arms. "Please. We can't have you taking such chances. Your family needs you." She nodded to their children.

"She's right." Sam spoke up. "No need for a family man to take this on. I'll go."

"Thanks, Sam, but you're a stranger here," John said. "You don't even know where Doc practices, which happens to be on the other side of Main Street. Seems to me I'm the logical choice."

"You? John, no." Fanny startled the others and rose from her chair. "You can't be seriously considering doing this." She walked over to John and grabbed his hand. "You can't leave me here *alone*, in this terrible situation. What would I do if something happened to you? You can't go." Her voice was tremulous as she added, "I forbid it."

It happened in an instant and was hardly perceptible, but Lila saw it. The flash of disbelief or perhaps resentment in John's eyes disappeared as soon as he responded to the ultimatum. "Fanny, all of us want to get out of this situation as best we can. We have a man who needs a doctor. I can go across the street to the Hays House first, see how they're doing, maybe marshal our resources. They have a back door with access to both Doc's office and the sheriff's office. It's the best shot we have."

"You've been thinking about this awhile, haven't you." Lila's voice was almost a whisper.

"I have. I've made up my mind. There's no time to waste."

Chapter Eighteen

They stood in a group by the front door. Mrs. Bauer had found an old sheet she ripped into large squares, one which he now clutched in his hand. "Don't know if it'll do any good," he said, glancing at it, "but then again, it can't hurt." John gave a spirited smile to the grim faces around him. "It's been quiet for a good half hour. It's time."

"God speed, son." Pastor Johnson gave him a quick embrace.

"Keep your head down, John." Mr. Shaw squeezed his arm.

Fanny stepped forward, eyes filled with tears. "It's not too late to reconsider."

"It will turn out fine, Fanny. I'm sure." He kissed her cheek.

"You come back in one piece, you hear?" Mrs. Bauer gave him a gentle smile.

Lila hung back, pricked with fear. Her every impulse was to keep him from going, to talk him out of it, to physically block the door. Instead, a litany of prayers ran through her head, prayers for his safety, prayers that he'd return unharmed. She was terrified for his life and angry she still cared so deeply for his wellbeing. All she managed to utter was, "Be careful, John," before he was out the door.

They watched him hold up the white cloth and dash across the street. He banged on the front door of Hays House and waited while the seconds ticked by. He banged again, and a shout rang out from one end of the street. The front door opened, and John disappeared inside. The boarding house family took a collective breath.

Once John was inside Hays House, the group at the boarding house focused on staying safe inside and keeping busy. The women helped Mrs. Bauer in the kitchen, and Mr. Shaw and Sam brought in water from the pump out back when they weren't stationed at the front windows. If the children tired of stories, Lila found string and engaged them playing Cat's in the Cradle.

The men moved Ben onto a pallet in the parlor where Lila, Mrs. Bauer, and Mrs. Johnson took turns monitoring his condition. The instant there was commotion in the street, however, everyone inside the boarding house was on full alert. Lila didn't know which was worse—the explosive war whoops that raised the hair on her arms or the terror in the silence that followed.

Supper consisted of vegetable stew, and hungry or not, everyone ate in shifts in the kitchen. The setting sun cast long shadows on the wide, dusty Main Street and brought an end to the frightful day. In the fading light, Lila could make out the shapes of the Indians at both ends of the street, shadowy specters holding their ground. It brought to mind the night she first arrived in Council Grove and saw Indians watching the town in the twilight. A shiver went down her spine now just as it had on that night.

Mrs. Bauer and Lila gathered extra blankets and showed the Shaw family to Ben's unused bedroom upstairs. The children were uncharacteristically quiet as they settled in for the night, and Lila could only assume the stress weighed on them as well as the adults. The men took turns sleeping and left one to watch at the windows. Lila retired to her room, certain sleep would be hard to come by. Every sound whether near or far was magnified, alerting her to danger. A coyote yipping in the hills, a bug skittering across the floor, a board creaking in the hall set her heart pounding.

After an hour or two Lila gave up on sleeping, grabbed her shawl and left her room. The house was silent as she padded the hallway in her sock feet, her gown brushing the floor. She filled a tin cup with water and carried it to the parlor.

"Mr. Thornton," she whispered. There was enough light to make out his face. His eyes fluttered. "How you feeling? Would you like some water?"

"Yes." His voice was thin, scratchy.

She knelt and held the cup while he drank.

He returned his head to the pillow and with great effort said, "Enough."

Lila reached for one of the stuffed chairs across from the pallet. "I'll be sitting here for a spell, Mr. Thornton, if you want more water." She settled into the chair and pulled her shawl close. She watched the shadows on the walls and after a time felt her eyelids grow heavy. His voice was so weak she wasn't sure she heard it at all.

"Thank you."

**

She felt a hand on her shoulder and opened her eyes with a start, her heart pounding, not sure where she was.

"Lila," Mrs. Bauer whispered, "go back to bed. Get some proper sleep."

Lila got her bearings and stretched the kinks from her back. "Must have fallen asleep. What time is it?"

"I've started breakfast. Folks will be gettin' up soon."

Sam joined them with what smelled like a cup of coffee hot off the stove. "Mornin'" he nodded. His blond hair was tousled, and he looked exhausted. Lila was suddenly aware she was in her nightgown in front of a gentleman, one she barely knew, at that. She glanced at Mrs. Bauer and noticed her always perfect hair was hanging loosely, the hairpins askew and knew in this moment appearance and proprietary mattered not at all but surviving this horrible situation did.

Lila tightened her shawl and rose. "Anything happen overnight, Mr. Curtis?"

"Glad to say, quiet as can be."

"Thank goodness for that. I'll get dressed and help with breakfast, Mrs. Bauer." Lila left and readied for the day with a heavy heart weighed down with questions. How long would the standoff last? How long would they be safe in the boarding house? How long could Mr. Thornton hang on? And where in the world was John?

The morning passed uneventfully—no random gunshots, no arrows flying through the air, no bravado from the Indians. It was midafternoon when Sam's voice suddenly echoed from the dining room. "Somethin's goin' on."

Instantly the group gathered in the front rooms, positioning themselves for a view of the street.

"There's John." Fanny clutched Lila's arm.

Three figures appeared from the Last Chance Store—Thomas Hill, the owner, John, and Doc Watson. They walked to the middle of the street and stopped as John waved the white cloth. Doc motioned the Indians from both ends of the street to come forward.

"What are they doing, Noah?" Mrs. Shaw whispered.

"Don't know."

Nothing happened. John waved his makeshift flag again.

One Indian from the Kaw tribe rode forward and stopped in front of Doc. They spoke to each other.

"They're negotiating something," Sam said.

Thomas Hill handed two packages to the Indian who turned his mount and trotted back to his end of the street. The Indians conferred for several moments, their gazes returning to the men in the street, then with a whoop, the Kaws kneed their horses and took off south to their reservation.

"They're leaving." Mrs. Johnson was breathless with hope.

"But will they stay away?" Mrs. Shaw seemed doubtful.

"What about the Cheyenne?" Lila asked.

The boarding house family pressed against the windows when they saw Mr. Hill disappear into his store and reappear with more packages. He, John, and Doc ventured slowly down the street toward the Cheyenne, John waving the white flag.

Lila's insides quivered. The Cheyenne were known to be hostile not only to white settlers but to other tribes, and she felt certain the men were pushing their luck. The trio stopped just past the boarding house and were met by three Cheyenne braves, sitting tall on their horses, who circled them once, twice, three times, before holding their mounts. They appeared to negotiate and while the Cheyenne seemed much less eager, they took the packages, rode to the end of the street and left with the rest of their party.

The street was empty.

The boarding house family waited in nervous silence for something to happen.

Without fanfare John pushed through the front door into the welcoming arms of his friends. Fanny rushed to the front of the group and threw her arms around John. "You're safe. Thank God," she sobbed into his shoulder. Lila watched from afar, feeling every ounce of Fanny's relief and turned away to hide the tears that brimmed her eyes.

Everyone talked at once. "Is it over?" "Do you think they'll come back?" "Thank God you're safe."

John gave a weary smile. "I think the crisis is over—for now. Doc should be here soon. He's getting his bag."

"First things first. Let's get you something to eat, John." Mrs. Bauer led the way to the kitchen.

While they waited for Doc, John recounted the events since he left the day before. "It started with the Cheyenne invading the Kaw reservation night before last. There was over a hundred of them."

"Good heavens. That many?" Mrs. Shaw shot a troubled look at her husband.

John took a big slug of coffee. "The Cheyenne claimed the Kaw had stolen some horses, and they were reclaiming their rightful property. The Kaw were highly insulted at this, donned their finery, painted their faces and rode out to meet the Cheyenne the next morning on Main Street."

"But why on Council Grove's Main Street?" asked Pastor Johnson.

"I suppose because they wanted to put on a show of military prowess the Cheyenne and townspeople would witness. All those howls and curses, the bullets and arrows flying through the air—I guess they thought they made their point."

"What about the negotiations?" Sam asked. "We saw you talking with them."

"Coffee and sugar. Thomas thought that might help end the stalemate if the merchants offered something from the town."

The atmosphere in the kitchen was one of relief, but John gave them the sobering news that this might be only a temporary halt to the crisis. The sheriff didn't know the extent of hostilities between the tribes and had left town that afternoon for Topeka to ask for help from the governor. There might be more troubles ahead.

Doc arrived shortly after, examined Ben's wound, and made a quick diagnosis which surprised no one. "The bullet needs to come out. Even with that, I'm not sure he'll survive. If it's nicked the bowel, he's probably already septic. I'll do my best."

He methodically went to work requesting boiled water, clean cloths and as many lamps as possible brought to the parlor while he set out instruments from his medical bag. The boarding house family gave him space and privacy save for the Johnsons. Mrs. Johnson's years of experience as a midwife made her a willing and obvious choice to assist Doc, and the pastor insisted at being bedside during the procedure. The Shaws were eager to return home, but Mrs. Shaw convinced her husband to stay another night just to be cautious.

**

Two hours later Doc stood at the front door, medical bag in hand, his shirt bloodied from the surgery. "Bullet came out clean enough. He should sleep for a good while. There's nothing to do now but wait."

"Thanks, Doc. We sure needed your help." Mrs. Bauer thrust warm biscuits tied in a napkin into his hand.

John joined her. "Thanks for everything, Doc. The town is mighty grateful."

"We're grateful for the part you played as well." They shook hands before Doc left.

Mrs. Bauer and John turned their attention to Ben asleep on the parlor floor with Lila sitting at his side. The house was put to bed. Every soul in the boarding house family, alike in their weariness, had collapsed into bed after the exhausting two days.

"Lila, you need to rest." Mrs. Bauer patted her shoulder. "I'm turning in—you should too."

John hesitated then sat beside Lila. They were silent for a long while, watching Ben's breathing.

Lila spoke first. "He could die at any time, couldn't he?"

"Yes."

Lila watched Ben's chest rise and fall. "I don't know this man. I spoke harshly about him earlier, that I couldn't abide him. I meant it."

John didn't reply.

"I've been sitting here thinking, what if he dies? Where's his family? Who would come to bury him even if they knew he'd died?"

"Lila, you're getting ahead of yourself. Ben might pull through."

Lila faced John. "But he might not. He might die. It seems only right when a person dies there should be someone to grieve that person's death, to mourn his passing with their whole heart."

"Truth is, out here people die far away from kin and strangers are left to bury them. The family is left to grieve when they get the news weeks—even months—later. This is how it works when you come out West."

"I know. But my heart wishes that even the least should have someone there to mourn them. There should be *someone*."

"You have a kind heart, Lila."

Then he did an unexpected thing—he reached for her hand. Instead of withdrawing, Lila left her fingers in the cradle of this comfort. It had been a terrible two days, days with fear heaped on her and the people of her town, days where life and death hung in the balance, days where she thought she'd never see John Reynolds again. But the Indians had not turned against the townspeople, John had returned alive, and she rejoiced in all the lives spared. She left her hand in his palm and felt the healing power of the human touch as a single tear slid down her cheek.

Chapter Nineteen

The first rays of sun streamed through the bedroom window, momentarily stirring Lila before she rolled over and returned to sleep. Moments later she blinked her eyes open and bolted upright in bed, amazed at the late hour. The stress of the previous day was greater than she had realized. She found Mrs. Bauer in the kitchen feeding kindling to the stove and a pot of coffee simmering. "Sorry I overslept. What can I do? How is Mr. Thornton? Please tell me he did well last night."

"Calm down, child. John and Sam been up early but the place is still mostly asleep. Folks are done tired out after yesterday." Mrs. Bauer told Lila she had checked on Mr. Thornton twice and he was still in a groggy state, feeling the effect of the laudanum. "I 'spect the Shaws will leave this mornin'. Don't' have any eggs so it'll be biscuits and gravy."

Lila slipped her apron over her head and inhaled deeply. "Coffee smells specially good this morning, doesn't it."

Mrs. Bauer nodded with gratitude. "Indeed, it does."

The morning was quiet, and few people ventured out. The customary clop of horses and rumble of wagons were missing, and Lila wondered how long before Council Grove would return to normal. As if waiting for a signal, the noon arrival of the sheriff with half a dozen soldiers from Topeka gave the townspeople reason to release their tension. The bank opened its doors, the blacksmith fired up the bellows, and the trickle of business at Last Chance soon hummed a familiar tune.

With the departure of the Shaw family, Lila and Mrs. Bauer swept their bedroom, folded blankets and stored pillows. When the kitchen was tidied from breakfast, Lila warmed a pan of beef broth and poured a bowl for Mr. Thornton. Mrs. Bauer had been unable to get anything but water past his lips since the surgery.

Lila situated herself beside the pallet and held a spoonful of broth to his lips. "Mr. Thornton, you need your strength back. Try a little." He was propped up on a pillow, his eyes closed. At the sound of her voice his eyes opened, and he stared with an unseeing gaze. Lila slid the spoon between his lips, and he swallowed. Liquid ran down his chin, and Lila wondered if a thimbleful had made it to his stomach. She repeated the task with little success but told herself surely, he was getting some nourishment.

Lila remained at his side, encouraging him to eat but in the end, returned the soup bowl still half full of broth to the kitchen. "He didn't get much down, I'm afraid."

Mrs. Bauer sighed. "We'll try again later. That's all we can do."

Lila turned to go, then reconsidered. "I almost forgot to ask, have you heard how Stacy and her family are getting on?"

"With everything that happened yesterday, I didn't ask John."

"I didn't either. Would you mind if I ran over to see them?"

"'Course not. Ask Edna if she's got any eggs, and I'll buy some from her."

Lila didn't need to be told twice, and when she walked through the doors of Hays House, Stacy nearly knocked her over with a bear hug. "Am I ever glad to see you." The friends held each other in a sobering embrace.

"I was worried sick about you and your folks yesterday," Lila said. She spotted Mr. and Mrs. Hays preparing food for arriving customers. "I'm so glad you're all right."

"Pa kept Ma and me away from the windows because of all the shootin'. We couldn't tell what was happening." Stacy's voice dropped to a whisper. "I was never so scared in my life."

Lila clasped both of Stacy's hands. "Me either."

At that moment Stacy's eyes looked past Lila out the front windows. "Oh, no. What's goin' on now?"

"What do you mean?" Lila turned around in time to see two soldiers riding down Main Street. "Good heavens, you don't suppose there's new trouble brewing?" The girls moved to the windows and followed the progress of the soldiers. "They're heading to the blacksmith." Lila craned her neck. "Maybe one of their horses threw a shoe."

"I hope that's all it is. Mama and I have had the jitters something awful since the trouble started up." Stacy's face wore more worry than Lila had ever seen — even when her mother was ailing and unable to work.

"I think having the soldiers here will keep things calm." Lila kept her voice reassuring. "Remember, the Indians never did turn on the townspeople. That's something." She gave a small smile. "Oh, I almost forgot. Mrs. Bauer would like to buy eggs if you have any to spare. She's plumb out."

When Lila returned to the boarding house, she helped Mrs. Bauer prepare supper for the family which was smaller now that the Shaws were gone, and Ben was still recuperating. Mrs. Bauer said Ben appeared more alert this afternoon and had taken nearly a full bowl of broth.

"Good news indeed." Lila looked in on him asleep in the parlor, heartened John might be right that Mr. Thornton would recover. She gathered plates and cups for the evening meal, noting the boarded-up window in the dining room and wondered how long before it would be replaced. She propped open the front door to allow a welcome breeze even if it was a bit sultry. Lila hadn't noticed John and Fanny sitting in rockers out front until fragments of their conversation drifted through the doorway.

". . . fearful . . ."

"Of course."

". . . more time . . ."

Feeling guilty of eavesdropping, Lila looked for a way to obscure their words and clattered the tinware as she set the table. When that failed and the tone of the conversation intensified to one of discord, she finished the chore quickly and returned to the kitchen.

"Anything else?" Lila cast a glance at Mrs. Bauer and then caught herself staring at her. Mrs. Bauer looked completely exhausted, the natural lines in her face accentuated, her mouth drawn down, her posture bent. Even with extra help, the burden of providing food and lodging for the boarding house during the calamitous Indian uprising fell to her. In addition, she was nursing Mr. Thornton back to health, feeding him, checking on him during the night, and Lila hadn't noticed the toll all of this was taking until now.

"Mrs. Bauer, supper is well in hand. Why don't you rest a spell?"

"Nonsense. I'm fine."

"No arguing. Go put your feet up. I can manage."

Mrs. Bauer considered her offer. She returned Lila's steady gaze and her eyes watered. "Did anyone ever tell you . . ." her voice trailed off.

"Tell me what?"

Mrs. Bauer smiled. "Never mind. But I think I *will* put my feet up—for a minute, and then I'll be back."

Fanny, John, Sam, and the Johnsons found seats at the dining room table, and Lila served sausages, rye bread, and Mrs. Bauer's homemade applesauce. They ate heartily with friendly conversation, and Lila retreated down the hall to Mrs. Bauer's room. She lifted her hand to knock, heard gentle snoring on the other side of the door and smiled. "Good for you, Mrs. B." She returned to the kitchen for her own plate, contemplating the unfinished conversations of the afternoon: what was Mrs. Bauer about to say to her moments before she retired to her room. More curiously, what was going on between John and Fanny?

Chapter Twenty

"Mrs. Bauer, come quick!" Lila bent over Ben Thornton in the early hours the next morning with a cup of broth. She couldn't rouse him.

Mrs. Bauer was at her side first, then John appeared and Mrs. Johnson seconds later. Mrs. Bauer searched for a pulse in Ben's wrist. "John, go get Doc quick." John was out the door while she worked her fingers over his wrists searching for his pulse. "Not feeling anything."

"Try his throat, right about here." Mrs. Johnson reached in and placed her finger on the side of his throat.

The two women continued to search for a pulse until the moment Doc arrived and stepped in to examine Ben. By now Pastor Johnson, Sam and Fanny had made their way to the parlor and stood in the background. Lila hung back watching helplessly as Doc placed his stethoscope on Ben's chest and listened intently. He took great care waiting to hear the beat of life, but they could tell by his expression that he couldn't find it.

He removed his stethoscope and turned to them. "He's gone. I'm sorry."

"I don't understand," Lila challenged. "He was recovering, starting to get his strength back."

Doc didn't say anything for a moment. "It could have been a number of things—internal bleeding, infection. The body can only take so much, and Mr. Thornton's body had taken on too much, even though you had nursed him and taken good care of him. Of that I have no doubt." When Doc learned Mr. Thornton didn't have any relatives nearby, he offered to contact the undertaker to make arrangements.

Lila stood rooted in her spot and watched events play out before her. The undertaker came swiftly and took the body to the mortuary; Mrs. Bauer started laundering the sheets with help from Mrs. Johnson; John and Sam stowed the pallet. Even Fanny helped set the parlor back in order. Only she couldn't make her limbs move in a helpful way. Instead, she moved awkwardly through the kitchen to the back step, sat down, and stared at the open space of the prairie.

Pastor Johnson eased onto the step beside Lila. "Mind if I join you? You look like you could use some company."

Lila was pulled from her thoughts. "Oh, yes, sir."

"How are you doing, Miss Bonner—Lila, if you don't mind my asking?"

She considered his question. "Honestly, not so well."

"It's been a trying time, these past two days. Besides the troubles with the Indians, Mr. Thornton has passed on. It's no wonder the world seems upside down."

"I feel terrible about Mr. Thornton. I was so sure he was getting better. I still can't believe he's gone."

"Did you feel a special attachment to him?"

"No, just the opposite. I had bad feelings toward him. How selfish and unkind I thought he was. And now . . ."

"Now you feel guilty?"

Lila's voice was small. "Yes. And sad that there's no family to bury him."

Pastor Johnson covered Lila's hand with his. "But he does have a family. We're here, aren't we? We can hold a service for him at the graveside, pray for him, sing a hymn of thanks to God for his life. That's the right thing to do, and that will help all of us get past what we've just been through."

Lila looked into the pastor's eyes and saw them spark with life. In spite of everything, Pastor Johnson exuded hope. "I don't know how you find the right words at times like this."

"A lot of help from the Almighty." He smiled.

"I have no kin of my own here. Times like this is when I feel so alone, it's good to hear comforting words. I thank you kindly, sir."

By late afternoon in the oppressive July heat that threatened rain, the small family from Mrs. Bauer's boarding house stood at the graveside of Ben Thornton. Pastor Higgens from the Presbyterian Church was agreeable to have a guest pastor, Pastor Johnson, assist in the proceedings. There was a designation at the edge of the cemetery for deceased without local connection, not exactly a pauper's field, but neither was it with the first families of Council Grove. Doc said he would see to it that Ben's grave received a plank marker.

Lila wore her good dress, the green one, and polished her boots. It seemed the thing to do. Before the service Lila had picked wild sunflowers and purple coneflowers, handing a stem to each to lay on the coffin. They had pooled their resources to provide a pine box for Ben and stood beside it now while the two pastors read from Psalms and Philippians and spoke of the brevity of man's time on earth and God's promise of eternal life.

Thunder rumbled in the distance. Lila wondered if God was prompting her, and she asked Him to forgive her judgment of Ben Thornton. The wind picked up, and she held her bonnet steady in spite of the bow secured under her chin. Her gaze moved among the faces of the mourners who had become close knit while stranded together. She already felt a kinship with Mrs. Bauer and John, but Sam and the Johnsons would be checking out tomorrow continuing westward on their travels. The group would be splintering, and she felt the prick of sadness at their departure. They shared an uncommon bond, and she'd most likely never see them again. And what of Fanny? Lila couldn't know for sure. She was tired of being angry and resentful of her. But friendship? She was a long way from that.

"Lila?" Fanny laid her hand on Lila's arm. The mourners left the cemetery and walked together toward Main Street.

Lila raised her head. "Yes, what?"

"That was thoughtful, to think of flowers for Mr. Thornton."

"Oh, well, there they were, in bloom, and I . . ." Lila's voice slid into silence.

Fanny glanced at a loaded wagon rumbling the dusty Main Street and gave a quiet sigh. "It's so different here. From back east."

"I suppose it is, depending where you come from back east." Lila undid the top button at the neck of her dress, fighting the merciless heat. "Some things are the same, though. Folks is folks."

Fanny didn't respond immediately. "Yes and no. Folks have a different quality to them out here. I don't know how to put it, a rawness about them."

Lila frowned, not sure of Fanny's meaning, but she didn't think it was a compliment. "A rawness?"

Fanny jumped to correct the negative impression. "I mean, a frontier-like toughness. Able to face anything."

Even at the attempt to placate, Lila bristled. She knew what Fanny meant—the folks out here were ill-mannered and uneducated. Keeping an even tone in her voice, Lila said, "I think once you get to know us, you'll like us just fine."

Fanny lengthened her stride and caught up to John. She slipped her hand through his arm and Lila barely heard, "Maybe that won't be necessary," leaving Lila to wonder again what she meant.

When they arrived back at the boarding house, the sky opened up, and for two days the storm front dumped rain on the parched town, saving the farmers' crops from ruin. The temperature dropped and brought relief to the heat-stricken townspeople and travelers. Main Street became a marshy mess with mud to slog through and puddles to dodge. Mrs. Bauer and Lila fought the constant trail of mud into the boarding house with scrub brushes and buckets of water.

When the morning of day three arrived clear and sunny, Lila was tasked with rinsing rags and hanging them in the back yard. Suddenly Mrs. Bauer leaned out the door. "Lila, there's a boy out front asking for his teachers. He's most upset. Says you have to hurry and help him. Something about his pa."

Lila dropped the rags and ran inside to the front door. There stood Charley, out of breath, looking terrified.

"Charley?"

"Please come. Pa's real sick. He's breathin' funny."

"I'll get my satchel, Charley."

Chapter Twenty-One

Before they were out the door, Mrs. Bauer grabbed Lila's arm. "Shouldn't you wait for John?"

"Doesn't look like there's time. Send him to Bellmard's cabin when you see him. I want to stop by Doc's before we head out." She took Charley's hand and they left.

It took a lot of convincing to stop at the doctor's office. "Pa don't want no doctor. He'd be real mad iffin I brought one home." Charley pleaded with Lila. "Pa don't even know I'm fetchin' you."

"We won't take the doctor with us, Charley. I want to stop by for some advice."

After repeated reassurance from Lila it was alright to confide in her and Doc Watson, Charley told them his pa had been out trapping and got caught overnight in the thunderstorms a few days ago. When he returned home, he seemed fine, then a day ago he came down with the shakes and this morning he couldn't get out of bed.

"When he breaths he makes a whistle sound, in and out," said Charley. "And he's sweatin' too, even when he's shakin'."

Doc disappeared into his back room and returned with a small packet he handed to Lila. "Mustard seed powder. Make a plaster of it and put it on the chest. But be careful."

"Oh?" Lila raised her eyebrows.

"It can cause burns if you make it too strong."

"I'll be careful."

"I've got quinine but try this first."

When the day was fair, Lila always reveled in the walk to Bellmard's cabin, but not today. Every tangled root on the forest floor seemed purposely placed to impede their progress. Charley managed to run ahead of Lila until she called out for him to wait for her. Remembering John's warning, she knew it wise for them to be together, even on this innocent, sunny day.

Lila had never been inside the Bellmard cabin, and she blinked while her eyes adjusted to the darkness. Feed sacks were tacked over the two windows blocking the daylight. The large room had unfinished walls with a bedroom cordoned off by a blanket hanging on a nailed-up rope. A fireplace made of the same limestone that dotted the countryside held a weak flame and beside it a rough table and two chairs. The dirt floor was thick with dried mud.

Charley took Lila's hand. "Pa's over here." He led her to a rope bed on the other side of the hanging blanket. Lila could hear Mr. Bellmard's rattled breathing as she approached the bed. He was sleeping fitfully, moving from his back to his side, clutching a blanket under his chin.

"Charley, I'm going to make a plaster for your pa, to put on his chest. If you'd fetch me some water, I'll get started. Oh, and more wood, please. We need a good fire going."

Charley built up the fire that danced brightly and lit the room.

Lila made a paste of mustard powder and water she warmed in the fireplace. Careful not to overheat it, she wrapped it in a dish towel and brought it to Mr. Bellmard, hopeful it might begin to loosen the congestion in his chest. Lila wanted to move Mr. Bellmard next to the fireplace but could see no way she and Charley could move the burly six-foot man.

"Do you have any more blankets, Charley?"

"I think so." He disappeared into a dark corner of the room and retrieved a crazy quilt from an old blanket box.

"That'll do fine. We need to keep your pa nice and warm." Lila tucked the quilt around the shivering man thinking of other ways to keep him warm, when there was a knock at the door.

"Hello," came a voice. "It's Mr. Reynolds."

Charley threw open the door and Lila greeted him. "Am I ever glad to see you."

"That's the most cordial greeting from you in—"

Lila's scowl was fleeting. "Never mind that now. Charley's pa is sick, and we need your help." She filled John in on Mr. Bellmard's condition, and he agreed to move him near the fireplace. They pulled a straw mattress from under the bed alongside the hearth and managed to carry him from the bedroom. The bed linens needed washing in the worst way, but

Lila focused on the immediate concern for Mr. Bellmard to sweat out the poison in his body.

"Let's you and me bring in a good stack of wood, eh, Charley?" John said. With that the two headed outside, and Lila turned to the shelf with crockery and a few canned goods which looked rather dismal in their offerings. Then she remembered the chickens. Eggs and cornbread fried in a skillet would do for noon meal, supper too, if the chickens were obliging.

By late afternoon John was attentive to the sun's placement in the sky. He and Lila agreed he would stay the night with Bellmards, and she would return home. "I should walk you back to the boarding house before dark."

He and Lila sat outside on the wooden step with Charley to catch some fresh air. They had kept the fire roaring hot all day and the cabin was stifling—good for Mr. Bellmard but smothering for the three of them. John's sleeves were rolled up, his shirt damp. Perspiration dotted Lila's forehead as she flapped a dishtowel in front of her. The underarms of her bodice were wet.

"Things have been quiet for weeks since the troubles. I can go by myself."

"Absolutely not," John said. "I won't hear of it."

"I can walk Miss Bonner back to town," Charley piped up.

What a dear child, Lila thought, smiling at his offer. "Thank you, Charley, but I think Mr. Reynolds is being too cautious. Even Doc thought it safe for us to come through the woods."

"You don't want to tempt fate," countered John.

"And you don't want to be stubborn, do you?"

John rolled his eyes in response.

"Besides, it's too much for you to walk to town and back. Why not walk me to the edge of the woods—I'll be fine the rest of the way."

They had an early supper of scrambled eggs and left over cornbread. Before she left, Lila made a fresh mustard poultice and placed it on Mr. Bellmard's chest. She rinsed out a wash rag and wiped the slick sweat from his face and neck. Charley and John stood aside and watched. It wasn't the first time Lila had caught John watching her while she tended their patient, but his gaze always left the moment their eyes met.

"Miss Bonner?"

"Yes, Charley."

"You're comin' back tomorrow?"

"First thing in the morning. Mr. Reynolds will stay with you tonight, and I'll stay tomorrow night."

He looked down at the dirt floor, so forlorn, it was all Lila could do to keep the ache she felt for him from spilling over.

"Good," was all he said.

Lila reached out and pulled him into her arms. "It's going to be all right, Charley," she whispered. "We're going to take care of him." She ran her hand over his dark curls.

He buried his face in the folds of her skirt and held on to her.

**

Lila poured water into the bowl on her dresser, removed her undergarments and washed herself. The cool water felt heavenly on her sweaty skin after the day she'd spent at the cabin. She dried herself and slipped her nightgown over her head, then took extra care brushing out the damp tangles in her hair. She hadn't realized she was frowning until she caught her reflection in the mirror. Guilt seized her, then fear, and she set the brush aside.

You promised Charley everything would be all right. You had no right to do that. If his pa doesn't make it, he'll think you lied to him.

Lila didn't know what Mr. Bellmard's chances of survival were. She knew pneumonia could be fatal, but she wanted to assuage Charley's fears and offer hope. How could she have been so cavalier with her words? Lila curled up under her coverlet and tried to push away the worry with plans for returning to the cabin in the morning, praying the whistling in Mr. Bellmard's breathing was getting better at that very minute.

Lila slept soundly, but the moment sunshine brushed her eyelids, her feet hit the floor. Lila had explained Mr. Bellmard's illness to Mrs. Bauer the previous night, and she wholeheartedly agreed Lila should return to the cabin the next day to help. They cooked extra bacon and johnny cakes at breakfast that they packed in a basket along with jars of pickled beets, applesauce, a tin of lard, a sack of dried peaches and a bar of lye soap. Lila asked for extra bedding—blankets, quilts, sheets— whatever she could spare, patched, or mended made no difference. She had arranged with Mr. Hays to borrow his small wagon for the day, knowing it would be easier to have their bay, old Daisy, pull the load instead of lugging everything on foot through the woods.

"What's this?" Lila turned an inquisitive eye to an apothecary bottle tucked in the basket and turned to Mrs. Bauer.

"Thought it might help Mr. Bellmard. It's been in my medicine bag for a long while. Never used it, though, since I'm strong as an ox."

Lila read the label. "'Dr. Bridgewater's Digestive Activator.' Mrs. Bauer, what *is* this?"

"It's a cure-all. Says so on the back. Besides digestion, it cures headaches, chest ailments, bowel problems, and diseases of the heart."

"Is this from Doc Watson?"

"No. Got it from a traveling salesman who came through town before Doc moved here."

"I don't know—"

"Go on and take it," she insisted. "Sounds like Mr. Bellmard could use every bit of help he can get."

"Mrs. Bauer, Lila, excuse me." Fanny was standing in the kitchen doorway. "I couldn't help but overhear." She paused before continuing. "Would you mind if I came with you, Lila? I'd like to help the Bellmard family, too. It sounds like they need it."

Lila was at a loss for words. Fanny was the very last person she'd expect to offer help to folks she barely knew, one of whom was sick, possibly dying, living in the most primitive conditions on the edge of their frontier town. Lila was sure Fanny had no idea what was waiting for her at the Bellmard cabin.

"Fanny . . .that's kind of you to offer, but Mr. Bellmard's breathing is real bad. Are you sure you want to go? I was planning on doing laundry and putting the cabin straight. It'll be a long day."

"I don't mind. Really. It would give me something useful to do." She turned to leave. "I'll go change into my work skirt and blouse."

"But—"
"I'll be back in a minute," Fanny called over her shoulder. "Thank you, Lila."

Chapter Twenty-Two

Fanny chattered nonstop after they left the boarding house, which surprised Lila since Fanny was often aloof and seemed uninterested in those around her. She wanted to know all about Lila's family, where she came from, and how long she'd lived in Council Grove until Lila felt as though she was being evaluated. When that subject was exhausted, Fanny talked about herself, how her family and John's had known each other for generations. Their farmland lay side by side and she and John had grown up playing together as children. "I've always known I'd marry John," she declared in an off-handed way. "I've had my eye on him since we were nine years old." She laughed.

Did you indeed? Fanny was filling in an incomplete picture for Lila, one that explained John's family history.

Whenever the wagon jolted over a rut, Fanny grabbed hold of the seat with both hands and held her breath until the path evened out. When the conversation resumed with, "I missed John so much yesterday. I do hope he comes back with us tonight," Lila began to suspect Fanny had motives other than altruistic for coming to help. She probably wanted to find out what she and John had been doing the previous day at the Bellmards, and she also no doubt wanted to get John back to the boarding house *with her* where he belonged.

Lila guided the wagon into the clearing in front of the cabin and pushed the brake handle.

Charley charged out the front door. "Miss Teacher's here," he announced cheerfully.

John followed with a look of surprise when he saw Fanny. "I didn't expect to see you, Fanny."

"I heard you needed help, and I just had to come," she gushed. "Come help me down, John." She smiled demurely.

Lila lifted her skirts and climbed down from the wagon on her own, amused by Fanny's helplessly sweet tone. "Good morning, Charley. I've got things to unload. Give me a hand?"

John helped unload the bedding and food, then tended to Daisy. Fanny stopped short when she stepped inside the cabin's front door. "Gracious." She eyed the room in disbelief, and Lila desperately hoped Charley could not read the revulsion on her face. "How can you get anything done in this—" she waved her arm across the room, "this place?"

Not what I'd call a good start to the day, Lila thought but quickly dismissed Fanny's inconsiderate behavior. There were important things to accomplish. "We're going to need the water buckets filled so we can scrub down the table," she said. "I saw a large boiling pot out behind the cabin." Lila turned to John. "'S'pose you can bring that around front for the laundry? And—"

"And lay a fire? I can do that but only with Charley's help. It's a big job." John winked at Charley.

"What can I do?" Fanny asked, hanging back.

The dirt floor was layered with debris and mud. Lila handed her a broom. "Sweep the clods over to the door, and we'll toss em' out."

Lila untacked the feed sack curtains, and daylight poured into the darkened room. "Well, that makes seeing our work easier, but now we know there's a lot more to be done."

John and Charley carried water, laid a fire and filled the pot. Lila boiled Mr. Bellmard's sweaty sheets and Fanny helped hang them to dry, but when Lila tried to remove Mr. Bellmard's sweat-soaked shirt to launder, Fanny suddenly disappeared outside leaving Lila to change and wash him by herself.

"John, could you lend me a hand?" Lila called. Mr. Bellmard was over six feet tall and his years living on the frontier as a trapper made him a bull-strong man. With John's help they removed the shirt, Lila washed him, and they dressed him in clean clothes. Mr. Bellmard drank some water, nodded when they spoke to him, but Lila could still hear wheezing when he breathed.

"I was thinking last night," John said. "My ma used to tent us beside the fireplace when we had the croup. It helped with the cough."

"Let's do it. I brought an old sheet with me that would work."

John brought in some large branches from the yard. He made a lean-to around Mr. Bellmard with the sheet draped over the branches and left it open to the fireplace to catch the heat. As they stood back satisfied with their effort John said, "I had another idea."

"Oh?"

"How about Charley and I go to the river later on and catch us some supper?"

"Charley would love that. Poor child must be tied up in knots about his pa, and he's been acting so grown up about everything. It would do him good."

"What's going on in here? Who are you talking about?" Fanny entered the cabin, and the edge in her voice was unmistakable.

"We were saying Charley needs something to take his mind off his pa," John explained. Trying to redirect the conversation he added, "How does fresh fish sound for supper?"

**

The laundry pot simmered all day and Lila never ran out of dirty bedding or clothes to be laundered. By midafternoon their work had slowed, and John gave Charley the good news about fishing. Charley ran to collect his fishing rod which was a willow stick with string and a homemade hook that he kept in a box under his bed. Before they took off for the river, Lila gave John a bar of lye soap and an old towel, or what passed for one.

"That child needs a bath. Convince him he'll get an extra helping of fish if he cleans up good—especially round his neck. I could plant radishes there and they'd sprout overnight."

John let loose with a laugh. "I'll try."

Fanny wasn't as amused. In fact, Lila thought Fanny glowered at her for a split second before pasting a neutral look on her face.

With John and Charley gone to the river, Lila and Fanny hung the last of the laundry and took down the dry sheets that had flapped in the breeze since morning. They made up fresh beds for Charley and Mr. Bellmard, and when Fanny announced she needed to rest a spell, Lila cleaned and seasoned the iron skillet in preparation for the fish fry. "Glad I brought lard," she declared after she found a container of rancid lard in the kitchen cupboard. She went behind the cabin and milked Jolie, then poured the milk into a jar that she set in a pail of water to cool.

With their chores finally done, the two of them sat on log stools in front of the cabin, waiting for the boys to return. "I hope they bring back a mess of fish," Lila said. "I'm starving."

"You were right when you said today would be a long day," said Fanny. "I'm hungry *and* tired. I can't wait to get back to town and into my own bed."

"Hey, lookie what we got." It was Charley calling from across the clearing holding a string of fish in the air like a proud soldier bearing his country's colors. He ran to them with his bounty, jabbering details about how they made such a haul.

They feasted on catfish fried in cornmeal, hot biscuits with preserves and cold milk. Lila approved of Charley's bathing which included a hair wash, and he ate seconds of everything. Mr. Bellmard showed signs of having an appetite, and Lila fed him bits of biscuit sopped in warm milk. He ate a few bites and nodded weakly, then lay back and closed his eyes.

The sky was streaking shades of evening red as it lowered behind the trees in the western sky. Fanny was anxious to get back to Council Grove, but John insisted on making sure Lila and Charley were secure for the night. He built a robust fire and stacked enough wood by the fireplace to last till morning.

"Charley, where's your pa's rifle?" The two disappeared behind the hanging blanket into the bedroom area and returned with the rifle. John looked it over, cocked it and checked the ammunition. It was loaded. "You know how to shoot?" he asked Lila.

"I had four brothers, remember?"

"Keep this nearby. Anybody forces their way into the cabin, don't be afraid to use it."

"Nobody comes by here, Mr. Reynolds. We're always by ourselves," Charley said.

"Can't be too careful." John walked to the front door and eyed the wooden latch. "Looks sturdy enough. Latch it good and tight after we leave."

Lila put on a serious face. "Of course."

"John, we really should get going . . ." Fanny edged toward the door.

"Maybe this is a mistake, maybe I should come back here after I take you into town, Fanny."

A frown cut across Fanny's forehead. "For goodness' sake, you are making a mountain out of a mole hill, John Reynolds."

Lila moved to the door. "Fanny is right. Stop worrying and get yourself back to town. Go on now."

John and Fanny climbed into the wagon, and old Daisy pulled them out of the yard while Lila and Charley stood at the door and waved until they disappeared into the woods. Lila bolted the door securely and took stock of the day. Her arms ached, her hands were red and chapped. The day was nothing short of exhausting but at the same time satisfying. Charley was clean and fed, Mr. Bellmard was holding his own, and she was certain the cabin hadn't been this clean in years. She was pleased.

Then there was John. She had worked side by side with him all day, and it was not the least bit awkward or uncomfortable. She could think about him without it stabbing her heart, and that was a small victory. John and Fanny, however, were confounding. They didn't make sense to her. The more she got to know Fanny, the less suited she seemed as a wife for John, but she knew it wasn't her battle to fight or even understand. One thing that was *not* confounding was from now on she would guard her heart carefully and hold fast to her feelings. She knew that for certain.

Mr. Bellmard slept by the hearth to benefit from the fire's heat. Lila kicked off her boots and laid on Mr. Bellmard's clean bed across from Charley's cot. She kept her clothes on and pulled up a freshly washed blanket, relieved it was not infested with varmints. With the rifle on the floor beside her and the door firmly latched, Lila felt safe. She picked up the McGuffey Reader and read aloud to Charley until the tallow candles flickered low and both their heads nodded as rest came.

Chapter Twenty-Three

He was choking and she couldn't help him. "Take a breath, take a deep breath." She urged him again and again, but he kept struggling to get air into his lungs. She reached out to pound his back, to help loosen the strangle hold, but her arms hung immoveable at her sides. He was turning blue. "Somebody help him!"

Lila sat up in bed, frantic. What was that noise? She searched the strange surroundings, the dimly lit room, the timbered walls. Then she heard him. Mr. Bellmard. She planted her feet on the floor, pushed aside the hanging blanket and hurried to the hearth. He was leaning on one elbow, gagging. She grabbed a cloth from the kitchen table.

"Cough it up, Mr. Bellmard. Get rid of the poison."

He coughed repeatedly, turning red, spitting up globs of phlegm. When the spasms stopped, he was able to take a deep breath. "Chest hurts."

"I know, sir. But it's loosened up. My mama always said that's a good sign. You're starting to get better. I just know it."

"Is Pa all right?" Charley was standing beside her, fear in his eyes.

"Charley, pour your pa some water." She stood and went to the cupboard. "Gonna make you some coffee, Mr. Bellmard. Not too strong, but plenty hot. Be good for you."

Mr. Bellmard drank a few sips of water from the cup Charley offered and lay back on the mattress. "Miss . . . Bonner, is it?" His breathing was labored, and he paused. "You have cared for me. And Charley. Thank you." He closed his eyes. "Not sure what Charley would have done . . ." his voice drifted off.

"Your Charley is a bright boy, Mr. Bellmard. He figured out what to do."

Lila and Charley ate leftover johnny cakes for breakfast and started morning chores. Charley milked and fed Jolie, and Lila gathered eggs. She found a shirt of Charley's that needed mending and was searching for something resembling thread to repair it with when Charley came running into the cabin. "There's Indians comin'."

Lila's heart stopped beating. "How many?"

Before he could answer, two Indians appeared in the open doorway. One was an older woman with a broad face and dark eyes, skin the color of bronze and a single black braid that hung down her back. Her companion was a boy, maybe twelve years old with the same round face and eyes wearing a buckskin shirt and leggings.

Lila stood immobile. It was too late to run for the rifle. She gripped the table. "What do you want?" She didn't recognize the sound of her own voice.

The woman was wrapped in a blanket. She reached under it and produced a handful of stringed beads that she held out in her palm. She spoke words Lila didn't understand and waited for a response.

"I don't understand." Lila's heart was in her throat. If she couldn't understand, would the woman get angry with her? Would she retaliate? Lila glanced at the companion and saw a sheathed knife at his waist.

The woman repeated herself, her gaze fixed on Lila. She was neither menacing nor friendly, she simply repeated the same unintelligible words.

Lila turned helplessly to Charley. "Do you know what's she's saying?"

"I think," Charley said, "she wants food for her beads."

"Oh?" Lila faced the woman. "You want to trade?" Lila began looking for something to offer. The chickens had not laid well this morning and the basket on the table held three eggs. Lila held out the basket.

The woman nodded, gave Lila two strands of beads and took the eggs but remained where she stood.

"We have nothing more," Lila said. Knowing she couldn't understand, Lila shook her head. "No more."

The woman didn't move.

Lila' heart pounded. She was near tears but kept her voice steady. "Sorry. No more."

The woman scanned the cupboard before returning her gaze to Lila. She nodded again and with her younger companion left the cabin.

Lila stared at the empty doorway, afraid to breathe, astonished at what had just happened.

"You all right, teacher?" Charley moved beside Lila.

"I think so." Charley appeared so calm Lila was embarrassed at the panic raging inside her. "I had a bit of a fright at first. Never expected to see Indians at the door." She gave a weak smile. "I thought you said nobody came by the cabin."

"Nobody does. Never had Indians stop before."

"But you understood what she was saying."

"Pa knows the language. Sometimes we go to the reservation when Pa has skins to trade."

"You are wise beyond your years, Charley Bellmard. Do you know what that means?"

He gave her a quizzical look. "Not really."

A raspy voice from the hearth whispered, "Means you're grownup for a boy, son."

**

John arrived mid-morning. After he brought in two pails of well water, he sat at the table. "How did you get on last night?" Lila sat opposite him.

"Mr. Bellmard had a coughing spell this morning but overall, I think he's doing better." Then she told him about the Indians.

John listened intently, a deep frown creasing his forehead. "That was bold of them to come inside."

"Honestly, I was really scared. But they were never threatening."

"Makes me wonder, if they're willing to go to inside a white man's home for food, are they in a bad way? I wonder if some of them are going hungry?"

"Charley said it's the first time they've come by the cabin."

"It ended well. All the same, we'll have to be more careful from now on."

That was so like John, Lila thought. No overreaction, only careful assessment. He had a steadiness about him that exuded confidence. It was one of the things she still admired about him.

"Why are you looking at me like that?" John interrupted her thoughts.

"What?" Lila came back to the moment and felt herself blush. "I'm *not* looking at you. I was just thinking, that's all. A lot been going on around here."

"I agree." He paused and gave her that look she had grown so accustomed to. "I hope you rested last night. You've put in long hours caring for Mr. Bellmard and Charley. It's nothing short of remarkable." His eyes never left hers.

"It's been my pleasure to help Charley and his pa." She kept her eyes locked on his until she finally said, "Why are you looking at *me* like that?"

It was John who reddened and looked away.

By afternoon Mr. Bellmard felt able to sit up and eat applesauce. Lila scrambled eggs for supper and made a large batch of johnny cakes for Charley and his pa for breakfast the next morning. She and John planned to walk back to town after supper, making sure the Bellmards were supplied with firewood and food for the next two days. It took a lot of coaxing, but Mr. Bellmard agreed to have Doc come by to check on him the next day. Lila knew it was time she returned to help Mrs. Bauer at the boarding house, and John was to meet with the school superintendent to plan for the fall term.

"Mr. Reynolds." Mr. Bellmard was back in his own bed and extended his hand to John in appreciation. Lila and John had moved him from the hearth and stowed the straw mattress. "Never needed neighbors before." He paused to get his breath. "Appreciate your help. Thank you." He coughed quietly.

Lila marveled she had never heard more than two words out of the man's mouth at one time. In his time of need, Mr. Bellmard who was so guarded and mysterious, and often frightening, revealed himself to be human, just like the rest of them.

"One of us will be back day after tomorrow, Charley." He clung to Lila's hand, and she knelt beside him. "You're very brave. Your pa is feeling better every day."

"Doc Watson will be by tomorrow. You're doing a fine job caring for your pa." John leaned over and gave him a quick hug.

Lila and John walked in silence back to town, lost in their own thoughts. Lila caught John's profile as the sun slanted through the trees. His jaw was set. "What are you thinking, if you don't mind me asking?"

He seemed to consider his answer. "How quickly we pass through this life."

"Such serious thoughts."

"Facing death does that, makes one serious."

"I think," Lila replied slowly, "it also makes us grateful."

He nodded and finished her thought. "Grateful for the blessings one has." He glanced at her and then focused on the path.

Chapter Twenty-Four

"Wait till I tell you what's been goin' on," Stacy said. She sat with Lila on the wooden bench in front of Hays House the next evening after Lila returned from Bellmards. Now that it was August, the number freighters on the trail was slowing enough to allow the Hays family an occasional early closing. Lila and Mrs. Bauer had worked tirelessly all day and caught up with laundry and cleaning. A breeze out of the west worked its way down Main Street, not the gusting kind that brought dark clouds followed by rumbles of thunder, but a soft breeze that cooled the skin and stirred the loose strands of hair around Lila's face. It felt good.

"Remember the church ladies talking about planning a festival?" Stacy asked.

"Sure do. Been talking about it forever. To raise money, wasn't it?"

"For charity. Since neither of the churches have their own building, it's a problem. They've been trying to find a room in town big enough to hold the festival. No luck until—" she paused for dramatic effect.

"Until what?" Lila asked.

"Until Mr. Williams offered them a room—in his saloon!"

"No," Lila gasped. "He didn't."

"He did, and it's caused a ruckus like you wouldn't believe."

Lila knew Seth Williams was one of the original settlers of Council Grove who owned the blacksmith shop, a dry goods store, and the saloon. He was unmarried, "rough around the edges" as Mrs. Bauer put it, but very hospitable and well-liked. Easily recognized by his sizeable beard and felt hat, he was a pillar of the town.

"What are they going to do?" Lila asked.

"Fuss about it, most likely," Stacy giggled. "Pastor Higgins' wife thinks something can be worked out. Some of the other ladies don't take to the idea at all. They're horrified. They're having a meeting tonight. Ma is goin'. So's Mrs. Bauer."

"Mrs. Bauer? You sure?"

"Ma talked her into it at the last minute."

"Never thought Mrs. Bauer would take an interest community life."

"Ma is good at nudging people," Stacy gave a satisfied smile.

"I'm trying to picture this whole thing," Lila said. "The church ladies having tea in the saloon."

"Mr. Williams promised them a large crowd, so we'll see what happens. Battle lines are drawn though. As of yesterday, Harriet Piper wasn't' speaking to Mrs. Higgins all due to this."

It was Lila's turn to smile. It was good to consider less worrisome things than Mr. Bellmard's pneumonia or the threat of an Indian raid. Things like how the spiritual soul of Council Grove would fit into the Red Horse Saloon to benefit the poor and needy.

Lila and Stacy watched the sun dip behind the hill that arched above Council Grove before saying good night. Lila saw a light in Doc's office and walked down the street hoping to speak with him before he pulled the shade on the front door.

"Bellmard has a strong constitution," Doc said. "His vitals were good, and I left instructions on how to apply a mustard plaster with Charley should his pa need it."

"How's Charley?" Lila asked.

"A remarkable child. Seems capable beyond his years."

Relief rushed through Lila at this good news. "Thank you for calling on them, Doc. Knowing things are going well puts my mind at ease."

She no sooner returned to the boarding house than Mrs. Bauer came through the front door and announced, "Well, now that was somethin' else." She took off her bonnet and sat in one of the stuffed chairs in the parlor.

Lila quickly found a seat opposite her. "Tell me about it," she asked without hiding even a smidgen of her curiosity.

"I thought Harriet and Cora would come to blows," Mrs. Bauer said matter-of-factly. "Harriet thinks having the festival at the saloon will send us all to hell in a handbasket, and Cora thinks the Almighty is calling us to work anywhere He calls us."

"Goodness, gracious, what are they going do?" Lila asked.

"There was a lot of back and forth, both sides holding their ground," Mrs. Bauer explained. "A couple ladies walked out. In the end, Cora Higgins and the Red Horse Saloon won out. They're holding the festival at Seth's place."

"But how are they going to manage holding a church fund raiser in a saloon?"

"Don't rightly know, but Seth said he'd make the place look fit for the church event. And that's not the only mystery I learned about tonight."

"Whatever are you talking about?"

Mrs. Bauer lowered her voice and leaned over in a whisper. "Have you heard about the stranger living in a cave in the hills on the west side of town?"

Lila shook her head, eyes wide.

"Have I got a story for you—but I'm plum worn out and heading to bed." She rose. "It'll have to wait till morning."

"Mrs. Bauer, you can't leave without telling me—"

"Good night, Lila." Mrs. Bauer called over her shoulder as she left the parlor. "See you in the morning."

Which left Lila muttering to herself in frustration.

**

Two boarders ate an early breakfast and departed before seven o'clock, which suited Lila's plans. When boarding house demands were light, Mrs. Bauer and Lila sometimes ate breakfast in the dining room, and Lila found this a perfect opportunity for Mrs. Baur to tell the story she had begun the previous night. Even the presence of John and Fanny didn't deter her. They could listen in or not—it didn't matter.

With plates of sausage, eggs, biscuits, and gravy before them, the four sat at the dining table and Lila wasted no time. "So, Mrs. Bauer, you were saying last night about this stranger?"

"Oh, yes, indeed. It was Minnie Simpson who told the story. They live on the west side of town not far from Belfry Hill. Seems this stranger arrived in town about a month ago, walking alongside one of the wagon trains. Name's Matteo something. He's Italian and shortly after he got here, he climbed Belfry Hill and found an overhang in the outcroppings. Makes his home there."

"Really." Fanny paused eating. "He makes his home in a cave?"

"More or less," Mrs. Bauer said. "Rumor is he's some kind of Catholic cleric. Minnie's husband Thomas has spoken to him—or tried to. Besides English he speaks Spanish and Italian."

"An Italian priest out here on the Santa Fe Trail?" John asked.

"What does he do all day?" Lila wondered.

"Minnie said he sits in front of his makeshift home and reads from the books he brought with him. That's all."

"He sounds very odd to me," Fanny said.

"The only thing of consequence he owns is a mandolin," Mrs. Bauer said. "Minnie said if you listen carefully, you can hear mandolin music in the evenings while he's playing."

"How did he find his way from Italy to Council Grove?" Lila asked.

"There's a good question," Mrs. Bauer agreed.

"He must have had a classical education," John added.

"Speaking of education," Mrs. Bauer said, "it's getting close to school opening again, isn't it, Mr. Reynolds?"

"Two more weeks." He finished the last of his sausage and turned to Lila. "That reminds me, you are helping with reading again this term, as time allows of course."

"Yes, I'd love—"

"John, I have an idea," Fanny interrupted. "Why don't *I* help with reading since Lila is so busy here at the boarding house? I'm sure I could manage to help the children with their reading. I mean, what's there to know, really? What do you say, darling?" She placed her hand over John's and waited with a soft smile, her eyes expectant.

Lila wanted to throw something.

Of all the nerve of Fanny Elwood. This had nothing to do with past feelings about John and everything to do with losing her place in the school and the community. She loved those children and the part she played in their education. It was the brightest part of her day. It was what her dreams were built on, it was her future. How dare Fanny take that away from her.

John looked ready to choke, a crimson color creeping up his neck.

Lila stood and grabbed the table with both hands to keep from reaching for a missile to heave at Fanny's head. "I love my time with the children and won't be giving that up." She glared furiously at Fanny and left the room.

Mrs. Bauer followed her into the kitchen. "Well done, Lila," she whispered. "Well done."

**

The church ladies' Festival was set for the last Sunday afternoon in August. The final weeks leading up to the event were a flurry of public announcements, poster distribution, recipe selections, and a few snipes from opposing camps. The worst offense was Nellie Brinkman describing Grace Gardner as "lookin' like she'd been drawed through a knothole backwards" when it came to her fashion sense. When that uproar abated, civility prevailed, and excitement ladled with curiosity surrounded the event.

At precisely three o'clock Stacy and her mother walked with Lila and Mrs. Bauer toward the Red Horse Saloon. Lila and Stacy wore their good dresses and new hair ribbons while noticing many ladies on the boardwalk wore their Sunday finest with stylish hats for the occasion.

"I don't know what to expect, do you?" Lila asked Stacy. "Never been in a saloon before."

A smiling Mr. Williams who had relinquished his signature hat for a vest and tie met them at the door with a bow and showed them to a table. When the women employed at the Red Horse arrived, the church ladies greeted each one with warm hospitality, setting aside dismay at their attire. The Red Horse ladies wore ruffled knee-length skirts and petticoats in a profusion of pink, yellow and green. Bare arms and revealing bodices were draped with fringed shawls in an attempt at modesty. In lieu of Sunday bonnets they wore feathers and flowers in their hair. Lila and Stacy gaped at their lip rouge and powdered faces.

"They must think us very drab," Lila whispered to Stacy.

"Indeed," Stacy said, her eyes never leaving the Red Horse ladies. Mrs. Hays and Mrs. Bauer observed everything with wide eyes but said nothing.

The room had been transformed. Mr. Williams had curtained the bar with an enormous, covered wagon canvas to hide all evidence of the nature of his business. Not a bottle of alcohol nor the bar itself was visible. The church ladies had decorated the room with paper hearts strung from the ceiling. In the center space stood a round table draped with a white linen tablecloth laden with sandwiches, pies, cakes, and pitchers of lemonade.

Small tables with chairs were scattered about the room. Approval buzzed among the guests as they made their way around the refreshment table. At three fifteen every table was filled, and Minnie Simpson hurried home to make another dozen cucumber sandwiches. Cora Higgins beamed.

Mr. Williams had gone to great lengths to provide entertainment for the festival and hired a disheveled-looking character to play the bagpipes which looked as bedraggled as he did. After the tramp-turned-musician finished an interminable rendition of "Scotland the Brave," the distressed looks on guests faces told the church ladies the volume of the bagpipes was overpowering the room. With utmost tact Mr. Williams changed his agreement with the bagpiper to play for the Red Horse patrons on Tuesday nights instead of today's festival. The deal was made, and conversation was restored for the ladies.

"Well, now, that was right nice," Edna Hays declared to Sophia Bauer as they sipped the last of their lemonade. "I suspect they'll get a nice sum of money, seeing as how the crowd is so big."

"When I was at the serving table, I overheard Cora tell Minnie that even Harriet will have to admit this was a big success," Sophia replied.

"Turned out grand," Lila said. "First time saloon and church social circles have crossed paths, wouldn't you say, Mrs. Bauer?"

"Yes, it is," she replied. "Minnie said the Red Horse ladies were polite as could be."

"And no one came to blows," Stacy said.

Edna and Sophia rose with the girls, smiling their thanks to Mr. Williams and the church ladies as they made their departure.

Lila and Stacy linked arms as they walked home. "You know, I still can't say I've been in a saloon, not *really*," Lila said.

"Never you mind," Mrs. Bauer said.

Chapter Twenty-Five

Lila pulled Stacy aside. "What do you know about the stranger, this so-called hermit, who lives in a cave near Belfry Hill?" Hays House was humming with hungry passengers who had arrived on a stagecoach from the west. The aroma of frying bacon filled the dining room.

"I'm really busy, Lila. Folks wanting their breakfast before the stage pulls out again."

"I know how it works—hurry up and feed 'em and off they go." Lila was returning from an errand at Last Chance for Mrs. Bauer and stopped in at the restaurant. "I'm so curious about this man living in a cave. Would you have time to hike out that way later on today?"

"Maybe. Depends on business. And what Ma says. I'll let you know."

Truthfully, Lila wasn't sure she'd have time for such frivolity today either. With autumn approaching, Mrs. Bauer was "putting food by" as she liked to say and had plans to make and preserve applesauce today. Lila knew the day ahead included peeling and chopping apples between preparing meals for their boarders.

It wasn't until three days later that Stacy and Lila found time for the trek to Belfry Hill. Lila learned the townspeople had erected a large bell to be rung in the event of an Indian attack on the stone outcropping of the hill at the western edge of town. Council Grove was used to rumors of guerrilla raids during the Civil War and Indian attacks. The bell was part of the town's defense.

"Why didn't they ring the bell last June when we had the Indian troubles? Lila asked.

"Don't really know. I guess because the Indians weren't attacking us, just each other."

September had arrived but summer temperatures held steady. Lila and Stacy wore their coolest blouses and pushed up their sleeves. They followed the incline of a rocky path with some effort for a good while until they came to an open view. The whole of Council Grove lay at their feet. The rocky crag gave way to the lush greenery below, the distant roofs of the businesses on Main Street poked through the trees, and the shimmering Neosho and the forest of trees that clung to its banks blurred into the landscape. All of the pieces fit together like a mosaic creating a magnificent painting.

Lila put her hand to her chest. "Oh, my. This is beautiful."

"You can see forever," declared Stacy.

The girls took in the beauty with quiet reverence, not moving from where they stood. A chickadee whistled "fee-bee" in the hushed afternoon. "I don't want to leave," Lila whispered. "Whoever lives up here, I understand why."

"Come on," Stacy said. "The Belfry is up yonder, and the stranger's cave is close by it."

The copper bell was installed atop a limestone base beside the path. A rope was attached to the clapper to allow for ringing. "Have they rung the bell very often?" Lila asked.

"I've never heard it rung, not once," Stacy said. "But we've only had it a couple of years—"

"Good day."

The girls jumped simultaneously and turned to the source of the voice behind them. A weathered looking man with olive skin and wild dark hair that partially obscured his face bowed slightly at the greeting. He wore an oversized pullover cotton shirt tucked into buckskin pants and boots. He was dusty and unkempt but not in an off-putting way.

"Good day," Stacy said. "We were . . .that is . . ."

Lila intervened. "My name is Lila, and this is my friend Stacy. We wanted to meet you," and she extended her hand.

The man shook Lila's hand, then Stacy's. "I am Matteo Boccalini. You've heard of me? The one who lives in the cave?" He raised his dark eyebrows.

"Well, yes we have," Stacy admitted. "We wondered how you're getting on."

The man's face creased with a sage smile. "I am a curiosity, yes?"

Lila and Stacy nodded.

"I am fine living up here."

"Don't you get lonely?" Lila asked.

"Nature provides me with all the company I need. When I go out walking, I can see what's happening in your town. Sometimes I have visitors."

"You do?" Stacy asked, surprised.

"A little girl named Emma shares her lunch pail with me from time to time. She loves to talk—sometimes she never stops." His brown eyes showed amusement, then he became silent as though signaling their conversation was coming to an end.

"Mr. Bonna...Bocca..." Lila struggled.

"Matteo," he said.

"Matteo, it was very nice to meet you. We'd like to visit you again, if that's all right."

"*Si. Buona serra.*" Matteo disappeared as quietly as he had appeared, down the path into the foliage and was gone. Lila and Stacy stared at each other, reading each other's thoughts at their astonishing encounter.

"We just talked to the man who lives in the cave," Stacy said breathlessly.

"He wasn't scary at all," Lila offered. "Polite even."

"You can tell he likes to be by himself, though."

Lila nodded. "Like people said, a hermit. And who'd have thought little Emma Simpson had made friends with him, sharing her lunch."

"Let's come back another time."

"But not right away," Lila said. "Don't want to seem nosy."

The girls took one last look at the glorious landscape from their perch in the hills before turning around for the hike back to town. As they trudged down the path, Lila thought about the man who lived in the cave. In some ways he was less mysterious than before—he had a name— but in other ways it raised new questions.

The encounter planted an idea.

**

Lila was eager to tell John about her chance meeting with the hermit Matteo. It was the final week before the fall term started, and John was busy meeting with the school board, opening up the schoolhouse, and preparing lessons. Fanny floated around the boarding house looking for something to do, but not trying very hard, and Lila was occupied with chores and avoiding Fanny. The two said little to each other since Lila made it plain, she wasn't giving up her place helping at school. Mrs. Bauer tried to stay out of the fray but on occasion could be heard muttering under her breath, "A peacekeeper in my own establishment. Humph."

John was eating a late supper by himself the night before school opened when Lila had a chance to talk with him. She slid into a chair beside him at the dining table. "John, you have to meet Matteo. He's such an interesting person." Lila went on to describe the encounter in detail, and John listened intently as he ate. "As we were leaving, he spoke in another language, probably Italian. It was only a few words, but that's the first time anyone has spoken directly to me in another language. Made me think of your comment he must be very educated."

"If he's a cleric in the Catholic Church, he probably speaks Latin, too, because of their Masses."

"I know you're terribly busy right now, but if you could find the time to hike out that way maybe you'd meet him just like we did."

"What's your great interest in him, Lila?"

Lila was contemplating an idea she wasn't ready to share yet, so she spoke of a second and equally valid reason. "Matteo seems book smart like you, and I think you'd have a lot in common with him."

John raised his eyebrows and chuckled. "A lot in common with a hermit from Italy?"

Lila persisted, her expression earnest. "You know what I mean. You come from different places in the world but the same world of books and learning."

"Matteo does sound interesting." John pushed his plate away and leaned back in his chair. "When school gets under way and things have settled down, I might see if there's an opportunity to meet him."

Lila was pleased. Ever since meeting Matteo she had been consumed with curiosity about him. She had heard he owned books he read every day and wondered what they were about, what language they were printed in. If she had her druthers, she'd go back to Belfry Hill every evening and visit Matteo. Perhaps he'd tell her the story of where he was from and how he came to live in Council Grove.

"There you are." An irritated voice interrupted her thoughts. Fanny stood at the dining room entrance, hands on her hips. "What took you so long?" Fanny sat beside John and Lila took that as a cue for her to leave.

"I'll clear the dishes." Lila immediately gathered the plates and utensils and left the dining room, but not before she heard Fanny say, "Are you going to be this late every night once school starts?"

Chapter Twenty-Six

After the Indian troubles in June, Captain Mullins and a small company of soldiers had been sent to protect the town from further invasion. They set up camp outside Council Grove, and a sense of calm settled over the citizens. At first the soldiers came into town only when necessary, their presence attracting everyone's attention. Over time they became less conspicuous as they became part of the community, and no one was surprised when more than one young lady of the town was called on by a soldier of the regiment.

Mr. Bellmard was completely recovered from pneumonia, which allowed Charley to return to school for the fall term. Lila and John were relieved. Mr. Bellmard could enjoy good health, and Charley could resume the role of a child, something he had missed during his father's illness. Lila's visits to Bellmard's cabin were less frequent, but when she did call, she found Mr. Bellmard a changed man. His appreciation for the care he received from Lila and John made him a more congenial neighbor. He no longer objected to Charley's "book learnin'" and encouraged Charley to keep up his attendance at school.

When Lila wasn't busy with regular domestic chores, her newest adventure was climbing Belfry Hill. She took advantage of the extra daylight after supper and the opportunity for a chance meeting with Matteo. If she heard the mandolin's melody floating from the hillside, she knew her chances of finding Matteo were good.

Sometimes she hiked around the hills, never seeing him and instead would find an overlook to sit on and gaze across the valley to the east toward the river. Other times she found him sitting in front of his cave strumming his mandolin and asked to sit and listen. She began to take a pad of paper and pencil to sketch flowers, plants, birds—whatever caught her eye—while she sat for the impromptu concert.

One evening after Matteo had finished playing, Lila let the melody suspend in the air before breaking the spell. "Matteo, I have another friend I'd like you to meet some day."

"Oh?"

"He's the schoolteacher, Mr. Reynolds."

"John Reynolds?"

"Yes." Lila was surprised. "How do you know . . ."

"I have met John Reynolds." Matteo smiled.

"You have? When?"

"He has visited me several times. We talk. He's an interesting man. An intelligent man."

So, he's been coming to visit Matteo, Lila thought to herself. "I had hoped you would meet each other. He's a very good teacher and you . . ."

"And me? What about me?" Matteo asked.

"You are a very interesting man with many experiences. I thought you would find much to talk about. That's all." She dropped her gaze, fearful she had pressed too much.

Matteo set his mandolin to one side. "You are an interesting woman. Eager to learn. Curious. Good traits in a person."

Lila looked up and found Matteo studying her. "Thank you. I don't mean to pry. As you said, I'm curious." She gave a self-conscious smile.

"Evening is coming now, and I have to ask you to leave, if you please."

"Of course." Lila rose. "Thank you for this visit."

Matteo nodded. "*Buona serra, Lila curiosa.*"

**

Toward the middle of September, there was a noticeable change in the air. The humidity disappeared overnight, blown away by a breeze from the northwest that cleared the skies and gave renewed vigor to everyone in town. Lila felt her step energized and her lungs expanded with the crisp air. The grove of trees along the Neosho showed the first blush of autumn yellow.

At the close of school on a Wednesday afternoon, Lila was straightening books and John had brought in an armload of wood should the temperature drop overnight. Fanny hadn't come to school today, although she found an excuse to drop by nearly every day. Lila thought this was the perfect time to present her idea to John, the idea that had been swirling in her head for weeks.

"John," she began.

"Lila," he said at the same moment. They were amused at their unison speech. "What were you going to say?" John asked.

"You first," Lila answered.

"All right." John brushed dirt off his sleeve and sat at his desk. Lila slid into a pupil's desk across from him. "I have an idea."

John proceeded to tell Lila he'd been visiting Matteo for weeks, had gotten to know him and found him a man of uncommon knowledge. What did she think of inviting Matteo to school to share his experiences and knowledge with the children, if he were willing to come, of course?

Lila was dumbfounded. "John, this is exactly what I've been thinking for weeks, ever since I met him. I've been waiting for the right time to ask. I didn't know if it was a good idea or if you'd approve.

John's eyes lit up, as they always did when he was enthused about a new teaching opportunity. "Did you know he was born on the island of Capris?"

"Where's that?"

"Off the coast of Italy. That alone would make an interesting geography lesson."

Lila leaned forward. "He could bring his mandolin, show the children how to play it. I think they'd love that."

"Don't forget the languages—Italian, Spanish, Latin—he speaks all three." John stood and began pacing as the ideas poured out.

"What if Matteo doesn't want to do this?" Lila asked, causing John to pause.

"He might resist. Maybe some gentle persuasion?" He looked to Lila for confirmation, she nodded in agreement, and he resumed walking the path in front of his desk while offering up more ideas.

Time passed unnoticed and when Lila realized the late hour, she left quickly and ran without stopping to the boarding house to help prepare supper. Fortunately, there was little to do since Mrs. Bauer had made a large pot of beef soup that morning, so Lila threw herself into making cornbread before Mrs. Bauer had a chance to ask why she was late. As she served the dining table, Lila thought Fanny looked rather sour-faced, quite the opposite of John who was still animated from their discussion about Matteo visiting school.

Later, when supper was over, John and Fanny sat outside on the rockers while Lila and Mrs. Bauer washed the dishes. Suddenly their voices rose, first Fanny, then John, back and forth the voices went. Lila and Mrs. Bauer frowned at each other. This was highly unusual to have such a public display of private feelings. The conversation became an argument. The voices grew louder. Lila couldn't believe her ears.

John Reynolds, the epitome of thoughtfulness and good manners, the even-tempered, soft-spoken man Lila knew, was yelling.

Chapter Twenty-Seven

It was impossible not to hear them, their voices carried from the front boardwalk out into the street, and beyond. What was more astonishing, neither John nor Fanny seemed to care who heard them.

"Have you taken leave of your senses, John? You're having that—that filthy ruffian who sleeps in a cave come to school? To do what?" Fanny demanded.

"He's a very learned person, Fanny. I've come to know him. He can share his life experiences with the children—where he came from, the languages he speaks."

"And expose the children to whatever diseases he may have. Probably has lice at the very least." Her voice rose in a crescendo. "Really, John. Since you've come out here you've lost all sense of propriety. I scarcely recognize you anymore." Through the front window Lila saw passersby across the street stop and gawk.

"And what does that mean?" John challenged.

"You consort with all sorts now. Not like you used to."

"All sorts? All sorts of what?"

"Do I have to spell it out for you?" Fanny's voice was shrill. "Undesirables, John. Like this hermit. Like the Bellmards. Like half the people in the town."

Lila wanted to scratch her eyes out right there on Main Street in front of everyone in Council Grove. And in the same moment, she wanted to hide from the humiliation it brought everyone within earshot, herself included. They were all undesirables, unworthy of those like John and Fanny.

"I don't believe this!" John shouted. "How can you sit in judgment of people I've come to call my friends, people who are kind and hard working who would give you the shirt off their back. Maybe life has dealt some of them a bad hand, but they fight on for a better day."

"Been dealt a bad hand? *Have all* these people in Council Grove been dealt a bad hand? More like they made poor choices to come out west. They don't have enough sense to make a proper life for themselves," Fanny insisted. "This place isn't fit for man or beast—not to mention red savages ready to wreak havoc at any moment. John, you don't belong out here with these people. I saw it the moment I got here."

For the first time in the argument, John lowered his voice. "That's where you're wrong. I very much belong *out here*, as you say, with these undesirables teaching their children. In fact, I love this place." There was a pause. Mrs. Bauer and Lila tried desperately to unhear the bitter words—Mrs. Bauer staring at her hands, Lila holding her breath—but it was too late. The truth was made plain for all to hear. John spoke with clarity. "If anyone doesn't belong out here, I believe it's you, Fanny."

Lila and Mrs. Bauer finished the washing up without so much as three words between them. Engulfed with embarrassment, they couldn't get to their own rooms fast enough.

Lila was ripped to pieces. She'd never experienced so many emotions simultaneously. Pulling her quilt under her chin, she sorted through the anger, shame, and embarrassment she felt, not only for herself but for Mrs. Bauer, for John, for her Council Grove family. She stared at the ceiling, agitated and furious. She heard no slamming doors, no muffled voices—nothing but dead silence. Lila was sure her pounding heart would never slow down, but somewhere in the early morning hours her anger abated, her heart slowed, and she drifted off.

**

The next morning, she woke frazzled. With only a few hours of sleep, the weight of the argument still troubled her, but more than that, Lila dreaded facing Mrs. Bauer, John, and Fanny. On her way to the kitchen, she turned the matter over in her mind and decided she could only do what came natural to her—look everyone in the eye and be as pleasant as possible.

"Good morning, Mrs. Bauer." Lila pulled her apron over her head. "What are we fixing for breakfast?"

Mrs. Bauer was pouring buttermilk into a pitcher. She turned with a look of recognition on her face. "Good for you,

Lila," she whispered, "for movin' on past last night. No sense dwelling on it."

They grabbed onto the idea of making breakfast as normal as possible, not knowing if others in the boarding house had overheard John and Fanny's argument. Three men were seated for breakfast before John came into the dining room, and Lila passed a platter of bacon with a "Good morning" greeting to all of them.

The table was quiet, but boarders often kept to themselves when they ate. It was John's silence that was unusual. He barely made eye contact with Lila or Mrs. Bauer, ate quickly, and left for school. Watching John walk down Main Street, knowing what she knew, filled Lila with sadness.

Fanny never came for breakfast. Mrs. Bauer told Lila she stopped by the kitchen later in the morning and asked for a cup of tea. "Her eyes were all red and puffy. I know she'd been crying," Mrs. Bauer confided.

Lila couldn't help herself. *Serves her right for all the wicked things she said last night.* Lila immediately chided herself for her unkind thoughts even though a tiny part of her wasn't sorry for thinking them.

Lila and Mrs. Bauer busied themselves the rest of the day baking apple pies thanks to the Shaw family who delivered a bushel basket of apples from their farm. Mrs. Bauer rolled out the dough while Lila peeled and sliced apples. The repetition of the familiar task brought Lila comfort, and they both took pride in the finished product—pies with bubbling juice and golden crusts. "It's funny how doing a simple chore like baking pies can make you feel right again, isn't it Mrs. Bauer?"

"Nothing better than work to help right the ship," she replied. "I hope Mr. John is feeling better after his day at school."

The lingering aroma of the pies filled the boarding house when Fanny joined the boarders for supper. Lila didn't know what to expect but thought at least the mouthwatering whiff of baked apples should put everyone in a pleasant frame of mind.

Fanny sat next to John whose mood seemed improved from the morning. Conversation was polite and centered around the cooling weather. One of the men talked about his upcoming departure to Diamond Springs where he would settle and send for his wife. This caused John and Fanny to exchange dark glances but nothing more.

It wasn't until later that evening that Mrs. Bauer pulled Lila aside.

"I've got news," she whispered, visibly upset.

Lila frowned. "What's wrong?"

"John just told me Miss Fanny will be checking out on Saturday."

"What?" Lila gasped.

"That's what he said. I asked if she'd be returning and he said, 'No. She's takin' the stage back to St. Louis.'" Mrs. Bauer paused, her eyes wide. "I don't mean to talk out of school, but I think this means the engagement if off."

Chapter Twenty-Eight

The news spun wildly in Lila's head. What exactly *did* it mean?

Was Fanny leaving for good and was the engagement off as Mrs. Bauer suggested? Or was this a temporary separation to give both parties time to reconsider after their heated argument the other night? It was impossible to know. What Lila did know was John continued to be withdrawn and worked long hours at school the rest of the week.

Saturday morning the air in the boarding house was thick with tension. Fanny's trunk stood by the front door where it had been since the previous night. The only sounds at breakfast were the scaping of cutlery across plates or the mumbled, "Please pass the biscuits." Lila had started the meal by greeting everyone with, "Looks like a fine day today," but was met with silent nods and quickly decided to quit making conversation.

The stagecoach heading east was expected in the morning but was often unreliable due to bad weather or breakdowns. Fanny was ready after breakfast and wore the same blue skirt and jacket she had on the day of her arrival. Lila watched her from the kitchen finding it hard to believe three months had passed since the devastating day of Fanny's arrival. A great deal had happened to Lila in those months, some significant life lessons, not the least of which was safeguarding her heart. She had packed it up and stowed it away with the utmost care.

When the stage rumbled into town and pulled to a stop in front of the Hays House, John and Fanny walked through the parlor to the front door.

"Wait, Fanny." Lila came from the kitchen and caught up to them. Lila was not sorry to see Fanny leave. She had brought hard feelings and resentment to the boarding house family. Despite that, something inside Lila would not let her depart without some form of farewell. "Before you go, I wanted to say I hope you have a safe journey to St. Louis," and offered her hand.

Fanny stared at it as though contemplating what to do before grasping it. She spoke without emotion. "Thank you." She turned and left.

Lila and Mrs. Bauer watched the departure from the parlor windows. John and Fanny stood by the stagecoach, spoke a few words then looked away awkwardly before a farewell embrace. John held Fanny's hand as she climbed aboard and found a seat. Other passengers joined her, the door was shut, and the reinsman cracked his whip over his team of horses. The coach jolted away, clattering down the street, leaving John to watch it head east to St. Louis as he stood alone in a swirl of dust.

**

It was Sunday afternoon two days after Fanny had left, and Council Grove had been treated to something of a parade. People gawked from windows and doorways. The townspeople were used to caravans coming and going along the trail but had just witnessed an east bound caravan notable for its size. Freighters returning from Santa Fe had driven twenty-seven wagons, pulled by teams of mules, straining with their cargo down Main Street to the campgrounds.

Before they were fully encamped, rumors were flying through town that the wagons bore buffalo meat, furs, and most importantly, gold. The goods were heading to Independence, and the gossip was gathering momentum from mouth to mouth. Furs weighing hundreds of pounds and gold weighing in the thousands would be situated overnight in the campgrounds of their humble town on the plains. Or so people were saying.

"You'd think folks never saw a caravan before." Mrs. Bauer shook her head and finished sweeping the boardwalk in front of the boarding house.

For Lila, still the newcomer, the sight was thrilling. The rumble of wagon after wagon in the swirling dust, the teamsters shouting over their teams, horseback riders alongside the procession kept Lila and John riveted watching the caravan's progress down Main Street to the campground. Lila saw the Riley brothers chase after the last wagons with their friends, hollering and throwing rocks at the wheels.

"Those boys never stop, do they?" She sat in a rocker beside John.

He smiled, Lila noted with gratitude. "They are a pair, those two. Ornery as the day is long."

Lila didn't know where to start the conversation. She'd never found it difficult to talk with John. On the contrary, half the time she felt like he knew what she was thinking before she spoke. But his break-up with Fanny—if that's what it was—was deeply personal and none of her business. Still, they hadn't spoken in days, and it was time to break the silence.

Lila took a breath. "Are you all right?" She immediately felt herself redden. *Why did I say that?* "I'm so sorry. I shouldn't have said—"

His voice was calm, like it so often was in awkward situations. "Don't apologize. I'm all right."

"I'm glad. You've kept to yourself, and I . . . I was a bit worried."

"Worried about me and Fanny?"

"Yes."

"Things didn't turn out like we planned. But they turned out for the best, that I'm sure of."

It was good to hear him so confident, Lila thought. "And what is the best?"

"Our happiness won't be found together." He tipped back in the rocker. "I don't know if I've changed since I moved to Council Grove or if I simply came to realize things about myself that I never knew before. In any event, Fanny and I are on different paths and want different things out of life. I'm at peace with the way things have turned out."

"I'm relieved to hear that. So is Mrs. Bauer." Lila went on. "I have to say, though, you still don't seem yourself. Are you sure everything's all right?"

"I'm not entirely sure. I hope it's nothing." John proceeded to tell her the school superintendent had spoken with him on Friday and asked him to meet with the school board on Monday evening.

"You don't know what the meeting's about?" Lila asked.

"No. I've been wracking my brain. I can't imagine what." John's brow furrowed.

"'S'pose it has anything to do with asking Matteo to visit school?"

"Possibly. I simply don't know."

Lila could see he was more concerned about this than he was willing to admit. In fact, this meeting seemed more upsetting to him than Fanny's departure. "You're right. It may be nothing at all. Tomorrow night will be here before you know it, and you'll have your answer."

She rose and gave him a reassuring smile before heading to the kitchen to help prepare supper. Superintendent Piper had always impressed Lila as very supportive of John's teaching and his needs for the classroom. Like John, she couldn't imagine the reason for a meeting with all the school board members at such short notice. Did John have reason to worry, she wondered?

**

John's meeting with the school board didn't last long. He got home about 7:30 the next evening, walked through the front door to the kitchen and asked Mrs. Bauer if she minded if he sat on the back step. "Need to clear my head."

Lila and Mrs. Bauer were tidying up the kitchen and gave each other a look. "Course I don't mind." She eyed him critically "You look like you've been pestered something awful, John."

"I have." He pushed open the screen door and lowered himself to the steps.

In an urgent whisper Lila said, "What do you 's'pose happened?"

"Don't know, but he looks mighty upset." Mrs. Bauer glanced in John's direction. "Give him some air. Maybe he'll feel like talking in a bit."

Lila paced around the parlor until she tired of walking in circles, strode down the hall and back, walked across to the Hays House but Stacy was too busy to visit, and returned to the kitchen. She hoped that was enough air for John because she couldn't wait any longer.

"Feel like talking?" She sat next to John on the step and pulled her shawl loosely around her shoulders. It was a beautiful evening. The sun was streaking the sky orange, the air smelled of fresh cut hay and grass and apples. It was the kind of evening to be savored, not spoiled with worries of the day.

"I'm in trouble."

"What?"

The school board consisted of three people—Mr. Piper, Mr. Osgood the banker, and Mr. Brinkman. Mr. Brinkman had requested the meeting because certain citizens had come to him with a negative report about Mr. Reynolds. Last Wednesday evening several people witnessed a loud argument outside the boarding house between Mr. Reynolds and an unnamed woman. The argument lasted for at least twenty minutes, attracting the attention of many townspeople. Mr. Brinkman deemed this behavior unprofessional conduct for a school master and a poor example for both adults and children.

"He's recommending my suspension as school master."

"No!" Lila shot to her feet. "He can't do this."

"I'm afraid he can. I can continue teaching until they come to a unified conclusion as to my status."

"We have to stop this. We have to convince them the argument was nothing but two people having a difference of opinion."

"I wish it were that simple. I did everything I could to explain it in those terms, that it was out of character for me to show anger. I promised I would never display such an outburst in public again." John leaned over, his forearms resting on his legs, and stared at the ground. "I had no idea my argument with Fanny . . ." His voice trailed off.

Lila lowered herself to the step and spoke to the slumped figure beside her. "I'm not letting this stand. Council Grove is not firing the best teacher it ever had."

Chapter Twenty-Nine

Lila lost no time in spreading the news of John's plight. She hoped to garner support for John from the community. Mrs. Bauer was the first to know that evening, and the next morning Lila crossed the street to the Hays House to tell them. She went to Last Chance and spoke with Thomas Hill, the owner, and shoppers including Minnie Simpson. Doc Watson appreciated hearing the news, too.

She knew Mr. Bellmard would want to know and headed to their cabin after an early supper that evening. Charley ran out to greet her with his usual infectious grin. Behind him in the doorway stood his father.

"It's good to see you looking so well, Mr. Bellmard," Lila greeted him.

"Strong as I ever was, thanks to you and Mr. Reynolds."

"About Mr. Reynolds, that's why I'm here. He could use your help."

During the next week Lila sent word to every parent whose child attended school in Council Grove. John appreciated her efforts but was doubtful it would affect the outcome of the board's decision. Mr. Piper was squarely behind John, Mr. Osgood was uncommitted, and Mr. Brinkman was opposed to his staying on. The board was meeting next Monday, and Lila wanted to bring character witnesses for John to speak in his favor.

Indian summer lingered in Council Grove. It should have been a time to delight in autumn, each day the sky a deeper blue than the day before. The sun teased with golden warmth, the countryside glowed in shades of gold, amber, and burnt umber. Sumac blazed crimson along the riverbanks and meadowlarks sang with Matteo's mandolin at sunset.

Lila missed all of it. Instead, she forged ahead, counting each day with worry for John's appointment with the board. She had offered her own private prayers that John would keep his position as school master and on Sunday, hiked up Belfry Hill to ask Matteo for a special blessing for John.

Matteo nodded. "Curious Lila, I will offer a prayer for Mr. John."

Lila didn't understand Latin but bowed her head reverently as the two stood in front of Matteo's cave and prayed. When he was finished, Lila thanked him and walked away. She had done all she could.

**

Her stomach was in knots.

Lila sat in the third row of desks in the schoolhouse, a place that had become her second home. It was a sad irony, she thought, that tonight this beloved school room was more like a courtroom where John would learn his fate as a schoolteacher in Council Grove. Around her were friends of John's who had come to show their support.

Mr. Piper opened the meeting by welcoming everyone, assuring them the board was glad they were in attendance. The scowl on Mr. Brinkman's face communicated otherwise. As the meeting got underway, Lila felt relief as the agenda became a discussion rather than an indictment of John.

At one point Mr. Osgood said, "I'd like to hear from some of you who came to tonight's meeting. We weren't expecting a crowd." He nodded to the audience. "Please."

Lila was taken aback when the first person to stand was Louis Bellmard. He was a towering presence but soft-spoken. "I'm not much on speakin' at meetin's. Or even goin' to them." There was quiet laughter. "But in the case of Mr. Reynolds, he's done my boy well, teachin' him just fine even though it took me quite some time to see that." Mr. Bellmard shifted his weight. "Even more, he and Miss Bonner came when I was sick with fever and pneumonia. Took care of me and my boy. I'm much obliged." He nodded to John who sat by himself in a desk in the front row.

Doc Watson rose from his seat. "You all remember our Indian troubles in June? I hope you know John Reynolds played an important part in settling that dispute. He and Thomas Hill, sitting here beside me, negotiated with the Indians to help end the standoff. Then John took me to the boarding house to treat a gravely wounded boarder, all without any consideration for his own welfare. He's a man of rare integrity, and I, for one, hope the school board keeps him on as our school master." There was a smattering of applause which Lila joined in with enthusiasm.

The townspeople took turns, rising one by one, and spoke to John's integrity and high quality of teaching. Mr. Riley likened as how Mr. Reynolds was the first teacher to keep his boys in line long enough to learn anything. Minnie Simpson testified her Emma was blooming into a first-rate writer, thanks to Mr. Reynolds' tutelage, and Mrs. Bauer said in all her years running a boarding house, Mr. Reynolds was the most well-mannered, considerate young man she'd ever had under her roof.

Lila was encouraged by the support. She had glanced at John during the discussion, watching his demeanor, but he gave no indication of how he felt. After the testimonies, Lila made eye contact with him. The look on his face told her he was hopeful he wouldn't lose the job he so dearly loved. That gave her hope, too.

Then Mrs. Brinkman stood, and the atmosphere changed. "All of this doesn't explain away the argument that happened on Main Street in front of the whole town. In my opinion, that action is still as unprofessional now as it was a week ago." She stood tall and looked at the rows of faces, daring the next defender to stand.

"I have to agree with my wife." Mr. Brinkman spoke for the first time. He turned to John. "Mr. Reynolds, you were having a very heated argument, were you not?"

"Yes, I was," John answered.

"What was this argument about?"

Mr. Piper interrupted. "I don't believe that will help solve this situation, William."

Mr. Brinkman pressed on. "It might clear up the whole misunderstanding." He turned to John again. "What the argument about?"

John shifted in the desk. "I'd rather not say."

"Rather not say? What are we to make of it, then?" Mr. Brinkman held out both arms in a helpless gesture. He waited. "Again, what was the argument about?"

John looked Mr. Brinkman in the eye. "It was personal."

There was a murmur among the crowd.

Mr. Brinkman gave a smug look over his spectacles. "Well, I don't see how we can come to a conclusion—"

"Excuse me." Lila rose from her seat. "I'd like to say something." The clench in her stomach returned.

Lila took in the faces of the strangers and friends in the school room before beginning. "I was there that evening at the boarding house and was close enough to hear what the argument was about." She glanced at John and saw the barely perceptible shake of his head. It puzzled her. "I think the folks in this town should know what it was about. Mr. Reynolds—"

"Miss Bonner, please. This isn't necessary." It was John with an imploring look on his face.

She returned his steady gaze. "They should know, Mr. Reynolds, what you did. You see," Lila continued, turning back to the audience, "Mr. Reynolds was defending our town and everyone who lives here. He was defending you, Mr. Brinkman, and you, Mrs. Brinkman—and everyone in this room."

"I hardly think I need defending." Mr. Brinkman was indignant.

"Oh, but you did. From a very insulting attack. Mr. Reynolds had been told that we who live in Council Grove were 'less than,' that we were not good enough for a teacher like Mr. Reynolds, that the children he teaches are undesirables and their parents are incapable of making a good life for their families out here on the prairie. In my thinking it was a very wicked thing to say, and Mr. Reynolds would not let those words stand without a fight."

Lila took a breath. "That's what we all heard that night—Mr. Reynolds fighting for the dignity of every man, woman, and child in our town. He was right to do that, he was brave to do that, and we should thank him for that." Lila sat, and it wasn't until Mrs. Bauer leaned over and squeezed her hand that Lila realized she was shaking.

The room was silent as Lila's impassioned words hung in the air. Someone cleared their throat. Lila kept her eyes straight ahead, afraid to look anyone in the face lest she fall apart. Presently Mr. Piper spoke.

"Thank you, Miss Bonner. We appreciate what you've said. We appreciate what all of you have said. I will meet with Mr. Osgood and Mr. Brinkman to discuss this matter further. Mr. Reynolds, we'll give you our decision by Wednesday evening at the latest. Thank you." He stood, indicating the meeting was over.

Supporters clustered around John after the meeting, shaking his hand and wishing him well before they departed. Lila found herself receiving thanks for exposing the nature of the argument that caused the uproar in the first place. She pressed through those who lingered until she was beside John, anxious to get his reaction. "What do you think?" she asked.

He said nothing and waited for people to drift away.

Lila frowned. "What's wrong?"

His answer was clipped. "They have no right to know my personal business."

"What?" Lila thought she heard wrong. "But, John, your personal business was about *them*, the people if this town."

His eyes flashed. "Lila, why didn't you leave it alone?" His angry strides took him out the door and into the school yard before Lila caught up to him.

"John, wait." When she caught his elbow, he was forced to stop. "I don't understand." She shook her head in confusion. "Why are you angry? I thought you'd be relieved."

His face flushed with emotion. "My word should be enough; a man's word is a sacred pledge. When I said, 'it's personal', that should have been enough for Mr. Brinkman to trust me and not question my judgement or my character for the details of the argument."

"I was only trying to help. To explain how important the argument was for the folks in our town." Lila struggled to keep her voice steady. She was at the edge of tears. "I meant no harm."

"Don't you see how this exposes me? I feel like everyone in town has intruded into my personal life. Everything's changed. I can't go back to the way things were before." He strode away leaving Lila staring at his angry figure as he disappeared down the hill toward Main Street.

Chapter Thirty

Lila stood on the back porch staring at the empty night sky, trying to make sense of John's outburst. She understood that teachers in any community were held to a very high standard of conduct. They could be fired for the slightest appearance of a moral lapse. But a public display of anger? Lila disagreed with that notion.

In her own defense, it had taken every ounce of her courage to defend John publicly, never mind all those folks she brought to the meeting to speak on his behalf. It was her lack of standing in the community that gave her pause to defend him, not the merit of his cause. And what did she get for her trouble? John's anger.

At length the evening chill sent her inside with a mighty weight on her shoulders. She found Mrs. Bauer closing up the boarding house. "I've made a terrible mistake," Lila blurted out. "I don't rightly understand it, but I have."

"Made a mistake? What do you mean?" Mrs. Bauer latched the front door and turned down the lamps.

Lila explained John's behavior after the meeting. "He was so upset. Said now everyone knows about his personal life, and I should have left it alone. He just stormed away from me." She was near tears for the second time that night.

Mrs. Bauer laid a comforting hand on her arm. "Oh, come now. Couldn't be as bad as that."

"It was. Believe me, it was. The worst part is, I thought I was helping."

Mrs. Bauer studied Lila and released a sigh. "You know, Mr. Reynolds has been through some trying times lately. Miss Fanny left, and then all this nonsense with the school board happened. He's been mighty worried about his job."

Lila nodded. "Of course, he has."

"That Mr. Brinkman, he's trying to make a name for himself in town, setting himself up to be better than. *He's* the one should of left it alone and trusted John."

"Can't argue with that."

"And I 'spect John's pride's been hurt, too. You know how men are—don't need help from anyone. Having you come to his defense even though you meant to be nothing but helpful, maybe it smarted a bit."

Lila's shoulders sagged.

"Don't look so sad, child. He'll come around."

"What should I do?"

"Give him time. He'll feel better in a day or two—wait and see."

She had no choice but to wait and see. By this time Wednesday John would know if he was still employed as a teacher in Council Grove. What's done is done, for good or for bad.

She desperately hoped it was for good.

**

He's got to wait today and tomorrow before he knows the board's decision, Lila thought while she scrambled eggs for breakfast the following morning. She reasoned that going to the school to help that afternoon would be a good tonic for waiting out the verdict. She could be a distraction or at least a presence, and that might be a way to help.

But it didn't help. When she told John of her plans, he responded with, "Don't trouble yourself. The lessons are going quite well."

It was like someone kicked her in the gut. Unexpected. All the wind gone out of her. *Don't trouble yourself? So, this was how it was going to be?*

Lila didn't like the new rules of the game and wasn't about to play by them. "Mrs. Bauer, do you mind if I make an extra batch of muffins this morning? Thought I'd take them to the school children this afternoon? To cheer everyone up."

"You mean cheer up Mr. Reynolds, don't you?" Mrs. Bauer raised her eyebrows.

"You know me too well," Lila answered. "If you want to take the cost of the fixin's out of my pay—"

"Don't be silly, Lila. If it puts Mr. Reynolds on better footing, I'm all for it. Why don't you chop up some apples and toss 'em into the batter?"

After lunch Lila filled a basket with her baked goods, wrapped herself in a shawl and set out for school. The day was bright and breezy, the fresh air cool on her face. Clouds scudded across the sky, blotting the sun one minute then suddenly exposing its fiery brilliance the next in a heavenly chase.

As she climbed the hill, the sound of the children's laughter told her it was recess time. She walked around to the side of the schoolhouse and found John keeping one eye on the children, the other on a book he was attempting to read.

His head shot up. "Lila—Miss Bonner—I'm surprised to see you."

"I find it hard to stay away." She gave a half smile. "I was baking this morning." She lifted the checkered tea towel covering the muffins. "Thought the children might like a surprise, if it's all right with you."

"Of course. That's very thoughtful." His eyes shifted away, then back to her.

"It's so nice outside, why don't we eat out here?" she suggested.

Recess became an impromptu party. The children gathered round and began to gobble up the apple muffins, thrilled with the unexpected treat. While they ate, little Mary Shaw tugged on Lila's skirt. "Can you keep a secret?" she whispered.

Lila bent down. "I certainly can."

Mary wiped crumbs from her mouth with her sleeve and said, "Mr. Reynolds is sad." She spoke gravely, her brown eyes pooled with worry.

Lila had grown fond of Mary since her family had sought safety in the boarding house during the Indian troubles last summer. She was shy and very sensitive for a six-year-old, and Lila needed to hear more. "Why do you say that?"

"He never smiles anymore."

"Mary, Mr. Reynolds isn't sad. He's very busy with work." She put her arm around the child and drew her close. Lila realized even the children were aware something was amiss with their teacher. Maybe those muffins filled a need for the teacher *and* the students.

The younger ones insisted Lila play "Go In and Out the Window" with them until she tired of bending under their tiny, clasped arms as she wound her way around the circle. When they asked Mr. Reynolds to find someone to take Lila's place, he begged off by organizing all the children into teams for relay races. It was at the end of the races when Team B had been declared the winner amid shouts and hurrahs, while John and Lila stood in the swirl of excited, noisy children that John turned to Lila and said simply, "I'm sorry."

Lila needed no further explanation and accepted his apology with a nod of her head.

John wasn't finished. "It was good of you to come." He glanced at the happy mayhem around them. "I needed this. Thank you." He looked at her with such appreciation her breath caught. Lila struggled to hold his gaze and found enough voice to say, "You're welcome."

**

Lila glanced out the parlor window every five minutes.

"That won't make him get home any sooner," Mrs. Bauer said.

"I can't help it." Lila set aside the scraps she was braiding for a rug and went to the window, peered out, then returned, and sat beside Mrs. Bauer.

"And flittin' back and forth won't help neither," Mrs. Bauer rebuked. "He'll get home when he gets home."

Lila sighed. Tonight was the night Mr. Piper had promised a decision about John's employment, and the waiting had frayed Lila's nerves. She no longer held any illusion that she and John had a future together, but that didn't change the fact that she wanted him to succeed as a teacher in Council Grove or wherever life took him. In her eyes, John being fired would be a huge miscarriage of justice. He had to be retained. That's all there was to it.

She was at the window again. "I see him."

Mrs. Bauer put down her braiding. "How does he look?"

"Can't tell. Too far away. His step looks lively enough."

By the time John came through the front door, Lila was fit to be tied. Neither she nor Mrs. Bauer wanted to ask the obvious question, so they stood there, holding their breath.

John looked from one to the other, then burst into a wide grin. "I'm staying!" he shouted. "I'm staying, I'm staying." He grabbed Lila around the waist and twirled her in the air as she whooped her delight. He no sooner set Lila on her feet than he grabbed Mrs. Bauer and twirled her while she protested with laughter.

"Oh, this is such good news." Lila clapped her hands unable to contain her joy.

"We've been frettin' for you something fierce." Mrs. Bauer gave him another hug.

"Tell us what happened," Lila said. "What about Mr. Brinkman?"

"Before you do that," Mrs. Bauer interrupted, "I have a bottle of sarsaparilla that needs to be opened. I'll be right back with some glasses." Her eyes sparkled.

With that John flopped into the stuffed chair and heaved a huge sigh. "Sounds perfect, Mrs. Bauer."

The three spent the next hour discussing the school board's decision while they drank to John's reinstated status. It turned out there was no outcry from the public about his behavior but only one complaint—from Mrs. Brinkman who happened to hear the argument as she was passing by. She told her husband about it, and he ran with it to Mr. Piper. When Mr. Piper learned there was only one complaint, it didn't take long for him and Mr. Osgood to overrule Mr. Brinkman.

"I don't mind telling you, I felt great satisfaction leaving Mr. Brinkman red-faced and muttering to himself by the end of the meeting," John grinned.

"A fitting end to the whole sorry affair," Lila said.

"I couldn't be happier for you, Mr. John." Mrs. Bauer beamed like a proud parent.

An enormous burden had been lifted—they each felt it. With that shared bond their camaraderie deepened and allowed John to speak freely. He turned to Lila.

"I didn't mean everything I said that night, after the meeting. About things never being the same again."

"John, you don't need to explain."

"Yes, I do. I did feel exposed, even betrayed, but that feeling went away the more I thought about it. I don't feel compromised as a teacher. I think the good folks in town understand the situation for what it was and are ready to put this behind us. I hope Mr. Brinkman feels the same and doesn't hold a grudge."

"I hope so, too," Lila said.

He went on. "So now we can turn our attention to more important things—like planning for Matteo's visit to school. Lila, what do you say we go see him after school tomorrow?"

Chapter Thirty-One

The day had arrived. Lila was excited and also a little nervous, and John admitted he felt the same. It had taken coaxing and encouraging, but they had convinced Matteo it would be a wonderful opportunity for the school children if he came and shared his life experiences with them. They hoped it would broaden their view of the world beyond Council Grove in a tangible way. Yes, they had experience with travelers from other countries passing through their town. Some had even settled there. But Matteo's story was different. He was different.

It was already ten o'clock, and there was no sign of him. Lila leaned out the door to view the path from Main Street to the school yard, but it was empty. Her heart sank. Maybe he'd changed his mind. It was a lot to ask of this very private person, and she wouldn't blame him if their request had overwhelmed him. Discouraged, she settled into one of the desks beside Bobby Gardner to have him read to her, when the door opened. It was Matteo with his mandolin strung over his back. He smiled and gave a small bow.

Taking long strides, John met him at the door, his hand outstretched. "Welcome to our class, Mr. Boccalini. Come meet the children."

John and Lila had prepared the children for Matteo's visit, but only one of the children had seen him before. The Riley brothers exchanged a skeptical look at the unkempt, bearded man in odd clothes but said nothing. After a formal introduction, the lesson began when Matteo pointed to the island of Capri on a map of Italy tacked to the wall and said, "This is where I was born." The children leaned forward to better grasp his words. A few frowned at his unfamiliar accent, but the children gave the stranger their full attention.

"When I was eighteen, I went to Rome to study to become a priest."

"Where's Rome?" one of the children asked.

Matteo pointed to the city on the map. "I learned Latin and Spanish and three years later became a priest. Soon after that the Pope named me a secretary."

"What's that?" asked Emma Simpson.

"An important job to help the Pope."

"I know the Pope," said Mary Shaw. "He's the president of our church."

Matteo smiled at her. "Yes, he's the head of the Catholic Church."

From there Matteo explained he fell out of favor with some in the church because he was outspoken. He was found guilty of something he had not done, but before he could be sentenced, he fled Rome. "I feared for my life and became a wanderer. I left Italy and found my way to America and came west, eventually to Council Grove."

Lila could tell it was a lot for their young minds to absorb. Matteo and John took time to answer a flood of questions.

"What does outspoken mean?"

"What's a wanderer?'

"Who was after you, the law?"

Billy Riley asked, "Did you kill somebody?"

The younger children had more practical questions.

"What's it like to live in a cave?" and "What do you eat for supper?"

During the discussion, John told the class the American judicial system is based on the principle that a person is innocent until proven guilty. The older students, even the Riley brothers, appreciated how this may not have been applied in Matteo's case. As Lila watched from the back of the classroom, it was not lost on her that Matteo was a man searching for a place to belong, just as she had been when she first came to Council Grove. He was on the outside looking in.

One of the children raised his hand. "Are you gonna play that?" He pointed to the mandolin sitting on Mr. Reynolds' desk.

"I am. My mandolin goes with me wherever I go."

Matteo picked up the well-worn, eight stringed instrument and began plucking the strings. The children marveled at the speed of his fingers and the lively tune he created. The younger ones clapped in time to the music.

When Matteo finished, they asked for another song and with a change in tempo and mood, he strummed the strings in a slow ballad he sang in his native tongue. Lila had heard this tune on many evenings and hummed along quietly, wondering at the meaning of the words. Was it about a lost love? A lost family? Emotion surged through every phrase as the Italian rolled off his tongue, and when the last note was sung, Lila felt a tear in the corner of her eye.

Matteo sang one more song, then let the children take turns, if they promised to be *very* careful, plucking the mandolin strings. When it was time to conclude Matteo's visit, John stood before the class. "Children let's thank Mr. Boccalini for being our guest today," and led them in a round of applause, to which Matteo gave a small bow and smile.

**

"The morning couldn't have gone better, Mrs. Bauer." John leaned against the kitchen counter as she and Lila finished washing up after supper that evening.

"I agree completely." Lila folded the dish towel over the drying rack. "We didn't know what to expect—"

"Or if Matteo would even come," added John. "But the children were eager to hear what he had to say."

"Even the Riley brothers?" Mrs. Bauer quipped.

"Even the Riley brothers." John chuckled. He hung around the kitchen a while longer making small talk until Mrs. Bauer left. "Lila, would you mind . . ." he stumbled over his words and began again. "Would you like to take a walk?"

Surprised, it took Lila a moment to respond. "A walk? Sure. Let me grab my cloak."

The evening was chilly, and Lila pulled her cloak close. The October mornings were showing traces of frost, and there was a sense that the wild creatures in the woods were preparing for the cold months ahead. The wagon trains to Santa Fe had all but stopped. A handful of freighters came through town, and the campgrounds saw only a few hardy—or foolish—travelers.

Although the sun still hung on the horizon, John carried a lantern, and they walked to the end of Main Street into fields of grass in the rolling hills that surrounded the town.

"It's beautiful out here," Lila said turning in a slow circle.

"I think so, too." John watched her. "I've been wanting to talk to you for a long time, Lila. Taking a walk seemed like a good way to do that."

Lila stopped circling and faced him. "Talk about what?"

"Lots of things. Could we sit?"

They sat beside a hickory tree, the lowering sun before them, the town behind them. "I don't know where to begin," he said. "I suppose when Fanny came here." He took a deep breath. "I've been promised to Fanny for as long as I can remember, an arrangement between our families. Our fathers had adjoining property back east and were best friends, as were their fathers. I grew up knowing I'd marry Fanny someday."

"Like an arranged marriage?"

"Yes. And I accepted that, and we planned to start our life together here in Kansas once I got established." He took another breath and kept his eyes on the horizon. "And then I met you."

Lila stopped breathing.

"It started back at the Beatty's." John shook his head reliving the memory. "I've never seen such courage as when you put on a disguise and boarded a stagecoach to who-knows-where to get away from your father." He turned to her.

Lila held his gaze. "I don't know how courageous I was. Scared is more like it. Sometimes a bad situation makes you to do things you never thought you could."

"But it says so much about the kind of person you are." He looked at her long and hard, and Lila could have sworn those dark brown eyes were full of affection. He swallowed and continued. "When we got to Council Grove and spent time together, we became friends. I kept discovering wonderful qualities you possess, which was terrible for me because I was engaged."

Wonderful qualities I possess. Lila was speechless. All those times she saw glimmers of a deep connection with John were not her imagination, they were real, had been real all along. She hesitated, then spoke. "I had no idea that was how you felt."

"I couldn't tell you. I had no right to find you so attractive. I was ashamed."

They were silent for a time, letting the truth settle between them.

"Everything changed after Fanny arrived," John said. "It was clear to both of us we weren't the same people we used to be. It would have been a poor marriage had we gone forward with it."

Lila stared at the horizon. Stray clouds obscured the sinking sun sending beams of light shooting from its center into the sky. "So, what happens now?"

"I'm not sure. You've said very little. May I ask, what do you think about what I've said?"

"To be honest, I'm not sure what to say. I've changed too since Fanny came. I'm more cautious about the world, about relationships than I once was. Maybe we need time to sort this out."

"Of course, but there's one thing I don't need time to sort out."

"What is it?"

"You are more than just my friend."

Lila's breath caught again. John stood and offered his hand to help her up. He used the fading light as an excuse to hold her hand should she lose her footing in the twilight as they made their way back to the boarding house.

Chapter Thirty-Two

You are more than just my friend. What does he mean? Lila couldn't let go of John's candid revelation. She replayed their conversation countless times before falling asleep that night and again the next day and the next. It ran through her head constantly.

"You've plum wore out that johnny cake batter, Lila," Mrs. Bauer said while preparing breakfast two days later. "It was ready to cook ten minutes ago."

"Oh, I'm sorry." Lila quickly poured the batter onto the hot griddle where it bubbled and sizzled. "Don't know what I was thinking." She gave an embarrassed smile.

"I don't either, but you been wool-gathering these past few days like I don't know what. Want to tell me what's going on?"

"I can't go into it right now." She paused while she flipped the johnny cakes, "but John and I had a big talk." She grinned at Mrs. Bauer. "I think we have an understanding between us."

"It's about time. You two have been at odds long enough. That said, don't get scatter brained on me and forget what you're supposed to be doin'." Mrs. Bauer nodded as if to drive home her point.

After they cleared the table and washed the dishes, Lila grabbed her cloak and headed off to school. "I'll be back in an hour," she called over her shoulder, closing the front door.

Red oaks and yellow hickory blazed against a pristine blue sky making the autumn day picture perfect. It wasn't the first time she was grateful she had landed in Council Grove whether by accident or some grand design. Bit by bit she felt herself becoming part of the place she had been searching for.

When Lila arrived at school, she glanced at John who was standing at the head of the room leading the older students in their reading assignment. "Good morning, Miss Bonner," he nodded, the corners of his mouth turned up ever so slightly in a smile.

His smile warmed her cheeks. "Good morning, Mr. Reynolds," Lila replied. Wishing she could control her blushing, Lila took her place beside the group of youngest children reading from their primers. The four students took turns reading aloud as Lila listened, assisted as needed, and praised them when they finished.

"Well done," Lila said to the group when the lesson concluded. Her gaze lingered on eight-year-old Lucy Shaw, the oldest of the Shaw children. A very bright student, Lucy appeared distracted and had read with many errors, which was unusual for her.

When John finished the geography lesson, the children were dismissed for lunch and scrambled for their lunch pails lined up on the floor near the coat hooks. Lila made her way over to Lucy.

"How are you today, Lucy." Lila gave her an extra bright smile.

"Fine, Miss Bonner." Lucy made a feeble attempt to smile, then carried her lunch pail to her desk.

This is not like her, Lila thought.

The sound of laughter and chatter filled the schoolroom, but Lucy sat quietly at her desk, picking at her sandwich and fruit. Lila thought she would try once more to encourage Lucy to tell her what was bothering her before returning to the boarding house. Sitting in a desk across from Lucy she asked, "What kind of sandwich do you have today?"

"Ham."

"Looks very good."

Lucy lifted the slice of bread, inspected the ham, and let the bread drop. "Not very hungry."

It was then Lila looked closely at Lucy and noticed tiny red spots on her neck above the collar of her dress. Lila inhaled sharply and hoped Lucy hadn't noticed. "Are you feeling unwell, Lucy?"

Keeping her eyes on her uneaten sandwich, Lucy answered, "Um, no. Well, sort of." Lucy's big brown eyes began to fill with tears. "I don't feel good. The sun hurts my eyes."

Lila laid her hand on Lucy's forehead and felt heat radiating off it. "I'll be right back."

Coming to stand next to John's desk, Lila spoke in a whisper, "John, it's Lucy Shaw."

John looked over at the child. "What is it?"

"She has a rash on her neck."

"A rash?" He stood. "Should I be concerned?"

"Come see for yourself."

When they approached Lucy, she was resting her head on her desk. Her braids had fallen to one side giving them a full view of the flat red rash on her neck. John and Lila's eyes met in worried recognition and John mouthed silently, "measles."

**

John and Lila took their conversation to the back of the classroom while the children finished their lunches. "Do you really think it's measles?" Lila's forehead was wrinkled with concern.

"I had measles when I was about Lucy's age," John said. "That was a long time ago, but from what I remember it looked like that."

"I had measles, too," Lila said. "Me and my brothers. But I was little and don't recall much."

"I wonder if Doc is in the office," John said. "If he could stop by and see her, we'd know for sure."

"I was getting ready to leave," Lila said. "I'll fetch him."

"I'd be grateful. Thank you."

"What are we going to do with the other children? We can't have them running around in town or going home yet."

"Let's see what Doc has to say," John said. "Hopefully he can come before school lets out."

Lila fastened her cloak, went straight to Doc's office, and was relieved to find him sorting apothecary bottles in the back room. "Lila, what a pleasant surprise. What can I do for you today?" Lila explained Lucy's rash and the concerns she and John had. "A flat, reddish rash, you say?" Doc wasted no time gathering his medical bag and coat. "I'll have a look at her. Let's go."

It wasn't far to walk to the school, but Doc decided to take his horse with him, "just in case. I never know what I'm going to find when I make a visit." When they arrived at school, the children were at noon recess playing in the school yard. John brought Doc and Lila inside where they found Lucy asleep at her desk, her arms folded, making a pillow for her head on the desktop.

John gently shook her arm. "Doc is here to see what's making you feel so poorly."

"Hello, young lady. I'm Doctor Watson. Remember me?" He had treated the Shaw family over the years and delivered Lucy's last two siblings. "Mr. Reynolds says you're not feeling very well. I'd like to check you over and listen to your heart." Lucy was groggy and only nodded in response. Doc examined her eyes which were puffy, red, and watery. He took her pulse and listened to her heart. Then he looked inside her mouth where he noticed a spattering of grayish-white spots. Finally, he examined the rash on her neck and behind her ears.

When he was finished, Lila put a comforting hand on Lucy's shoulder, and John turned to Doc. "What do you think?"

He spoke in a hushed tone. "It's measles. Any other children showing symptoms?"

John and Lila shook their heads. "No. Not that we've seen. What should we do?"

"Measles can spread quickly." Doc explained he wanted to check the children one by one as they came in from recess for any signs of rash and examine inside their mouths for often accompanying white spots. Once done, he wanted to take Lucy home and check on the rest of the Shaw family. "Wouldn't be unusual for the whole family to come down with it if they haven't had it before." He leaned close to John and Lila, his expression grave. "The problem is keeping this from spreading."

**

When Lila returned to the boarding house, she was anxious to tell Mrs. Bauer about Lucy Shaw's measles.

"Measles? Oh, gracious," Mrs. Bauer said. "Never had it. But then, as I've said before, I'm as healthy as an ox."

"I had measles as a toddler," Lila said. "Wonder if I can catch it again?"

"What did Doc say about Lucy?"

"He was going to take her home and check on the family. I'm eager to hear how the rest of the day went for John."

During the afternoon Lila and Mrs. Bauer checked in two land speculators heading west, made up their beds, and baked a walnut cake to serve with the hash and carrots for supper. Since there was ample room at the supper table, Lila and Mrs. Bauer sat with John and the boarders after serving steaming cups of coffee.

Lila wasn't sure she should ask in front of the new boarders, but she wanted to know. "What happened after I left?" she asked, passing the bowl of carrots to John.

"Doc took both Lucy and little Mary home from school even though Mary seemed fine. I stopped by his office on my way here. He said the Shaw's baby has the measles' rash, too. He told Mrs. Shaw the whole family might catch it and to stay home and not send any of the children to school or into town until he says it's all right."

"Poor woman," Mrs. Bauer said. "Two sick children to care for. She doesn't have the rash, too, does she?"

"Doc didn't say so. It's a worry, that's for certain." John stared at his plate of food.

Lila eyed John with concern. "There's not much to be done once you have it, right? I was so little when I had measles, I have no memory."

"Other than trying to keep the fever down, no," John said.

"Excuse me," one of the land speculators spoke. He had the look of a businessman, wearing a good quality vested suit. "What's this about measles?"

"One of our school children has come down with the measles rash," Mrs. Bauer replied. "Just this afternoon." She looked from John to Lila, eager to change the subject. "There's plenty more hash, sir. Help yourself," she said with an encouraging smile.

The man made no reply, but a frown crossed his face. He finished his meal quickly and excused himself without further conversation.

After supper Lila and Mrs. Bauer were putting tinware into kitchen cupboards when they heard Stacy call from the front door. She appeared at the kitchen doorway out of breath, cheeks flushed.

Lila paused her work, staring at her friend. "What's wrong?"

"Ma thinks we might have a problem."

"What do you mean?" Lila asked.

"A mother and father from the campground came to the restaurant asking if there was a doctor in town. Their little boy is sick."

"Did they say what's wrong with him?" Mrs. Bauer asked.

"He has a fever and a rash. Ma told them where Doc Watson's office is, and they flew out of there to find him."

Lila and Mrs. Bauer exchanged a look but didn't say anything.

"After they left," Stacy went on, "Ma said something that really worried me. She said she couldn't be sure, but it sounded like their little boy might have measles."

"Your mother might be right." It was John, standing in the hallway, listening to their conversation. He joined them and told Stacy about the measles case at school earlier that day.

"Then maybe that little boy does have measles." Stacy looked doubly frightened.

"Doc is aware of the situation with the Shaws, but not at the campgrounds . . ." John's voice trailed off, and the friends were forced to consider a new threat. Maybe this wasn't simply a case of one farm family having measles. If the disease was at the campgrounds, this might be something much more serious.

Chapter Thirty-Three

The next morning Lila sensed an undercurrent of tension at the boarding house. John left for school earlier than usual, then the two land speculators abruptly checked out after breakfast, hoping to catch the next stage west. "I thought they were staying two days," Lila said to Mrs. Bauer as they stripped the bed sheets and carried the bundles to the kitchen.

"So did I, but they changed their minds. Couldn't get out of here fast enough."

That gave Lila pause. "Suppose it had anything to do with our talk about measles last night at supper?" she asked.

Mrs. Bauer considered for a moment. "Maybe we shouldn't have said anything, but what's done is done." She eyed the pile of laundry with a sigh. "Let's start the water."

The weather was favorable for drying sheets outside. The kitchen smelled of boiling water and lye soap as they washed in large tubs, then pegged the sheets on lines behind the boarding house. Since they had only themselves to feed, Lila and Mrs. Bauer made quick work of the noon meal and reheated the hash in the frying pan.

"I'd like to go to school and see how John's getting on, if that's all right?" Lila asked.

"Do that and come back with a good report." Mrs. Bauer gave her best effort to smile.

**

To her relief, Lila found all the children in attendance except the Shaw girls. John said everyone seemed in good health and classes had been running smoothly. He did notice Bobby Gardner had a runny nose, but that was often the case with the seven-year-old who cared nothing about cleanliness. The children had a short afternoon recess playing tag and hopscotch and then settled into their handwriting lesson after returning inside.

Lila sat beside the youngest child, Abby, still learning to print her name. The room was quiet. All heads were bent over writing tablets while the children practiced the curls and swoops of the handwriting lesson displayed on the chalk board, all the heads except for one—Bobby Gardner. He was rubbing his forearms between each stroke of his pen. John took notice and went to Bobby's desk.

"What seems to be the matter?" John asked.

"It's my arms. I have an itch." Bobby rubbed his arms to prove his point.

Hearing the word itch drew Lila's attention to Bobby. She rose and moved beside the boy's desk.

"Could I have a look at your arms please?" John asked Bobby.

Bobby rolled up his shirt sleeves and revealed a red rash on both outstretched arms.

Lila's heart sank.

"Could I have a look at your neck, too?" John asked. Bobby's neck was not as red as Lucy's had been, but the rash was there, nevertheless. John felt Bobby's forehead. "How do you feel?"

"Throat hurts some."

John raised his eyes and met Lila's. "Another one?" she asked in a whisper.

John nodded, his face grim.

Since Bobby seemed well enough to walk, John and Lila decided Lila would accompany him to the Gardner's home in town. Mr. Gardner ran a mercantile that catered largely to locals and homesteaders rather than travelers on the Santa Fe Trail. Mrs. Gardner opened the door with two youngsters clinging to her skirts. Her eyebrows arched over wide set brown eyes, and she was surprised to see Bobby. Then alarmed.

"Miss Bonner? Bobby, what are you doing here?" She opened the door wide to let them in and took hold of Bobby. "Are you sick?"

"I got a rash, Mama." Bobby hung his head looking more embarrassed than ill.

"I'm afraid he *is* sick, Mrs. Gardner," Lila replied.

Mrs. Gardner felt Bobby's forehead. "He never complains when he doesn't feel good. He must be feeling real poorly if you brought him home."

"It's not only Bobby that Mr. Reynolds is concerned about, but the other children, too."

"What do you mean?"

"We think Bobby has measles. Doc Watson has warned us it spreads very quickly."

"Measles? Should Doc see him?"

"I can fetch him if you like. Doc said bed rest is important and to keep him home from school."

Mrs. Gardner looked away distressed. "What are the other signs of measles?" She took a breath and returned her gaze to Lila. "What about headache?"

It was then Lila suspected Mrs. Gardner might be experiencing symptoms of the disease herself. "Let me see if Doc is in his office," Lila offered.

"I'd appreciate that very much."

Lila saw Mrs. Shaw's lower lip tremble as she drew Bobby into her arms for a comforting hug.

Lila left and walked with determined strides to Doc's office only to find his shade pulled down on the front door. She exhaled in frustration. There was nothing to do but come by later, but in the meantime, she decided to stop by Hays House and ask Stacy for news about the little boy at the campground. She rounded the corner onto Main Street contemplating her mission when she walked head-on into Doc.

"Lila, where you off to in such a hurry?"

"It's you I want to see," Lila replied. "Have a moment?"

Back in his office Doc filled Lila in on the past twenty-four hours. "Just came back from the campgrounds. A boy came down with measles last night and two more youngsters this morning. I'm afraid it will spread like wildfire out there. Folks are sleeping in tents and wagons without proper bedding." Doc raked his fingers through his hair. "It's hard enough to keep up with the cases in town, never mind the campgrounds. I'm going back to the Shaws this afternoon, and I heard a rumor the Rileys have come down with it, too."

"I've got more bad news," Lila said. "I just came from Gardner's. We think Bobby has measles and when I saw his mother, she may have it, too. She'd like you to pay a visit whenever you can."

Doc shook his head wearily. "I was hoping this wouldn't get out of hand."

"I wish I could help." Lila felt useless as the number of cases mounted. Something had been weighing on her since the day Lucy came down with measles, something she needed an answer to and now was the time to ask. "Doc, can I get measles again if I've already had it?"

"My experience is once you've had measles, you won't catch it again. Why?"

"Well, maybe there's a way I can help. I had measles as a young child. Since there's a good chance I won't catch it again, maybe I could visit some of the sick families, check on them to see how they're doing. That would lessen your load, wouldn't it?"

Doc tilted his head and gave Lila a tired smile. "You'd do that?"

"I would."

"The way the disease is spreading, I may accept your offer."

"Doc, do you think John should close the school until this has passed?"

Doc slowly nodded his head. "That's worth considering."

**

Lila's chance to help Doc came sooner than expected. She had finished bringing in the sheets from the clothesline when Doc sent word asking if Lila could please check on the Shaws that afternoon. He was overwhelmed making house calls.

Lila borrowed the Hays' wagon and sat behind Daisy who clopped down the road to the Shaw's farm. She brought a pan of corn bread and found Mrs. Shaw caring for all five children who were in various stages of measles. She and Mrs. Shaw sat at a round table in the kitchen. The strain was evident in Mrs. Shaw's exhausted face, but she nevertheless rocked the baby in her arms as they visited.

"How are the children?" Lila asked.

Mrs. Shaw looked down at her baby. "It's this one I'm most worried about—little Will. He's burnin' up with fever." Lila heard the fear in her voice. "I've tried everything."

"You've given him a cool bath?"

"Yes. Does no good."

"Is he drinking?"

"Can't keep my milk down."

Lila tried to remember Mama's remedies when she and her brothers were sick "Have you tried weak tea with sugar or honey?"

"No." Her eyes flickered with hope. "Think that would help?"

"Might be worth a try." With Lila's help Mrs. Shaw made a tea concoction and spoon fed the baby. He took a few swallows as Lila held cool compresses to his forehead, and Mrs. Shaw tended to the other children.

Lucy and Mary were in bed with fevers but were no worse than the day before. Mrs. Shaw changed their nightgowns and bedding, then wiped their foreheads with a cool damp cloth. She brought a cup of water to the bedroom for Lucy who seemed to be thirsty all the time. The two toddlers had rashes but otherwise hardly seemed ill as they played with blocks on the kitchen floor.

"It's so kind of you to come by." Mrs. Shaw returned to her chair, took her baby boy from Lila, and cradled him in her arms. He was quiet and barely moved. She stroked his head, brushing his damp locks with her fingers. "You know, the tea has got me to thinking."

"About what?"

"I remember hearing about an Indian cure for fever using some kind of bark. Don't know what kind. You don't happen to know, do you?"

"Sorry, no."

Mrs. Shaw's shoulders slumped. "Maybe Jonah remembers. I'll ask when he comes in for supper."

"I'll tell Doc about the baby's fever." Lila stood. "I should be heading back home and get the wagon back to Mr. Hays. Next time, I'll bring more than cornbread. Maybe help with the laundry, too." She gave Mrs. Shaw a departing smile.

On the way home Lila thought about Mrs. Shaw struggling to care for all her children suffering from measles, especially the baby who was burning up with fever. It brought to mind something Mrs. Bauer once said to her. "Our troubles have meaning beyond our understanding." Mrs. Bauer had certainly experienced crushing losses since settling in America—the deaths of her young daughter, her son, and her husband. Mrs. Shaw was facing her own troubles with all five children sick with measles, one of them gravely so.

Lila thought their troubles having meaning beyond their understanding was an understatement.

Chapter Thirty-Four

Pounding on the front door jolted Lila and Mrs. Bauer early the next morning while they were preparing breakfast.

"What in the world?" Lila hurried to the door and opened it to a distraught Jonah Shaw. "What's wrong?"

"It's our baby. I need help," he pleaded. He began talking so fast Lila told him to slow down and start over. The baby's fever remained high all night. By morning his wife, Catherine, was beside herself with worry and insisted on going to the Kaw Reservation to ask for their cure for fever. She was ready to hitch up the wagon and go by herself if her husband refused to accompany her. To keep her from going he promised to fetch Doc from town.

"Just my luck, Doc's not in the office," he said, "but I remember you came by yesterday. Could you come with me and calm her? Please?"

Lila's mind spun. Doc was gone for any number or reasons—taking care of someone with measles or delivering a baby but gone all the same. Mrs. Shaw was surely at the end of her rope if she was considering going to the reservation by herself. Lila knew Indians used plants as natural cures for illnesses but knew nothing about which plants cured which ailments. Then she thought of someone who might have some answers.

"Mr. Shaw, I'll come with you, but first let's stop by Louis Bellmard's cabin. He's a friend. He might be able to help."

The sun poked through the early morning clouds as Lila and Mr. Shaw arrived at Bellmard's cabin. "I don't know how I can help." Louis was apologetic. "My wife used to make tonics from different plants, but it's been so many years, I don't remember what she used."

"I wonder," Lila said, "if the Kaw would be more willing to share their cure for fever if Mrs. Shaw came to the reservation herself with the request?"

"I'll not have Catherine go," Mr. Shaw interrupted. "It's not safe."

Louis didn't hesitate. "She'd be safe if I went with her. I've traded furs with the Kaw for years—they know me."

Mr. Shaw protested. "We had trouble with the Indians last summer."

"But no harm came to any of the settlers," Lila reminded him. "What if I went too, as moral support for your wife?" Lila could see the doubt in Mr. Shaw's eyes. "Mr. Bellmard would be our interpreter, and the Kaw would see me and your wife as women seeking a cure for a sick baby. Surely that might tip the balance in our favor."

**

Louis Bellmard drove the wagon and shared the seat with Lila and Mrs. Shaw. Lila had never been to a reservation before, and her stomach tightened with apprehension about how the request would be received. Mrs. Shaw kept her eyes straight ahead, her hands clasped firmly in her lap. The three of them spoke little.

The sun rode high in the midday sky, and Lila was glad for the shade from her bonnet. They passed cultivated fields owned by farmers on the outskirts of Council Grove which gave way to open prairie and barren hills with scattered trees. The wagon creaked over the bumpy terrain. When they glimpsed the Kaw teepees with smoke hovering above them from the noon cooking, Lila inhaled slowly to steady her nerves. She told herself this was the right thing to do, that this was a chance to help baby Will.

They approached the outer circle of teepees and were met by two Indians on foot who stopped their progress and grabbed the halter of their horse. They were bare chested and wore deerskin breeches and moccasins. Their dark, narrow eyes bore no welcome. Lila gulped involuntarily even though her throat was dry as dust.

Louis raised his hand in greeting and spoke first. One of the Indians gave a two-syllable reply. Self-assured and relaxed, Louis climbed down from the wagon and retrieved a gunny sack of corn from the wagon bed. It had been his idea to bring something to trade in a show of good faith and to encourage a cordial exchange of goods. As he walked over to the Indians, Lila held her breath and laid her hand on Mrs. Shaw's clutched fingers.

Louis spoke briefly, and one of the Indians left. He returned a few moments later with a third Indian who recognized Louis. They exchanged greetings and spoke at length.

"I think they know each other," Lila whispered to Mrs. Shaw.

"I hope that helps," she replied.

They watched Louis, and at one point he gestured toward Mrs. Shaw, causing all three Indians to stare at her, then return to their conversation, seeming to grasp the situation. Lila couldn't gage the Indian's reaction to the trade for their faces showed no emotion.

The Indian who knew Louis left with the sack of corn, and the other two remained holding their horse. Louis walked back to the wagon, and Lila leaned down from her seat and whispered, "What's happening?"

"He's going to get one of their women."

"That's good then?" Mrs. Shaw asked, holding her emotions in check.

"We'll see what happens next," said Louis, "but I think that's a good sign."

Lila noticed a handful of children edging towards them, curious. They stopped and stared from a distance. A dog trotted around their wagon, sniffed the wheels and then left.

The day was not hot, but the sun's heat intensified as they sat and waited.

"What's taking so long?" Mrs. Shaw asked.

"I don't know," Louis answered.

"They won't leave us sitting here, will they?" Lila asked.

"No. We'll hear from them."

Wishing the trade would reach a conclusion, Lila and her friends felt themselves a spectacle and grew uneasy, as several adults joined the growing crowd of curious children.

The Indian whom Louis had spoken to returned with a woman wearing a buckskin dress fringed at the bottom and led her to the wagon. When she came close, Lila saw strands of gray in her black hair and lines etched on her weathered face. She carried a small leather pouch and handed it to Louis as she spoke to him. He listened carefully and nodded, then reached up and handed the pouch to Mrs. Shaw.

"It's sassafras root bark."

The Indian woman turned to go. "Wait, please." Mrs. Shaw climbed down from the wagon and reached toward the woman. "I know you can't understand me, but I must thank you. It's for my baby boy. He's very sick." Tears glistened in her eyes. She extended her hand. "Thank you."

The Indian woman did not shake her hand, she did not need to. The trade had been completed and both parties were satisfied. The Indian woman did, however, give a perceptible nod of her head, and when Lila searched her face, the woman's dark eyes showed a glimmer of understanding. Was this exchange more than from one person to another? Was it from one mother to another? Lila had no way of knowing, but she wanted to believe that was what she saw.

Louis Bellmard had barely turned the wagon around when Mrs. Shaw eagerly opened the pouch with Lila looking over her shoulder. The contents looked like shredded bark and was cinnamon brown in color.

"Root bark from the sassafras tree? How do I use it?"

"Boil some water and let the roots steep until it's the color of tea," Louis answered. "Add a few drops of honey and feed it to the baby or anyone else with a fever."

Mrs. Shaw turned toward him. "I can't thank you enough for taking us to the reservation, Mr. Bellmard. I have been at my wits end. I'll never forget your kindness." She looked at the pouch in her lap with reverence. "Now that we've gone to such lengths to get this, there's only one thing left to do."

"What's that?" Lila asked.

"Pray it works."

She held the pouch as though life itself depended on it, all the way back to the farm.

Chapter Thirty-Five

It was the fourth day since Lucy Shaw had come down with measles. When John took attendance at school that Thursday morning, four students sat before him. Eleven were absent. John asked each student if anyone in their families was sick with measles and two said yes.

During the morning, he gave it some thought and by afternoon had come up with a plan. He wrote a brief letter for each student to take home stating there would be no school tomorrow, and he would get word to them when classes resumed. He prepared extra lessons for each child to take home for study.

"I imagined coming to school tomorrow and having no students," John told Lila after supper that night. "It seemed the right thing to do."

Lila nodded. "More than half your students are sick."

"Grownups are sick, too," Mrs. Bauer said. "Measles is all anyone can talk about. I was at Last Chance this morning and heard about folks at the campground havin' the measles. Terrible to be on the trail and come down with that."

The three friends sat in the boarding house parlor finishing their coffee. It was strangely quiet as they hadn't had any boarders since the land developers left on Monday.

"Are people avoiding us?" Lila asked.

Mrs. Bauer leaned forward in her chair. "Feels to me like someone's hung out a big sign somewhere that says, 'Stay away from Council Grove, they have the measles.'"

"Word gets around," John said. He set his mug on the side table. "There's no school tomorrow. What can I do to help?"

"I'm going to the Shaws and then the Gardners if there's time. Come with me," Lila said. "I'm anxious to see how baby Will is getting on."

**

Lila and Mrs. Bauer put together a large basket of food for the Shaw family—a kettle of ham and bean soup with biscuits, jars of chicken broth for the children, a loaf of rye bread, and a blackberry cobbler. John set it in the back of the Hays' wagon before he and Lila set off for the farm early the next morning.

Words spilled out of Lila's mouth the minute she came through the doorway. "How's the baby?"

Catherine Shaw was sitting in the rocking chair beside the stove, holding Will against her shoulder, stoking his back. "About the same. I was hoping the fever would have broke by now." She rose with a weary sigh and began to pace the kitchen.

Lila was at her side and felt the baby's forehead. "Not as hot as the other day, don't you think?"

Catherine blinked away tears. "I'm not sure anymore . . . it's all a muddle. I was up and down all night."

"Let me hold that sweet baby," Lila said. "I'll take care of him while you sit in the rocker and rest."

Catherine sank into the chair, closing her eyes immediately. "I'll rest for a minute," she murmured. "Thank you."

Lila watched as John headed to the field wearing work clothes and a wide brimmed hat to help Jonah harvest the wheat. Bouncing Will in one arm, she waited for the kettle to boil, then dropped in sassafras root to steep. A spicy-sweet aroma filled the kitchen. The girls appeared to be recovering and were content to rest in their beds or amuse themselves with their rag dolls. Lila spoon fed the tea to the baby, as much as he could tolerate, followed by a bath in cool water in a kitchen tub.

When he was changed into a clean gown, she fed him warm chicken broth and walked about the house with him in her arms from room to room, cooing, humming, and bouncing him until every muscle in her arms and shoulders ached. When his eyelids finally closed, and he grew heavy with sleep, she laid him in his crib beside his parents' bed. Catherine hadn't woken from her nap, even when the youngest toddler, Emily, had crawled onto her lap and fallen asleep.

At noon, Lila heated the soup, set out pitchers of milk and water and a dish of butter for the biscuits. John and Jonah washed up outside at the pump and brushed off the dust and chaff from their clothes. Catherine woke up as they entered the kitchen.

"How's the baby?" Jonah asked the minute he came inside.

"Still sleeping," Lila answered. "He's having a good nap."

"I had a bit of rest, too." Catherine gave her husband an encouraging smile. The girls joined the grownups, and everyone sat to eat.

John and Jonah discussed the wheat harvest while Lila and Catherine took turns feeding the youngest girls.

When the cobbler was served, Catherine rose. "I'm going to check on Will. I'll only be a minute." She was gone a few minutes before they heard her call out from the bedroom. "Jonah, come!"

Jonah's fork clattered to the floor, and he rushed to the bedroom. Lila and John looked at each other fearing something dreadful had happened and followed him.

Catherine was holding the baby nestled onto her shoulder. Tears streamed down her face. "The fever," she began, "the fever broke. Come feel him." She reached out to her husband.

Jonah was at her side and laid his palm on the baby's head. He wrapped them both in his arms and his shoulders shook as he shed tears.

**

They rode for a long while on the way home without speaking. Lila was turning the day's events over in her mind, and she assumed John was doing the same. The sun was lowering in the western sky wrapped in shades of red and gold. There was not a whisper of wind which made for a peaceful ride. It was as though Mother Nature was putting her approval on the events of the day saying, "Well done."

Finally, Lila spoke. "We had quite a day, didn't we?"

John nodded. "I'm so glad we were able to help Jonah and Catherine," then added, "and do it together." He gave her a sideways smile, serious and sweet at the same time.

Lila gave John a smile in return. She studied him for a moment and saw someone so unlike the teacher she had always known. Dust covered every inch of his body and clothing. His shirt was soaked through with perspiration. He smelled of sweat and hay. Chaff clung to his dark wet hair which was plastered against his head. At one point in the afternoon, Lila had caught herself watching the men work. John's sleeves were rolled up, and Lila realized John had arms that were muscular and strong. He had broad shoulders. This was a John Reynolds she had never seen before, one of strength and grit, sweat and dirt, and she found these new discoveries about him oddly and utterly captivating.

They arrived home tired after the long day but felt certain all the Shaw children were recovering from measles and confident Jonah had the wheat harvest well in hand.

"That reminds me," Mrs. Bauer said, "Doc stopped by while you were gone. Said he'd have time to visit the Gardners today."

Lila heaved a grateful sigh. "Glad for that. I'm exhausted."

They'd no sooner collapsed into chairs when Doc leaned through the front doorway.

"Doc, come and have a sit down with us," Mrs. Bauer said.

He remained where he was. "Would love to but don't have time. Wanted to let you know—" He stopped speaking, and a pained expression crossed his face.

John got to his feet, frowning. "What's wrong?"

"A baby at the campgrounds died this morning. Was five months old. Had measles."

"Dear Lord, no." Mrs. Bauer clamped her hand to her chest."

"Five months—that's the same age as baby Will," Lila said. "If the Shaws hadn't gotten that sassafras root . . ." She left the sentence unfinished as the horrifying thought took hold.

"I'm afraid that's not the only bad news," Doc continued. "Stopped by Gardners. Billy's had a high fever for a several days. His mother thinks measles is affecting his hearing. She told me when she asked Bobby a simple question while her back was turned to him, he didn't answer. I can't be sure yet, but Bobby might have lost his hearing."

Chapter Thirty-Six

From the back steps of the boarding house Lila had a clear view of the cemetery at the end of the street. A white picket fence surrounded the orderly rows of graves identified by wooden planks or limestone markers. Pastor Higgins officiated at the graveside service for the infant from the campground. Lila thought it sad no one else attended, but folks were either ill or keeping to themselves. Or afraid. He stood with the parents beside the tiny pine coffin that held their precious baby, waiting to be lowered into the earth. The father had a supportive arm around his wife who leaned heavily against him.

Pastor Higgins read from the Bible, then they bowed their heads in prayer. He spoke to the parents, their faces masked in pain, and left them to grieve in private. The father and mother stood with heads bent and shoulders slumped, unable to walk away. Even from a distance the sorrow washed over Lila. She thought there must be nothing worse than burying your child unless you were burying your child in a far-away place where you'd never return. At least this baby would rest beneath a marker in a place with a name and not become lost in a nameless grave somewhere along the Santa Fe Trail. This was the first funeral since measles had stricken the town. Lila wondered, would there be more?

Most everyone in Council Grove understood the seriousness of what was happening. If you hadn't had measles and encountered someone who did, you could get the disease. Still there were skeptics. Mr. Chapman, who ran the blacksmith and harness shop, saw no need for Mr. Reynolds to cancel lessons.

"We pay you a good salary, Mr. Reynolds, and school should be open." He spoke at the boarding house door, the irritation rising in his voice. "My young 'uns ain't sick, and I'm sending 'em to school tomorrow." He turned on his heel and stormed away, leaving John with his mouth hanging open.

The next morning John had no choice but to meet the Chapman children at school. When they didn't arrive after an hour, he walked down the hill to Chapman's shop on Main Street.

"Your children didn't come to school, Mr. Chapman. Why?" John asked.

Mr. Chapman kept his eyes on a harness he was repairing and spoke in a barely audible voice. "Woke up with the rash."

"I beg your pardon," John said. "Did you say they woke with a rash?"

"They did." Chapman spit out the words. "Wife said they should stay home."

"Your wife is right. Doc says the sick should stay home until the rash and fever are gone. Understood?"

Mr. Chapman grunted.

"Mr. Chapman, did you know a baby at the campgrounds died yesterday from measles?"

Mr. Chapman stiffened but kept his eyes down.

"That's right, the child died." John paused to let this news make an impression. "I hope your children recover with no problems. Good day to you, sir." He turned and left.

**

Doc was worried about all his patients, but especially Bobby Gardner.

When Bobby's temperature returned to normal, Doc gave him a simple hearing test and determined he had hearing loss but was hopeful one ear was somewhat functional.

"I'll write to an expert I've read about in St. Louis for more information," he told Mrs. Gardner. Quietly, Doc was baffled. It was the first time he'd encountered a patient suffering hearing loss after having measles, and he needed the wisdom of doctors more experienced with the disease than he was.

"Bobby's not going to be deaf, is he?" Mrs. Gardner asked, terrified of the answer.

"I can't be certain, but I'll do everything I can to help your son," Doc promised.

John promised to help Bobby, too, but he wasn't sure how to do that. At the end of the second week, new cases of measles in town had all but stopped. Everyone was hopeful the worst was behind them, and John decided classes would resume the following Monday.

"Things are returning to normal," John told Lila after his first day back. "I checked each student as they arrived to be sure they were healthy. No traces of rash, no runny noses, no fevers. I was actually glad to see the glint in Billy Riley's eyes if you can believe that." He chuckled, then turned serious. "I don't know what I'm going to do when Bobby returns. His mother sent me a note saying he wasn't ready to come to school yet. I may have to write out all his lessons from now on."

"Maybe I could help out," Lila said. "Work with him one on one till you figure out what he needs."

"I've never taught a student with hearing loss before," John said. "I'm not sure what to do."

"We're all uncertain—Doc, his parents, you." Lila gave John a reassuring look and reached for his hand. Her gesture was very bold, but she didn't care. She couldn't ignore the distressed look on his face. "I have faith you'll figure out what Bobby needs."

While the situation in town improved, measles continued to spread on the campgrounds. Doc went every day without fail and brought sassafras root with him hoping it would help control the fever. "The ones hardest hit are children under the age of two," he reported. "The good news is the campgrounds will clear out for the winter soon. There're fewer travelers each day."

By the middle of October, just like the rashes that faded from the arms and necks of its victims, measles crept away from Council Grove. Mothers turned from nursing sick children to harvesting gardens and preserving fruits and vegetables for winter. Lila and Mrs. Bauer picked wild choke cherries for jelly and shredded cabbage to preserve as sauerkraut. The corn and wheat harvest in nearby farms concluded with storage bins bulging, and Mrs. Bauer declared order fully restored when travelers checked into the boarding house once again.

Chapter Thirty-Seven

Lila planned on making two visits this morning—one to Hays House and the other to Bellmards. Charley had missed two days of school, and while she suspected he was hunting with his pa, she wanted to check on him. She hadn't been to their cabin for weeks, and decided it was high time to pay the Bellmards a visit.

Lila wrapped herself in her wool cloak. Her mother had sewn a pocket inside the lining for gloves, and that's where she slipped a copy of McGuffey's Reader for Charley. She dashed across the street to Hays House where a handful of customers were eating breakfast and quickly caught Stacy's eye.

"How can I help you, ma'am," Stacy teased with coffee pot in hand.

"I'm headin' to the Bellmards and don't want to go empty handed," Lila said. "Boarders ate everything in sight this morning. Could I have two buttermilk biscuits?"

"Sure thing." She grabbed two biscuits from a basket and brought them to the counter. She cocked her head to one side. "Anything else on your mind?"

"No time for gossip now. I want to get to Bellmards and back before lunch." Lila gave Stacy a parting wave. "We'll have time to talk later." She placed coins on the counter before putting the biscuits in her basket and walked out the door.

Lila followed the boardwalk down Main Street until it ended, then took the path to the north that led to the woods. The morning was frosty, and Lila pulled the hood up on her cloak, glad for its warmth and glad for the wool skirt she had chosen to wear.

She kept up a brisk pace through the wooded path as the sun peaked in and out of the clouds, shifting the shadows of the trees. Some of the trees had shed their leaves, but the mighty oaks still clung to theirs, and they rattled in the breeze. She kept her arms under her cloak for warmth but slowed momentarily when the sound of the rattling changed.

She did a quick turnaround but saw nothing. "Must have been some critter scampering about," she said, and picked up her pace again. She couldn't help but remember the day last summer when she'd been frightened walking home from Bellmards. It turned out to be nothing so why should it be any different now? She pushed worrisome thoughts from her mind.

It happened so fast it scarcely registered.

Large hands overpowered her and grabbed her from behind, one covered her mouth, the other circled her waist. A surge of adrenaline triggered a painful heartbeat in her chest. She screamed through the clamped hand, but the sound was choked off. Lila struggled to free her arms from inside her cloak while she wildly kicked backwards. The harder she fought, the fiercer the grip. Lila raised her leg and shot it backwards again, this time hitting a shin. A rough voice cursed in her ear.

She was lifted off her feet and shoved against a tree, snapping the side of her head against the trunk. Pain shot through her head. Dazed, she made a feeble attempt to grab the arms. A hand slapped hard against her face. Spots danced before her eyes with the disappearing daylight, then nothing.

**

When Lila came out of the fog of unconsciousness, she found herself in darkness. She was blindfolded. She was on a horse with someone sitting behind her, someone with unspeakable body odor whose breath reeked of whiskey. *What was happening? Who has done this?* She had a throbbing headache, made worse with each step of the horse over the uneven ground.

Reaching for her head, she realized her hands were bound together. *Why am I tied up? This makes no sense.* She was a captive and there was nothing she could do to give herself any advantage. The realization sent her into a frenzy of fear, and tears swelled under her blindfold. *Dear God, what am I to do?*

Now fully awake, her heart pounded as she tried to clear her head. She had no idea how long she'd been unconscious, no idea where she was, no idea who sat behind her in the saddle. She shuddered to think who her captor was and what he had in mind.

Lila had heard the stories—everyone had—about white children kidnapped by Indians who never returned to their families. Or if they had returned, their experience had altered them so much that reclaiming their former life was never fully achieved. Kidnapping hadn't happened as often in Missouri and Kansas as it had during the Sioux Uprising in Minnesota a few years back. Putting together what she knew, Lila didn't think an Indian sat behind her. Indians didn't use saddles and this person's lack of horsemanship told her he was a white man, and a foul smelling one at that.

I have no money, no family. Why would I be taken? Lila began to think she had been mistaken for someone else, and her abduction was a monstrous error. How else to explain this? But she thought deeper and knew women and children were kidnapped for other reasons. For sale, for profit, and for inhumane reasons that sickened her. Ignoring the intermittent dizziness from the blow to her head, Lila focused on who may have wanted to abduct her. She could think of no one. Then suddenly—

"No! It can't be," she said aloud. There *was* one person who would want to kidnap her.

"Awake, are 'ya?" Before she knew it, the man reached around and stuffed a gag in her mouth. "That oughta take care of hollerin' for help," he grunted.

Her supply of air seemed cut in half with the rag in her mouth, and her pulse raced as she struggled to breathe. This wicked person preying on her, whoever he was, was playing for keeps. No time for tears, no time for half measures. If she wanted to come out of this alive, she'd have to start thinking like a survivor and outwit her captor any way she could.

Lila felt the warmth of the sun come and go and sensed they were traveling on a path surrounded by trees. There were no specific smells to give her clues as to where they might be other than the woods—no whiff of the river, no breeze from the open spaces of the prairie. She hoped for some scent to stir a memory of place.

Lila recounted the timeline as best as she could remember. She had left for Bellmards around nine o'clock and been taken shortly after that. She'd carried a basket and only now realized it was missing. No doubt it had been knocked about during the abduction, but more importantly, where was it now? Had this evil man hidden it in the underbrush before taking her off on horseback? She hoped against hope he had been careless enough to leave it exposed as a clue to the place of the abduction.

The rope securing her hands bit into her wrists, but she maneuvered her hands and felt the primer still safe in her cloak pocket. A grim irony, Lila thought, that something she cherished so much could be totally useless now given the circumstances facing her.

Surely Mrs. Bauer would be concerned about her by now. Was school out for the day? Was John back at the boarding house? She had lost all sense of time. *Mrs. Bauer, I need John. Send him to find me. Do it now!*

Chapter Thirty-Eight

Mrs. Bauer waited for John at the front door of the boarding house when he came home from school that afternoon. Her words tumbled out. "Somethin's wrong, John. I just know it." Her face was flushed, and her tone was desperate.

He frowned as he took off his jacket. "What's wrong?"

"It's Lila. She was supposed to be here to help with the noon meal, promised to be back from Bellmards in plenty of time." Mrs. Bauer all but wrung her hands. "She hasn't come back. I haven't seen her since morning. This isn't like her."

John glanced at his pocket watch. It was four o'clock. "Maybe Charley's sick, and she's helping out. She's done that before."

Mrs. Bauer was unconvinced. "I know, but somethin' doesn't feel right. I'm worried." She paused. "You don't suppose . . ." She gave a pleading look.

"I'll go to Bellmards and check on them. I'm sure there's nothing to be worried about," John reassured her.

Mrs. Bauer gave a relieved sigh. "Thank you, John. I'll feel so much better if you go. Oh, and stop by Hays House on your way. Lila was going to see Stacy before she left for Bellmards. Maybe Lila said something to her."

When John talked with the Hays family, he didn't learn much from Stacy other than Lila had bought a couple of biscuits before she left for Bellmards, and the two of them planned to see each other later in the day. When Mr. Hays learned John was walking to Bellmards cabin, he told him to take Daisy. "You'll get there and back with daylight to spare."

Late afternoon sun slanted through the tree branches as Daisy trotted down the path strewn with fallen leaves. John smelled wood smoke from the cabin's chimney when he reached the clearing, dismounted, and tied Daisy to a post near the front step. Before he could knock, Charley was at the door with a wide grin.

"Hello, Charley. May I come in?"

"Mr. Reynolds." Mr. Bellmard joined his son at the door and extended his hand in greeting. "Come in. What brings you out this way?"

John cast a puzzled look around the room. "I came to check on you and Miss Bonner. Has she left?"

Mr. Bellmard returned an equally puzzled look. "Has she left? She hasn't been here."

It took a moment for Mr. Bellmard's words to register. "You mean, Miss Bonner hasn't been here at all?"

"No. Charley saw her at school last week, of course. Why did you think she'd be here?"

"Because she left the boarding house this morning on her way to visit you." John felt a chill of fear move down his spine. "If she didn't come here, then where . . . " He left the thought unfinished and ran his fingers through his hair. "This doesn't make sense." He spoke to himself as much as to Mr. Bellmard.

"Well now," Mr. Bellmard said, "seems to me we should try and retrace her steps from this morning. She'd come down the path from town like she always did, right?"

"Yes," John nodded.

"Let's you and me ride down the path and see what we find." He turned to Charley. "You stay here, son. I won't be gone long."

The two men mounted their horses and slow walked the path through the woods. They kept their eyes fixed to the ground, sweeping across the trail and along both sides, looking for anything that might shed light on where Lila had been earlier in the day. Nothing was out of the ordinary—the woods were quiet, there were no signs of a disturbance anywhere. They reached the end of the path where the woods parted, and Main Street was visible in the distance.

"Nothing," John said, his voice heavy with disappointment.

"Let's turn around and work our way back to the cabin," Mr. Bellmard said. "Things can look different from the opposite direction."

They turned their horses around and resumed their careful search. They rode in silence for a time. "I can't thank you enough, Mr. Bellmard," John said.

"Call me Louis," he said. "I'm glad to help out any way I can."

John could tell by the sun's shadows they had about an hour before the sun would set. He pushed away unwanted thoughts of night approaching and Lila unaccounted for. They passed a thicket of cedars when Louis pulled up his horse. "I think I see something." He dismounted and made his way through the brush to the trees.

John quickly dismounted and followed. "I don't see anything."

Louis pulled something from the underbrush and held it up. "Recognize this?"

John's blood ran cold. It was Lila's basket.

There was no mistaking it belonged to Lila. John retrieved it from Louis and stood immobile, staring at it. Louis was taking stock of where he found the basket and began a deliberate search of the underbrush which yielded nothing. He circled back to the path and knelt down for a closer look.

"Over here," he called to John.

When John joined him, Louis pointed out boot prints in the dirt. They were a confusing cluster of partial prints and left no trail. "Looks like a scuffle happened right here." He moved along the path's edge and found clearer prints made from deeper impressions. "Somebody was carrying something heavy to leave an imprint like this." He found hoof prints nearby that disappeared under fallen leaves.

John watched while Louis's keen eye made observations he had missed. The natural world was where Louis Bellmard lived, and John had renewed appreciation for that. If he had any hope of tracking down Lila, he would need Louis to help him. John bent over to study the boot prints and said, "Was somebody carrying . . ." He didn't want to say it out loud.

"Miss Bonner? Maybe, probably. We don't know. But it looks like she might have been taken and near as I can tell there's a horse to follow." He stared evenly at John. "I know this is hard to hear, but we need to get together a search party. I think Miss Bonner's been kidnapped."

**

John rode back to town and returned with Sheriff Jenkins. Daylight was fading quickly, but Louis thought they could follow the path beyond his cabin for another hour before night fell. John could tell by the looks on their faces they didn't hold much hope of finding a good trail to follow tonight. They rode in silence, scouring the ground and surrounding brush along the path.

"There's no other way through the woods?" John asked.

"No," Louis answered. "Too dense to ride through. A horse would have to follow this path."

When the woods became too dark to yield any more clues, the sheriff said, "I think we'd best halt for the night and start again at daybreak."

"What about using lanterns?" John insisted.

"Shadows play tricks on you. Won't really help us, Mr. Reynolds," Louis said. "Sheriff's right. We'll start again first thing in the morning."

Sheriff Jenkins had come to Council Grove three years ago but had been a lawman for twenty years and had a comfortable way with town folk. His dark hair was streaked with silver, but his lanky frame was strong and muscular. "Mr. Reynolds—"

"Please, no need to be formal. Not now. Both of you, call me John."

"All right, John. I understand you're right worried about Miss Bonner. With good reason. We can do our best for her starting early in the morning. Whoever has her will most likely have to stop and rest tonight, so he won't be getting that far ahead of us. Let's call it a night."

John knew they were right, but everything in him wanted to press on, to keep looking for Lila until they found her. They turned their horses around and headed back to what John knew would be a worrisome night where he doubted he would sleep a wink. It was more than he could bear to think Lila was out there unprotected, alone, and afraid with the scum who had taken her. Lord help that miscreant if he ever got his hands on him. At that moment John thought, if given the chance, he would kill him with his bare hands.

Chapter Thirty-Nine

Lila needed to relieve herself so badly she thought her bladder would burst. If they didn't stop soon, the next time the horse stepped in a hole, she'd wet everything.

"Looks like as good a place as any," the voice said and reined in the horse. He dismounted and grabbed Lila from the horse. The gag was pulled from her mouth and her blindfold removed. She blinked at the sudden light, disoriented, and looked about. They were beside a stand of trees in a countryside of sloping hills and scattered rocks. She guessed from the sun it was late afternoon.

"Guess you'll be needing to do your privacies."

Lila held out her bound hands, and to her surprise he untied the rope. "Don't be thinkin' about runnin' cuz there's nowhere to go. You'll not git far."

It was her first look at her captor. His weathered face made him appear old. The brown hair sticking from under his hat was stringy, his beard dirty and matted. The buckskin shirt revealed a slight paunch that hung over his belt buckle, but it was his eyes that were most frightening. She'd never seen such empty, lifeless eyes. Then she looked at his shirt again, and it brought something to mind.

Lila squinted at the man. "Do I know you?"

"Not likely."

"I've seen you before. Somewhere." Lila forgot her need to relieve herself as her thought gained momentum. "At the Hays House in town. I saw you there once. I know it."

"Well, now ain't you the smart one."

"You were there with another man. You had a funny sounding name—Crags?"

"*Skaggs*," he corrected.

She took a tentative step toward him. "What do you want with me?" Her voice rose. "Why have you done this?"

"Let's just say I have a business agreement."

"What are you talking about? I don't have any money."

"No, but somebody's willing to pay for ya, and I'm the lucky one who's gonna score," the man scoffed.

Lila shuddered and stepped back. She knew who would pay for her. She thought she'd out-run him, that she'd left him behind for good. She knew it was Pa.

The man watched her reaction. "That's right. It's your own Pa wantin' you brought back. Says you're his property." He snorted with satisfaction. "Want to know what yer worth?"

Lila felt the sting of furious tears threatening. "Whatever he's agreed to, Pa's got no money."

"Well, now, I happen to know different," Skaggs said. "I play poker with yer pa. He won the table awhile back. That's how our business deal come about."

Lila was speechless. She turned and strode into the nearby brush before he could see her eyes filling.

"Fifty dollars," he hollered as she walked away. "Twenty-five up front and twenty-five when I deliver you."

Lila didn't' answer. She knew if she spoke, she'd start sobbing. Lila made sure she was out of the man's line of sight before squatting in the bushes. Swiping away angry tears, she sized up the situation the best she could. This scoundrel appeared motivated to keep his end of the deal and take her back to Pa for the rest of his money. So far, he'd made no advances toward her, but she feared that could change on a whim. As she stood and straightened her clothing, her hand ran over the primer still secure in her cloak pocket.

If only there was a way to use this to my advantage. I certainly can't whack him over the head with it.

And then for some odd reason a fairy tale from childhood came to mind about two lost children. Hansel and Gretel, wasn't it? And a trail of breadcrumbs that were to guide them out of the forest to find their way home. Lila didn't have any breadcrumbs, but she did have a book. Suddenly she dropped to her knees, pulled the primer out and ripped pages from the book. She tore each of those pages in half and returned the pieces along with the book safely to her pocket, then stood and walked back where the man waited.

"We'll camp here tonight and start early in the morning. No fire. It attracts attention." He took the saddle blanket from the horse and tossed it to the ground in front of her. "Got hard tack and jerky." The man handed Lila food and held out his canteen which she greedily accepted. Her tongue was dry and thick, and she would have gladly downed the entire contents if he hadn't grabbed it from her. She watched him stretch out on the ground not three feet from where she stood, his head pillowed by his saddle, his gun at his side, his hat pulled down over his eyes.

She knew he wasn't going to sleep—at least not until she fell asleep. Lila wrapped the coarse blanket around her shoulders, knowing it would be a very cold night with no fire. She sat and looked up into the darkening sky as she chewed the jerky. The stars were barely visible, and she tried mightily to find the Big Dipper but couldn't.

If he was taking her back to Pa, they would have traveled east unless he was taking a circuitous route to confuse anyone trying to follow them. What had John called the Big Dipper? The Great Bear. If only she could see it now, at least that would be some reassurance that the entire universe hadn't gone mad, that God's heavens were still as they should be, even if she was caught up in an evil scheme between people acting on the worst of human impulses.

Lila curled up, pulling the blanket tight with the hood of her cloak over her ears. She was exhausted yet unable to calm her nerves and jumped at every whistle of the wind or creak of a tree branch. She thought of the pieces of paper in her pocket and where to leave them so they wouldn't blow away, yet still be found when John came looking for her.

I know you're coming, John. I know it.

**

John had no time to spare.

He stopped first at Hays House to return Daisy. She was a good old girl in her heyday, but John needed a strong horse for what lay ahead. He told Herbert and Edna to tell Mrs. Bauer what had happened to Lila and that he'd return to the boarding house in about an hour. It was late but the livery was still open. Clive Jenson, in an uncommonly gracious gesture, told John to borrow one of his horses and they'd work out the details later.

"Can't imagine someone going after that slip of a girl. Taint right a 'tall."

The second stop was to see Matteo. He took a lantern from Clive and rode into the hills to Matteo's cave.

"It's about Lila," John explained hurriedly.

"My friend, you are agitated." Matteo's brow creased in concern.

"Lila's been taken, kidnapped we think, this morning. You know the hills and caves around here better than anyone. Keep an eye out. If there's any chance whoever took her comes back to hide out around here, let Thomas Hill at the mercantile know. He'll be in charge while the sheriff is gone."

A look of horror spread over Matteo's face. "Not our *Lila curiosa*. You must find her, my friend." He grabbed John's hand. "We will say a prayer for her, just as she asked for a special blessing for you when your job was threatened."

It took a moment for John to fully grasp Matteo's words. "She did that? For me?"

"In the very place we're standing now."

Matteo's blessing for Lila gave John much needed reassurance as he returned to town. That hopefulness would bolster him when he reached the boarding house to face Mrs. Bauer. She would be devastated, but he had one more stop to make before he saw her — the school superintendent, Mr. Piper.

"John, this is horrible. I scarcely can believe something like this is happening here. Do whatever you must to find Miss Bonner."

"I don't know how long it will take," John said.

"I'll see to the children's lessons. Don't worry about that." Mr. Piper warmly grasped John's hand. "Godspeed, John."

John returned to the boarding house and found Mrs. Bauer in the parlor waiting quietly on the davenport, her hands folded in her lap. "Edna came over and told me." She looked up at him with such sadness in her eyes it nearly broke his heart. "I don't know what I'll do if . . ." She didn't finish. She didn't need to.

Forgetting his own fear and apprehension, he went to her side. "Sheriff Jenkins is riding with me, so is Louis Bellmard, one of the best hunters around here. He can track a horse through brush better than anybody I know." He laid his hand on hers. "We'll find her, Mrs. Bauer. We'll bring her back safely."

She held tight and nodded.

Before John returned to the cabin, Mrs. Bauer supplied him with as much food as he could stuff into his knapsack—bacon, jerky, beans, and dried fruit. Providing him with sustenance gave her purpose. "You'll need your energy," she declared, gathering items from the pantry. Then she gave him a warm hug before he rode off into the night.

At Bellmard's cabin the next morning, John woke before dawn to an argument between Louis and the sheriff. Both men stood before the fireplace with coffee cups in hand as a small fire warmed the room. "We can't take the boy with us," the sheriff said, a resolute look on his face. "Hunting down someone who's been kidnapped is serious business and no place for a child."

Charley stood at his father's side, waiting for him to respond. "Hear me out," Louis said. "I understand hunting down bad people. I've done it before. Charley won't be any trouble—he'll do exactly as he's told."

The sheriff persisted. "This could take days. Is the boy up to that? Will two riders slow your horse?"

"Charley won't burden my horse," Louis insisted. "And I've taken my son out trapping for a lot longer than a few days."

The sheriff turned to John. "I'm not convinced. Are you?"

John needed the experience both men possessed if he had any hope of finding Lila, and he couldn't afford a fracture in their search party. Before he could respond, Charley spoke.

"I can help you find Miss Teacher. Four is better than three." He looked hopefully into each of their faces.

The sheriff softened at Charley's words. "I understand you want to help, son, but it's just not practical."

Louis spoke again. "If I don't take him with us, he'll pack his own bag and follow us on foot, alone. Miss Teacher, as he likes to call Miss Bonner, is the closest thing he's had to a *maman* since his own died when he was a baby. There's nothing I can say that will keep him from lookin' for her."

The three men were silent and looked from one to another while Louis' words weighed on each of them. Presently John said, "It's decided then. Charley goes with us."

Chapter Forty

Exhaustion prevailed over fear. Lila slept on the cold, hard ground until the sharp nudge of a boot in her back woke her as the sky brightened the next morning. "Get up. Need to find water for the horse."

Chilled to the bone, Lila squatted in the brush not far from where they camped and used the opportunity to wedge one of the pieces of paper between some wild grass and weeds, pushing dirt on it to hold it in place. She worked quickly because her captor seemed short tempered and eager to get moving.

Skaggs bound her wrists but didn't blindfold her today, perhaps because he assumed they were far enough away from familiar surroundings. He'd be right about that, Lila thought. The landscape looked like no place she'd seen before, even though they'd only traveled one day.

Skaggs was right about another thing, too. Where would she run? There was nothing but rolling hills as far as she could see, broken only by an occasional thicket of cedars or clusters of trees. They followed a rocky gully with scattered vegetation until an outcrop of rocks eventually yielded a spring where they stopped to water the horse and fill the canteens. They ate hardtack and drank from the spring.

It was while they waited for the horse to have his fill that Lila felt the man's eyes on her. They sat by the spring, and the man's stare never left her. Up until now he'd either ignored her or treated her like a huge inconvenience, both of which were fine by her. When she couldn't take his eyes boring through her any longer, Lila looked directly at him.

"Why the stare?"

"Humph." His eyes narrowed. "Yer a fine-lookin' woman. Better 'n I remembered."

Every nerve in Lila's body tensed. "Remembered? From where? How'd you find me in Council Grove anyway?"

"Yer Pa described you in good detail. Said you'd taken off west and couldn't have gotten far. That you'd probably be a cook or some such in the first place you landed."

Pa was wrong about most everything. Why did he have to be right about this, Lila thought bitterly.

"I spied you months ago at Hays House. Even came close to gettin' you once before." He gave a satisfied laugh.

Lila's heart thudded. "You *what*?"

"In the woods . . . that cabin you visit. Almost got you last summer, 'cept those two Injun boys got in the way."

So, she had been followed that day. And this scoundrel had been waiting for another chance ever since. Lila's fear turned to anger. "You've spent all this time—days, months—waiting to get your hands on me?"

"Yes and no. Worked odd jobs on a ranch in Diamond Springs once I saw you weren't goin' anywhere. Just bidin' my time waitin' for the right moment." His laugh was smug, then his smile disappeared. "I'm in this for the money. The more I look at you, the more I see what you're worth, and it's a lot more than another twenty-five dollars."

What this soulless man had in mind was darker than Lila dared imagine.

"I'm changin' my plans. Forget Pa. Think we'll head to Denver. There's fancy whore houses out there, and I can git a lot more for you. You'd fit in right fine."

Denver.

Lila was stunned into silence. Did this man have the cunning and the resources to take her all the way to Denver? Her mind raced with ugly scenarios. She thought of the girls at the Red Horse Saloon in Council Grove and the life they lived. They were called soiled doves. She couldn't believe any of this, but like everything else in this nightmare, she was forced to.

Denver changed everything. Knowing she might be taken back to Pa was a logical choice for anyone searching for her. Even Lila had resigned herself that if she was returned to Pa, she had escaped from him once, and she could do it again. But Denver? It might as well be California or Oregon or another country altogether. She'd get swallowed up in the vastness of the

West and never be found again. She wanted to weep but the terror of this new prospect wouldn't allow it.

With the excuse she needed to relieve herself, Lila walked behind the overhang of rocks. She hunched down and pulled another torn page from her pocket while keeping her eyes peeled for Skaggs should he leave his place beside the spring. She slid the paper between two rocks and returned to where the man waited.

"Horse done finished. Let's git movin'."

The wind picked up and blew clouds from the north. At least Lila thought it was the north. They were riding at an angle into the wind, and without the sun Lila couldn't be sure of their direction. In spite of her bound hands, she pulled her hood up which gave some protection from the cold.

She decided to be forthright. "How many days to Denver?"

"None a yer damn business. Don't be askin' no questions."

It is my business. My life depends on it.

**

The wind was relentless. It kicked up dirt that stung Lila's eyes and she did her best to keep her head down as the horse covered the uneven trail. She didn't think they made as much progress the second day as they had the first, and that thought gave her hope. Whoever was following them might be gaining ground. They camped near a clump of fir trees which provided a barrier from the wind. The man gathered wood and built a fire.

"Gonna shoot us somethin' for supper." He hobbled his horse, left Lila's wrists bound and disappeared over a sandy hill with his gun. After he left, Lila looked at her options. She tried to untie the hobbled horse, but the rope was thick and unyielding. In addition, her wrists were raw from the rope that bound them, the abrasions near bleeding. When Skaggs returned, she would ask him if he had any salve, which seemed highly unlikely. She resigned herself to sitting by the fire and leaned into its meager warmth.

She jumped at the crack of a gunshot and moments later Skaggs appeared at the rim of the hill carrying a rabbit. He came back to the campfire, skinned the rabbit and fashioned a spit for roasting. While it cooked, Lila took a chance and approached the subject of her bound wrists.

"My wrists are in a bad way." She held up her bindings. "'S'pose you could take these off?"

"You forgotten yer my prisoner?"

"How could I forget? But my wrists are about to bleed, and I'd be mighty grateful if you'd undo these ropes. I'm not running anywhere, I promise."

He came to where Lila sat and inspected her wrists, grunted with disapproval and untied them.

Lila shook out her hands and flexed her fingers and said simply, "Thank you." Not waiting for permission, she took the canteen and poured water onto a corner of her petticoat, then held that to the deepest cut on her wrist. The cool sting was soothing.

The meat browned and sizzled. They'd eaten so little, and Lila was famished. The warm food brought a measure of comfort considering the dwindling rations the man appeared to have left. The hardtack was gone, the jerky nearly so. Lila wondered if the man would be forced to shoot all their food from now on. And what about rations for the horse? Skaggs had a small amount of feed in one of his saddle bags but that wouldn't go far. No, it seemed to Lila that he would need to find a place to buy supplies if they were going to Denver and that meant a town. With a store. And something she hoped might be a lifeline.

People.

**

John and his companions made good time riding through the woods past the cabin since they had searched it the previous night. When they arrived at the open plains, they slowed their pace and began to follow the tracks of a single horse. Louis and the sheriff kept them on course until the tracks suddenly disappeared.

"We've lost 'em," the sheriff said, puzzled.

Louis said, "Let's circle back and pick up the trail again.

With watchful eyes, Louis picked up the tracks again as they angled away from where they had been riding. "This way," he shouted to the others, and they pressed on.

They stopped at midday to rest the horses. They sat while they ate cold johnny cakes and cast their eyes over the desolate prairie hills.

"I've been wondering," said the sheriff, "if our outlaw would be looking for a waterin' hole about now, this being the second day of riding."

"Good to keep in mind," Louis said. "Keep an eye out for vegetation. Might find more tracks if we're lucky."

About two hours later they spotted a stand of trees and rode to it. They searched the area thoroughly, but it yielded nothing. "Let's keep going in the same direction," the sheriff said. John could tell he was trying to sound positive when all of them were disappointed at the scarcity of tracks. John pulled his collar up against the brisk wind and wondered for the millionth time if Lila was alright and if he would find her in time.

It was late afternoon when they found a rocky gulch and followed it to a spring.

John was beside himself with hope. "They had to have been here," he exclaimed and dismounted. The others followed and began looking for tracks, each going at his own pace, studying the ground as they circled the spring.

Louis crouched on his haunches. "There's hoof prints here," he said. "Maybe theirs, maybe not." He moved closer to the spring. "And boot prints here," he said pointing to markings in the earth.

"Can you tell how recent?" John asked.

A shout interrupted them. "Over here!" It was Charley. The three men made their way to the limestone overhang not far from some scrub bushes where Charley stood holding what looked like a piece of paper in his hand.

"What have you got there, son?" asked the sheriff.

"Found it stuck in the bushes." Charley handed the paper to John who glanced at it. An astonished look passed between John and Charley.

"There can only be one explanation for this," John said as he looked into Charley's wide eyes. The two spoke in unison. "It's a primer page."

"What? Out here? But how?" Louis asked.

John's heart pounded with joy. "I don't know. But it's Lila's." His voice choked. "She left it here for us to find, for us to follow." He passed the torn page to Louis and the sheriff.

"It is for sure," Louis said.

"That's a page from my primer, Pa," Charley said. "The one I'm readin' at school. Miss Teacher must have had it when she got took by the bad man."

"Quite something using your wits like that," the sheriff said. "Miss Bonner's taken it on herself to outsmart this outlaw. A lot of spunk, that one."

"A lot of spunk and a lot of courage," John murmured.

While the sheriff and John debated about camping for the night at the spring, Louis circled the area one more time, studying tracks.

"Found something over here," he called. The others joined him. "There's a trail," he said, pointing to the hoofprints. "We've been following them east, but these head off to the west."

"That makes no sense," John said.

"No, it doesn't," sheriff agreed. "Unless this guy has changed his destination."

"These are the only tracks that leave the spring. It has to be them," Louis said.

The three scoured the ground around the spring and were convinced this was the trail to follow. With another hour of daylight left, they could close the gap on the head start of Lila's captor. John felt certain and the others agreed, every mile and every hour could mean the difference between life or death to Lila. Privately, John prayed Lila would not be the victim of outrage, if she hadn't been already. That thought propelled him like none other.

Chapter Forty-One

They crested a rise and looked down on what appeared to be a small town in the distance. As they rode closer, a livery, blacksmith shop, mercantile, boarding house, and a smattering of houses came into view. It was early morning, and few people were about. Each daybreak seemed more frigid than the one before, and Lila trembled under her cloak. Skaggs still smelled rank, but at least he provided some body heat when they rode next to each other.

She wondered if he had any idea where he was going or if he stumbled onto this town by accident. One thing he'd made very clear before they went into the mercantile, however, was her behavior once inside the establishment.

"We're gettin' supplies. In and out fast. You got that? If you so much as *think* about raisin' a ruckus, it'll be the last thing you do." Then he'd leaned within an inch of her face, his rancid breath watering her eyes. "I ain't so desperate for money I can't find me another way to make a buck. You're replaceable, honey. Remember that."

Lila took stock of the store the moment they stepped inside, especially the people. It was about the same size as Last Chance and offered a variety of merchandise. A middle-aged man in work clothes was busy stacking bags of coffee and cornmeal on shelves behind a pot belly stove radiating a welcoming heat. Lila gravitated to the stove and could have stayed there forever, so frozen were her arms and legs. A woman behind the counter with a kind face and hair pulled back in a bun nodded at them as they entered.

"Good mornin'. What can I help you with?" she asked.

"We're passin' through. Need a few things, then we'll be on our way." Skaggs grabbed Lila's arm, his fingers clamped into her flesh, and guided her down the store aisles while he made selections.

"You folks not from around here?" the woman came out from behind the counter to offer help.

"Like I said, we're just passin' through."

Lila noticed the window at the back of the store that looked out on the prairie, but her interest piqued when she saw an outhouse not ten yards from the back door. She turned to Skaggs. "Husband, I should like to use the outhouse while we're here, if that's all right with you ma'am?" She directed her question to the woman.

"Of course. Folks use it all the time."

"But—" Skaggs was caught off guard by Lila's request, and his protest got no heed.

"Thank you so much." Lila wrenched her arm free from his grip and strode to the back door.

"You'll be needing paper," said the woman and met her at the door with a sheet of newspaper.

Thinking fast, Lila turned her back on Skaggs and raised her sleeves to reveal the abrasions on her wrists. The woman looked at them with a mixture of confusion and concern before Lila covered them and went out the door, her heart pounding. She had taken a chance and didn't think Skaggs had seen her defiance.

It had been three days since this horrible man had taken her. Using the privy gave her a moment's release from his constant presence. Afterwards, Lila rinsed her hands at the pump beside the back door and splashed cold water on her face, a jolt of needed courage. When she stepped inside the store, Skaggs gave her a hate-filled look that took the breath right out of her chest. Maybe he *had* seen her show her wrists, or he was simply furious that she left on her own to the outhouse.

The woman at the counter gave them a tentative smile and tallied their purchase of coffee, rice, salt pork, a plug of tobacco, horse feed, and a pint of spirits. Lila winced at the sight of the whiskey bottle knowing this brought new worries—her captor getting drunk.

Lila had a last-minute thought before Skaggs paid. "'Scuse me, ma'am, but do you have any salve?"

"Sure do." The woman reached for a small tin from a shelf behind her and added it to the purchases.

Skaggs glared at her, but she did her best to ignore it. "Thank you kindly."

"You have a safe journey, ya hear," the woman said when Skaggs paid. "Where did ya say you were headed?"

Before he could answer, Lila said, "Denver."

When they got outside, Skaggs looked around at the nearly empty street before he turned to Lila and slapped her hard across the face. She staggered back but kept her balance, her hand to her burning cheek. "I told you no funny business, you little whore," he snarled. "You told her where we're goin'. Don't think I didn't notice." He raised his hand again but didn't strike. "One more stupid move like that . . ."

**

The sun lifted above the clouds and gave Lila a sense of direction—they were heading due west as they left the town behind. The saddlebags were laden with supplies, and Lila thought the extra weight plus the wind buffeting them from the north slowed the horse. Good, she thought. Good news for whoever was trying to catch up with them. Her cheek throbbed. She raised her hand and felt the swelling. This horrible man must be very worried about being followed to have resorted to striking her for revealing their destination. Being followed was the only glimmer of hope she had, and she clung to it.

They had been riding all morning and spoken not a word when they came to a muddy watering hole surrounded by forlorn, leafless trees. They dismounted to give the horse a drink and a brief rest. They hadn't been there but a few minutes when a mounted figure appeared on the horizon from the opposite direction riding toward them. Skaggs gave her one look of warning before the rider arrived, and she understood his meaning.

"Howdy." The young man was in his twenties wearing a felt hat, sheepskin jacket, chaps, and pointed boots. He dismounted and walked his horse to the water's edge. "Always glad to find water. You folks just get here?"

Skaggs said, "Long enough for the horse to drink, then we're on our way."

The cowboy touched his hat and nodded to Lila. "How do, ma'am. Don't often see ladies out this way." He smiled.

Lila nodded and looked away.

"Where y'all headed?"

"Out west," the man said.

"Sure," the cowboy said, "but anywhere in particular? The west is pretty big."

"You ask a lot of questions that don't concern you."

"Well now, I don't mean to pry, only makin' conversation. That all right with you, ma'am?"

Lila met the cowboy's eyes with a pleading look but turned away again.

The cowboy frowned at Lila, turned and looked at Skaggs, then back at Lila. "Is everything all right? I'm gettin' a strange feeling about. . ."

Before the cowboy finished speaking, Skaggs whipped out his gun and shot him point blank in the chest. Lila screamed. The cowboy fell backwards to the ground and his terrified horse bolted and galloped away.

"What have you done?" Lila shrieked. She ran to the young man and knelt at his side. He lay motionless, his chest still, his eyes open to the sky. "Dear God, you've killed him!" She stood and rushed her captor with fists balled. "What's wrong with you? You didn't have to shoot him." She beat his chest, ignoring the smoking gun still in his hand. "You are an evil, evil man," she sobbed as tears streamed down her face.

Skaggs flung her aside like a limp doll and holstered his gun. "We gotta get out of here. Now!" They mounted his horse and rode away as fast as the animal could go.

Chapter Forty-Two

Skaggs pushed his horse until the animal showed signs of laboring before he backed off to a slow gallop. Horrified by what she had just witnessed, Lila felt waves of nausea rising from her stomach. She had thought nothing was worse than being kidnapped, but she was wrong. She was now riding with a cold-blooded killer.

When Skaggs seemed satisfied they had covered enough distance from the watering hole, he found a spot to give the horse a rest. The minute they dismounted, Lila leaned over and retched, splattering her boots. Shaking from head to toe, she gagged and vomited a second time.

Skaggs tied the horse to one of the evergreen trees clinging to a limestone ledge. He eyed her with disgust. "Not gettin' sick, are ya?"

Lila wiped her mouth with the back of her hand. "Canteen." She couldn't stop shaking.

He tossed her the canteen which she opened, took a mouthful of water, and spat on the ground. "I'm all right," she lied, trying to steady her voice.

"Better be. Soon as the horse is rested, we have some more miles to go before nightfall."

He failed to notice dark clouds gathering in the west while they rested the horse. Before they could get on the trail, the clouds opened up and dumped rain mixed with sleet, forcing them to stay put. They found a carved-out place along the ledge large enough to shelter themselves and the horse and leaned into the dry space while the wind whipped around them. Lightning shot across the sky through the black clouds followed by crashing thunder that shook the ground beneath them.

Cold and wet, knees pulled to her chest, Lila huddled against the rock wall and watched nature unleash a furious storm. She tried to come to terms with the violence she'd just witnessed but couldn't rid herself of the young man's ghostly death stare. When lightning lit up the sky, his lifeless face appeared.

She turned her thoughts to John, hoping to lift herself out of the nightmare. While she watched the angry skies, she was struck with a thought like the thunder bolts exploding around her: she'd never told John how she felt about him. Not once.

How could this be?

Lila clearly remembered the evening John had confided his feelings for her and had said, "You are more than just my friend." She'd replayed that phrase a million times in her head. He'd even asked for a response from her. And what had she said? "Maybe we need time to sort this out." What a weak, non-committal thing to say. Tears welled in her eyes.

This was the third time she was faced with losing John—once when Fanny arrived as his fiancé, again during the Indian troubles, and now. What was she waiting for? A fourth time? Here she was hoping he was on his way to rescue her without so much as a token expression of her feelings toward him. She had closed off her heart, wrapped it up and put it away for far too long.

I hope I'm not too late. I can't be too late. When I see you again John, I will fix this. I promise.

**

Collars up, hats pulled down, the four riders hunched into their jackets against the bursts of wind. The squall came in fits and starts, swirling rain and sleet, slowing their progress to a walk for the past hour.

"Up ahead," the sheriff hollered above the storm. He was pointing to buildings in the near distance, and they urged their horses forward to the welcoming sight of a town. Pale light from the windows of the mercantile shone through the gloom as they dismounted and tied their horses.

Once inside, a woman greeted them from the front counter of the store. "Goodness, gracious. You folks must be soaked."

"You'd be right about that, ma'am," John said removing his dripping hat and giving it a shake. Cold rivulets ran down the back of his neck.

"Come on over here and git yerselfs warmed up." She gestured to the stove. "And look at you," she exclaimed at seeing Charley. "Such a little one out in this storm. Do you all have time to get dry?"

"Thank you, ma'am," the sheriff said. "We were so anxious to get out of the rain, didn't notice if you have a place to hold up overnight? Weather doesn't look like it's letting up any time soon."

"There's a boarding house across the street. I know there's room — most always is."

Louis nodded in agreement after looking at Charley. "The boy needs to dry out. We all do."

John hated to stop, but with night closing in and the four of them drenched and cold, it made sense to get lodging. He further justified stopping for the fact that Lila and her captor would be held up as well, so foul was the weather. "What about a livery?"

"Just down the street." A man from the back of the store joined them. "Name's Joseph Mather, this is my wife, Agnes. Welcome to Salina." He extended his hand to the men who introduced themselves. "You folks a long way from home?"

John, Louis, and the sheriff exchanged glances. They had agreed at the outset of their search to spread the word about Lila's abduction. The more people who knew, the better their chances of finding her.

John spoke first. "We're not traveling home, we're on the trail a kidnapper."

Mrs. Mather shrank back in horror. "Good heavens, no. What happened?"

The sheriff relayed the story, and when he gave a description of Lila, all the color drained from Mrs. Mather's face. She reached for her husband's arm. "Dear God. I knew something was wrong, Joseph, I knew it. We should have done something." Tear sprang to her eyes.

Mr. Mather clasped his wife's hand. "We didn't know, Agnes. How could we help her if we didn't know?"

"Help her?" John was suddenly fully alert. "Help who? What do you mean?"

"She was in our store, right here, this morning," the woman's voice rose as she held back a sob. "The woman you're looking for."

"Lila was here?" John burst, hardly believing their good fortune. "About this tall," he said, holding his arm out as a measure of her height.

Charley elbowed his way into the circle of grownups. "You saw Miss Teacher?" he asked, his face full of hope.

"Miss Bonner works in our school," Louis said. "My son is very fond of her."

"We're looking for her," Charley said eagerly. "Been lookin' for three days. Is she all right?"

"She's doing fine, son," said Mr. Mather with a forced smile for Charley's benefit.

But when Charley returned to warm himself at the stove, the couple gave a detailed description of her captor and what had transpired while they were in the store. Mrs. Mather described the rope burns Lila had risked showing her.

"I'd say she's holding up the best she can," Mrs. Mather said, "but she's not fine. That's one mean lookin' man that's got her. He slapped her hard across the face outside our store before they rode off."

Every muscle in John's body tensed with this information.

"Can you tell us anything else, anything at all?" the sheriff asked.

Mrs. Mather responded. "Your friend let it slip where they were heading, and I don't think that mean one was none too pleased about it."

"What did she say?" John asked nearly breathless.

"Denver. He's taking her to Denver."

**

John paid for two rooms at the boarding house for the night. It was the least he could do for the sheriff and Louis. He would be nowhere without them. True, Sheriff Jenkins was there in an official capacity, but he was extending the time for a search beyond what he'd normally do. This kidnapping was personal for him and everyone in Council Grove. He wanted to see it through to a satisfactory conclusion — the apprehension of the kidnapper and the safe return of Lila Bonner.

The men bought a few items at the mercantile before taking their horses to the livery and sitting down to a hot meal at the boarding house. The wind had calmed but the rain continued in a steady downpour while they ate their fill of stew and drank fresh buttermilk. Before retiring, they shed their wet clothes to dry beside the stove in the front room.

John shared a room with the sheriff. When he turned down the lamp and lay back in bed, he knew sleep would be hard to come by — his mind was sorting through what they had learned from the Mathers. He was alternately relieved and fearful with the new information. Relieved and deliriously happy to know Lila had been here only hours ago, and her captor was less than a day ahead of them. They were gaining on him. Relieved she appeared unharmed except for her bound wrists. Fearful when he learned this fiend planned to take her to Denver. *Denver.* They had to close the gap and get to Lila soon. He had to get to her before she was lost in Denver, or he might never see her again.

**

They woke to a clear, crisp day, and after an early breakfast they mounted up, eager to resume their search. The Mathers suggested following the trail west out of town which would take them through ranching country in western Kansas and eventually to Denver. This was helpful advice as the heavy rains had obliterated any trail left by Lila's captor.

"Why Denver?" John asked as they rode. "That's at least a week of hard riding, maybe ten days.

"I can think of several reasons, none that you want to hear," replied the sheriff.

John fell silent. Sheriff was right — he could imagine the worst that awaited Lila and couldn't bear to hear it spoken aloud.

"Don't worry about what waits in Denver, John," Louis said. "We'll find Lila long before then."

After several hours of riding Charley noticed birds circling in the distant sky. "Pa, are those buzzards?"

"Think so, son," Louis said. The men exchanged concerned glances and kneed their horses forward. John's pulse quickened, dreading what they might find.

They pulled up short of a watering hole and discovered the reason for the scavengers: a man's crumpled body with a hole in his chest. Buzzards sat poised over the lifeless body with their ugly, featherless heads of red skin, something akin to the Devil, waiting for the right moment to start scavenging.

"Get away!" John jumped off his horse, waving off the buzzards with his arms. Louis and the sheriff followed suit, hollering and flapping their arms at the stubborn birds who eventually soared into the air.

The sheriff knelt beside the body for a cursory look. "He appears to be shot from close up. Not too long ago, but it rained so much last night, can't tell for sure."

"Horse probably got spooked by the gunshot," Louis said. "Looks to be a cattle driver or rancher."

"Who is he, Pa?" Charley stood a distance from the body, unwilling to come close.

"Don't know, Charley."

"What do we do now?" John asked.

The sheriff ran his hand over the stubble covering his jaw. "I don't feel right about just leaving him here. We don't have any way to bury him . . ."

"Maybe we do," Louis said. He removed from his saddle bag what resembled a short-handled spade. "We could dig a shallow grave with this. That would work for the time being."

"That's our best choice. Otherwise, what?" John asked again.

"Otherwise, I'd have to take the body back to Salina, turn it over to their undertaker. You two would go on without me, and I'd try to catch up."

"Let's start digging," John said. "We need to stick together."

"What do you think happened here?" Louis asked.

"Hard to say," answered the sheriff. "But since we're tracking a known kidnapper, and a ruthless one at that, it's my guess he's got something to do with this."

John felt sick to his stomach. "Give me the shovel. I'll go first."

Chapter Forty-Three

She had been so cold her teeth chattered, still Lila fell asleep sitting against the wall of the limestone outcropping. The physical and emotional toll left her exhausted. When she opened her eyes the next morning, Skaggs was still asleep, only a few feet from her, propped up against the same ledge. The rain had stopped, the sun shone in a clear sky.

Her throat was raw and hurt when she swallowed. Sleeping exposed to the elements and wearing wet clothes through the cold night could easily cause the croup. She didn't feel feverish but ached in every muscle and joint.

Skaggs stirred and sat up. "Could do with some vittles." He gathered what dry kindling and brush he could find and built a fire. "Ain't nobody on our heels after a storm like last night. Gonna find us somethin' to eat."

Lila held her hands toward the fire, appreciating its warmth along with the fact that Skaggs was gone from sight. Since he'd killed the cowboy, his presence sickened her even more than it had before. And terrified her. She didn't know how much longer she could bear being his captive. Early on she'd contemplated trying for his gun while he slept, but since he'd so callously murdered that young man, she'd given up the idea.

How had it come to this, being the captive of a murderer? She shook her head in disbelief at where she found herself. All she had wanted was to get away from Pa. That's all. But the answer to her question circled back to him. Lila still couldn't believe—not really—that even Pa in a drunken state would stoop so low as to pay someone like Skaggs to track her down.

It forced her to think back to living on the farm in Indiana. Her real father had died when she was eleven, killed at the Battle of Wilson's Creek somewhere in Missouri in the early days of the Civil War, fighting for the Union. Mama wasn't a widow for long and married Pa. He took care of the family and was good to Lila and her brothers. Lila searched her memories, sifting through holidays, birthdays, and all the everydays of their life together. They had been happy, hadn't they? She hadn't made up a favorable family history to suit her needs, had she?

Lila couldn't answer her own question about her history with Pa. The only thing she knew for certain was she wanted to get out of this nightmare alive. With her spirits at a breaking point, she found a place to partially hide a torn page from the primer before Skaggs returned.

They rode into the afternoon without stopping until her captor pulled to a halt at a rise in the trail. About a half mile to the north was a farmhouse with a barn next to it. He eyed it for several moments, then gave a sinister laugh. "Ain't that funny how the Lord provides?"

"What would you know about the Lord?" Lila asked, her voice laced with anger.

"Shut up! I know plenty." He kept his eyes on the house. "I think we need to pay us a visit. Find us a roof for our heads."

Lila's mind raced. If they went to the farmhouse, their trail might be lost. She needed to indicate where they were going, and she needed to do it fast. "We've been riding since morning. Can we stop here? I have to go."

"You can wait till we git up there." He nodded toward the farmhouse.

"This horse takes another step, and I'll wet myself," Lila said.

Skaggs grunted, walked the horse to some brush and dismounted. Lila slid down and ran for cover. She grabbed a few rocks, pushed them together at the edge of the brush to point toward the farmhouse before she squatted.

"Hurry up," the man hollered.

"Be right there."

They rode slowly up the path to the farmhouse, sizing up the place. It was limestone with a small front porch, probably built in the last year or two. "Newly acquired land, I'd say," Skaggs said. He swung down from the horse at the hitching post by the front steps and glared up at Lila. "Not a word out of you. Understand?" Before he could knock at the door a voice called from the barn.

"Can I help you?"

They both turned to a woman standing at the barn door with a shotgun trained on them.

"Whoa, ma'am." Skaggs raised his hands in a submissive gesture. "No need for the gun. We're friendly folk travelin' to Denver in need of a place to bed down for a night. Was hopin' maybe you wouldn't mind if we slept in your barn. We'd be on our way come mornin'."

The woman crossed the barn yard to the house, eyeing Lila, then the man, her shotgun still raised. "Denver. That's a long ways from here. Where you from?" she demanded. Lila guessed she was in her twenties, wearing a heavy coat over workpants and boots, her hair pulled back in a long blond braid.

"I—we're from Council Grove," Lila offered against strict orders from her captor.

Skaggs threw her a threatening glance, then said, "It's been gettin' mighty cold the past few nights. Like I said, we'd be real glad for a night out of the elements."

The woman was quiet for a moment, thinking over their request. "My husband will be comin' in from the pasture shortly. If he says it's all right, then you can stay. In the meantime, the pumps over there." She pointed to the side of the house. "You can wait in the barn." With that, she withdrew into the house and left them alone.

Once inside the barn, Lila lowered herself onto a bale of hay. She had cupped her hands under the pump and swallowed water in spite of the pain in her throat. Although it was warmer in the barn due to bales of hay stacked against one wall and heat from a couple of milk cows, Lila kept her cloak on to ward off chills that were coming in waves. She watched Skaggs unhitch the horse and remove the saddle bags, fearful of what he had in mind for this family.

"What's the plan?" she asked, her voice wavering.

"Just askin' for a night's sleep here."

Please, Lord, let it be only that.

**

John, Louis, and Sheriff Jenkins dug a shallow grave and buried the poor soul where he had died—beside the trail.

Lacking the time and materials to make a cross, they piled stones at the head of his grave to mark his final resting place. John spoke a few words while they bowed their heads, then they mounted up and rode off at a steady gallop to find Lila's kidnapper, whom they suspected had killed the man they just buried.

They rode hard all morning, stopping briefly to rest the horses and eat salt pork and biscuits before continuing down the trail. The sky was clear, but the temperature dropped as the miles fell by. John stole a glance at his companions, grateful they were as steadfast in their purpose of finding Lila as he was. He quit torturing himself with worry about what Lila was going through—was she being abused, was she sleeping on the cold ground? It did no good. His only thought now was to find her.

**

The barn door opened and a lanky man with reddish-blond hair and beard stepped inside. He wore work clothes and a heavy coat and approached Lila and Skaggs.

"Wife tells me you're travelin' to Denver, want to stay the night in our barn."

Skaggs stood. "That's right. We'd appreciate a night out of the cold."

The rancher looked them over with a steady gaze, up and down, first Skaggs, then Lila.

"Denver's a mighty long way from here. You have any idea how long that's gonna take?" he asked.

Lila watched the color in Skaggs' neck redden. *Please don't hurt him. Please.*

"We'll be fine. Out of here early tomorrow." He kept his voice even.

"Well, all right then. Wife says you should come in for supper. You could probably use some hot food."

"That's right nice of you," the man said.

Lila had been silent during the exchange. "Thank you kindly. We'd appreciate that." They followed the rancher into the house while Lila silently prayed they would get through the meal with no one getting harmed. Or killed.

**

It might have been the best meal Lila had even eaten. She savored every mouthful of the slow simmered stew with chunks of beef and potatoes in thick, rich gravy, the fresh baked rolls with butter, and warm applesauce. Their hosts were Rolf and Miriam Lundstrom, new to Kansas two years ago after the war ended. Lila and Skaggs ate silently at first in their eagerness for a decent meal, but eventually the men did most of the talking.

Skaggs said they were Mr. and Mrs. Moore and made up an outlandish story of meeting up with a brother in Denver who was a rancher. How easily the lies fell from his lips. How smooth he was at hiding his coarse, ruthless nature. Lila nodded politely as she ate, while desperately looking for an opportunity to speak with the wife away from her captor. She had to be very careful revealing the truth. All this weighed on her while the rawness in her throat intensified and her chills increased.

"Let me help clear the dishes," Lila offered when the meal was over. "It's the least we can do for your hospitality."

"Thank you. That's right kind," replied Miriam.

When Lila carried plates to the counter, the tinware rattled in her shaky hands.

Miriam steadied Lila's hand, then studied her face. "You're flushed, Mrs. Moore. You feel all right?"

"Oh, yes," Lila lied. "It's nothing."

Miriam put her hand to Lila's forehead. "You're burning up. Go sit down and I'll brew some tea, put some spirits in it."

Skaggs rose from the table. "Somethin' wrong with the missus?" he frowned.

"It's nothing, husband," Lila replied returning to the table. "She's brewing tea for me."

His frown deepened. "We should turn in. Have to get an early start in the mornin'."

"Mr. Moore," Miriam began, "your wife's not well. She's got a fever and should sleep in the house tonight at the very least."

"I won't hear of it." Skaggs' voice rose, and Lila saw the telltale creep of red in his neck.

Alarmed, Lila interceded quickly. "Thank you, Mrs. Lundstrom, but I'll be fine in the barn. The tea will be good enough."

Mrs. Lundstrom looked at her husband, bewildered. He returned a confused look. "All right," she said, "but I'll send a quilt with you. Wrap up good in it."

Chapter Forty-Four

Lila burrowed into the hay with the quilt wrapped around her. Mrs. Lindstrom had made a home remedy for colds that warmed Lila from the inside out. Before she drifted off to sleep, she saw Skaggs open his bottle of whiskey for the first time since he'd bought it. He took several pulls of drink, but Lila was too drowsy to care and fell into a deep sleep.

It was dark, and rough hands were pulling her awake. She smelled whiskey. Half dazed Lila jerked with a start. "Stop it, Pa! Stop it."

The clumsy groping stopped abruptly, then sickening laughter. "So tha's how it was," the voice slurred. Lila sat up, fully awake and stared at Skaggs leaning over her. "No wonder he wanted you back." He smirked as he reached for her and pitched forward. Lila rolled out of the way, and he landed face down in the hay beside her. She jumped to her feet, heart pounding and waited for his next move. He lay still.

Lila stood holding her breath, her eyes fixed on him, but he didn't move. The next sound she heard was snoring. Too drunk to stay awake, she thought, or maybe divine intervention had saved her. She exhaled, safe in the belief he wouldn't bother her again—at least not tonight.

Lila found a safer place to sleep in the barn—away from Skaggs, but close enough to keep an eye on him. She watched him sleep and wondered if he, like Pa, would sleep hard after a drinking binge. Would he sleep long enough for her to run to the farmhouse and tell the Lundstroms what was really happening? That would put the Lundstroms in danger, too, but Lila knew she couldn't get away from Skaggs on her own. She was burning up with fever, her throat painful and raw, and she needed help. Skaggs was a determined kidnapper. Even if she took his ammunition while he snored, he still possessed a knife strapped to his leg and could ride out of here with her as his captive.

She weighed her options as the first streaks of daylight appeared. Skaggs had not moved from where he lay sleeping in the hay. In spite of feeling lightheaded and weak, Lila knew this was her one and only chance. She was sorry to involve the Lundstroms but could see no other choice. Lila rose silently and treaded softly across the barn floor to the door. She released the latch, pushed the door open enough to slip through, then closed the door behind her.

Once out in the open she ran to the farmhouse and pounded on the door. "Mr. Lindstrom. Mrs. Linstrom. I need your help!" She pounded again.

The door opened and Mr. Lindstrom stood there, confused by the commotion. "What's all this about?"

"Please, I need your help. There's no time." Lila pushed past him into the house. Miriam was cooking breakfast. Begging to be heard Lila turned to Mr. Lindstrom. "Mr. Moore is not who he says he is. And we're not married. Four days ago he kidnapped me in Council Grove."

Miriam's spatula clattered to the floor. "Kidnapped?" She came from the stove to Lila's side.

Lila clutched Miriam's hand. "We've been on the run ever since. He's taking me to Denver to . . ." she paused before forcing out the truth, "to work in a brothel. I have to get away from him. Can you help me, please?"

"This is unbelievable!" Miriam turned to her husband. "We have to do something."

"Does he have a gun?" Rolfe asked.

"Yes, and he's dangerous, capable of anything."

"Good Lord," said Rolfe. "I don't suppose he'd listen to reason."

The front door opened with a bang, and Skaggs walked in. "Would who listen to reason? Me? What's goin' on here?" His eyes narrowed as he eyed the Lundstroms. "My wife been tellin' tall tales again?" He smirked. "Let me guess. She said I kidnapped her and am keepin' her against her will, right?" He gave a chilling laugh. "What a story. You see, my poor wife has these bouts of trouble with her mind. Doesn't know up from down, if ya know what I mean."

"That's—that's not true," Lila cried. Her pulse raced. She implored the Lundstroms. "You have to believe me."

"Or you can believe me." Skaggs raised his eyebrows.

Lila watched the Lundstrom's expressions change. She could read doubt creep into their eyes and knew there was only one thing that might change their mind. "Look at these," she demanded and rolled up her sleeves revealing the rope burns on her wrists. "He kept me bound for days. I'm not making up this story." Tears sprang in her eyes as she forced them to look at her wrists.

Rolfe Lundstrom's face turned grim. "Mr. Moore, or whoever you are, clear off my property—" A loud knocking at the door startled everyone.

Skaggs pulled his gun from under his coat and pointed it at Mr. Lundstrom. "Answer the door and get rid of whoever it is. I'll have my gun on your wife, understand?"

Rolfe Lundstrom's jaw dropped. For a moment he stood unable to move. With the gun pointed at him, his face like stone, Rolfe approached the door with tentative steps. Lila and Miriam grasped hands, afraid to breathe. Rolfe opened the door.

"Sorry to bother you so early. Name is Sheriff Jenkins, Council Grove. Wanted to have a word with you."

Rolfe stood frozen for a moment before he spoke. "Of course. What do you want?" He stepped out onto the front porch. Before he closed the door, Lila caught of glimpse in the early morning light of two other men with the sheriff. Wearing dust from the trail and looking weary from what must have been hard riding stood John and Louis Bellmard. She could have wept for joy.

I knew you'd come, John. I knew it.

They heard bits and pieces of the conversation between Rolfe and the sheriff through the closed door. Rolfe raised his voice Lila thought, so Skaggs could hear what was being said, so he'd know Rolfe was following orders.

"No, haven't been any strangers out this way," Rolfe explained to the sheriff. They talked a while longer and when the sheriff asked if they could look in the barn, Rolfe got defensive and said there was no need, and they should be on their way. The sheriff started to argue, then let it drop, and he and his friends mounted up and rode off.

No, don't go. You can't go. I'm right here! Lila wanted to run out on the porch and scream at their disappearing figures. This can't be happening, she thought. Not after everything I've been through. They can't have come all this way to have this horrid man slip through their fingers.

Rolfe came back inside and stared with fury at the captor. "Satisfied? They're gone. Now clear out and leave us alone." He crossed the room to his wife and pulled her to his side.

"That's not how it works," replied Skaggs.

A minute ago, Lila had been beside herself with joy. Now she feared the worst.

**

They rode away from the farmhouse until the rise in the trail hid them from view. They pulled up. "Do you believe him?" John asked the sheriff.

"No." He glanced back toward the farmhouse.

"Neither do I," Louis said.

"That makes three of us," John agreed. "Especially after finding that pile of rocks on the trail to the house. I'm sure that was Lila's doing."

"Let's go back and check the barn. Maybe there's something there," the sheriff said. "We'll ride off the trail to the west and circle back toward the barn from behind so we can't be seen from the house."

They approached the barn and dismounted, leading their horses through the pasture on foot. John's horse whickered, and he gently stroked his nose to quiet him. After tying their horses to brush on the back side of the barn, they edged their way to the barn door and darted inside.

Besides the cows, farm tools and bales of hay, they found one horse tied up by itself with saddle bags full of supplies lying on the barn floor, an empty whiskey bottle, and a quilt.

"Somebody's been sleeping out here, and I don't think it was Mr. Lundstrom," Louis said.

"I have a hunch you're right, Louis," John said.

"My guess, whoever this was, is still in the house. And if we're lucky, Lila is with him," the sheriff said. He thought a moment before continuing. "Let's split up. Louis, go round to the back. I 's'pose there's a back door. John, you and I will take the front. Charley," the sheriff looked kindly at the youngster, "you've been a mighty good help. Best thing for you to do now is lay low here in the barn, understand?"

Charley nodded solemnly, his brow knitted with worry.

"Another thing," the sheriff said. "John, I don't suppose you've had to hunt down a man before like Louis here has. Be alert when we get to the house. We don't know what we'll find. Could turn out to be a life-or-death situation where even a split second could cost a man his shot. Be ready, all right?"

"I'll be ready," John said. "Before we go, I want you to know how much I—"

The sheriff cut him off. "Not yet, John. Not till we get our man."

"And we get our Miss Teacher back." Louis gave a serious smile.

"All right then," the sheriff said, "let's see what's in that house. Maybe we can git us a kidnapper."

The three men nodded with a resolve that hadn't wavered since they began their worried search for Lila. They left the barn and approached the house keeping low to the ground.

**

Lila was buying time, arguing with Skaggs.

He kept repeating, "Doesn't pay to leave eyewitnesses behind."

"These folks have been nothing but kind to us. They fed us, gave us a warm place in their barn. Once we're out of here, they're miles away from reporting this."

"My wife and I won't say anything to anybody, just leave us be." Rolfe was putting up a brave front, but Lila could tell Miriam was near collapse with fright.

Lila stood in front of the wretched man who had ripped her life to shreds in a matter of days. Knowing his erratic temper, it took every ounce of courage to confront him. "You said this was about money, that this was a business deal. So go on about your business and don't make it about anything else. You don't need that kind of grief and the Lundstroms surely don't."

Suddenly a voice called from outside, and the captor wheeled around toward the source of the sound. "Mr. Lundstrom. It's the sheriff. We've got reason to believe there's someone inside your house we need to talk to, someone we've been tracking."

"Dammit, they came back," Skaggs muttered and grabbed Lila by the arm. Waving his gun, he directed the Lundstroms to stand by the front door. "If either of you move, the girl gets it, understand?" He opened the door and stepped onto the porch, the gun pointed at Lila's head. "What did you want to talk about?"

The sheriff was crouched on one side of the porch, gun drawn, and John held the same position on the opposite side. "Nobody has to get hurt, mister," the sheriff said. "We want this to end peacefully."

"Not likely from where I stand," replied the man. "Unless I can leave with the girl, and nobody stops me."

Chapter Forty-Five

Lila stood rigidly beside her captor who was pressing the gun to her temple. She saw someone out of the corner of her eye, someone crouched beside the porch. It was John, head cocked to one side, his gun trained on the captor, hands steady. She'd never seen John go hunting, never watched him shoot a rabbit or even a prairie chicken, yet there he was poised to kill the man he had helped track down in order to save her.

The sheriff tried to reason with the captor. "If you surrender, all you'll face is kidnapping charges. You don't want to make things worse for yourself."

Lila knew his response before he uttered it. "Not gonna happen. You have to let me go and the girl too—and there's two more inside. I got hostages."

At that moment a single shot gun blast erupted from inside the house, came through the open door, and hit Skaggs, grazing his shoulder and shredding his jacket. He and Lila ducked as the sheriff and John took shots that missed their moving target. Skaggs held Lila fast and dragged her back inside.

Skaggs then turned on Rolfe and grabbed the smoldering shotgun. "You don't listen very well. I've a mind to put you out of your misery right now." He hit him across the face with the butt of his gun, and blood spurted from Rolfe's nose. "Not gonna do it yet, though. You're a bargaining chip."

He returned to the front door, and hollered, "Seems we have a stalemate. If you don't agree to let me and the girl go, one of these two homesteaders is gonna get shot. You got ten minutes." He slammed the door shut.

**

John and the sheriff inched their way around to the back of the house where Louis waited. "I think he's crazy enough to start killing those folks," John said. "What should we do?"

"Let him think we'll go along with letting him go. See what he does," the sheriff said.

Louis shook his head. "I don't know. He's a mean one. If we hear any ruckus from the house, I think we should be ready to rush the place."

"Agreed," the sheriff nodded. "I'll go round front and tell him to pack up and leave. Do you think there's a way we could corner him in the barn? I can't think he'd take all three of them as hostages."

"This gives me an idea," Louis said. "He might want the three of us to account for ourselves when he's ready to leave. But he doesn't know we have a fourth one."

"A fourth one? You mean Charley?" the sheriff asked. "How can he help?"

Louis said, "He may be just a kid, but it might be the advantage we need." They came up with a plan, based more on hope than tactics, but they were desperate. Staying out of direct sight of the house, Louis crossed the yard to the barn while the sheriff returned to the front of the house to talk to the captor.

"Listen up," he hollered. "If we let you and the girl go, you've got to do something for us. Otherwise, no deal."

The house was dead still. Finally, Skaggs answered. "What do you want?"

"Leave those homesteaders unharmed. If we hear so much as a peep coming from the house, all bets are off. We're coming in, guns blazing. You got that?"

More silence. Then, "All right. Here's what's gonna happen. You three come in here, hands up, guns holstered. No funny business. I got my gun pointed on these three and I can take 'em out any time. Understand?"

"Understood." Louis hadn't returned from the barn and the sheriff needed to stall. "We'll be coming soon as one of my boys relieves himself," he hollered.

No response. Then, "What's takin' so long?" shouted Skaggs.

"Can't hurry nature. We'll be there."

None too soon Louis returned from the barn, and the three men holstered their guns and approached the front porch with their hands up. Skaggs threw open the front door, Lila at his side, his gun to her head. "Get in here," he thundered. As they came through the door, he grabbed each of their guns, stuck two in his waistband and kicked the last across the kitchen floor into a corner.

When John stepped through the door, seeing Lila for the first time after this long search, a gun to her head, nearly undid him. He held her terrified gaze, willing her to be strong for a little longer. There was no way on God's green earth this horrible man was going to kill Lila. He would not allow that to happen.

Waving his gun, Skaggs lined up his hostages.

"What are you doing?" the sheriff asked.

"What do you think?" he answered. "You think I'm gonna leave you all here alive to come after me?"

"Now hold on—" the sheriff began.

Frantic, Lila interrupted, "You said you wouldn't hurt them."

"Maybe you can't count, mister," Louis said, "but there's five of us and one of you."

"If you get one shot off, we'll be all over you." John dared take a step toward the man.

"But I'll still get one shot off—"

A gun blast shattered the front window spraying shards of glass into the room, launching the three friends into action. Skaggs was caught off guard long enough for John to dive toward him, knocking him to the floor while the sheriff wrestled for his gun. As they fought, the gun went off and a bullet ricocheted off the ceiling. Louis grabbed the extra gun lying on the floor and trained it on the struggling criminal as Rolfe jumped on top of him alongside John.

"Miriam," Rolfe shouted, "get rope from the porch."

They forced Skaggs onto his stomach, his arms twisted behind his back with Rolfe sitting on top of him. "Quit fighting, you miserable excuse for a human," the sheriff shouted.

Louis cocked his gun. "Or we could end this right now." With the click of the hammer, the man quit fighting and the room grew quiet. That's when the door opened and there stood Charley, gun in hand.

He ran to his father and threw his arms around him. "How'd I do, Pa?"

"You did fine, son." Louis held his son in a tight hug and murmured, "You helped save Miss Teacher."

John rose from the floor and hurried to Lila, pale and shaking, and pulled her into his arms. She spoke through tears. "John, I knew you'd come. I knew—" Her head rolled back, and John caught her before she slumped to the floor.

Blood trickled from her head. John eased her to the floor away from the broken glass and tenderly brushed back her hair. Her scalp had been grazed by the bullet that ricocheted off the ceiling, leaving a flesh wound but fortunately nothing more. Still, it was bleeding steadily, and he knew it had to be staunched.

He spoke to Mrs. Lundstrom. "Ma'am, I could use some help here. She's got a head wound."

Mrs. Lundstrom quickly untied her apron and knelt beside John, pressing the cloth against the wound. "Hold this, I'll get more," and went to a cupboard. The two of them attended to Lila while the sheriff finished binding the hands and feet of their prisoner and sat him on the kitchen floor propped up against a wall.

"What are we gonna do with him?" Louis asked, nodding toward the prisoner.

"Take him back to Council Grove where he'll face charges of kidnapping and, if we can get proof, murder," the sheriff. "Gives me great satisfaction." He turned to the Lundstroms. "Sorry you folks got dragged into this mess. Looks like this outlaw gave you a broken nose."

"My nose will heal," Rolfe said. "Miriam and I are all right. That's what matters."

Slowly, they began to put things right in the farmhouse. Miriam cleaned and wrapped Lila's wound. John and Louis carried her to bed in a small room at the back of the house where she continued to sleep undisturbed. The men swept up the broken glass and boarded up the open window.

Later the group sat around the kitchen table, and the sheriff gave the Lundstroms details about Lila's kidnapping and their search for her over the past week.

"She's going to be all right, isn't she?" Charley looked at the adults around the table, his young face drawn with worry.

"She's going to be fine, thanks to you, Charley," John said. "You did a very brave thing. We couldn't have saved her without you."

Charley blinked away tears that threatened to fill his eyes. "But she didn't wake up. When you carried her to bed, she was still asleep."

"Miss Teacher is very weak, son. She needs to rest," his father added.

"She's very special to all of you," Rolfe said. "She's welcome to stay here while she recovers."

Miriam nodded. "As long as needed." She paused, looking into the faces of the men who had come to find Lila. "Thank you for rescuing your friend—and us. We are in your debt."

John felt a surge of gratitude for the Lundstroms and especially for his companions. Against great odds, they had found their quarry and would bring him to justice. But that wasn't the end of the mission for John. Like Charley, he worried when Lila had not woken after they treated her head wound. The longer she slept, the more concerned he became. It wasn't a good sign.

Chapter Forty-Six

After a persuasive interrogation by the sheriff with Louis and John looking on, the kidnapper revealed his identity as Bill Skaggs, hired by Charles Bonner to return his daughter to him for the sum of fifty dollars.

"Bonner told me she was his only kin, that she stole his money when she run off," Skaggs said.

"I know for a fact Lila didn't steal from her stepfather," John said, infuriated.

"Why were you heading to Denver?" the sheriff asked Skaggs.

Skaggs hesitated a beat before answering. "To git more money for her."

No sooner were those words uttered than John lunged at Skaggs and wrapped both his hands around the man's throat. "You miserable—"

It took both Louis and the sheriff to pry John's hands loose and pull him off Skaggs. Countless times since this nightmare began, he'd imagined serving his own brand of justice to this scoundrel. When he finally cooled down, he walked the hobbled prisoner to the barn with Louis and the sheriff where they took shifts guarding Skaggs during the night.

When John wasn't on duty in the barn, he returned to the room where Lila slept in a small bed beside a single window that looked out onto the prairie. He kept watch at her bedside until sleep overtook him and he lay down on his bedroll.

Early the next morning after a rancher's breakfast, as Miriam liked to call it, Louis and the sheriff mounted up for the return to Council Grove. The prisoner, hands bound tight, sat on his horse that trailed the sheriff's, and Charley assumed his usual place riding with his pa. The Lundstroms sent them off with ample provisions in their saddlebags.

Frost covered the ground and chilled the air as John bid farewell from the porch steps. "Lila and I will be along as soon as she's strong enough to travel."

"Hope that's soon, my friend." Louis tipped his hat. Charley imitated his dad, and the gesture brought a smile to John's lips.

"Safe travel, sheriff. I'll rest easy when I know our prisoner is behind bars," John said.

"You and me both. Take care," the sheriff nodded in farewell. The riders turned their horses and took to the trail in a steady gallop.

John stood with Lundstroms, watching until they were out of sight and headed back inside. "Care for any more breakfast?" Miriam asked the two men.

"Time to start chores," Rolfe answered. He gave Miriam a kiss on the cheek and pulled a wool cap over his head. "See you around noon." He gave his wife a reassuring smile and left for the barn.

"I wouldn't mind more coffee, thank you." John said.

He carried his cup to Lila's room and sat by her bed watching her sleep, then gazing out the window, all the while willing her to wake up.

By afternoon John was stir crazy. There was no change in Lila's condition, and he felt helpless in caring for her. He asked the Lundstroms if he should find a doctor. Was there even a doctor to be had in the vicinity? Miriam said they had a friend in the next town, the wife of their minster, who was a midwife and helped out with medical matters whenever she could. Maybe she could help. John was willing to try anything and planned to go the next morning.

"Who do I ask for?"

"Mrs. Johnson," Miriam replied.

"Mrs. Johnson? Wait. And her husband's a minister?" John pieced the information together. "Have they been here long?"

"Only a few months. Why?"

"It can't be . . . but maybe it is. I think I know them," he grinned, "from Council Grove."

The next morning, with spirits high, he rode the two miles to the tiny town of Baxter. He hoped knowing Lila and having shared past experiences would somehow give Mrs. Johnson insight into healing Lila. He found the Johnsons easily enough in one of the few frame buildings on the Main Street which served as a church. Miriam said the Johnsons lived upstairs.

The door opened. "Yes? Can I help you?"

"Mrs. Johnson, it's John Reynolds from Council Grove. From the boarding house. Remember me?"

A moment's hesitation and the recognition flooded back. "Oh, my gracious! John Reynolds. Of course." She reached up and pulled him into a hug. "George," she called over her shoulder. "Come see who's here." She held the door wide. "Whatever brings you to Baxter?"

John's breath caught. "It's Lila. I need your help."

John unwound the story of Lila's abduction, the capture of Bill Skaggs, and Lila's head wound suffered during the ordeal.

"Of course, I'll do what I can," Mrs. Johnson said. I'll pack my case, and we can go after we have something proper to eat."

Pastor Johnson smiled. "Thelma always makes sure the stomach is full before taking on a big task such as this one. We'll take our wagon after we eat."

They arrived at Lundstroms early afternoon, and Miriam spoke with Mrs. Johnson before taking her to Lila's room. "She swallowed some water for the first time," Miriam said. "Her eyelids fluttered, too. Both good signs."

"Indeed, that is," agreed Mrs. Johnson. She bent over Lila. "My dear girl, what has happened to you?" She held Lila's wrist, taking her pulse and ran her fingers over her abrasions. "I suppose this happened during her kidnapping."

John nodded.

She shook her head in disgust at the treatment Lila received at the hands of her abductor. She listened to Lila's heart and checked the wound on her head. "Her heart sounds good. The human body can often heal itself. How many days were they on the run?"

"Caught up with them on the fifth day," John said.

"Exposed to the elements at night with little nourishment for four days, I suspect she needs more time to rest and recuperate after all she's been through." Mrs. Johnson leaned over Lila again and cupped her cheek with tenderness. "If there's no change in the morning, we'll give her a stimulant, if that's all right with you, John. In the meantime, I'll make up some beef broth and see if she'll swallow some of it."

**

Lila stared at the ceiling in the darkness not knowing where she was. The bed was comfortable, the pillow stuffed with feathers she thought, the quilt snug and warm. It was safe here. No light came through the window near her bed. She blinked and rolled her head to one side. There was a person, sleeping peacefully on the floor beside her bed. She couldn't tell who it was, but she had felt the presence before. Maybe they would bring water. Her throat was parched.

"Water." She didn't recognize her raspy voice.

The person on the floor stirred, then sat upright in an instant. "Lila." He was on his knees, beside her bed, cradling her. He was weeping.

"John?"

He swallowed before attempting to speak. "I'm here."

"Oh, John, it's you . . ." she stopped to take a breath. "I'm so glad it's you." She gathered her strength, pulling him close as the memories returned and filled her eyes with tears. "I remember now, I remember everything."

He held her gently and whispered, "Everything's going to be all right." He reached for the cup on the nightstand and brought it to her lips.

She sipped the water, then looked into his eyes. "I was so afraid I'd never see you again." The tears spilled over.

"I wasn't going to let that happen."

"Don't leave."

"Never." He supported her head next to his, his fingers gently wound through her hair.

Her voice was stronger. "Because I don't know what I'd do if I lost you."

They held on to each other in the darkness, in the stillness, and the only thing that mattered was the presence of the other.

**

John woke before Lundstroms and Johnsons the next morning and waited impatiently to tell them the good news. "She woke up in the night. She remembers everything." The words tumbled out in joyous relief. "I think she's going to be all right." He couldn't stop smiling, nor could he sit still.

"That's very good news indeed," Mrs. Johnson said. "Miriam, why don't you and I check on her and see if she has an appetite?"

"Mrs. Johnson, is it really you?" Lila couldn't believe her eyes upon seeing her old friend. "I'm not dreaming, am I?"

"I'm here in the flesh, Lila, and George is here, too. John brought us from Baxter to help in your recovery." She smiled fondly at Lila. "Now, what would you like for breakfast?"

Miriam prepared bacon and eggs while Mrs. Johnson brewed tea with ginger root sweetened with honey.

John brought her tray of food to the bedroom. "This may sound silly," he began with some hesitation, "but do you mind if I sit with you while you eat?" He lowered into the chair beside her bed. "Seeing you awake—it's all I've hoped for the past two days, and now that your eyes are open, I don't want to miss a minute." Without being obvious, he studied her as though reassuring himself she was fully awake and finally safe from the torment she had endured.

Propped up with pillows, Lila spoke between forkfuls of food. "This would be embarrassing if I wasn't so hungry that I don't care." She buttered a biscuit and ate it between sips of the soothing tea. After finishing her plate, she leaned back against the headboard and let her eyes rest on John, taking in his every detail. It brought comfort. "There's something I have to tell you, something I promised myself I'd do if I ever saw you again."

John heard the seriousness in her voice and waited.

"After all this time, after everything that's happened, I've never told you how I feel about you." She glanced down at her hands, folded in her lap, then returned her gaze to John. "I've been afraid to admit how much you mean to me. Afraid because I've cared for you for a long time—since we won the three-legged race at the school picnic. Since we sat together on the blanket and ate fried chicken. Since Fanny came and the two of you broke my heart, and I swore I'd never let anyone hurt me the way losing you hurt me then."

"Lila—"

"Please, let me finish. Then Fanny left but I was still afraid, that is, until I was kidnapped, and I was faced with never seeing you again and you never knowing . . ."

"That I am more than just your friend?" If Lila had never seen hope in John's face, she did in this moment.

Lila's lips trembled. "So much more."

John leaned forward and took her hand. "Lila, there's something I must tell you. You may think I chose Fanny before I chose you. That's not true. You are not my second choice, you are my first and only choice. I've known from the moment you first asked me what I was reading in the dining room at Beatty's stagecoach stop. I've known since I looked you in the eye and saw the fear and courage of someone escaping a frightful father. I may not have been ready to admit it then—"

"Me neither. But I am a now," Lila said.

They spoke at the same moment, their voices in unison. "I love you."

John held her in his gaze until Lila's breath caught in her chest. "There's something I've been wanting to do for a very long time . . ." He reached under her chin and gently drew her face toward his until their lips met in a warm and tender kiss that Lila wished would last forever.

Chapter Forty-Seven

After caring for Lila for two days, assisting with wound care and providing hearty meals, the Johnsons returned to Baxter confident she was making a more than satisfactory recovery. The graze on her scalp showed no signs of infection, but Mrs. Johnson left an extra bar of lye soap for cleaning the wound should it be required. Everyday Lila's strength improved. The weather remained fair, and she borrowed a warm wool coat from Miriam for short walks with John, lengthening them as she felt stronger. The color returned to her cheeks. By the end of the week, she convinced John she was ready to return to Council Grove.

The next morning before the sun was up, John and Lila said goodbye to the Lundstroms. Miriam gave Lila long underwear and wool stockings which she gladly wore under a wool sweater and skirt. John bought a small ax and ammunition at the tiny mercantile in Baxter the day before. Rolfe and Miriam made sure their saddle bags were bulging with food.

Lila hugged Miriam. "I'll never be able to repay your kindness. Thank you from the bottom of my heart."

"Seeing you healthy again is all the thanks we need." Miriam pulled back and studied Lila. "You know, if there's something going on between you two," she nodded toward John, "Rolfe and I want to know about it. Hear me?" She grinned.

"I'll write you a letter. I promise." Lila hugged her again.

John grasped Rolfe's hand. "Thank you, Rolfe, for everything. We certainly didn't mean to cause you and Miriam trouble. We are grateful for your help."

"You are fine folks. We wish you every good fortune." He slapped John on the back. "God speed."

They mounted John's horse, Lila in front, and waved one final time before turning down the road to the trail that led back to Council Grove.

**

The return trip home was the opposite of her forced travel west as a captive. What had been a nightmare with her abductor was now a journey of reassurance and contentment with John. Where she had endured a disgusting, ruthless reprobate for five days, John's company was kind and considerate. He was nothing short of a prince. He inquired into her well-being nearly every mile until she protested, she was doing fine, thank you very much, and asked him not to fuss over her. Lila rode in front of him, his one arm holding the reins, the other around her waist while they covered the miles at a steady lope.

The morning cooperated with unseasonable warmth so late in the autumn. "Enjoy it while it lasts," John cautioned. "We both know what November is really like."

After a full day of riding, they camped near a grove of cedar trees which provided shelter from the wind that had picked up. They both felt a drop in temperature. John hacked branches from a tree to build a fire and Lila boiled coffee and cooked beans they ate with corn bread. He added what little wood was available to the fire, worrying the nighttime exposure would cause Lila to relapse so soon after her recovery. When it was time to turn in, they lay down beside the campfire and John wrapped the two of them together in a wool blanket.

"This may seem highly improper, Miss Bonner," he explained, sounding every bit the school master. "I'm doing this for altruistic reasons, your health being the most important."

Lila leaned into him and whispered, "Body heat is important, Mr. Reynolds, in this cold night air."

He wrapped his arms around her and pulled her close to his body.

A divine way to spend the night, she thought, wrapped in John Reynolds' arms.

The mild weather disappeared overnight. They woke to a brisk wind out of the north which persisted all morning while they rode east under a sky thick with clouds. Swirls of dirt kicked up in their faces. With bent heads, John pulled his bandanna over his nose, and Lila covered her mouth and nose with her scarf. Whenever the wind died down, they raised their heads, took stock of their location, and pressed on until the next gust of wind took their breath away. Lila knew to answer John before he asked. "I'm doing fine," she'd say, but Lila didn't think he believed her.

It was midday when they heard the train whistle.

"There's a train?" Lila shouted through her scarf.

John pulled the reins to halt the horse. "Over that way somewhere," he hollered back to her, looking to where the sound had come from.

"Why are you stopping?" The wind sucked her words away.

"I have an idea." He turned the horse to the north, nudged its flanks, and they galloped across the prairie toward the sound of the train.

**

John and Lila stood on the platform beside the hissing train in the tiny town of Ellsworth having a heated discussion with the conductor.

"You don't seem to understand," John continued, undeterred. "My companion is recovering from an illness, and it's important for her health that we continue our journey to Council Grove on the train."

"I understand, sir. What *you* don't understand is we don't run a charity. If you can't pay for your tickets, you can't ride the train." The young man squared his shoulders with an air of authority, flashing the buttons of his uniform.

"I can pay for one ticket now and I assure you, I will wire money for the other ticket when we reach Council Grove."

"What seems to be the hold up, Harry?" The station master appeared from inside the small frame building that served as the station for the Kansas Pacific Line.

"These folks were asking about riding the train but don't have enough money for two tickets, sir." The young conductor resumed his rigid stance.

The station master scrutinized John and Lila with an experienced eye. "Where you folks heading?"

"Council Grove," John replied. "My companion, Miss Bonner, is recovering from an illness. I assure you, I'm good for the other ticket once we reach home."

"Council Grove, you say? You must know my brother, Jeremy Watson."

John brightened in recognition. "You mean Doc Watson? Of course, we know him. One of the finest men in our town."

"Well, now isn't it a small world." The station master stroked his bearded chin. "Your friend been ill, you say?"

"Yes sir. She's been through quite an ordeal."

Lila stood at John's side and gave a polite nod.

"Hmm." He scratched the back of his head in contemplation. "Come inside with me. Let's see if we can work something out."

Ten minutes later Lila climbed aboard the train with the assistance of the surly conductor, her ticket in hand, while John was securing his horse in the livestock car. Lila sat next to a window and heaved a sigh of relief so audible, other passengers turned to stare.

When John slid into the seat beside her, he said, "Now, isn't this better?"

She beamed. "How were we lucky enough to manage this?"

"I wrote a note of debt to a kind-hearted station master who believes in an honest man's word." John continued, "He said we should get off at Abilene. That would leave about forty miles as the crow flies to Council Grove. A long day's ride but maybe we could do it with a horse that's rested."

Lila gave a contented sigh and leaned against him, her head on his shoulder. He took her hand in his. "This is nice," she said. They stared out the window as the train jerked away from the station with a long blast of the whistle.

As the train gained speed, the rolling hills flew by. The motion of the train rocked Lila, and her eyelids grew heavy until she caught sight of a dark cloud on the horizon. She sat up and blinked. "John, what's that?" She pointed out the window at the cloud which was growing larger and was moving toward the train.

John leaned over her shoulder and peered out the window. "I can't be sure. Looks like a dust storm." By now other passengers noticed the same phenomenon and spoke up in curious and excited voices. In the next moments everyone in their car saw the cloud for what it was—dust and dirt thrown into the air by stampeding buffalo.

"Good heavens," Lila gasped, "they're headed straight for us!" Even through the closed windows and over the sound of the locomotive, they heard the heavy rumble of beating hooves. "John, are we doomed?" Lila asked frantically as she watched the approaching herd.

John's face tensed as he gripped her hand. "I don't think they'll charge headlong into the train." The engineer blew the whistle repeatedly, and just as the buffalo reached the train, they changed course, running alongside the tracks. Through the cloud of dust Lila and John watched the shaggy heads and powerful bodies race by their window in a deafening noise.

The beasts ran, wave after wave, as though trained to keep in stride for if one faltered, it would have been trampled. The engineer blew the whistle again and again, and the herd veered off at an angle away from the tracks. When they saw the last of the herd thundering away from the train into the distance, Lila and John fell back against their seats exhausted.

"That was terrifying!" Lila's heart pounded in her chest.

John looked awe struck. "I've never seen anything like it. Absolutely amazing."

Passengers who had grouped by the windows to witness the stampede shared their amazement. They calmed themselves and without hurry returned to their seats. Relief was palpable. An elderly man coughed and opened a newspaper he'd been reading. A mother shushed a crying baby. Conversations resumed.

"I hope I'm *never* that close to a stampede again," Lila declared.

"It was frightening," John agreed, "but, I have to admit, a bit exciting."

"Exciting? I've had enough excitement for nine lives, don't you think?"

"When you put it that way . . ." John put his arm around her with a reassuring smile.

**

The sun rode high overhead as John's horse ambled down Main Street in Council Grove, its two riders taking in every aspect of the town. There were people shopping on this late Saturday morning at Last Chance loading bags of flour and corn meal into a wagon, and Lila observed townspeople exchanging greetings in front of the bank. Two boys chased each other around a water trough. Somewhere a dog barked. Nothing looked sweeter in that moment than Council Grove, Kansas.

It had taken a day and a half from Abilene since following the trail made for a longer journey than they initially thought. John rode up to the boarding house and dismounted. Lila slid down into his arms before she noticed a handmade sign in the front window. It read, "Welcome home Lila."

At that moment, the door flew open, and Mrs. Bauer stood there, her arms open, her eyes glistening with tears. "Lila—" she choked on her name.

Lila dissolved into tears and fell into her arms. "Mrs. B," she sobbed.

Mrs. Bauer wrapped Lila in her arms. "You're home," she murmured again and again. "You've no idea how I've been praying for you."

Lila heard a shriek from across the street. "Lila, Lila!" Stacy ran full speed from Hays House and encircled Lila and Mrs. Bauer in her arms.

The next thing Lila knew, Mr. and Mrs. Hays were at her side. Moments later Superintendent Piper and his wife appeared, then Sheriff Jenkins and Doc Watson, Pastor Higgins and Thomas Hill, Louis Bellmard and Seth Williams—it seemed the whole town appeared out of nowhere, smiling, hugging, laughing, and cheering to welcome her home. Through her flood of tears, she saw children, parents, neighbors, and acquaintances. One small body pushed through the crowd and rushed forward, grabbing her in a fierce hug around the waist.

Charley Bellmard.

He looked up at her, not letting go. "Miss Teacher, are you better?"

"I'm much better, Charley." She bent down and hugged him for a long while. When she finally straightened, she said, "I understand I owe you a big thank you. You helped save my life."

Charlie blushed with an embarrassed grin.

Lila linked arms with Mrs. Bauer and faced the gathering. She took a big breath. "It's so good to be home. I—" Her voice broke, and the crowd applauded while she swiped away tears. "I'm overwhelmed by your kindness. Truly." She took another deep breath and turned to John. "There's some folks I want to thank for rescuing me. Without them, I wouldn't be standing here now. They are brave men who'd never call themselves heroes. But I will."

Lila paused before she called out her rescuers. "Sheriff Jenkins, Mr. Bellmard, Charley, and Mr. Reynolds I owe you—" her voice wavered again, "I owe you my life. If I spend the rest of my days thanking you, it won't be enough. God bless you. And bless the folks of Council Grove for kindly giving me such a warm welcome home."

The crowd clapped with emotion as raw as Lila's, the ladies fighting back tears, some of the men spiking the crowd with "hurrahs." She looked across the crowd and saw Matteo standing off to one side, alone. She waved her arm and called his name, and he waved back with a broad smile. Lila shook every hand, receiving hugs and good wishes, before the townsfolk slowly dispersed to go about their business. When she looked for Matteo again, he was gone.

Lila, John, and Mrs. Bauer retired to the boarding house kitchen where Lila and John shed their heavy coats, sinking wearily into chairs, and Mrs. Bauer lit a fire before filling the teakettle.

She looked at them, her face flooded with joy that they were safe once again, snug in the kitchen at the boarding house. "Would you like some tea?"

The simple, ordinary question brought a fresh flow of tears to Lila. "It's so good to be home," was all she could utter.

Mrs. Bauer pulled Lila into her arms again. "It's ever so good to have you home, my dear."

Chapter Forty-Eight

"You two are baking up a storm." John peered over Lila's shoulder while she measured raisins and poured them into a mixing bowl.

She wiped her hands on her apron, humming softly. "That we are." She reached for a large knife and began chopping walnuts.

"What are you making?"

"Fruit cake," Mrs. Bauer replied. "My mother's recipe." She nodded toward a yellowed paper with faded ink script laying on the counter while she buttered two baking pans.

"But Christmas is three weeks away. Isn't it too soon?" John asked.

"Not for fruit cake. It needs to cure about a month. We're cutting the time short by a week, but it'll still be delicious, you can count on that." Mrs. Bauer gave a decisive nod.

With Lila's return to Council Grove, the whole town had turned its attention to Thanksgiving and now Christmas. Lila would have gladly forgotten the whole ordeal of kidnapping and focused on the holidays but, with Mrs. Bauer's help, understood something so traumatic might leave lingering scars. She fell into her routine with ease and embraced her work at the boarding house with Mrs. Bauer—mopping, cooking, and laundering—as a new lease on life and her hours at school with John and the children as the greater joy it had always been. The visible scars on her wrists and scalp would fade in due time.

It was the invisible scars John worried about.

"There's something I want to talk over with you," John said as they sat in the parlor that evening. It was particularly cold, and the kindling popped as it burned in the stove. "I know we'd like to think that awful kidnapping business is behind us, now that you're home safe." He leaned forward, his forearms on his knees, and studied the braided rug.

Lila pulled her shawl tighter around her shoulders and waited.

He turned to her. "Truth is, I think there's unfinished business for me to take care of."

Lila looked at him evenly. "What kind of unfinished business?"

"Your pa. He's still out there, and he's still a problem."

Lila was silent, then spoke. "What would you do about Pa?" Her voice quivered ever so slightly.

"Go see him. Tell him you are off limits, that he has to answer to me from now on."

"See him?" Lila put her hand to her chest. "Oh, John, I don't think so. Couldn't we send word to the Beattys instead? Tell him any further plots against me are useless?"

"That's not the same, Lila. I want to see him face to face, make certain he understands."

"And if he doesn't?" Lila's voice was barely audible.

"I'll find a way to make him understand."

The mantel clock marked time in the silence. "When would you go?" Lila asked, not really wanting to know.

"The sooner the better. Maybe before Christmas." John waited for Lila's reaction.

"But the weather? In December . . . is that wise?" A frown creased her forehead.

John took her hand in his. "I'll take the stage. That way I won't be as exposed to the elements, and it takes less than two days.

"I'm coming with you."

"What? No. You've been through enough." John was adamant.

"I'm the reason for all this," Lila said. "If you're determined to go, I'm determined to go with you."

John saw the look in her eyes, the set of her chin, and knew the odds of his winning the argument were slim to none.

**

Unfinished business. That was what John had called her pa.

Lila turned it over in her mind and knew he was right. As much as she didn't want to admit it, facing Pa and her past was something she had to do. She had to put an end to it once and for all. On the way back to Council Grove, there had been another troublesome worry she and John had not spoken about. Lila dreaded testifying at Bill Skaggs' kidnapping and murder trial. There was no way she couldn't testify—she was the victim of the kidnapping and the only witness to the murder.

The afternoon they returned home, Sheriff Jenkins pulled them aside and said he needed to talk to them as soon as possible. He came by the boarding house that evening.

"Sheriff, good of you to stop by." John and the sheriff shook hands warmly.

"A lot has happened since we left you at the Lundstroms."

Lila arched her eyebrows. "Oh?"

"You haven't heard?" the sheriff asked.

"Heard what?" John asked.

"It happened the second night after we left," the sheriff explained. He sat stiffly in one of the parlor chairs. "Everyone was bedded down for the night—Louis, Charley, and Skaggs. It was my turn to watch Skaggs. I must have dozed off. Next thing I knew, he was sneaking for Louis' gun and grabbed it even though his hands were bound. He came at me, gun pointed, and I shot him through the heart where he stood."

John and Lila sat with their mouths agape.

Lila found her voice. "He's dead then." She blinked as the words sank in.

"Most surely he is," the sheriff said. "I regret not bringing him back to Council Grove. He took one of our own and should have faced justice here." The sheriff looked away momentarily. "Was my fault he tried to escape."

John expelled a breath. "There's no fault on your part, sheriff. The man was evil through and through. It was a fitting end if you ask me." He stroked the dark stubble on his face. "You know, I was close to stringing him up to one of those cottonwoods on the Lundstroms ranch the night before you left."

The sheriff gave a harsh laugh. "Thought as much myself."

"So, it's over," Lila said. "No more Bill Skaggs. Ever again."

"He's six feet under in the Kansas prairie, Miss Bonner. And just between us, it gives me great pleasure to say that."

A look of understanding passed silently among the three friends.

**

Lila knew John and Mrs. Bauer were up to something. The following week whenever she happened upon them whether it was in the kitchen before breakfast or during clean up after supper, they abruptly stopped talking the minute she appeared. She ignored it for a few days and decided it was none of her business until, as Matteo would call her, *Lila curioso* could stand it no longer. When she confronted them, they brushed it off as nothing for her to be concerned about, exchanged a smile, and went about their business.

"Nothing for me to be concerned about? Humph. I'll decide that when I find out what's going on." Lila discussed it with the pillowcase she had been patching. She folded the rest of the laundry and stacked the sheets in the cupboard in Mrs. Bauer's room. "What could the two of them possibly be up to?"

That Saturday morning Lila found a note slipped under her door when she woke. Wrapped in her shawl, she sat on her bed and read it:

> Miss Bonner,
> The pleasure of your company is requested at four o'clock this afternoon in the parlor. Wear your cloak and gloves for a short walk to our destination.
> Yours truly,
> John Reynolds

Lila couldn't suppress a grin while she waited for John in the parlor, nearly overcome with curiosity. It was early December, and they were walking somewhere—for what purpose, she had no idea. She loved the mystery of it all and had to credit John and Mrs. Bauer. They had kept their secret quite well.

"Miss Bonner, punctual as always." John swept into the parlor wearing his heavy coat with a lantern in his hand and a grin on his face.

"John, what is all this?" Lila sounded exactly like an excited schoolgirl and gathered her composure. "I mean, Mr. Reynolds, what have you planned?"

"You shall see, Miss Bonner," and extended his elbow.

The frosty air nipped their noses as they walked down Main Street, but Lila was more interested in the need for a lantern since the sun was out. When they turned their steps and mounted the hill toward the school, she had to admit her disappointment.

"We're going to school? There's something new to show me?"

"Something different," John answered mysteriously.

Lila kept her hand tucked in the crook of his arm until he opened the school door and ushered her inside.

Fading afternoon light from the windows slanted across the room. At the front stood the school Christmas tree the older boys had been tasked to cut down earlier in the week, decorated by the children in red and green paper chains and hand-crafted snowflakes. Two flickering lanterns flanked John's desk which was covered with an ivory tablecloth, a wicker basket placed in the center, and a chair on each side. A fire burned in the stove.

Lila didn't move. "The room looks beautiful." She turned to him. "How did you do all this?"

"I had help," he smiled shyly. "I know how much you like picnics, and we never got around to having one last summer. So, Mrs. Bauer and I—"

"—succeeded in surprising me," Lila finished with a laugh.

John guided her to the table and took her cloak. "Stacy helped, too."

"Stacy? Did everyone in town know about this?"

John poured glasses of homemade wine compliments of Mrs. Bauer's friends, the Hoffmans, and they ate the delicious contents of the basket—fried chicken and apple turnovers. "This reminds me of the school picnic last spring," Lila said between bites, "watching you lick your fingers while you ate fried chicken. I couldn't take my eyes off you, even then." She felt herself redden under John's amused gaze.

"And I remember when you arrived at the picnic wearing that green dress. You took my breath away, Lila." She saw color creep into his cheeks and loved him for it. "I think it was the first time I really noticed those beautiful eyes of yours. Did you know they have flecks of gold?"

They talked as they ate, discussing plans for the next school term, the upcoming holidays, the approaching winter, and poured a second glass of the fruity wine. The conversation flowed easily as it always did between them.

"I'll have time over the Christmas holiday to see how many requirements you have left for graduation," John said. "You're almost finished."

"Math and geography exams left if I remember right," Lila said. "I should have time to catch up on my studies during the break." She stared into the flickering lanterns and released a contented sigh. "You went to a lot of trouble for our picnic today, John. We should have a toast, don't you think?"

"I agree. But before we do that . . .there was another reason I wanted to have a special dinner tonight."

Lila tilted her head. "Oh?"

John rose and walked around the table to her chair. He stood awkwardly for a moment, a look of hesitation on his face.

Lila frowned. "What is it?"

John bent on one knee, and Lila's breath caught. He cleared his throat and took her hand in his. "Lila, I can't promise you riches or a life with no hardships. The one thing I can promise, you will always be loved. I will love you every day with all my heart for the rest of my life. Will you do me the honor of being my wife and making me the happiest man in the world?"

She held his hand tight, lost in his deep brown eyes that were so honest and reassuring, reflecting the man of strength and honor she had grown to love. "Yes, yes, yes, I will be your wife," she whispered through her tears and fell into his arms.

When he released her and leaned back, John held her face and wiped away the tears on her cheek with his thumb. "I have something I want to give you." From his pocket he pulled a bracelet of braided ribbons—gold, green, and burgundy—he slipped over Lila's wrist. "I wanted you to have something pretty on your wrist, something from me in the way of a promise." He paused. "These colors remind me of you."

Lila ran her fingers over the silky ribbons. "I will cherish it, John."

John brought Lila to her feet and slowly gathered her into his arms. His kiss sent shivers cascading over her from head to toe, his breath sweet and warm, his lips lingering on hers. He whispered in her ear, "I will never tire of this."

"Nor I," Lila answered, her body quivering, the room spinning, her heart singing.

Chapter Forty-Nine

The stagecoach pulled away from Hays House with a full load of passengers, the team of horses snorting frosty streams into the frigid air under the crack of the reinsman's whip. Lila and John, bundled in layers of warm clothing, huddled under a buffalo robe with their feet resting on hot bricks wrapped in an old wool blanket. The canvass curtains were securely tied, but the bitter wind persisted in blowing in around its edges.

Insulated by the thick buffalo fur, Lila leaned against John for reassurance. She had written to Mrs. Beatty saying she was coming to visit but hadn't explained the reason why, nor did she know if her letter would reach the Beattys before she and John arrived. Even though Lila had been certain she wanted to accompany John on this trip, the closer it came to reality, the more nervous she became.

She caught a glimpse of the frozen landscape through the edge of the canvas. The sun peeked in and out of clouds casting momentary sunshine across the snow-dusted hills, much like her mood shifting from hopeful to fearful of what lay ahead in confronting Pa. Had it only been nine months since she had run away? More like a lifetime. She had left out of fear and desperation; she was returning as the fiancé of John Reynolds. But before she could take the next step and become Mrs. Reynolds, she had to face the girl left behind, that vulnerable girl still buried deep inside that she had left at Beatty's stagecoach stop—Lila Bonner.

**

Lila cast a quick glance in the gathering dusk at the horse handlers after the stage pulled into the stable yard at the Beattys. Pa wasn't there. Clutching her cloak against the wind, she dashed out of the cold into the house, John close behind carrying their bags. Once inside she came to an abrupt stop, unprepared for the wave of memories that swept over her inside the Beatty's house—the happy days with Mama serving meals to Santa Fe travelers but also those last desperate hours under this roof before she decided to run away from Pa.

Mrs. Beatty was bent over a boiling pot on the stove. "Sit anywhere," she directed the travelers without looking up, her oldest daughter Alice working at her side. "Food will be on the table right quick."

"Mrs. Beatty," Lila called out from where she stood.

The woman straightened and turned. Her eyes widened. "Sakes alive, is that you, Lila Bonner?"

Lila crossed the room, and Mrs. Beatty hugged Lila to her ample bosom. "What a surprise this is. Welcome back, darlin."

Lila returned Mrs. Beatty's affectionate bear hug. "It's so good to see you," she managed to say while her dear friend squeezed the breath out of her.

Mrs. Beatty peppered Lila and John with questions while she served the meal, and they did their best to answer while diving into the hearty food and comforting warmth of the room. Yes, John had been here months before as a passenger traveling west at the same time Lila decided to run away. "And now we're engaged to be married," Lila beamed.

"Engaged to be married?" Mrs. Beatty gasped and caught the pan of biscuits before they slipped from her grasp. "I'm thrilled for you, my dear. You deserve every happiness," and began another round of hugs for Lila and this time included John.

Twenty minutes later, right on schedule, all the passengers heading east were loaded onto the stage, and the dining room settled into the quiet of the evening. Alice helped with clean up and was on her way upstairs when Mrs. Beatty called after her, "Tell those young 'uns to get their night shirts on, and I'll be up soon." She sat with Lila and John at one of the trestle tables. "So what brought on this visit?" She wore an expectant look. "You could have written us about your engagement."

"Nothing gets past you," Lila said, then hesitated. "I came to see Pa."

"I see." Mrs. Beatty frowned. "Do you think that's a good idea? I mean, the way you left and all."

"I need to clear the air, set things right with him. I didn't see him when we pulled in just now."

"He's in the barn I 'spect. Should be coming in for supper soon. He hasn't been well."

"Hasn't been well or drinking too much?"

"Nothin' gets past you either, Lila." She heaved a sigh. "Truth is, he's been goin' downhill since you left. Sleeps in the barn now or in the storeroom when it's too cold. That place you were living in has all but fallen to the ground. He's not the worker he used to be, but Mr. Beatty doesn't have the heart to let him go."

"If I may," John interrupted, "Mr. Beatty might think differently if he knew what Lila's Pa has been up to." He caught Lila's glance and reached for her hand.

Mrs. Beatty's eyebrows shot up. "Oh?"

Lila began with the morning of her kidnapping and recounted her harrowing experience. John added his perspective of the pursuit of Bill Skaggs with Sheriff Jenkins and the Bellmards. Mrs. Beatty's astonishment grew as the story unfolded. She was furious one minute, in tears the next. "This is beyond belief. It's like a made-up story, Lila." Her face grew grim, her jaw set. "And to think your pa who lives under this very roof set that evilness in motion." She slammed her fist to the table. "I'll not abide such a thing!" She stood, looking about the room, not sure where to direct her anger. "Somethin' has to be done. I'm not sure what, but somethin'."

"That's why I'm here," Lila said. "To face him one last time and put an end to his foolish and evil notions."

"Do what you have to, child," she said. "And we'll do what we have to do." She left the dining room and climbed the stairs to the family quarters.

**

"Maybe he's not coming in tonight," Lila said. She paced beside the table glancing toward the door with every rattling gust of wind.

"I should think he'd come in for supper *and* a warm place to sleep," John countered and in a gentle voice added, "Come sit, Lila. No sense in getting worked up."

The dining room door burst open with a freezing blast of air. It was Pa. He leaned against the door, forcing it shut and turned around. Lila stood motionless, staring at him.

"Li—la?" Her name stumbled on his tongue. "What . . . what are you doin' here?" He squinted at her as though trying to determine whether her visage was real or imagined. He took an unsteady step toward her. "I never thought—"

"You'd see me again? Or see me unless Bill Skaggs brought me here?"

Pa frowned. "Who?"

"Stop it, Pa. I know all about it. About how you hired him to bring me back here, how you *paid* him to do it. Twenty-five dollars down and twenty-five on delivery. Wasn't that the deal you made?" She spat the words out like bile in her throat. "How does a father do that, Pa? To a child. How?"

Pa moved forward on shaky legs and lowered himself to the table. The flickering kerosene lamps revealed deep lines in his face. His eyes were milky. He cleared his throat with a phlegmy cough, but his rattling wheeze persisted. "This Skaggs fellow told you a bunch of lies, Lila. You can't believe I'd do such a thing."

"You're too late, Pa. Skaggs knew too much to be lying." Lila sat opposite him at the table. "It's time you looked at yourself and see what I see."

Pa stuck his chin out. "And what's that?"

"A drunk old man who used to be my pa." Lila hoped the barb in her words would cut into his flesh. "We had a nice family once. Seven of us. Happy memories on the farm in Indiana." She leaned toward him, her voice rising. "You stole that from me. That's unforgivable." Her hands clenched on the table.

Pa leaned into her stare. "That's no way to talk to your pa."

"You're not my pa, not anymore. My pa's gone—drowned in a bottle of whiskey." Tears gathered in her eyes and spilled down her face.

"After Mama died, you were supposed to take care of me, but you didn't. You put your hands on me. Do you know what that does to a child? I was terrified of you. You forced me to run away from the last bit of family I had out here. I was all alone with no one to turn to. If that wasn't bad enough, you hired someone to kidnap me—*your supposed kin*—to force me back here with you. And for what reason? To live off my wages so you wouldn't have to work? To be your caretaker? To control my coming and going? To make my life a never-ending misery?" She was shaking with rage. "Whatever it was, Pa, it's over. You don't own me. I'm done with you!"

Pa didn't move. He looked to have grown smaller from the words Lila spoke.

John rose from the table and stood over Pa. "If Lila hadn't come with me, there's no telling if you'd still be breathing right now. I'll do anything to protect her, don't think I won't. That includes taking a life. You understand?"

Pa opened his mouth, then closed it and nodded.

"There's an end to it then," John said. "Lila and I will be leaving in the morning. You are to have nothing to do with her ever again."

"Just so you know," Lila said, "that friend of yours, Bill Skaggs, was a miserable human being. Our sheriff shot him dead when he tried to escape. You can take that as a warning." She rose, straightened her shoulders, and slipped her arm through John's. They turned their backs on Pa and climbed the stairs.

**

Lila slept deep and undisturbed. After breakfast they said goodbye to the Beattys and when the next stage heading west rattled into the stable yard, she and John gathered their bags, their buffalo robe, and readied for their return trip. As they boarded the stage, Pa left his place holding the lead horse and came to Lila.

"Lila, you can't leave like this." His voice was pleading.

"I have nothing more to say, Pa."

He persisted. "What did you say to Mr. Beatty?" Pa's voice had an edge. "He told me to clear out by the end of the week. He fired me. I have nowhere to go."

Lila leveled her gaze at Pa. "Looks like you have some fences to mend."

"But Lila, honey—"

John interceded and steadied Lila's elbow as she hoisted herself into the stage. John took his seat beside her and closed the door. The reinsman cracked his whip, and the coach jerked away.

Lila watched her father gaping at the departing coach. "He looks pitiful, doesn't he?"

John saw tears in Lila's eyes and reached for her hand. "Yes, he does. But it's his own doing."

"Mama always said we're supposed to forgive those who hurt us."

"I wish I could have known your mother. She sounds very wise—a lot like the daughter she raised." He gave Lila a tender smile.

Lila sniffed away her tears. "I can't forgive Pa. Not today. Maybe someday, but not today." She pulled the buffalo robe under her chin and leaned close to John, her heart overflowing with love for this wonderful man she was to marry.

Confronting Pa released Lila from a control she hadn't known was there. She had cleared out refuse from a dirty cellar, and now her house was in order. She was free to stake her claim on the future. With her head on John's shoulder, she recalled the hope she had when she ran away from Pa, how the words from her favorite poem gave her encouragement. Once again, she could hear the words ringing in her ear, not as the girl sewing and washing but the young lady cooking and cleaning—and teaching. Lila smiled at the addition to her poem. Soon she would become the "young wife at work" building a life with John.

As her thoughts clarified, Lila remembered something the sheriff had said about Bill Skaggs after the kidnapping: "He took one of our own and should have faced justice here." The sheriff was talking about *her*. Council Grove claimed her. She belonged to them, and they belonged to her.

The stagecoach bumped over the frozen ground through the spitting snow, and Lila warmed to a new idea—she was going home. To Council Grove.

Chapter Fifty

For Lila, it was a Christmas unlike any other.

On a frosty Christmas Eve parishioners crowded into the parlor at Pastor Higgins' home where he led the service with his wife, Cora, playing hymns on their old upright piano. The mood was buoyant, and Lila didn't think she'd ever heard *Good Christian Men Rejoyce* sung with such gusto or so off key. Even the *Silent Night* lullaby sounded strong and true as the melody soared through the little frame house.

Christmas Day the Hays family roasted turkeys and hosted Council Grove at their restaurant with everyone contributing whatever they could, however grand or simple: hams, potatoes, green beans, corn, relishes, apples and dried peaches, rolls and breads, cakes, pies, and fruitcake, and a hodge-podge of homebrewed beer and wine.

After dinner Mrs. Bauer, Lila and John returned to the parlor at the boarding house. John had cut down a cedar from the bluff not far from the Neosha for their Christmas tree. Mrs. Bauer searched through her sewing basket and found odds and ends of ribbon she and Lila tied to the branches of the tree. From a piece of tin John fashioned six candle holders they attached to the tree branches.

They watched Mrs. Bauer transform the tree as she lit the candles. "It's magical," Lila whispered. "We never had a tree like this. Truth be told, we didn't always have a tree."

"The candles are a tradition in Germany," Mrs. Bauer said, staring at the tiny flames. "I haven't had a tree for years. But thanks to the two of you . . ." her voice faltered.

They sat around the tree under the spell of the candlelight. John and Lila had agreed not to exchange gifts after incurring the unplanned cost of the coach fare to meet with Pa. They had a lifetime of Christmases to look forward to and were more than content with that. But Mrs. Bauer disappeared to her room and surprised them with gifts wrapped in plain brown paper tied in bright red ribbon. Her eyes sparkled. "Just a little something for each of you. Open them."

Lila went first and unwrapped a forest green wool hat and matching mittens. "Mrs. B, they're beautiful." She hopped up and twirled around the room, the new hat on her head as she waved her mittened hands in the air. "Thank you so much."

John opened his gift and unwound the longest, warmest muffler he'd ever seen. "I can wrap this around my neck three times," he exclaimed and proceeded to do just that. "It's ever so nice, Mrs. B, thank you."

"When did you find time to make these?" Lila asked.

"While I was waiting for you and John to come home. I had to do something with my worry. Turned to my knitting needles." She gave a brief sad smile. "It helped."

They ate molasses gingersnap cookies and kept a mindful eye on the glowing candles until the mantel clock struck eleven o'clock, the candles flamed low, and with warm embraces they said good night to each other and to Christmas.

**

The first week in January a snowstorm blew in from the west and buried Council Grove.

"Good thing we had such a grand time at Christmas," Lila said, looking out the window as the snow swirled into drifts up and down Main Street. "We may be stuck inside for a while."

Whenever there was a pause in the weather, the townspeople would hitch up their wagons and plow through the snow to Last Chance, the dry goods store, or wherever they had to travel, their horses beating down a path that would be obliterated with a second and third round of snow.

School was canceled until the weather improved and roads were passable since the children came to school on foot or by horseback or wagon. John kept busy chopping wood for the stoves, digging a path to the outhouse, and clearing the front boardwalk along Main Street. On the third day after the storm, he was able to make his way across Main Street to Last Chance and offered to help Thomas whenever his shipments arrived.

Travel on the Santa Fe Trail was at a standstill. The only lodgers at the boarding house were a woman and her elderly mother traveling back to Missouri after visiting family in western Kansas. Snowbound until the weather improved, they were quiet, undemanding boarders, affording Mrs. Bauer and Lila precious time for other projects.

"Maybe I can set a spell and work on this," Mrs. Bauer said. It was midday, a time when she never sat down, but here she was in the parlor beside the stove, her feet resting on a stool.

Lila poked her head into the room. "What are you working on?"

Mrs. Bauer smiled. "Something for you and John."

Lila came close and leaned over the handiwork. Mrs. Bauer was crocheting a delicate edge on a pair of pillowcases. "They're beautiful."

"For your hope chest, my dear." She continued skillfully hooking the thread in an intricate pattern. "Who knows, might have time to do more than one pair. Course Edna and I have to get started on your wedding quilt, too. There's so much to do."

Indeed, there was. Lila and John had set June 20 as their wedding day, and Lila was making lists. Mrs. Bauer offered them the largest bedroom in the boarding house after they were married, and Lila planned to create a homey space for them: a double bed, a dresser, two chairs, and a side table — all of which were begging for a cheerful rag rug which she was in the process of making. It would be a perfect place for the two of them to share an occasional supper in the privacy of their own cozy room.

Being snowbound gave Lila time to make wedding plans and finish requirements for graduation in May. One evening after the second snowstorm, she and John sat down at the dining room table surrounded by textbooks to determine what she had left to complete.

John read through his grade book. "You are lacking the final geography exam and two math exams. I'll help with algebra if you need it."

Lila groaned. "I do need help. I wish math was as easy as English."

"You'll figure it out." He flipped to a page in the math book. "Exercises on this page should help." Lila pulled out her tablet and began working through the problems. When she finished, he corrected her work and went over the mistakes she had made. "You have a better understanding of this than you think." He watched as she studied the corrections. "You know," he paused, "you might qualify as a substitute teacher when you receive your Kansas certificate."

Lila leaned forward. "Do you think so?"

"Some schools hire teachers with less education than you'll have when you graduate."

Lila expelled a burst of air with that dizzying thought. "Someday I could, perhaps, substitute here? In Council Grove?"

"If the occasion arises. I'll ask Mr. Piper. Besides," he continued, "this town is only going to grow. We should plan on the school growing, too."

Lila sat up, alert. "Any more of these annoying algebra problems left for me?"

**

Snow and freezing temperatures held Council Grove in a wintry grip during January and February. When school resumed, John did his best to continue lessons in spite of heavy rounds of snowfall which disrupted everyone's lives. Whenever the roads were passable, John and Lila checked on Matteo and the Bellmards. They put together a basket of food, bundled up in their warmest clothing, and rode old Daisy to either the Bellmard cabin or Matteo's cave. Bellmards were faring well during the bad weather. Louis did his trapping nearby and rarely left Charley alone. He made sure Charley attended school when the weather allowed, even taking him there by horseback on occasion.

Matteo was another matter. He insisted he was fine in his cave, and although the temperature inside was more moderate than outside, John and Lila were worried.

"Thomas Simpson is offering you a place in his barn any time you want to stay there," John said. "Come and go as you like—they don't mind." They stood near the entrance of Matteo's cave where he had a small fire burning.

"I appreciate the offer, but it's not necessary," Matteo countered.

Lila studied her stubborn friend. His eyes looked glassy, and underneath the layers of clothes he wore, she could tell he'd lost weight. She took his hand. It was frigid. "Would you spend just one night in their barn? If not for yourself, for me?"

Matteo looked down at his ragged shoes and was silent.

"I'd bring a pot of soup. Any kind you like."

"There's nothing to be worried about," John added. "I don't think you know how much folks in town care about you."

Matteo looked up, curious, interested. "Well, maybe—"

"I'll take that as a yes," Lila threw her arms around Matteo. "Come on. We'll walk there with you."

**

Winter relented and spring arrived in a muddy embrace—sloppy, overdue, and unpredictable. The townsfolk and farm families welcomed the fair weather and even smiled in the rain and gusty winds of March. Lila circled May fifteenth and June twentieth on her calendar at the turn of the new year and focused on those two days that would forever change her life. She was nervous about the May graduation because she and Molly Brinkman, the other graduate, were expected to speak at commencement.

"I'm not a public speaker," she objected to John.

"Don't think of it as a speech," John answered. "Tell the audience what graduation means to you."

Lila fretted over what to say and scribbled ideas down whenever they came to her while doing laundry or watching the children during recess. As the weeks slipped by, her ideas took shape, and she grew more comfortable with the daunting task of public speaking.

Commencement was Sunday afternoon at the schoolhouse and when the benches were filled, parents and friends stood along the walls. Superintendent Piper gave the opening remarks, the children sang "America the Beautiful," and John recognized students for specific achievements during the school year. Lila's stomach flip-flopped while she waited for her turn to speak, but when she approached the podium, she looked at her audience of mothers and fathers, friends and neighbors and felt a wave of familiarity wash over her.

She began by confiding in them. "My family didn't have much. We worked hard to take care of ourselves, much as you do. I never ever expected to go back to school after I left the fourth grade. Then I came to Council Grove, and everything changed." She told the story they partially knew about how she helped at school, tutoring students when she could be spared at the boarding house, about how much that opportunity informed her decision to graduate from common school and hopefully become a teacher.

"It started with a single poem by Walt Whitman called "I Hear America Singing." I thought that poem was written just for me. I loved how the poet made me feel a part of something bigger than myself, something important like being part of this country. I never knew poetry or book learning could have that effect on me. I hope our children in Council Grove can find that same excitement getting an education."

Lila paused and reached for a book she had placed under the podium. "There's another reason I'll cherish books." She held the book aloft. "Some of you might recognize McGuffey's Reader. What you might not know is this book saved my life." There was a stir in the audience. "When I was kidnapped, the only thing I had with me was this reader. I kept it hidden from my captor in the pocket of my cloak. The idea came to me to rip pages from the reader and hide them along the trail, hoping someone would follow them and find me." She turned to John. "Someone did." The room hushed. "So, you see," she turned back to the audience with a smile, "books can save lives." Laughter rippled through the crowd. Lila thanked them and took her seat while the audience clapped with heart-warming enthusiasm.

The applause rang in her ears days later when she hung her framed diploma on the wall in her bedroom. That piece of paper, that pronouncement, was an assurance of someone whose purpose had been found and whose course was steady and sure. "You have come so far, my dear," Mrs. Bauer had said with pride after the ceremony. Lila was already making plans to hang it in their new living space once she and John were married. "That's not being boastful, is it?" she asked John.

"Of course not. You're recognizing an achievement that's well earned. You have every right to say, "Well done."

Chapter Fifty-One

June 20, 1867

They wanted a simple ceremony and the only place that would hold all their friends was the great outdoors. They decided on a shady location off Main Street slated to be the future home of the Presbyterian Church. Mrs. Piper insisted they use her garden arch as the altar they decorated with pink hollyhocks, positioned under a canopy of elm and oak trees.

At first, Lila's spirits fell when she realized neither she nor John would have any family attending the wedding. She had written to her brothers in Indiana who sent their best wishes for her approaching marriage even if they couldn't attend. That's when she turned to those who shared her life now, her new family. She invited the Lundstroms and the Johnsons from Baxter, who arrived days before the wedding and stayed at the boarding house.

Lila asked Mrs. Bauer and the Hays family to stand with her during the ceremony. Stacy was thrilled to be tasked with holding Lila's bouquet during the exchange of vows. Mrs. Bauer wept at the invitation. "Of course, my dear. Standing beside you would be like seeing my Gretchen get married."

When John wrote his family in St. Louis announcing his wedding, he couldn't help but wonder if they would disown him after what had happened between Fanny and himself. Not that it mattered to him. But the fact that his father replied by blessing the marriage set John's heart at ease and made the approaching wedding day perfect. After the unwavering support of Louis and Sheriff Jenkins in the pursuit of Lila, John asked both of them to stand with him.

"You sure you want a rough old woodsman like me to stand up in front of God and everybody?" Louis asked, scratching his head.

"No doubt in my mind," John answered. "I'd be honored if you and the sheriff would stand with me."

Their friends gathered before the ceremony, visiting in an easy, comfortable way while Matteo, wearing a freshly laundered tunic, stood near the flowered arch and strummed Italian folk songs on his mandolin. Lila and John were thrilled he was there because it hadn't been easy to convince him to play.

"Play at your wedding? I couldn't possibly," he protested. "Look at me." He gestured at his thread bare clothes.

"Your clothes don't matter," John answered. "It will be outside under the trees, nothing fancy."

"But—"

"If you don't play for us, there won't be *any* music," Lila said, "and we must have music." She gave a pleading look he couldn't refuse.

The ceremony began when Lila and John approached from opposite sides of the gathering and met in front of the arch, their faces lit with smiles.

"You look beautiful," John whispered, his eyes never leaving hers. She was a vision of loveliness, wearing a dress of pale blue with puffed sleeves and tiny buttons down the front bodice, a full skirt with petticoat and a white lace collar around her neck. A circle of daisies crowned her brown hair that was lifted in a soft coil; loose strands curled near her cheeks. She carried a bouquet of wildflowers the Shaw girls had gathered— blue hearts, yellow coreopsis, and white daisies.

"You are utterly handsome," Lila whispered to John. He was clean shaven but for a neatly trimmed mustache, his dark hair damp and combed in place. He wore a white shirt and necktie under his gray jacket, and a single daisy in his lapel.

Pastor Higgens dispensed with convention once again and agreed to have Pastor Johnson assist with the wedding ceremony. "Seems everything is a bit unconventional about this wedding," he said, amused. "We're having the ceremony outside under the trees, and the bride herself was rescued from the clutches of a kidnapper not long ago. That doesn't happen every day, does it."

Pastor Johnson stood before Lila and John and gave them a loving smile, his eyes crinkling. He read from I Corinthians:

"Love is patient, love is kind. It does not envy, it does not boast, it is not proud. It does not dishonor others . ." It was Lila's favorite Bible verse, and she savored every word. When it was time to repeat their vows, Lila looked into John's eyes, and her heart was ready to burst. Promising to love and cherish this man for the rest of her life was the easiest thing she'd ever done.

Charley stood at attention near the couple, waiting for his part in the ceremony. He was barely recognizable with his shirt tucked in and his mop of unruly hair plastered in place. Pastor Higgens nodded to Charley. "Now?" Charley asked, eyebrows raised.

"Now," Lila said with a wink. He stepped forward holding a dainty white pillow Mrs. Hays had sewn to hold Lila's ring fastened by a satin ribbon. The plain band slid into place on her finger with ease, as though it had always belonged there. John held both her hands firmly in his as he stared into her eyes and when Pastor Higgens said, "I now pronounce you husband and wife," his eyes misted over before their lips met in a sealing promise. A hurrah rose from the crowd, followed by clapping and more cheers as Lila slipped her hand through John's arm and they walked toward the smiling faces of their friends.

The ladies of Council Grove created a stunning vanilla wedding cake they served to the guests. Lila and John walked among their friends, greeting each one before they moved away from the crowd for a private moment.

"A penny for your thoughts, Mrs. Reynolds?" John gently squeezed Lila's hand nestled in the crook of his arm.

She turned and smiled, loving the sound of her new name. "So many thoughts are running through my head, John. But especially about what I wanted when I first came here." Her eyes wandered over the crowd and stopped at Mrs. Bauer. "I was so frightened. I wanted a place to belong, a place like Council Grove. I didn't know it at the time, but more than a place, I wanted a family. I wanted one to replace the family I had lost." She caught Mrs. Bauer's glance and waved with a smile. "Who would have imagined that irritable land lady at the boarding house would fill the void in my heart."

"You've become like a daughter to her," John added. "Mrs. B is a changed person from the one we met a year ago."

"Mrs. Bauer asked me once why I came to Council Grove."

"What did you say?"

"That I wanted to make my own way. But I discovered something in the process—I found out who I am. I discovered that in the most unexpected places."

"What places?"

"At Bellmards' cabin and Matteo's cave. At the schoolhouse and the livery." She paused. "And at the Lundstrom's farmhouse in the most frightening moments of my life." John pressed her hand tighter at the memory. "I never expected to find out who I was in those places."

"You are an extraordinary person, Lila Bonner Reynolds." John put his arm around Lila's waist and kissed her lightly on the lips. "I love all the versions of you, from the moment I first met you, until now, until . . . forever."

Lila put her hand on John's cheek and stared into his eyes. "And then there's you. While I was making my own way, discovering who I was, I found you. I love all the versions of you, Johnathan Zachary Reynolds, a devoted schoolteacher, a man of his word who defends his friends, a man who makes a mess eating fried chicken, and . . ." her breath caught before she continued, "the brave man who came looking for me, who saved my life." She blinked away sudden tears. "Let's share many years together. I should like that very much."

"As would I." John took her hand from his cheek and kissed it.

"Now, husband, before it's all eaten, could I interest you in some wedding cake?"

"I'd love some."

They clasped hands and walked back to join the celebration under the endless expanse of sunny blue sky. Strains of the mandolin floated over the laughter of children. The scent of fresh earth and sweet clover drifted on the prairie breeze to the place—their place—blooming with promise.

The End

Fact or Fiction in *Lila's Journey*

Beatty's Stagecoach Stop: The real name is **Mahaffie Stagecoach Stop and Farm** (which I named for the owner James "Beatty" Mahaffie) and is the only working stagecoach stop remaining on the Santa Fe Trail. The farm is located on the Westport Route of the trail in Olathe, Kansas, and carried travelers to the Oregon and California Trails as well as the Santa Fe Trail. The site is a component of the Santa Fe National Historical Trail. Today's visitors are invited to take a stagecoach ride, visit the 1865 limestone farmhouse, view the blacksmith at work, visit the horses, oxen, sheep, and goats, and enjoy the Heritage Center and gift shop.

Hays House Restaurant: The restaurant where Lila first hoped to find employment was built circa 1857 and lays claim to being the oldest, continuously operating restaurant west of the Mississippi River. It has been recognized by the Kansas Sampler Foundation as one of the Eight Wonders of Kansas Cuisine and is on the Santa Fe National Historic Trail and the Council Grove National Historic Landmark District.

 **Last Chance Trading Store:** The store was built in 1857 and is the oldest remaining commercial building in Council Grove. For a time, it was the last place to purchase supplies en route to Santa Fe providing its long-lasting nickname. It's registered on the National Register of Historic Places and the Santa Fe National Historic Trail.

Church Ladies Festival: Before Council Grove had churches, the local church ladies needed a room to hold a festival. Seth M. Hays (Seth Williams in the book) was the first permanent settler in Council Grove. He was prominent in the community and owned considerable property including a saloon. He offered the use of his saloon for the festival, promising to keep all liquor out of sight. Some of the ladies were horrified at the idea, but one woman knew Seth would keep his promise and convinced the others to accept his offer. The bar was curtained with wagon covers, the room was decorated, food was served, and the affair was a social and financial success for the ladies of the church and the community. The attendance of Red Horse employees at this event is fictional.

Matteo Boccalini, Hermit Priest of the Santa Fe Trail: I had to include the fascinating Matteo Boccalini in *Lila's Journey*, although for the sake of storytelling I gave him social attributes he probably did not possess in real life. According to historian David Dary in *The Santa Fe Trail*, Matteo Boccalini arrived in Council Grove in the spring of 1863 walking beside a wagon train. Soon after his arrival, he climbed the eastern face of Belfry Hill on the western edge of town, near where the townspeople had erected a large bell to be rung in the event of an Indian attack. North of the bell Boccalini found an overhang in the stone outcropping and made his home there. His belongings consisted of a few religious articles, a half dozen small volumes and an old mandolin. In the evenings the music of his mandolin floated down over the town.

Boccalini's account is also chronicled in *The Story of Council Grove on the Santa Fe Trail* by Lalla Maloy Brigham as recorded by the Morris County Historical Society. Residents of the town learned he was born on the island of Capri in about 1808 where he lived until age eighteen and was sent to Rome to study for the priesthood. At age twenty-one he was ordained Father Francesco. An eloquent and bold speaker, he drew the attention of the Pope and was appointed one of his secretaries. Some of his colleagues did not like him and plotted his downfall, accusing him of falling in love with one of his flock. Before he could be sentenced, Boccalini fled Rome, fearing for his life and made his way to America around 1850.

Five months after arriving in Council Grove, Boccalini saw a man in clerical garb and believed the man was looking for him. Early the next morning he quietly joined a caravan bound for New Mexico. For the next four years he reportedly made his home in a cave in the mountains near Las Vegas, New Mexico, working among the poor Mexicans living in the valley below. His death in 1869 remains a mystery when his body was discovered at his cave, a knife through his heart. The Hermit Priest's Cave in Council Grove is on the National Register of Historic Places and the Santa Fe National Historic Trail.

Indian Troubles in Council Grove: Among the Plains Indians of North America Counting Coup is the warrior tradition of winning prestige against an enemy in battle. It involves intimidating him and persuading him to admit defeat without having to kill him. It was considered braver to touch an enemy with a hand or bow and escape than to kill him. In Chapter Sixteen the Kaw and Cheyenne face off on Main Street, intimidating each other by displaying their prowess.

A similar event took place in Council Grove on June 1,1868 when the Cheyeene invaded the Kaw reservation accusing them of stealing horses. The Kaw responded by confronting the Cheyenne in full regalia and face paint on Council Grove's Main Street. After four hours of both sides displaying prowess or counting coup, the merchants offered coffee and sugar as a peace offering and the Indians left. The skirmish continued outside of town. One Kaw was injured, one Cheyenne was killed.

Discussion Questions

1. The book begins with the very serious subject of abuse. Lila felt her only choice was to escape her situation. Have you known someone who's experienced physical or emotional abuse? How was it addressed?
2. Lila receives unexpected financial help from Mr. Reynolds on her journey. What impact does this have on Lila's future? Have you given or received financial aid in a similar situation?
3. Lila is desperate to find work when she arrives in Council Grove. Describe a time in your life when you had difficulty finding a job or lost your job.
4. Were you surprised John had a fiancé? Did it change your opinion of him? How would you have reacted were you in Lila's position?
5. Discuss Lila's relationships with Louis and Charley Bellmard. How does Lila's selfless caring for them affect events in the novel? Have you ever been asked to nurse a friend or relative who was seriously ill? What was that experience like?
6. Measles vaccine wasn't available until 1960. In 1867 would you have trusted an Indian remedy as Mrs. Shaw did? Why or why not?
7. When Lila was abducted, what was your reaction? Did you suspect Pa was behind it?
8. Explain how the relationship between Lila and Mrs. Bauer changes during the novel. Have you ever changed your opinion of someone once you got to know them?
9. The importance of education is a theme throughout the novel. Do you think Lila will realize her dream and become a teacher? Will she be satisfied if she doesn't realize this dream?
10. Why do you think it took Lila so long to recognize her true feelings for John?
11. Lila was inspired by Walt Whitman's "I Hear America Singing." Its theme is everyone has their own unique work and completing that work provides personal dignity as well as for the greater good. Has a book or poem inspired you or had an impact on your life? Share it with your group.

To the Reader

Dear Reader,

Lila asked me to write this novel.

Several years ago, I visited Mahaffie Stagecoach Stop and Farm in Olathe, Kansas (Beatty's Stagecoach Stop in the novel), the only working stagecoach stop remaining on the old Santa Fe Trail. While touring the basement kitchen of this historic home, an idea for a story came to me. What would it have been like to cook in that kitchen for travelers who rode the stagecoaches along that busy trail during its heyday in the 1860's? And what if a young kitchen girl wanted to secretly board one of those coaches to escape a troubled life and find a new one?

What followed was a short story, *Lila' Song*, which resulted in the 2021 Laura Award for Short Fiction from Women Writing the West. Thrilled as I was with this recognition, Lila wasn't done with me. In the story, she had only enough money for passage to Council Grove, Kansas, and Lila wanted me to continue writing about her journey. Thank you, Lila, for nudging me forward.

Advice abounds for writers, and I read somewhere we write to entertain, to educate, or to escape. I hope *Lila's Journey* was an adventure that entertained you till the very end, perhaps an escape from your reality, and along the way you gained a deeper appreciation for life in the 1860's on the Santa Fe Trail. I hope we all continue to study our history, learn from the past, and appreciate its lessons.

Thank you, my wonderful readers, for joining me in Lila's journey. None of this would be possible without you. Like Lila, may you find your own adventure and live it to the fullest.

Blessings,

Jane

About the Author

Award winning author Jane Coletti Perry's second novel, *Lila's Journey*, will be released summer 2024. Her short story "Lila's Song" won Women Writing the West LAURA Award (2021) and is the prequel to *Lila's Journey*. Her previous historical fiction novel, *Marcello's Promise* (2019), was inspired by her family's immigrant story. She loves nothing more than digging into history and discovering unique stories unless it's bringing those stories to life through writing. An English major, Perry graduated from Iowa State University and participates in writer's workshops, conferences, and local writing groups.

When she's not writing, Jane is singing in a choir, exercising in some fashion, or soaking up nature in a shady spot in the yard with a good book. She and her husband live in Kansas and have two children and six grandchildren. She treasures time spent with their far-flung family and still entertains the fantasy of appearing on *Dancing with the Stars for Grandmas*, although the clock is ticking. . .

Website: www.janecolettiperry.com
Blog: www.janecolettiperry.com/blog/
Facebook: www.facebook.com/JaneColettiPerry/

Read about another journey in
Marcello's Promise!

Chapter One

Monastero, Northern Italy

July

"Get more water! Hurry!"

Marcello ran down the hillside to the well beside the church, his mother's words ringing in his ears. His hands shook as he lowered the bucket deep into the well, then pulled hard on the rope, raising the brimming bucket back to the surface. He hurried back up the hill to his parents' house, splashing water over the edge of the bucket as he lengthened his stride up the dirt path. When he reached the door, his legs burned, and he bent over to catch his breath.

"Mama," he asked, panting, "how is she? Is she all right?"

His mother emptied warm water from the fireplace kettle into a basin. "Shouldn't be much longer." She walked quickly to the bedroom at the back of the house, closing the door behind her. No sooner had she disappeared than the door opened again, and Marcello's mother-in-law emerged.

"Is there anything I can do?"

She took no notice of him, gathered cloths and towels from the cupboard, and hurried back to the bedroom. He stared after her as the bedroom door closed once again.

Marcello felt sweat clinging to his forehead. He ran trembling fingers through his damp hair, then emptied the bucket of water into the kettle to heat before stepping outside. The yard was deserted. Marcello's two younger brothers were gone for the day, tending the family's cows grazing in the summer pasture farther up into the hills. If this were an ordinary day, he would be with them.

But this wasn't an ordinary day.

A breeze off the mountains stirred the thick July air. He thrust his hands deep into his pockets and paced in front of the house. *Please be all right. Please be all right.* Back and forth he traveled on the dusty path, repeating his incantation. He stopped short and stared vacantly at the family home where he and his siblings had been born and raised. The whitewashed cement walls and timber roof were typical of the houses clinging to the mountains. Crumbling around the edges, the three stories leaned into the rocky hillside as though born of the earth.

How long has it been? Marcello tossed his head back and gauged the sun. *Three hours? Is that too long? Should the baby be here by now?* A sense of dread sent him back inside.

Through the bedroom door he heard his mother's voice rise. "Luisa, push now! His stomach knotted. *Please, Holy Mother, take care of Luisa and the baby.*

His legs weak, he sank into a chair and leaned forward, elbows on his knees. He wanted a boy, a son to carry on the family name. Luisa had predicted they would have a son who would grow up to look just like him—lean and muscular with a sunny smile that would make his brown eyes sparkle beneath an unruly mop of dark hair. But more than that, she wanted him to have Marcello's optimism and penchant for hard work, his way of looking people in the eye when he spoke, humble and earnest, his easy smile. Her opinion of him was flattering and kind, but that was like her. Luisa saw the best in everyone.

A shriek split the silence, sending a jolt through Marcello's body. He sucked in the sultry air and held it, afraid to breathe, his body rigid.

Silence.

Marcello's chest tightened. He forgot all about his selfish desire for a son and pleaded for the lives of Luisa and their baby. *Please be all right. Holy Mother, let her and the baby be all right.*

The bedroom door opened.

"Come see your son." His mother nodded, and a smile spread across her face. Marcello leaped to his feet and strode to the bedroom.

His mother-in-law bent over Luisa and gently wiped perspiration from her daughter's forehead. Marcello knelt beside Luisa and clasped her hand. Her unbraided raven hair spilled across the white pillow in dark ribbons. She opened her eyes with a weary smile. His gaze went from her eyes to the tiny baby wrapped in a white cloth snuggling in the crook of her arm.

He marveled at the miracle. "Our baby," he whispered. He brought Luisa's hand to his lips and kissed it, pained with the knowledge that all too soon, he would be leaving them...

@copyright 2020 Jane Coletti Perry

Buy *Marcello's Promise* on Amazon